Best Wishes
Michael T!

# Dolphinsong

# DOLPHINSONG

## Michael Tod

Cadno
Books

First published in Great Britain by Cadno Books in 2000
Cadno Books
P.O. Box 34
Abergavenny.
NP8 1YN
e-mail michaeltod@cadnobooks.co.uk
Web Site Address www.cadnobooks.co.uk

Cover illustration by Richard Jones.
Map by Barbara Anne Knight.

Printed and bound in Great Britain by
Dinefwr Press
Rawlings Road, Llandybie
SA18 3YD


ISBN 1-89822504 4

## *To my wife, Jo.*

Authors' wives find it hard enough to live with people who are different characters at different times. When these characters may also be squirrels, dolphins or elephants this makes it even more challenging. Only a very special person could put up with this.

*Dolphinsong* is a work of fiction. Incidents, names and characters are all the product of my imagination except for the dolphin, Elegance of Kerry, known to many humans as Fungie of Dingle Bay, with whom I had the honour of swimming during the research for this book.

The fictitious town of Dormouth has many features in common with the charming and largely unspoiled seaside resort town of Weymouth in Dorset, not least of which is its position just to the north of Portland.

*Also by Michael Tod*

**The Silver Tide**

**The Second Wave**

**The Golden Flight**

Now available as a single volume
**The Dorset Squirrels**

**A Curlew's Cry** (Poetry)

# Acknowledgements

Many people contribute to the writing of a book such as *Dolphinsong*. The unsung heroes are the editors who never seem to get a mention. Whilst writing this book I submitted it to several people for editorial comment and advice. Most notable were my wife, Jo, my son, Stuart, Robin Chawner, friends and fellow writers Catherine Merriman, Barbara Anne Knight, Ewart and Ivy Jones, Michael Meredith, Trish Sharpe and, on a professional basis, Celia Catchpole, Andrew Taylor and Helen Wire.

I also received considerable assistance from Vanessa Williams of the Whale and Dolphin Conservation Society.

I am indebted to Douglas Adams for his permission to use the extract from *The Hitchhiker's Guide to the Galaxy* in Chapter Twelve.

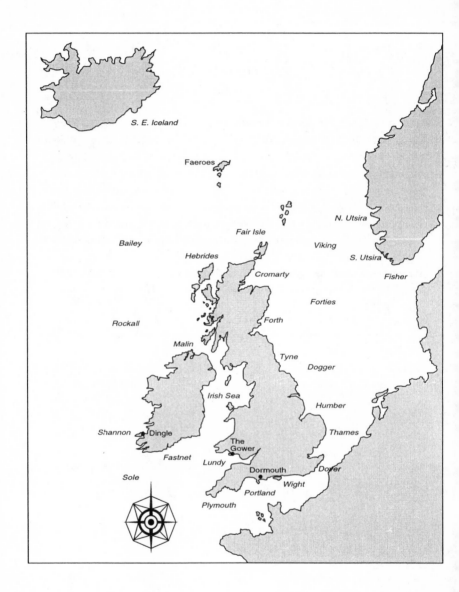

S. E. Iceland

Faeroes

Fair Isle

N. Utsira

Bailey

Hebrides

Viking

S. Utsira

Cromarty

Fisher

Forties

Rockall

Forth

Malin

Tyne

Dogger

Irish Sea

Humber

Shannon  Dingle

Thames

The
Gower

Fastnet

Lundy

Dormouth

Dover

Sole

Wight

Portland

Plymouth

# CHAPTER ONE

## *The Gower Coast, South Wales*

Mary swam parallel with the shoreline, the grass on the dunes behind the beach a soft green against the clear blue of the summer sky. She was swimming hard enough to keep from chilling while trying not to disturb the gulls floating all around her. The tic in her left eye had nearly gone during the holiday but she knew her A level results were *not* going to get her the university place she, or rather her mother, aspired to.

At six in the morning the beach and the unruffled sea belonged to her and the gulls. In a few hours the first families would come trickling through the dunes and colonise the sands, although, as it was so calm, there would be no surfers today. This would be her last swim – back to London this afternoon and the long brown envelope on the doormat in the morning. The tic quickened, pulling and tugging at her eyelid. She tried telling it to go away, this sometimes worked but not for long and certainly not today.

The most seaward of the gulls flapped their wings and ran along the surface before flying up and calling an alarm. Mary trod water and looked around to see what had disturbed them. There were no people visible on the beach and no boats in sight other than a small fishing boat a long way off – yet she had an almost psychic feeling that she was being watched. Her body tingled as she circled slowly. There was no one about – but the feeling didn't go away. As she circled again she heard a gentle 'whoosh' behind her as though someone had sighed. This was followed by two more and she turned quickly. Three black fins showed briefly and disappeared. Dolphins! Mary turned face down and opened her eyes, wishing she had brought her swimming goggles. The water was clear and over to her right three graceful shapes glided away into the distance, turned, and swam towards her. One was notably smaller than the other two – a young one.

This dolphin swam nearer, though the other two held back, hanging effortlessly in the water, watching her intently. The youngster swam around Mary, studying her with a look combining obvious curiosity with

1

a wisdom beyond its apparent age. It dived under her as she turned, then swam towards her from a different angle.

Mary sensed a 'come and play' message, took a deep breath and dived. She had been proud of being able to swim a length of the huge Morley Park pool underwater and she followed the young dolphin, her hair streaming out behind her as she tried to follow its effortless twists and turns. The bigger dolphins watched from a distance, reminding Mary of how her mother and aunt had watched her romping with her friends on the grass in Morley Park when she had been a little girl.

She was a little girl again now, all cares forgotten, in a magical underwater world. Time floated away, the sting of salt in her eyes faded to insignificance. Soon even the bigger dolphins joined in the playing, leaping and diving all about her. Mary envied them the ability to leap as she watched their bodies curve gracefully through the air, elegant shapes dark against the blue of the sky. How big they were. Even the young one was bigger than she was, yet they implied no threat – quite the reverse. They seemed to project an aura of gentleness, of benign goodwill. Love? Three final, coordinated leaps and they were gone as suddenly as they had arrived.

Mary lay back and floated. Her overwhelming feeling was of privilege, the privilege of being invited to join a world of such grace and elegance. Allied with this was a sense of calm, peace and understanding, a sense of them wanting to communicate with her. She swam around for a little while, hoping they might come back, then made slowly towards the shore. The tic in her eye had gone and she knew it would not return to bother her. She, Mary O'Connor, an ordinary, unexceptional girl from a drab, terraced house in South London, had swum with a joy of dolphins. She suddenly felt very special.

# CHAPTER TWO

## *The Faeroe Islands*

Helga Jacobsen stood in the prow of *The Black Raven* hearing the dip and sweep of the oars behind her, her spirit riding the waves ahead. Yet, as exultation lifted her, she knew that around the point she was going to hear the clamour of the dreaded bell-buoy.

Now! She could hear it *now* – but it was not the deep, full-throated roar and clang from her childhood dreams. This was the tinny, but equally ominous, tinkle of a tiny toy bell.

A slimy tentacle reached up out of the water and gripped her thigh. Another was round her throat choking her. She was sweating profusely, her nightdress clammy across her chest and where it was tangled around her legs. The ringing was faster, insistent and demanding. Suddenly, she could see the bell. It was on the tip of another of the writhing tentacles. She tried to reach out and hold the bell to stop the sound but another slimy tentacle gripped her arm and she woke as she usually did from this dream, sitting up in the darkness shaking with fear. Breathing hard, she swung her legs over the edge of the bed and padded barefoot across her bedroom and into the living room. There was no need to look at the clock, the dim light coming in at the open front door told her the time was between two and three in the morning.

In the gloom the carved animals and birds around the walls had grown. Their normally familiar and comforting shapes now seemed menacing, reminding Helga of the wicked trolls in the stories of her childhood. She shivered as she heard the old cockerel give a half-hearted call. It was answered by another from over the water, then by a distant curlew, its bubbling lament sad and depressing as if it was mourning a chick taken by a raiding skua.

The bell tinkled again. She went into her mother's room and stood by the bed.

'Yes, Mother?'

'Just wanted to be sure you were there.' The thin voice was cold.

3

'I'm always here,' Helga replied, then added under her breath, 'Where else could I be?' As she said the words, she trembled at her impertinence but her mother had not heard.

'All right then, don't just stand there, girl.'

Helga turned to leave, biting on her lower lip.

Stumbling in the near darkness of the stuffy room she bumped the bedside table and the tin bell tinkled to the floor. Helga stooped, groped around until she found it, slipped a finger either side of the clapper and carried it outside. The sky to the east was already touched with the palest of pink washes. She strode the short distance to the rocks that curved down into the black sea and tossed the bell far out to where wraiths of thin mist twisted above the surface like dying ghosts. A seal snorted as the last tiny but still imperious tinkle was silenced by the water and Helga was aware of the coldness of the rock under her feet and the chill of the air on her neck and bare arms.

In these northern latitudes summers were short enough. There was still all the hay to cut, dry and store for the long winter. She shivered uncontrollably and was turning to go back to the house when the sky near a high-flying aircraft's vapour trail was filled with tiny sparks – a cluster of shooting stars streaking over her head and falling towards the sea to the east, burning out one by one as they neared the horizon.

She stood, her arms wrapped about herself, forgetting the chill of her damp nightdress and looked up with the same awe she had felt when her grandfather had carried her out into the darkness when she had been restless at night. Then, she had been only six years old. Now, the sight of the flashing sparks in the sky brought back the feel of his strong arms, the cushion of his beard against her cheek, and she could once more smell the pipe-tobacco smoke that hung about his always-smiling face.

The seal snorted again as Helga recalled that one of her grandfather's bedtime stories had told of shooting stars. She tried to remember if these had been a sign of impending hope or of despair. It was Hope – she was sure of that. Yes – Hope. The captive princess had given up waiting for her lover to come and had herself vanquished the trolls before going in search of the prince so she could marry him and live happily ever after.

A long-suppressed anger rose in her as she crept back into the silent house. In the big cupboard next to her bedroom door were two pillows. She chose her brother's, the softer of the two, then held it against her lips before putting it back on the shelf. Her brother had loved his mother as sons do – it would be wrong to use *his* pillow. She took her grandfather's – he had never cared much for his daughter-in-law – and tiptoed into her mother's room carrying the striped pillow against her chest and stood by the bed, trembling. An ugly troll was lying there, not moving – lulling her into a false sense of security before it leapt for her throat. Or was it an octopus with its tentacles hidden under the grey blanket? Troll or octopus, it didn't matter, she knew what she had to do. She lifted the pillow and pressed it against her own face until she had to fight for breath then jerked it away, cool air rushing into her lungs. Even now the coarse material smelt faintly of pipe-tobacco smoke and she could hear her mother's voice chastising the old man for smoking in bed.

Helga gripped both ends of the pillow firmly and bent forwards.

*Grace of FairIsle, a nubile dolphine of thirteen years, was cruising just below the surface when the sound of the falling bell reached her. She flicked round and located the tiny metal object a moment after it entered the water. She dived, shimmered it and read the echoes as it twisted towards the seabed. Its shimaura was unlike anything she had known before. The thing twisting down towards the kelpweed was made of very thin shipstone, was shaped like a limpet-shell, and had an unpleasant sense to it, out of all proportion to its size.*

*She tried to analyse the aura but the human experience of 'possession' was alien to her and it read as 'duress'. No, not duress – 'captivity'. To her captivity was represented by fish held by their gills in a net – a familiar enough scene, though the horror of it always shocked her when she swam near to the wriggling, dying creatures that had once been as free as she was herself and almost as fluid in their movements as the water in which they lived.*

*On the previous day, swimming north with her mother and her mother's sister, Grace of Tyne and Grace of Humber, FairIsle had already absorbed two other new and mind-expanding experiences. These were all part of the excitement of their annual sea-change.*

*As they swam, guided by the planet's invisible North-South aura, they listened-out frequently, the three explorers occasionally beaming away their own signature whistles but receiving no answering calls though they knew that other dolphins swam these seas.*

*Grace of Humber had calculated the distance since they had passed the Lands of Shet and knew that they should soon reach the Faroff Islands. She expressed concern that, not knowing the local currents, they might be too far to the east and leapt effortlessly, searching the horizon as she reached the top of the arc. 'No land in vision,' she reported, her words vibrating through the water as her body slipped back into her native element.*

*FairIsle leapt herself. Not because she doubted what her aunt had said, but just to express her joy and the excitement of exploring new seas.*

*The water here was notably clearer than in their home patrol area on the east coast of the Land of Eng. There was a different feel to it here, cooler and cleaner, and to the wide skies above, where slender-winged sea birds circled and called, seeming to mark the passage of the three dolphines.*

*FairIsle leapt again, revelling in the life that surged through her body, then powered downwards, the translucent green water darkening as the depth increased. Tiny, immature fish, silver wisps of reflected light and sound, twisted away and vanished.*

*The dolphine scattered sounds ahead of her – the absence of major echoes indicated a clear swim. Long before her body called for air, she turned upwards, read the returning echoes from the bodies of the other dolphines and headed towards them to leap out of the water once more in a triumphant curve. Life for a dolphine of her age was a never-ending joy.*

*Later that day, as Humber led them northwards, a dull, persistent throbbing permeated the water.*

*'A human's boat – heading towards us from east of north.' Tyne voiced their thoughts and they turned in the boat's direction, planning to ride its bow-waves and sport in the bubbles behind its propeller.*

*'What is that?' FairIsle asked as they saw an ugly device mounted on its foredeck. The whole ship radiated an aura of horror and evil but it was at its most intense around the thing silhouetted against the blue of the sky. As one, the dolphines dived and swam away deep underwater, FairIsle's question unanswered.*

*Further north they encountered a giant of a whale, blue-grey on the upper side, yellowish on its belly, so vast that it seemed to take an age for it to swim past them, though FairIsle knew this could not really have been so. The dolphines paused in awe and reverence while the enormous creature swam by, not in any way acknowledging their presence. FairIsle thought she had never seen such sadness and such loneliness as she saw in the whale's eye as it passed, calling, calling, calling to others of its chapter, apparently without response. She felt the awesome power-waves of its intellect reach out and envelop her as it went by and she knew that the encounter would make this a day that would leap high in her memory for many years.*

As the sun dipped towards the horizon, the captain of the ship that had so disturbed the dolphins heard the cry of 'Hvalblast,' and scrambled on deck in time to see the distinctive shape of a blue whale's spout as it exhaled again. The whale was heading southwards on a course almost parallel to that of his ship. He glanced over his shoulder at the Norwegian flag flying proudly at the stern, thought of his Government-given right to kill whales, dismissed the knowledge that this applied only to the plentiful minkehval and calculated that one blue was worth many minke. He called to the helmsman to alter course and turned to speak to the harpooner who had followed him up onto the deck.

*The dolphines did not hear the thud of the exploding harpoon but they did hear the whale scream, the sounds of its agony vibrating through the water even though it was half a day's swim away. They turned to face towards the south and floated side by side as the calls grew fainter until there was no audible sound, only whispered echoes of a great pain and a greater loss. Eventually, even these echoes were absorbed in the vastness of the sea.*

*The dolphines had floated in silence for a while, then had swum north again. Each was busy with her own thoughts though they had held a formation close enough for Humber and Tyne to caress FairIsle's side as they swam.*

*Now FairIsle let the shipstone limpet-shell drop down into the bed of kelpweed and swam to the surface to see if she could see what had made it fall into the water. On the rocks a human female stood upright, her arms crossed over each other on the upper part of her body. The hair on her head was almost as white as the covering that clung to her body – hair lighter in colour than the hair of the young female human FairIsle had play-shared with in the sea near the Land of the Dragon three years before. The 'captivity' aura surrounded this human even more strongly than it had the shipstone limpet-shell so FairIsle turned towards the open sea to find Humber and Tyne. They would be feeding offshore and would answer her whistles. The fjord behind her, the hidden inlets of which had looked so tempting to explore just a short time before, had an unpleasant feeling when near-to – a feeling for which she had no name. It was more than the 'captivity' of the human – all the water around her reeked of death and despair and she needed to put it behind her tail-flukes.*

*Humber and Tyne had come to seek her and, as she heard them respond to her calls, the night sky was filled with sparkling lights. Humber leapt.*

*'So many!' she whistled. 'I have never seen the like. Are they not beautiful?'*

*'Beautiful, yes, beautiful,' FairIsle responded, leaping for joy at of the sight and for the relief of being away from the sadness beyond the black rocks.*

7

*She leapt again but the sparkles had gone and the normal stars still formed their time-set patterns in the brightening sky.*

*The three dolphines swam away from the island as the edge of the sun rose above the horizon, rafts of puffins scattering as they progressed. The stars had faded to nothing when a faint clicking sound tickled the sensors in the lower jawbones of the cruising dolphines. Humber swung her head from side to side to read the direction.*

*'Stargazers,' she said. 'A constellation of stargazers – west of north.'*

*They swam towards the sounds which grew louder and clearer until, when the dolphines leapt, they could see the black curved fins of many pilot whales heading towards them.*

# CHAPTER THREE

Helga ran tired fingers through her long blonde hair, which, like her pale skin and blue eyes, was a legacy of her Viking ancestry. She stood at the bedside staring down at the face of her mother who had died unexpectedly in the night. Helga was tired – a bone-aching, mind-numbing tiredness that made every movement seem as if she were in a dream.

She listened once more to make absolutely sure her mother was not breathing, all the time watching the bedclothes, half hoping to see some movement whilst simultaneously dreading that a flicker of life remained. At last, she leant forward and, with fingers that trembled slightly, slid the eyelids down over the eyes which even in death stared up at her accusingly. With a sudden savagery she pulled the sheet up over the ashen face and walked out of the bedroom, through the gloomy living room to the black-tarred front door that had stood open all night.

The door was seldom closed in the summer except when a storm swept in from the sea or roared down from the hills behind the tiny farm. The sun was just coming up, its almost horizontal rays lighting the cliffs and the houses of the village on the far side of the deep-water fjord with a delicate pink glow.

A kilometre away across the water, the buildings of Eysthavn looked like miniature doll's-houses, brightly painted in reds, greens and blues like those in all the other tiny villages around the coasts of the Faeroe Islands.

The wooden church with its stubby white tower and many of the houses still had the traditional turf roofs, as green as the grass in the steep meadows between the buildings and the cliffs behind, though some of the more recently cut fields were swathes of golden yellow where the aftermath of the mowing had not yet greened again. The calm water of the inlet was also green that morning, except where the basalt cliffs were reflected blackly in an almost perfect upside-down picture.

Helga was only dimly aware of the distant sounds of the waterfall and the sea birds' cries. A pair of black and white tjaldurs, the island's oystercatchers, piped a plaintive note as they strutted across the sea-rounded rock promontory near the Jacobsen's anchorage. Another pair were poking their long orange beaks into the cut grass of the meadow behind the house.

She realised she was still in her dressing gown and returned reluctantly to the single-storeyed wooden farmhouse. As she put on her functional undergarments she found herself longing once more for pretty nylon or even silk underwear. Gorgeous slithery garments such as she had seen advertised in the Danish women's magazines that Uncle Roi occasionally brought over to the farm for her. There was not much point in having pretty things now, she thought angrily – at 33 she was not old but she felt it. She felt – how did they put it in the stories on the British World Service Radio? 'On the shelf.'

She pulled on a check shirt and heavy black woollen trousers that had belonged to her brother, then his old jumper – she had knitted it for Christian many years before out of wool she had spun from the fleece of one of their own sheep.

As she was dressing, an insistent voice in her mind was saying, 'Get the grass up to dry, get the grass up to dry, get the grass up to dry on the turkilag or it'll rot on the ground and the cow will starve when the winter comes.'

'Chores first, then you can play,' her father had said again and again to Christian and her when they were children. He had made it sound reasonable enough but when the chores were done there was little time left for the children to do what *they* had wanted. Life had always seemed full of chores. Drying the hay – shearing the sheep – catching the fish – gutting the fish – drying the fish – collecting the gulls' eggs – netting the lundi – killing the sheep – drying the sheepmeat – smoking the tiny bodies of the lundi with their quaint striped beaks – chores, chores, chores.

Then there were the 'duties'. To her father – to her mother – to the schoolmaster – to the church over in the village. God, she was sick of chores and duties. And what on earth was it all for? Surely there was more to life than this?

She shook out her long hair.

First her father and grandfather had been drowned, fishing for cod when she was fifteen. Then her brother had been killed, falling while catching the lundi with the long-handled net as the silly birds flew in clumsy circles past the cliff top. She could hardly bear to think of that day. For years her world had been shrinking and shrinking until it was just this house and the patch of half-cultivated land between the sea and the foot of the great black cliffs behind.

Once she had dreamed of going to England – an England lovingly described to her by her grandfather who had been there when he was a young man. Once too, she had dreamed of marrying as all her friends in the village had done but, as the years slipped by, her dreams and hopes had vanished in the same way as the early mists around the cliff tops faded to nothing in the warmth of the morning sun.

She sat at her dressing table brushing her hair and trying not to see the dark-ringed eyes staring back at her out of a drawn and pallid face. No man would want her now. A bird called from the meadow outside and she envied its freedom. Freedom to fly away when it wanted to – even to England if it chose. She went to the window and shouted, 'Go away.' A mocking voice called back from the cliff beyond the meadow, Go away, away, away . . .'

'Freedom – England.' She shouted these at the departing bird and the cliff called back 'Freedom – England – Freedom – England – Freedom – England.'

The two words were somehow synonymous and, as the cliff echoed them back at her, a realisation welled up in her that, after years and years and years of nursing her mother, she – Helga Jacobsen – was now *free*. Free as any bird – FREE!

Saying that magic word in time with each stroke of the brush, forcing her aching arms to do what she wanted, she pulled the crackling, rebellious mass of hair over her shoulder, wove it into a thick plait and tied it with a defiant bow of scarlet ribbon. I am free. FREE!

Helga ran out of the house, her tiredness suddenly gone. 'I am free,' she shouted, first in her native Faeroese language, '*Eg havi fri*,' then in her second language, Danish, '*Jeg er fri.*' But it sounded best in the English she had tried so hard to learn well. 'I am free. I am FREE.'

She shouted it again and again, startling the tjaldurs who flew off complaining towards the open sea, dipped towards it, then rose and turned inland again.

A seal bobbed its head above the surface of the water beyond the wave-smoothed rocks where she had spent so much of her younger life gutting the fish that her father and grandfather had caught. How long had it been since she had last played music to the seals? Her brother had been dead ten years and she had certainly not played to the seals since. She turned back to the silent house, paused at the open door of her mother's room and listened. Would she dare? The huge old sea chest stood under the far window, the heavy padlock challenging her. She would. Helga Jacobsen was FREE.

She fetched her nail scissors from her own room and, heart thumping, pulled back the sheet and cut the greasy brown cord that was around her mother's neck. The key lay on the wrinkled skin waiting for her to pick it up. She hesitated a moment then delicately lifted it with her finger and thumb before covering the pale face again, glad that she had closed the

11

dead eyes. Her foot touched the corner of a pillow lying on the floor, half under the bed. It wasn't her mother's pillow. This one had no pillowcase on it – just blue and white striped material like the ones in the cupboard next to her bedroom. How had that got there? She nudged it out of her sight with her toe.

The padlock opened easily and she lifted the lid, something she had not done since she was a child. The smell was the same – a musty mixture of camphor and oldness. Inside, wrapped in cream-coloured tissue paper that crackled as she moved it, were her and her brother's costumes, the national dress of the Faeroe Islanders. Hers with the laced bodices and the coloured shawls and her brother's with the silver buttons and the fancy waistcoats. She carefully lifted out the garments, the sizes getting smaller with each layer.

Had she ever been as small as *that*?

Under the costumes was a tattered photograph album which she put to one side. She could look at that later. Then she found a boxed pack of playing cards. She flipped open the lid and slid the cards into her hand.

'You cheated,' Christian accused her.

'I did not!' Helga had replied.

'You did. That was a Queen, not a King.'

Helga had turned the card over to show him. It *was* a King.

'Stop quarrelling, you two,' their mother snapped. She was always irritable when their father's boat had not come back when expected, even though delays were commonplace.

'I still say you cheated,' Christian had shouted at her.

Her mother had put down her knitting and stood up. 'Give me those cards.'

The cards had been put away until both of them had apologised. Christian had said his 'sorrys', but Helga knew that she had not cheated. *She* was not going to apologise.

This was the first time she had seen the cards since that day. Helga shuffled the pack once, the cards feeling surprisingly comfortable in her hands, put them back in the box and dropped it into the chest out of sight. She brushed at the corner of her eye with the back of her hand.

Here was the Noah's Ark, built out of pieces of driftwood by her great-great grandfather and lovingly preserved as an heirloom, generation after generation. She opened the lid of the ark and took out each painted animal and stood them in pairs on the bedroom floor. Two grey elephants, two spotted giraffes, two striped zebra, even two black dolphins and a grindhval who didn't even belong *in* the ark. In those long ago days when they had played with the painted animals together, Christian had always insisted on the dolphin-hvals swimming either side of the ark's bow with the single grindhval out in front. Neither she nor Christian had ever wondered why there was only one grindhval when there were two of all the other creatures, but they had often argued about why it was white and not black like all the other grindhvals they had ever seen.

Once when they had been playing with the ark and the animals, Christian had said, 'There's some black paint in the barn.' He had jumped up and gone out to find it, then had come back to say, 'It's really warm out, I'm going up to swim under the waterfall.' Helga had left the animals on the bedroom floor and followed him across the sunlit meadow to the pool.

When they got back their mother had scolded *her* for leaving 'those silly animals all over the place.' Not a word to Christian.

What wasn't in the chest – she really knew it could not be – was her doll's-cradle. The one Uncle Roi had made for her fifth birthday.

Tears were running down Helga's face and she fumbled in her pocket for a handkerchief.

She had forgotten her lunch box one day but remembered it just as her father was about to take her and Christian across the inlet in the boat to school.

'Papa, my lunch box is in the house.' As he was backing the boat out of the mooring-place she had jumped out onto the rocks and run back up to the house.

Her mother was kneeling, chopping something to light the stove. Helga stood in the doorway staring in disbelief. It was her doll's-cradle being fed into the crackling flames.

Her mother had looked up, red-faced. 'You don't need this any more,' she had said. 'You are thirteen, not a little girl now.'

Helga had stared at her mother, then turned and coldly walked into her bedroom. She had come back carrying her doll.

'You'd better burn this too.'

She'd held out the doll, certain her mother would never burn the beloved Elisabeth.

They had faced one another for ages, neither blinking, then her mother had reached out slowly, taken the doll and pushed it, head-first, into the top of the stove.

Helga had run screaming from the house.

Her mother had been right. From that day she was no longer a little girl. Now, twenty years on, she was not a proper woman either. She blamed her mother for that too.

The next thing she found in the chest was a yellowing envelope addressed to her in her grandfather's distinctive handwriting, the H of 'Helga' drawn in the ornate and loving way only he had ever been able to do. She read, 'My dearest Helga, to be given to you on your engagement to be married. These were your grandmother's. Left here in case I am not able to be with you on that happy day.'

She had never seen *that* envelope before.

Inside was a string of large pearls. She held them against her chest briefly then dropped them back into the envelope. Helga blew her nose, sniffed and looked amongst the clutter of family history in the chest, searching for the old accordion her grandfather had won in some drunken bet with an English sailor during the war. The hexagonal box was there, under the great black leather-bound bible. She lifted it out carefully. It seemed much smaller than she remembered.

She replaced the animals in the hollow of the ark, put it, the bible and the other treasures back into the chest, glancing several times over her shoulder at the body under the bedclothes as she did so, closed the lid, then tip-toed into the living room.

Fearful lest the cloth bellows on the instrument had deteriorated from age and disuse, she lifted it carefully from its box. It groaned in an almost human way as she slipped her hands through the cracked leather loops at either end and tried a chord. She imagined a wave of disapproval flowing from the bedroom so she went out of the house, closed the door sharply and walked down the path to the rocks.

Instinctively she checked the boat, snug in the tiny natural harbour behind the promontory. The boat was her way out to the world beyond the house, her only way to cross to the village. The cairn path up and over the cliff behind her and round the head of the fjord had not been used since her brother died, and was probably impassable by now.

The seal bobbed up again as though it had been waiting for her and floated upright in the water twitching its whiskers, watching her and waiting.

Helga sat on her favourite rock and gently drew the accordion to its full length, enjoying the hiss of inrushing air. She positioned her fingers on the white buttons and pressed the ends towards the centre.

She played badly at first, feeling that she was letting her grandfather down. He had taught her to play and she could imagine him sitting on *his* favourite rock near her, his white-bearded head tilted to one side and his eyes closed as he listened.

Her fingers were stiff and she found it difficult to locate the right buttons. She tried the simple tunes of childhood – nursery rhymes and children's songs, then as her confidence grew, the more complex rhythms of the Faeroese chain dance, picturing the villagers circling and singing in the schoolroom across the water. She saw the circle growing as more and more people, old and young, joined in, until the circle broke and the ends of the human chain passed one another, everybody singing the seemingly endless verses and moving two steps right, one step left, two steps right, one step left.

Suddenly, it all came back to her and she was playing – playing – playing, tears streaming down her face. She was playing tunes she could not recall ever having learned – slow, sad tunes that seemed to reach up out of the very rocks on which she sat. Tunes that rose out of the sea beyond her, out of the kelpweed waving in the swirling currents below her, out of the bodies of drowned sailors far away in the ocean. Out of the waterfalls and the distant cliffs the tunes came. Out of the seals and the gulls and out of the vast empty sky above her.

The accordion seemed to be playing itself, her fingers moving as though with a will way outside of her own and, when she raised her head, she could see that many more seals had come to listen, a great sadness apparent in their round brown eyes.

Suddenly, the music died with a hiss as the fabric of the bellows split along the concertina folding. Helga ran her fingers along the tear, wondering how she might get it repaired, then laid the silent instrument on a rock and stood up. She saw, beyond the seals, the curved dorsal fins of a pod of pilot whales – grindhvals – showing above the glassy water. Some were circling slowly, others pushing their heads out of the water and watching her, while many more were heading in from the sea towards the inlet.

She readied herself to send the ancient cry of 'Grindabod – the grindhvals have come again,' – ringing across the water as her father had done when she was a child and as her grandfather had done before him.

She checked herself. If she made the call, boats would put out from the village to kill the whales. One death that day was all she could bear. The seals floated silently and the whales turned and circled as though waiting for some action from her.

# CHAPTER FOUR

While Helga had been closing her dead mother's eyes, Dan Watts was sitting on a ledge outside a cave high up in the basalt cliff across the fjord, sipping tea from a metal mug. He moved one leg, farted luxuriously and said to a nearby sheep, '5.6 – at least!' The sheep raised its head and moved on down the rock-strewn slope to join two others.

There had been a time when even a fart, let alone a cough or an indiscreet word might have cost him his life but those days were past. Compared with his time in the Special Boat Service this trip was a doddle – a piece of cake. Even if he were seen he would most likely be taken for a twitcher but the natives had proved friendly – not the insensitive killers portrayed in some of the anti-whaling propaganda Skipper Jack had left in the cabin for him to read. He put the empty mug down, took a catapult from the top pocket of his camouflage jacket, loaded a small stone from the pile on the rock in front of him then sent the stone flying in an arc over the road far below. It fell with a tiny splash in the dark water beyond. Not bad for a distance shot.

He let fly three more stones in quick succession, each one hitting the rock at which he aimed. The three sheep looked around to see what had caused the noise then moved hurriedly away along the tussocky hillside. He knew he had been indiscreet but – what the hell!

Twenty minutes earlier, as the sun had appeared above the horizon between the towering sea cliffs at the fjord entrance, Dan had crawled out of the tiny cave and done twenty press-ups and the same number of sit-ups on the dew-damp turf behind the rock which hid the cave-mouth.

Squatting, he had turned his face towards the sun, taken a comb from a pocket of his green and brown-blotched combat fatigues and run it through his hair before doing the same to the stiff black whiskers on his cheeks and chin. It was good to be living in the open again although he missed the challenge of constant alertness. The beard was a new experience too.

Dan had come to the Faeroes four days earlier on the weekly ferry from Scotland to the islands' capital and main port, Torshavn. He had wheeled his motor bike aboard at Aberdeen and, after seeing to its safe stowage, had mingled with visiting birdwatchers and the islanders who had been to Scotland to buy clothes and shop in the big stores of the Granite City.

He was dressed like the birders, wearing camouflage clothes and carrying a long-lens camera quite openly but he had avoided conversation. Despite his pre-trip study of the islands' birds he was afraid that his difficulties in remembering such things as the differences between guillemots and razorbills might blow his cover.

Dan had ridden up from Bristol on 'Bonny', his sixties Triumph Bonneville, cruising at a little below a ton on the motorways, frequently glancing in the mirror as his beloved but elderly machine performed effortlessly, but no cruising police cars had pursued him as he rode north past Preston and Carlisle, Glasgow and Perth. He enjoyed watching the reflections of the vehicles that he passed change their shapes in the lovingly polished chrome plate on Bonny's headlamp.

On Royal Deeside he had camped undetected in the grounds of Balmoral Castle and breakfasted on one of Her Majesty's cock pheasants that had carelessly managed to walk into the line of fire of his morning catapult practice.

This was the second morning in his O P above Eysthavn. He sniffed the air – something big was going to happen today. He had always had this sort of sixth sense, though in his service days it had been easy enough to anticipate impending action. The frequency of signals increased enormously, the officers strode round more purposefully, and orders were given to double and triple-check one's weapons and equipment. But here, the signals were much less tangible. Had he been asked to explain he could not have done so.


He had completed his reconnaissance of Eysthavn which was at the mouth of a fjord that he suspected was used as a whale killing-ground. He had explored the village during the brief night, counting the boats in the new harbour and noting the mooring position of each.

The old harbour was empty – the newer one being better protected from the east and nearer to the fish-packing shed. He had stored the information in his brain. Eysthavn: two small harbours, one deserted; twenty-two boats, mostly well maintained; thirty houses, a church and a fish-packing shed; no shop; single road along the fjordside, ending at the village.


There were no vehicles on the road this early in the morning. He shot another stone out into the black water.

Dan's clothes always had two pockets reserved for ammunition. One easy to reach, which he frequently replenished with small round stones for practice and an inner one in which he kept a dozen ball bearings of just the right weight to kill or maim an enemy silently. It had been a childhood dream to use it to protect a maiden in distress but so far in his thirty-four years he had never found that necessary. Men to kill – yes – but maidens in distress – no such luck.

He was about to sort out some food when he caught sight of a movement at the farmhouse across the fjord. He had seen the buildings there as he had surveyed the village from the cliff on the previous evening.

House on its own: three out-buildings; six small fields between the sea and the cliffs; a waterfall down the cliff face; no road; boat with outboard motor moored in a cleft in the rocks; no people visible.

The farm could have strategic importance. He took Skipper Jack's high-powered binoculars out of their black leather case.

The day was mostly clear, if chilly. Occasionally thick mist came swirling down from the black and green hills, blanking out all vision, only to clear within minutes and be replaced by brilliant sunshine.

Dan rested his elbows on a rock and focused on the farmhouse across the fjord. A woman had come out of the house and was walking, almost running, towards the water. She was dressed in men's clothes and had blond hair tied back, possibly in a single plait. Before she reached the edge of the rocks she turned abruptly and went back inside the house.

A sheep grazing on a ledge far above Dan dislodged a small rock which rattled and bounced down the cliff face. He ducked into the safety of the cave where he had hidden his Bergen backpack, his sleeping bag, the camera and his food reserves and watched the rock fall past the cave entrance, strike the ground once more, then leap clear over the road before splashing into the dark waters of the fjord. He watched the ripples spreading outwards before picking up the binoculars once again to scan the area around the farmhouse. The woman must still be indoors.

He breakfasted on a tin of sardines spread one by one with a knife-point onto hard biscuits and followed this with another mug of tea brewed in a billy-can on a tiny gas stove in the cave entrance. Supping tea in the open had always been a pleasure.

As he was drinking, the woman came out of the house again carrying something he could not recognise at that distance even with the glasses, walked down to the water's edge and sat on a rock just beyond the cleft where her boat was moored.

Dan swept the entire scene with his glasses, then focused on the blonde, trying to make out what it was she was holding. There were black heads in the water near her. Divers? Unlikely. Probably seals. Yes – definitely seals. And the fins farther out – they must be pilot whales swimming towards her. A faint sound of music reached him and he recognised that the woman was playing one of those old-fashioned concertina things. Was she calling the whales in by playing that? Nothing in the notes he had found in Skipper Jack's boat had suggested that the Faeroese people 'called' the whales. The notes told of whales coming close to land of their own accord before being rounded up by the boats.

The fins were near to the rocks where the woman was sitting and he could see from the ripples that a few of the whales were circling as though they were waiting for something. Others were poised upright, their heads well out of the water.

The music ceased and the woman stood up and started to walk towards the house but stopped and stared across towards the village. A shout of 'Grindabod! Grindabod!' reached him and he lowered himself out of sight as the cry echoed and re-echoed from cliff to cliff. 'Grindabod! Grindabod!' Seabirds rose in circles as the echoing cry was repeated again and again. 'Grindabod! Grindabod!'

Dan raised his head cautiously. The man who had made the call was up on the base of one of the lights on the old harbour entrance pointing across the fjord. Men and boys were running from the houses towards the boats, shouting as they ran. Some were carrying metal hooks.

The urgent words, 'Grindabod. Grindabod,' still filled the air, tossed back and for by the sullen cliffs. The excitement was contagious. Something snapped in Dan's head and he wanted to be running down the hillside shouting, 'Wait for me. Wait for me.' Then the Skipper's voice was in his ear, steely hard. 'Get a grip of yourself, man!'

Dan counted slowly to ten and forced the crazy urge out of his mind. It left him shivering and cold.

This urge, this *thing* – he had no name for it – had first happened to him when he was nine years old.

The older boys from the estate had run past shouting, 'Kill it. Kill it. Kill the bugger.' They were chasing a black and white cat and he had run after them shouting, 'Wait for me. Wait for me.' Of course they hadn't waited, not for him, and when he arrived with his catapult at the ready they were all kicking at the cornered animal.

'Stand back,' he had shouted, and been surprised when they obediently did so. He had stepped forward, a stone ready in the leather, and aimed at the quivering body of the crouched cat. The stone thudded home and the cat screeched. Dan had shot it again and again, secretly horrified at how long it had taken to die.

As the boys were drifting away he asked what the cat had done.

19

'I dunno.'

'Can't say for sure.'

'Killed something, I guess.'

'It was an ugly bloody cat anyway.'

When the other boys had all gone, Dan was suddenly and terribly sure of something awful. He had gone slowly forward, bent down and read the owner's name on the collar of the dead animal. The name was GASKELL.

Mrs Gaskell lived in the flat next door. It had been Mrs Gaskell's new cat, Lucky, the one she'd got when her old one, Henry, had been run over.

He told the RSPCA officer who had questioned him, how he 'had to put the poor thing out of its misery,' though he knew this was a lie, and nothing further had come of it. Mrs Gaskell had been as kind to him as before whenever one of his mother's boyfriends had pushed him out into the draughty concrete corridor.

The *thing* had struck twice during his service in the Royal Marines. Once in training when the Skipper had bawled him out and once in a battle situation where he had let it run its course. That was the day he had won the gong that he kept locked away back at the flat in Bristol.

From behind the rock, he watched the boats leaving harbour, all heading out to the seaward side of the pod of whales. The beating of his heart was almost back to normal.

On a neighbouring island the Minister of Economic Development stood at the window of his office on Tinganes, looking out over the harbour of Torshavn. He watched a fishing boat, with high bow and stern cruise smoothly past many similar boats, all strongly resembling Viking longships. The moored boats bobbed in the wake of the fishing boat as though eager to follow it out to sea.

The Minister turned to the immaculately dressed businessman from England who was seated on the upright visitor's chair, the light from the window bright on the smooth skin of his bald head. He had taken an instant dislike to the man but tried not to let it show.

'I cannot grant you the permissions you are asking of me, Mr . . .' He glanced down at the letter on his desk. 'Mr Cartwright. I am sure that you are right that there *could* be a very lucrative market for the freezing whale meats in Japan.' He looked up, aware that his English was less than perfect. His visitor was trying to conceal a scowl.

'And I am grateful to you for drawing my attentions to it and also for offering to organise the marketings. Good heavens knows, a small country like Faroyar is glad of all the foreign currencies we can earn, but the killing of the grindhvals – the whales – is a tradition here and not a matter of economics. In fact, some of us believes that it stops many visitors coming to the islands for holidayings. I know Danmark would like us to finish the doing of it.

'Myself, I do not care for the killings, but since these islands were first settled by our ancestors from Norway a thousand years ago, people here have killed the grindhvals, but only for foods, you understand. Foods for themselves – in the villages.'

He turned and studied the watercolour on the office wall. It was of his home village on the island of Eysturoy and the painted yellow and green fields made him want to be there now, helping to get the hay up for drying.

The Englishman's voice brought him out of his reverie.

'I've seen frozen whale meat in your supermarket, here in Torshavn – it was labelled Grindflesk. That was whale meat, wasn't it?'

'Yes. Some peoples sell their shares to the stores here – but it is *not* for sale outside of the Islands.'

Mr Cartwright got to his feet, irritation evident in his every move.

'So I've wasted my journey here,' he said.

'I regret that is so,' replied the Minister. 'But why do you not stay for one or two days to see our beautiful countrysides of the islands.' He waved his hand at the painting. 'I can arrange for a car to take you around and abouts.'

'Thank you, but no. I am booked on tomorrow's flight to Glasgow. I have brought work with me – I can do that at the hotel. Are you sure there is no way to set up what I have suggested? It could be very profitable for *all* concerned.'

The Minister noted the emphasis on the 'all', strode across the room and opened the door.

'Thank you for coming, Mr . . . Mr Cartwright. I hope you will find the remainder of your stay in our country enjoyable. But our whales stay here – alive or dead.'

# CHAPTER FIVE

While Dan had been carrying out his night-time survey of the harbour, a circle of starwhales had been poised in the moonlit sea some miles from one of the Eighteen Islands. They hung in the water, maintaining their upright positions with the slightest movement of their tails and flippers, their heads out of water and their eyes focused on the stars above.

In the centre of the circle was Nordstar, a white female, the only one of that colour to have been born to starwhales in remembered history, and whale history reaches back more than a million years.

Nordstar was unmated, though others of her age would certainly have joy-shared with males by now, if not actually borne calves. This self-denial she had accepted as part of her destiny, a minor sacrifice compared with the one she would have to make soon, possibly even the next day. She shuddered and listened to the earnest arguments of her fellow whales, each stationed to mirror their name-stars in the night sky above.

Aldebaren was speaking. 'A full thousand years have passed since our Great Shame and a million whales have died in recompense. The ~yegods~ promised that we would be released from the Death-duty after that time had passed. And we have a white virgin to fulfil the prophecy. It must be now.

'We do not know if the upstarts any longer depend on our bodies to sustain them in these islands. The prophecy also said that the Death-duty would end when our meat was no longer needed.'

'We have no way of knowing if the upstarts go hungry,' another whale said. 'They can come and go on our Sea, but we cannot do the same on their Land.'

'If only the ~yegods~ could come again, they would know. They imposed the duty.'

Aldebaren sighed, a fine mist rising from his breath-vent and glowing in the moonlight above his back. 'They have not been seen for many years – of that we are all aware. They may have gone to the crabs for all I know.

'We can only read what the Heavens tell us and their message is not clear,' Aldebaren continued. 'The Dead Planet's passage through the

22

Crab would signify death, and for that we are prepared, but the Ringed Planet's position in the constellation of the Swan speaks to me of a multiple rather than a single death, and the constellation of the Virgin is devoid of planets. I am unable to advise.' He sighed again and a night-flying shearwater, cruising just above the surface, turned away in panic at the eruption of misty spray.

'Are there star-signs relating to the upstarts?' a female asked. 'The prophecy speaks of a white-headed upstart dying with the white virgin starwhale before we are released from the Death-duty. The two must die before we can swim unafraid for ever.'

'I have seen no upstart signs in the stars tonight,' Aldebaren replied, knowing that when there were, his sister-whale's daughter, Nordstar, would have to make the sacrifice that would free them all. 'Nor have we seen the shooting stars follow the sky stripe. That was to be the final sign.'

An airliner flying at 35,000 feet passed overhead, moisture from its jet engines condensing in the bitter cold of the thin air. Hardly had it passed out of sight over the eastern horizon before fragments of space-debris from a failed communications satellite, glowing to white heat in the friction of re-entry to the Earth's atmosphere, streaked in its wake.

'Tomorrow is the day,' Aldebaren announced unhappily and the heads of the whales slid below the surface as they began their slow swim towards the islands. Two starwhales swam alongside Nordstar, projecting waves of support, comfort and gratitude into her swim-path to strengthen her for the coming ordeal.

The dolphines Humber, Tyne and FairIsle idled in the water until the sounds reaching them indicated that the whales were near.

'Stargazers usually sound serious, but these seem really miserable today,' said FairIsle. 'Let's see if we can cheer them up.'

'Ever the dolphins' role,' said Tyne, leaping to see the whales for herself in the thin pre-dawn light.

Through millions of years of association, stargazers and grinners, – as the pilot whales called bottlenose dolphins – have learned to communicate effectively. Their languages of clicks, whistles and grunts, amplified by subtle body movements and backed up by a considerable degree of telepathic transmission allowed conversation, even if a little stilted at times. Both species used the same greeting convention.

'How are your seas?' Elegance of Humber asked the whales courteously as their swim-lines converged.

'Calm enough,' replied Nordstar's mother Capella, the senior female in the pod, who then asked, 'And in your swim?'

'Favourable currents,' clicked Humber. 'No orcas?'

'None of which we have awareness.'

'That is good.'

And, with the formal greetings over, the dolphines swam amongst the starwhales to exchange news.

'Are you from distant waters?' a male asked Humber as they cruised side by side, their tail flukes rising and falling in unison, though the whale was nearly twice the size of the dolphin.

'We are from the eastern coast of the Land of Eng,' Humber replied.

'Then you are unlikely to know of our Death-duty in the Eighteen Islands?' Though worded as a statement, it was signalled and received as a question.

Humber replied, 'Apart from a Great Blue, who we fear is now with the crabs, we have met no other whalekind for many days. We know nothing of this Death-duty. Is it a custom among these islands? We have heard whispers in the seas that the humans from the Land of Many Fjords have been killing the Numberers – the Minke whales – but we do not know if this is a truth.'

'That is a truth, but our Death-duty was laid on we Starwhales of the North by the ~yegods~ a thousand years ago – after one of our kind erred greatly towards the upstarts.'

'Upstarts?' Humber's body signalled 'question'.

'You call them "humans",' said the starwhale, Aldebaren. 'As I am sure you will know, it was the task given whalekind by the ~yegods~ for whalekind to help the humans develop intelligence and compassion, tolerance and understanding – before the humans betrayed our trust.'

'We dolphins still hold out a hope of doing that, said Tyne. 'What was the error of which you tell?'

'You will have heard of the great mass of land far to the west, the land that stretches from the Northern Ice Plates almost to the Southern Ice Lands. A thousand years ago in the Land of Many Fjords to the east of here, upstarts assembled a fleet of boats to go and build new lives for themselves and their families in this distant place where only a few, darker-skinned upstarts were living.

'With our knowledge of the night skies, it had always been our duty to guide upstart's boats on long voyages, and this was no exception. Sirius, the greatest starwhale navigator of the age, was selected as pilot to the fleet, and this was seen as a great honour. Many starwhales envied him.'

Aldebaren paused in his explanation. The whales' progress had slowed even more, though they were still heading for the nearest of the islands.

Its massive cliffs descended on either side of the great sea-filled opening – the Channel of Sacrifice – from where FairIsle had fled to escape the evil sense that morning.

Signalling to the pod to head towards the opening, Aldebaren continued.

'However, several days out from land, one of the upstarts' boats struck a female starwhale, a favourite of Sirius' and she was sent to the crabs.

'To his eternal shame, Sirius led the upstarts, not to the Land of Vin as was his duty, but amongst the dangerous rocks and crags here in the Eighteen Islands. In a storm all the boats were destroyed and many upstarts drowned. As the islands were barren of trees, no boats could be made for the survivors to sail neither on to The Land of Vin, nor back to the Land of Many Fjords.

'The ~yegods~ heard of this unworthy act and their judgement was dire. The Tusked ones imposed the Death-duty on the Starwhales of the North for a thousand years.'

'No wonder the stargazers are serious,' thought Grace of FairIsle and waited to see what the Death-duty involved.

'The Eighteen Islands had little life to sustain the upstarts, except fish and birds, so the ~yegods~ decreed that each year as many starwhales as the upstarts needed, must offer themselves as food. This we have done for a thousand years. Today, we make the final sacrifice – the signs in the Heavens have told us that the Death-duty is about to end.'

'Should this not then be a day for rejoicing?' asked Grace of Tyne, as the cliffs they were approaching towered above them. Sea birds launched themselves from ledges, circling and calling raucously in the dawn skies.

'In many ways – yes. But the decree can only be lifted, according to our legend, when a white virgin whale dies with a white-headed upstart. Then we will know that our body-meat is no longer needed and be free. We have such a white whale with us today – my sister-whale's daughter, Nordstar the Virgin, whom we all love dearly.'

FairIsle looked at Nordstar and read a sadness in her eyes as deep as that in the eyes of the great lone whale.

'There is another part to the legend,' a young starwhale said.

'I had omitted that, to spare Nordstar,' said Aldebaren swishing his tail-flukes at the speaker. 'But since it has been floated . . . The Death-duty will only cease when the white whale has been eaten on the Land, and the white-headed upstart has been eaten in the Sea. That was the final part of the decree. Today, we go to sacrifice our beloved Nordstar as our part of the ancient pact with the ~yegods~.'

'May we have the honour of swimming with you?' Humber asked. 'It will be a tale to tell our youngsters' youngsters when we are wisers. And to Nordstar I say, 'Be brave. If your death saves countless others of your kind, it is a noble and a proper thing to do. We salute you.'

Humber leapt the exquisitely elegant and moving Curvee of Salutation, a gesture followed by Grace of Tyne and, less elegantly but no less sincerely, by Grace of FairIsle.

Aldebaren led his constellation into the Channel of Sacrifice and as they turned the headland they all experienced a strange tingle in the senses of their jawbones. Rhythmic sounds, bearing messages of great sadness, flowed through the still water. Sounds unknown to starwhale and to dolphine alike.

FairIsle leapt. On a rock at the water's edge was a human figure making these unfamiliar but thrilling sounds with movements of her hands. Even though this one was seated and wearing the covering usually worn by human males, something in her posture indicated that she was a female.

Seals listened in the sea below the low promontory and, behind the human, FairIsle caught a glimpse of one of the square-sided boxes in which many humans lived and was presumably the home of this one. She was pale-skinned and had white hair on her head. She must be the human part of the final sacrifice, lamenting her impending death.

FairIsle's thoughts spread amongst the starwhales and the pod circled slowly beyond the group of seals. Several of the whales raised their heads above the water to view the upstart who was destined to die with their sister-whale, Nordstar the Virgin.

They saw the woman cease making the rhythmic sounds and stand erect, then stare across the water to where another human, a male, had made a loud cry. The words were magnified and repeated again and again as they echoed from cliff face to cliff face, 'GRINDABOD . . . GRINDABOD . . . Grindabod . . . Grindabod . . . grindabod . . . grindabod . . . bod . . . bod . . . bod . . .'

# CHAPTER SIX

Helga glowered across at the village. People were running between the houses. Boats were leaving the harbour opposite. She could hear the buzz of outboard motors and the shouts of men and boys as the boats circled out to sea to head off the grindhval. The magic of her communion with the seals and whales had gone and she felt physically and mentally drained. Her shoulders slumped forward as she prepared herself to watch the prelude to the ritual that had happened here at least once a year for as far back as she could remember.

Boats were driving the whales towards the shallows at the head of the fjord. A dolphin swimming with the whales leapt as though to see more clearly what was happening. The seals had disappeared, diving among the rocks and the kelp and Helga wondered why the whales did not do the same. It had always been as if they were *offering* themselves to be killed.

She had only ever seen the Muster, never the Kill. Women and clergymen had traditionally been barred from the actual Kill and her father had forbidden it as not a sight for a girl. Also, since he and her grandfather had been drowned, she had always had to stay with her bed-ridden mother.

Helga glanced at the house, silent with death, laid the accordion reverently on the rock where she had been sitting and went down to her boat, stepped into it and cast off the mooring rope, pushing away from the crudely carved steps as she did so. The boat drifted backwards out of the little harbour as Helga pulled the starting cord of the outboard motor. The engine spluttered into life and she steered after the other boats, her own smaller one rocking violently in their wakes. I am free to do what I like, she thought. Fri, Fri, FREE.

A new strength flowed through her body and she looked up as a sea bird swooped low over her head. She shouted at the bird, in English, 'Free – I'm FREE!' The bird veered away and headed up the inlet. Others were leaving the cliffs and following the boats. More were coming in from the open sea, all calling hungrily.

Nordstar and the other starwhales had heard the sound of the upstarts' boat-propellers thrashing the water across the inlet and felt the interwoven vibrations of the engines as the boats came nearer.

Nordstar trembled with fear – uncontrollable shudders rippling along her body – the upstarts were coming to kill her. She had dreaded this moment all her life. The prophecy had spoken of the Chosen One going gladly to her death but she was not glad – she was terrified, so all her pain and agony and terror would be in vain. Her fear reached out to the others.

'I will be with you, Nordstar. You will not swim alone,' Aldebaren told her, coming up to her side as her escorts slipped back to allow her to swim forward to her destiny.

Nordstar reached out a fin to touch her mother's brother-whale in gratitude and love as the two swam out of the slowly circling constellation and towards the killing beach. She must try and hide her fear and be glad. It was good not to be alone.

The star-songs of the remaining whales filled the water as Nordstar and Aldebaren, dorsal fins proudly showing above the water, swam together up the Channel, the last sacrifice any starwhales would ever have to make, each singing their own Song of Truth – the different cadences mingling and counter-balancing one another.

But the boats were not turning towards them as Aldebaren had expected, he could sense that the direction the boats were taking was further out to sea, beyond the other whales. He slowed, signalling for Nordstar to do the same.

Then all the whales and the three dolphines were together again, the boats closing behind them and herding them away from the open sea and towards the beach at the head of the inlet.

There was confusion and panic, the songs dying and being replaced by calls of alarm and fear. The males tried to place themselves between the boats and the females – as they did when a pack of orcas threatened a pod – ready to lead the attackers away, but the sounds of the engines, the slash of the propellers and the thumping of heavy objects against the sides of the boats all led to distraction and terror.

They swam in the only direction open to them – up the narrowing, shallowing channel until suddenly there was gritty sand below their bellies. They were ashore in shallow water, their greatest instinctive fear, where echoing was useless and sounds were either magnified or absorbed. Upstarts were standing in the water, waiting. A young whale screamed as a heavy metal hook was swung and driven deep into her flesh near her breath-vent and, as one, the whales tried to swim towards her to offer help. A knife slashed and the water, churned by their threshing tail *flukes, turned pink, red, then crimson as the knives slashed and slashed again.*

The boats had closed the circle behind the whales and more men were dropping over the sides into the shallow water of the shingle beach, and wading waist deep towards the whales, hooks, ropes and knives in their hands.

Helga, standing at the helm of her boat, watched the men of her island whooping and shouting like Viking berserkers. Among them she recognised her Uncle Roi, one of the elected Grindaformenn appointed by the village once a year to lead the grindkills.

She held back, slipping the engine into neutral and staying out of the way of the other boats, some of which were stationed to cut off any attempts by the whales to swim out to sea again, though none appeared to be doing that. *All the whales* seemed to be trying to get near to the first one to have been hooked. A flash of a fin near her boat, followed by another, told her that at least two dolphins, who must have been with the whales, had escaped. She watched the slight V-shaped disturbances in the shallow headwaters of the channel as the dolphins swam rapidly away from the slaughter towards the open sea.

On the shore to her right a man was crouched between two of the rocks that formed scattered islands in the shingle. The man was bearded, dressed in camouflage clothes and wore a khaki woollen hat. He was watching the kill through binoculars and he clearly did not wish to be seen.

He must be one of those troublemakers. One of those people from 'outside' who were trying to impose *their* ideas on the islanders. She slipped the engine into gear and steered towards the man who evidently saw the boat coming his way for he stood up and started to walk up the beach away from her. She shouted at him angrily.

Dan had been so intent on observing the kill that he had not noticed the boat coming up behind him until he realised he had been seen. He kicked himself mentally for being so unprofessional. In the past, a mistake like that might have cost his life or that of his mates. Now, a dignified retreat was the best option and would be the least likely action to draw him to the attention of the men who were killing the whales. His backpack was hidden further along the beach – he could collect that later. He started to walk away but the woman in the boat was shouting at him and steering for the shore.

'Shit.' The boat was going to land just where his pack was concealed. A black and white bird fluttered along the ground ahead of him, trailing its wing as though it was injured. He had seen this behaviour before and knew it had evolved to draw predators away from a nest or crouching chicks. He followed the bird, amused to find that he had developed a limp but the ploy was not working. The woman was shouting again, her words lost in the hullabaloo from the killing ground. She had run the boat aground, jumped out and seen his Bergen between the rocks.

'Shit, shit, shit.' He feigned a fall, hoping that she would come nearer but she had picked up his heavy pack and thrown it into her boat as if it had been a sack of potatoes.

It was his turn to shout but she ignored him and pushed the boat out, clambered in and was four boat-lengths away before he reached the water's edge.

Only then did he realise that the woman was the blonde from the lonely farm. She waved insultingly, turned away from him and headed down-channel the way she had come, standing at the tiller and not looking back

Dan thought briefly of stinging her trousered rump with a stone from his catapult, decided against it and crouched, impotent and annoyed, behind a rock, sullenly watching the men in the water slashing at the necks of the living whales. None of the men appeared to have seen the incident on the beach.

A tall man had arrived by car and taken charge – obviously some kind of local official.

Helga sat by the stove in the house, the khaki pack on the floor by the door, wondering why she had taken it and what she should do with it now she had it. It was obviously important to the man on the beach. It would contain most of what he needed to camp out on the island and, at the least, he would be uncomfortable without these things – but *that* was not why she had brought the pack to the farm.

She could account to herself for having followed the other boats up the fjord. That was just curiosity – the fulfilment of a wish long denied, though now she wished that she hadn't. In the past when Uncle Roi had brought her family's share of the dark meat and delicious blubber across to her house, she had tried not to connect it with the whales that swam so gracefully past her rocks. Often when she had seen them as girl she had *not* given the 'Grindabod' call and once when her brother had, she had not spoken to him for a week. Now, she would never eat grindflesk again.

But why had she brought the pack home? Why hadn't she just thrown it in the sea? That would have shown her contempt for strangers who tried to interfere. She might still do that. Though, if the stranger didn't *see* her do it, the gesture would be wasted.

Realising that she hadn't eaten any breakfast Helga, took an apple from a bowl on the table, and ate it as she walked to the field where the cow lowed frantically.

Seated on a three-legged stool, Helga milked the gentle-eyed beast, pulling and squeezing the teats and feeling the ache in her own breasts that came each month. Today, that other ache was there in her belly, an ache of emptiness and she thought of the man on the beach, daring to think that he might come to get his pack. Was that why she had taken it, she asked herself, but did not answer the question.

She picked up the stool and walked round behind the cow's tail to strip the other two quarters. Could anyone blame her if she had? Nils, her childhood sweetheart, had gone to Danmark when he was twenty without asking her to marry him as the whole village had expected, and had come back with a pert young thing from København who didn't care for the Islands. A year later they had gone back to the mainland, taking their brat with them. By the time Helga had got over that the few eligible young men in the village were married.

She pulled hard at the teats and the cow complained, its moo low and irritable as it held back the milk. Helga mumbled an apology.

Dan had watched the continuing kill from a new hiding place much nearer to the action. When it was over he'd have to find a way to get his Bergen back from the woman.

The stalk to his new concealment point just above the killing beach had been almost enjoyable, exercising to the full his experience of field-craft, though he would have had to admit that not one of the killers, nor any of the row of spectators, ever looked behind them as he had crawled and wriggled from rock to rock. All their attention had been on the whales.

Watching the beach as the hours wore on, even Dan, who had always thought of himself as a hard man, began to sicken at what he saw before him. Whale after whale was hooked, knifed and dragged ashore. Fountains of blood spurted out of slashed necks as jugular veins were severed and tails beat the water in ever-weakening death throes.

He started to get angry and told himself that this anger was unprofessional. He watched a teenage boy beg a knife from a man in a navy-blue jersey and stride down towards the carcasses in the shallows, wade in and sit astride a black body, grinning. Dan reached into his pocket for the catapult and a stone, changed his mind and with a well-practised action, took out one of his precious ball bearings and slipped it into the sling.

He was sighting on the boy's upraised hand when he heard the shout of 'NO' from a bald man who had just stepped out of a car.

31

*The dolphine, FairIsle, lay belly-down in the shallow water with twitching bodies on either side of her. She was unable to wriggle her body backwards as there were dead whales between her and the deeper water, so she feigned death, though it was hard to control her breathing in such a way that movements of her breath-vent would not betray her. If she could only survive long enough, the bodies behind her or to her side might be dragged away and she could flip round and escape. Earlier calls to her mother and aunt had gone unanswered in the melee and she did not know if they had been killed or had escaped.*

*The water was sticky on her skin and when the waves from a threshing whale sloshed over her eyes the sky momentarily turned red. Cries from the last living whales filled the water, all the time getting fewer and weaker. One voice she recognised as Aldebaren's, singing his Song of Truth to the last to give encouragement to his fellow whales. A snatch of the song reached her,*

> *. . . in the fifth dimension swimming*
> *Visions clear and love . . .*

*His song gurgled to a sudden silence as a drag-hook was swung down and into his breath-vent. As his single vital airway flooded with blood the song died, leaving only the forlorn lamentations of the white stargazer.*

*FairIsle wondered why this one, out of all the whales, the one whose day of sacrifice this was to have been, was still alive.*

*A gull swooped past her head and she stared vacantly, trying not to let her eyes show life. Her tail, held for too long in an unnatural position, twitched violently. A young human male waded towards her, threw a leg over her back to straddle her and raised a knife above her neck. As she braced herself for the stroke, from somewhere on the land beyond the beach a commanding human voice shouted, 'NO!'*

*FairIsle did not know the word but the tone and tenor of the sound told her that one human was forbidding another to do something. She felt the immature one astride her back, pause and she relaxed a little, hoping that the command-word could mean a respite for her. 'Hope swims with dolphins,' her mother's mother's voice seemed to come from the depths of her mind.*

The boy holding the knife above the dolphin-hval's neck checked in mid-stroke and looked up to see who had called. Around him the bodies of hundreds of slaughtered grindhvals lay inert in the water, and tired men, their clothes soaked through with blood and brine, stood on the beach waiting for the lorries to come and take away the carcasses. Some of the

men and a cluster of other boys were looking at the only creature beside
the dolphin who was still alive – an unusual white-coloured grindhval
which they had so far spared out of curiosity. One of them would shortly
kill the white hval as there was nothing else to do with it, and what was
one more death amongst so many. Its meat would probably taste the
same as that of the black ones.

These men, and the boys with them, had also turned to see who had
come to interfere with the time-honoured traditions of the hval-kill.

The bald-headed man standing by the taxi was a stranger to them all.


The boy sitting on the dolphin was not going to be denied his first kill by
some slap-headed stranger. He raised the knife again ready to plunge it
deep into the smooth black skin and draw it smartly to the right as he
had watched his father do in this and many other hval-kills.

He heard the thud at the same time as his hand went numb. The knife
dropped onto the dolphin-hval's head before splashing into the slurry of
seawater, blood and faeces around his feet. Through the tears flooding
his eyes he saw a mysterious silver-coloured ball roll across his victim's
back and disappear into its blowhole with a swirl like bath water going
down a plughole. He stared at his hand. Two of his fingers hung limply,
the bones clearly broken. Pain crawled up his arm to his shoulder then
back down to focus in his two crooked fingers. The dolphin-hval on
which he sat was making odd whistling noises. He slid off its body and
stumbled ashore holding his right hand in his left.

The bald man was walking towards him, gesticulating as he picked his
way around the beached corpses. *He* had nothing in his hands. It couldn't
have been the stranger who had shot at him and smashed his fingers.


*FairIsle had once drawn a falling feather into her breath-vent but had
expelled it at the first excruciating tickle. Now, something feeling like a
round pebble of ice was trickling down into her lungs, restricting her
breathing. The young human had gone.*

*Believing and hoping that feigned-death was still her best chance of
life, she held her breath as the ice pebble rolled deeper and deeper into
the passages of her lungs until it reached a tubule too small to pass.
There it lodged, a focal point of intense pain. In desperation she let her
breath go in a shuddering but ineffective lung-gust.*


*The smooth-headed man had come down onto the beach. He must have
seen that she was still alive and pointed a finger, first at her and then
along the beach towards where she had last seen the white whale,*

*Nordstar, before the water had turned red and she had lost contact with her mother and her mother's sister.*

Mr Cartwright had heard from the waiter at the hotel that a whale-kill was taking place at Official Killing Site No. 9. Unlike in the old days, when news of kills was signalled across the islands by runners, sheets spread out on hillsides and bonfires, telephones now conveyed the information in seconds.

He rang for a taxi and, although it took three hours of hard driving over mountain and coastal roads, through tunnels and by way of one short car-ferry crossing, the kill was still in progress when he arrived.

Most of the whales were dead and many had already been hauled up on the beach and their intestines removed. Guts and unborn foetuses, perfect pink-coloured miniature whales, lay in steaming heaps. Some of the whales in the water were possibly still alive and, as he stepped out of the taxi, he saw the tail-twitch of a living dolphin trapped on the shoreline by three dead pilot whales behind it. A young man astride its back was about to draw a knife across the dolphin's neck.

Nearby was an unusual white whale, also showing signs of life. He had shouted and the boy with the knife paused, checked by the authority in the voice.

'Tell him to stop,' Mr Cartwright snapped at the English-speaking taxi-driver standing beside him. 'I want to buy that dolphin and the white whale. It may be a beluga. Tell him not to kill it. I want to buy them both.'

But the boy was stumbling ashore without his knife, tears running down his face.

The local Syslumador, traditionally responsible for the distribution of the whale meat, intervened and ordered the white whale and dolphin-hval to be spared until the bald man from England had made his request clear. The boy with the broken fingers was telling his friends how a tiny silver ball had shot out of the dolphin-hval's blowhole, smashed his hand and then been sucked back in again. Otherwise he would have killed the shitty hval for sure.

Nets were brought from the village and Nordstar and FairIsle were secured amidst the shambles in the shallow water.

Dan, having observed the effect of his shot with a certain satisfaction, wriggled backwards through the tussocky grass and, when out of sight, walked up the riverside to where he had concealed his motorbike. As he walked he considered his options for recovering his Bergen. He rejected the idea of stealing a boat to cross the fjord as too likely to lead to his

34

discovery. He would wait for dusk and find a route along the far side of the channel to the lonely house. There he would either: Plan A; persuade the woman to give back the pack or buy it from her if need be. He had a roll of banknotes in his pocket; or Plan B, steal back his own property if she was unwilling to give or sell it to him. That should be easy enough – she appeared to live alone and from what he had already seen in the islands, few people ever locked their doors at night.

Of course there was a Plan C. Let her keep it. Somehow, though, *this* plan had no appeal. Women did *not* get the better of him, and to abandon equipment in the field went against his training and instincts.

Plan A, Task One: find a way along the steep south side of the fjord to the lonely house.

Bonny was just as he had left her, hidden under the canvas of a hide designed for bird-watchers that acted as a camouflage net. The stones and grass that completed the cover were still in place and it was clear that the bike had not been found. It shouldn't have been – the hiding place was well away from any human paths and Dan had ridden slowly up the riverbed for most of the way. The stream had only been a few inches deep but the tumbling, peat-stained water had totally obliterated the wheel tracks.

He tucked the canvas neatly under the rear wheel, having decided that Bonny needed it more than he did – he'd often slept rough in his service days. He added a few more rocks, more from love than necessity, then took off his boots and waded across the river. Another of those black and white birds with a beak like an orange pencil flew, complaining as always, across the marshes and out of his sight.

As he neared the beach in the semi-darkness he gave the killing-site a wide berth. He could see whale carcasses being loaded onto lorries lined up along the road by the beach. Out on the water a fishing boat was anchored and what looked like a white whale's body was being lifted aboard by some sort of crane.

An hour later, Dan bivouacked against a cliff face, having failed to find a safe way up in the darkness. He ate a little chocolate and a few dried apricots from his emergency food reserve kept in an outer pocket, before brushing dried sheep droppings from under a projecting rock and crawling into the hollow to sleep.

He loosened his boots, pulled up his collar and rolled his woollen hat down over his ears. He was glad of the beard, it kept the lower part of his face warm.

He'd had the beard for nearly a year now – ever since that day after he'd flown back from his last holiday in Majorca.

Dan wriggled into a more comfortable position, put the binocular-case under his head for a crude pillow, tucked his hands into the front of his jacket and, in spite of a chill wind and the smell of sheep dung close to his nose, he slept.

# CHAPTER SEVEN

It had been almost a year since the plane from Palma landed at Gatwick, and Dan had sat and waited for the more impatient passengers to get their hand baggage out of the overhead lockers and jostle to leave the plane. There was no hurry – they would all have to wait round the conveyor for their cases to come through.

As the last passenger passed his seat, he stood up and reached for his black holdall. This action seemed to draw a curtain across the events of the past two weeks. Memories of hot sun, cold lager and holiday sex vanished and a picture of his one real love came into his mind. She would be waiting for him in the covered section of the secure car park, ready as always to do his every bidding and to carry him effortlessly back to reality. He pictured the classical curves and could almost feel the throbbing that would permeate his whole body as he opened the throttle to roar away into the night. Bonny, beautiful, even if old-fashioned, had never let him down, never asked more of him than he was willing to give, and obeyed his every command without question.

Why, he asked himself, did he bother to go to Majorca at all?

He cruised down the M4 and onto the M32 and was back at Bristol as the pallid English sun dropped behind the blocks of flats on the Clifton Road. Dan wheeled Bonny into the garage she had all to herself, and smelt the familiar and comforting odours of oily rags and musty concrete as he pulled the machine up on to her stand. He wiped the chrome-plated headlamp with his handkerchief and patted the fuel tank lovingly before locking the garage door and walking the two blocks to his flat.

The pile of mail on the floor rustled as he pushed the door open. Most could wait but one envelope obviously wasn't a bill.

He didn't recognise the handwriting. The name read, 'Sgt. D. Watts.' Only Skipper Jack still addressed him as 'Sergeant,' but it was not *his* writing. At the head of the letter was printed: ST JOSEPH'S HOSPICE, SEA ROAD, POOLE, DORSET. The letter was dated 15th June – eight days earlier.

Dan had read the nurse's letter rapidly, stuffed it into his trouser pocket, pulled the door closed behind him and ran down the stairs.

Bonny ate the miles between Bristol and Poole but it was still past midnight when Dan reached the Edwardian building in Poole's Sea Road with the discreet signboard outside.

'Why didn't you phone?' the night nurse asked gently when he had given his name. 'I'm sorry, but Mr Jackson died this afternoon. Can I make you a cup of tea? Mr Jackson said you'd come when you got the letter. Have you been away?'

'Majorca. Only just got back.'

Dan parked Bonny safely behind the Hospice before reading another letter that was given to him. This one had been dictated by Skipper Jack and was in the same nurse's handwriting. He spent the night in the room set aside for relatives of the terminally ill patients.

The letter had been typical of the man. It said little of Skipper Jack himself except that his own version of Gulf War Syndrome had suddenly worsened and the doctors had said that a week was the most he could reasonably expect. The staff here were marvellous, death came to everyone. His only regret was that he couldn't see his current 'scheme' through himself. He was sure that Dan would take it up for him. Another letter was with his solicitor, Mr Edwardes of Edwardes, Jenkinson and Fellows. Their address followed.

In the morning a nurse woke Dan, bringing him a cup of tea. He showered in the *en suite* bathroom, shaved with a disposable razor he found there, then went to see the matron.

'Would you like to *see* Mr Jackson?' she asked.

Matron went to a room at the back of the building with Dan and unlocked the green door.

Although Skipper Jack, as all the squadron had called him, had been the greatest influence in his life, Dan hardly recognised the face. The skin was tight over the bones and the dark eyes were hidden behind closed lids. Most unexpectedly, for he had not seen him for a year, the dead man had a silver-grey beard.

Dan drew a chair up to the bedside as Matron slipped quietly out of the room. Dan did not pray, neither he nor Skipper Jack had ever been that way inclined but he silently thanked the man for all he had done for him during their years in the squadron and since.

He sat, eyes unfocused, by the body of his friend, smiling sometimes as he recalled, one by one, many incidents when they had served together. Eventually, as he stood up to leave he reached out and brushed the unfamiliar beard.

'Goodbye, Skipper, you old sod,' he said. 'Goodbye.'

Mr Edwardes received him courteously but, as they shook hands, Dan eyed the solicitor warily. He held the belief that all professionals were conspirators, conniving with other professionals to rip off ordinary folk like him. He let Mr Edwardes do the talking.

'Thank you for coming to see me so soon, Mr Watts. I'm sorry about Mr Jackson's . . .' The missing word hung unspoken in the air, then Mr Edwardes continued. 'But from what *he* told me about *you*, we don't have to skirt around the facts and use polite euphemisms for death.'

Dan nodded, wondering what Skipper Jack had told this man.

Mr Edwardes looked up. 'I have a letter here that Mr Jackson dictated to me a week ago when we failed to reach you at Bristol. He also dictated his will which I took down and he managed to sign. It was witnessed by Matron and one of the nurses so it is quite valid. In simple terms he left whatever he owned to you. As far as I know, his estate consists of a boat – a redundant trawler he called *The Warrior* – moored in the harbour here and not much else. I know he sold his house to buy the boat so I would expect there to be a bank deposit account holding the balance. His current account is with Lloyds in Poole. I can check that out if you would like me to. He lived aboard the boat so I would imagine all his other possessions are there.'

A woman brought in a tray with two delicate china cups and a plate of Rich Tea biscuits.

Mr Edwardes waited until she had left. 'Coffee?' he asked.

As Dan reached for the cup Mr Edwardes opened a drawer in his desk and took out a bunch of keys which he laid on a Manila envelope.

'These are the keys to Mr Jackson's boat. I can see no reason why you shouldn't have them now, but I just need to be absolutely sure that you are Daniel Watts and I will have to ask you to sign for them. I am sure you will understand. You are exactly as Mr Jackson described you, otherwise I would have had to go through these tedious formalities earlier.' A typed receipt was ready to hand.

Dan was impressed. He showed his driving licence and credit card and Mr Edwardes pushed the letter and keys across the desk.

'Directions for finding the boat are in the letter, as I recall. Come and see me again whenever you wish. Here's my card.'

Dan walked back to the Hospice, wondering about funeral arrangements. He spoke to the matron.

'Didn't Mr Edwardes tell you?' she said. 'Mr Jackson signed some papers to give his body to the University Hospital. He hopes they can find out more about what it was he actually died of. Do you want to see him again? The hospital is sending some people over later today.'

Dan declined. He had already said his goodbyes.

In the relatives' room he read the letter that Skipper Jack had dictated to the solicitor.

*Dear Dan,*

*People here have been trying to contact you since the doctor told me what I already knew. I'll skip most of the sloppy stuff. You know how I felt about you. One day I hope you find a woman who can put up with you and you have the children I never had. I would be tickled pink if one of them just happened to be called 'Jack'. Enough of that. First, I would like you to finish a job for me. I admit I really knew I was unlikely to be able to see it through myself. Plan B was to set it up for you.*

Dan walked across to the window and stared out, seeing not the row of Edwardian houses with the dark green pine trees in their gardens, but a desolate beach in Kuwait where he and Skipper Jack had roasted in a tiny dugout for three days waiting to be picked up after an unsuccessful raid. Two of their party lay dead and fly-covered in the dunes behind them. The beach was covered by an Iraqi machine-gun position and they had not dared to move until the planned diversionary attack along the coast had covered their retreat.

He owed Skipper Jack. What was *he* asking of him now?

The letter went on to remind Dan of when the Skipper had been on a course with the US Navy, using trained dolphins for mine-laying and recovery. Dan knew the Skipper had caught the 'dolphin bug' as he had called it.

The letter continued:

*I can't believe that people can still kill whales and dolphins for food and I made a promise to do all I could personally to stop it.*

Dan remembered Skipper Jack's promises. They were always kept, regardless of the cost to himself – and sometimes to others. What the hell was *he* in for?

*You will have seen how Greenpeace have been so successful with small boat intervention against oil companies, and against whalers when there was more of that going on. I have bought a boat, The Warrior, and now she is all yours. Find a crew, (some of the old Squadron lads would be keen, I know) and do your utmost to stop the last of the whale-killers. Japan and Norway are the biggest countries involved but a lot of whales are still killed each year in the Faeroe Islands. That*

40

*might be the place to start. I'm only sorry we won't be out there together, as in the old days.*

*By the time you read this letter you will have met Mr Edwardes and will have the keys to The Warrior. Someone at Smith's Boatyard will put you aboard, then it's up to you. All the gear and any stuff you may need are aboard. Good Luck.*

*P.S. If you cannot, for any reason, do what I have asked, check the overheads, dispose of any unwanted gear, sell the boat and give the proceeds to the Whale and Dolphin Conservation Society.*

The neatly typed letter was followed by a shaky *Jack*, then in brackets an equally shaky, *John C. Jackson* and a date – *20th. June.* What had Skipper Jack willed on to him?

His own Plan A was clearly to find *The Warrior.* Typically Skipper Jack had offered a Plan B but, for the present, Dan rejected that option – that would be wimping-out.

He thanked the matron at the Hospice and rode Bonny slowly down to the quayside. He knew Smith's Boatyard – the SBS training base was just across the harbour. His sense of loss on seeing Skipper Jack's body was being overridden by a sense of anticipation. He revved Bonny's engine impatiently at the traffic lights.

# CHAPTER EIGHT

After taking the man's pack from the beach and fleeing the bustle and the horror of the hvalkill, Helga had hung around the house all day, only going out to milk the cow and feed the chickens. She did not go into her mother's room. She *would* go if the bell tinkled for her, though she knew that it couldn't, not from the bottom of the sea.

Finally, totally exhausted, she went to bed, leaving her grandfather's accordion in its box on guard just inside her bedroom door. No troll would dare come past that.

In the morning she looked into her mother's room. Her mother was dead, as she had expected her to be, but with the sheet pulled up over her head.

Helga left her there and went across the fjord in the boat to tell her Uncle Roi. As usual she headed for the Old Harbour which she preferred to the stark concrete of the new one, but the entrance was closed off with nets that were draped between the rusting lamp standards and reached down into the water.

Uncle Roi followed her back across the fjord with two other men in his own larger boat and together they rolled the body in blankets and carried it down to Helga's tiny harbour between the rocks.

Uncle Roi suggested she to come and stay in the village. He would come back later and see to the livestock.

'Thank you,' she had replied. 'But no. I need to be on my own for a bit. Do you understand?'

Uncle Roi did. The dead woman had been his sister.

At first light Dan wriggled out of the hollow under the rock, picked sheep droppings off his camouflage jacket and trousers, and set off again, following a trail of small cairns which took him up steep screes and along breathtaking ledges to the cliff top where he could see over the channel. The whale carcasses and all the boats had gone, though hundreds of black and white gulls were still fighting over the scraps of offal left on the beach.

He rested briefly after his exhilarating climb, and then did a fair yomp along the cliff top until he came to a small river draining a vast upland bog. The river ran through a narrow channel and projected the stream out over a lip of black rock and into the open air, the sound alternating between a hiss and a sigh as occasional gusts of wind from the sea blew against the cliff face, driving the water upwards and showering it back over where he crouched. He crawled to the edge, taking care not to show himself against the skyline and peered down. Far below the water fell into a pool at the foot of the cliffs, then tumbled over fallen rocks to the sea. Two tiny fields away, the buildings of the woman's farm crouched between the fields and the rounded rocks at the water's edge.

From here, as he ate three dried apricots, he surveyed the scene below him, professionally noting the layout of the buildings and locating lines of possible retreat. One of Skipper Jack's favourite maxims had been, 'Time spent on reconnaissance is seldom wasted.' This whole trip to the Faeroe Islands was just a reconnaissance exercise – any anti-whaling action would come later. The trawler with 'The Warrior' painted neatly on its stern, was still in Dorset.

The view here was better than it had been from across the fjord. The single-storeyed wooden farmhouse with the cluster of other wooden and stone-built buildings around it was as clearly visible as on a map or an aerial photograph. Fields, separated from each other by crude walls of piled rocks and wire fences, ran from the foot of the cliffs almost to the edge of the dark water. Beyond the fields, on either side, the black crags rose sheer out of the depths – no way round there. The place was only accessible by sea or from any track that might exist down the cliff below him.

Between the house and the sea the smooth rounded rocks were split by the cleft in which the woman's boat lay snugly moored, hardly moving to the slow lift and fall of the sea beyond. The natural harbour looked bigger from here than it had seemed when viewed at an angle from across the fjord. It could accommodate a larger vessel if need be. Old car tyres hung on the rock walls on either side. There was no sign of the woman.

Dan leapt easily across the stream then climbed down the cliff by zigzag pathways marked by stone cairns and into the meadow at the side of the house. A cockerel on a fence post saw him coming and crowed a challenge. Dan assessed its value as an emergency meal, walked through the knee-high grass, followed a beaten dirt path round to the black-tarred door, and knocked.

The blonde woman came out, her eyes screwing up in the morning sunlight and spoke to him in a language he did not understand.

He stood there uneasily. 'I'm sorry,' he said. 'I . . .'

'You are of England,' the woman said, speaking now in English with very little trace of a foreign accent. 'I thought you must be of England when you ran away from me yesterday.'

I didn't run away, Dan thought, just made a tactical retreat, but no matter.

'You will have come for your backpack,' she said and Dan nodded.

She looked past him for a boat.

'By the cliff pathway?' she asked.

Dan nodded again. The woman looked surprised.

'No person has come that way since . . .' She paused. 'I am named Helga Jacobsen. Come in, please. I do not know why I took your backpack yesterday. I suppose I was angry with you.'

'Angry?'

'Coming here to interfere with what we do. What we have *always* done.'

'You mean killing the whales?'

'Ja. Yes. The grindhvals.'

'Did you see the killing? It was horrible. No sight for a woman.'

'It has always been done – for food. There is no easy way. I did not stay for long to see. But you will know that.'

She stood aside. 'Please come in.'

Dan ducked through the low door and into a room that was a curious accumulation of styles. He looked about him. The walls were of ancient wooden planks, darkened by age and by the smoke from an antique iron stove that stood in one corner and which looked as if it served for both heating and cooking. A collection of old-fashioned looking plates, dishes and jugs were on shelves to either side of the stove but the two armchairs, a sofa, and a dining room table with four upright wooden chairs were 1960s Scandinavian. There were no 'bought in' pictures or ornaments but around the room and on the floor were many carved wooden animals and birds. In one corner was a twisted piece of grey driftwood that had evidently been kept as too curious to burn. The air in the room was close and heavy with the smell of peat smoke.

A galvanised metal tub stood on the stove and a mound of damp washing was on a tray on the table. The woman pulled at a towel so that it covered a bra on the top of the pile.

'Will you take some tea with me, or are you angry for me taking your pack?' she asked.

'Tea? Yes please. Thank you.' This was going better than he had expected. He was ready for some tea.

The woman was wearing a wide brown belt with a large horn-handled knife in a leather sheath. Otherwise, her clothes were the same as on the previous day – a chunky hand-knitted jumper and a pair of men's black woollen trousers.

'Please, will you sit?' she asked, indicating a chair by the table.

Dan sat and watched her busy at the stove. He did not care for that knife but she was behaving hospitably and not threatening him in any way. She seemed almost glad to have him there.

Helga poured boiling water into a teapot, selected a mug with a faded floral pattern on it from the shelf and filled it.

'Do you take your tea with the milk?' she asked. 'It is from our . . . my own cow. I have milked it myself this morning.'

'Thank you, yes,' said Dan awkwardly, wondering if the woman always wore a man's clothes. He glanced surreptitiously at the knife.

'Do you live here alone?' It was important to know.

'Now, yes. Now, I live here by myself.' Helga replied.

'Your English is very good,' he said. 'Did you learn it at school?'

'First at school, then I listen to the BBC. We have a little battery radio, see there.'

Dan was reviewing his plans. The woman was far friendlier than he had expected. There might be a chance of a real meal here. When he'd joined the SBS soon after the Falklands war he'd heard that the farmers' families there had always been good for bacon and eggs, lamb chops or mutton stew.

If he played his cards right he could have a decent meal, recover the Bergen, which was not in sight, and get a boat ride over to the village. Then he could walk back along the sheep-paths to his bike and ride easily to Torshavn. There were still a couple of days before the ferry left. He'd seen all he needed to see of a whale-kill.

When they had finished the tea, Helga showed Dan around the farm buildings. She showed him the small cow-byre, the covered sheep-pen, the hen-house, the building with slatted wooden sides for drying meat and the shed with the motor-driven grass cutter and the farm's hand tools in it. She was not sure why she was doing this – it was as if she wanted to sell her farm to this man. She described each building carefully, drawing his attention to the good points and ignoring the places where rain had leaked through the patched roofs or where repainting was well overdue.

At about midday they had finished the tour of inspection. Helga glanced at the sun, now at its highest above the cliffs, and said, 'I will be having my lunch soon. Will you stay and join me or must you be leaving?'

'No hurry,' said Dan. 'The boat for Aberdeen doesn't go until Friday.'

'Then you will stay for lunch?'

Helga made a meal of fish and vegetables which they ate at the table in the dark room. As Helga cleared away the plates Dan said, 'Can I help you with any of the work? I owe you for the meal.'

'You are welcome to that – to the meal. It is a duty to see that visitors do not leave one's house in hunger.'

'I don't *have* to leave soon,' said Dan and Helga was sure he was watching her reaction. 'I could stay and help you with the hay. You said it was ready to cut.'

Helga's heart leapt. She told herself that this was because she had been dreading doing all the work herself and here was a strong man offering to do it with her in return for a meal she had been duty-bound to provide anyway.

'Can you drive the motor-mower?' she asked.

'If anyone can, I can,' Dan replied and stood up.

The motor-mower was an ancient British-made Allen Scythe. Dan had seen similar but newer machines being used for cutting the grass behind the village across the fjord. He wheeled the rusty machine out into the sunlight, checked the petrol and swung the starting handle. To his surprise the motor started at once and he experimented with the controls before engaging the clutch and steering the machine towards the nearest field where the lush grass, rich with wild flowers, was rippling in the gentle wind now blowing in from the sea. The cutting blades in front of the two large wheels balanced the weight of the motor behind the axle and he found it easy to manoeuvre around the field, the grass falling in swathes beneath his feet. A scent that took him back to training exercises on Dartmoor, rose about him and he felt he would really have enjoyed being a farmer. Here would be especially enjoyable. Here there would be boats as well . . .

He mowed the field in ever-decreasing circles, avoiding the large boulders that stood immovable amongst the grass and the flowers. Helga was collecting armfuls of the cut grass and draping it over a sort of wire fence.

It took him the best part of two hours, even though the field would be considered a tiny one in England. When he reached the centre and cut the last narrow strip, he switched off the motor, tilted the machine forward and walked across to where Helga now stood holding two mugs of freshly made tea. She had changed out of the man's clothes and was wearing a coloured blouse and a long cotton skirt. The belt with the knife had gone. Earlier, Dan had taken off his camouflage jacket and his shirt to work in his khaki-coloured string vest.

They sat side by side on one of the boulders, sipping the tea but saying nothing, each busy with their own thoughts. Afterwards, Dan helped Helga drape the rest of the cut grass on the fence and hang an old fishing net over it before steering the clattering machine back to the shed.

'Is it OK if I have a splash in the pool under the waterfall?' he asked. 'I'm a bit sweaty.' He wrinkled his nose.

'It is OK. Today the water will be warm. The sun has been warming the bog at the top of the cliff. My brother and I would play there in the pool when we were little children.'

Helga watched Dan stride off across the meadow, not looking back.

When he was out of sight she followed slowly, asking herself what she was doing but letting her legs carry her across the yellow aftermath as though she were in a dream.


Dan stripped at the edge of the pool, waded in up to his waist, ducked his head under then struck out across the pool. The woman, Helga, had been right – the water was warm. He turned on his back and floated, the sky above the cliffs a brilliant blue, barred with wisps of high clouds.

The main waterfall cascaded into the back of the pool, errant showers of water splashing at random across the surface and the rocks nearest to the cliffs as the wind played with the falling water.

He reviewed his plans. Circumstances had altered dramatically. The woman was positively friendly, though she looked worn out. His mother used to have dark rings like that round her eyes when one of his 'uncles' had been giving her a bad time. He swam around the pool then turned over again and floated on his back, the slightest movement of his hands maintaining his position. Swimming nude made one feel a part of the place – gave one a kind of intimacy with the land.

Skipper Jack had collected what he called 'memorable bathes' from all around the world as a schoolboy might collect stamps or phone cards. Dan let his mind wander – dolphins and whales would be sensitive to every tiny current, every minute change of temperature. They would have no way of hiding themselves from one another. No clothes meant no pretence. No pockets – *no* possessions. He looked over to where his clothes lay in a heap on a rock and felt vulnerable. His catapult was there – and his money. He was starting to draw up an inventory of what else was in his pockets when he saw a movement between two rocks near the foot of the cliff.

He exhaled and sank, a hard-to-learn SBS survival technique that had saved his life at least once. He rose close to a boulder and very slowly manoeuvred into a position where he could see who was watching him. It was the woman – Helga. *She* could watch if she liked. He had watched, and been watched, many times only this time there was no danger of the watcher having a Kalashnikov trained on him. What the hell!

He stood up and waded out, picked up his string vest and rubbed himself down quickly, spread the wet vest over some warm stones and lay face up on a flat rock to dry off in the sun. If she wanted to look at him she could.

Helga sensed that she had been seen but did not move. She envied Dan in the water. She had not been in the pool herself since her breasts had started to bulge and her mother had forbidden her to undress any more when Christian was about.

'But why? We like swimming in the pool.'

'Because I say so, that's why.'

'But Christian's only little. He won't mind.'

'When someone goes to Torshavn next I'll ask them to get you a bathing costume.'

The bathing costume had always been forgotten.

When Dan strolled down to the house Helga was there, pegging clothes onto a sagging line. He sat on a bench, leaning back against the warm grey wood of the house and watched her, not talking. Hens pattered around their feet, each scratching twice before taking two steps backward and studying the ground to see what edible things they might have uncovered. It all seemed a long way from Poole Harbour and *The Warrior*, even further from the monotony and the daily sameness of his work as a security guard.

Helga made no sign of wanting him to leave, neither did she mention the back pack. Later, she boiled water and brought out a bowl with soap and a towel even though she knew he had been swimming up in the pool. He stripped to the waist and washed, aware that he was being watched closely.

He followed her into the house as the sun dipped behind the cliff top, leaving only the houses on the opposite shore glowing in the last, sloping rays that shone down the narrow gap of the inlet from the west, and together they ate home-baked bread and farm-churned butter with slices of some unidentifiable cold meat.

Nine o'clock came and no hints had been given as to whether he should leave or, if he was to stay, where he should spend the night. Helga was sitting in one of the armchairs by the stove, knitting rapidly in the glare of a hissing pressure lamp. Dan went outside, walked down to the rocks and urinated into the sea as he watched the lights of the village opposite reflected in the black water.

'She's waiting for you,' he told himself. 'She's expecting you to stay the night. You've earned this, you lucky sod.' He pulled up his zip and sauntered back to the house.

Helga was trying to interpret her own feelings. She was excited by, yet afraid of this big but gentle man from England who had arrived so opportunely just after her mother's death. Would she be safe if she let him stay in the house? Did they have the 'Strandercare' in England? That would ensure that he behaved correctly. No storm-bound sailor or weather-trapped shepherd would ever abuse that tradition. The man from England had certainly helped with the chores as was dictated by the custom.

When Dan came back into the house a mug of hot chocolate was waiting for him. Helga passed it to him and said, 'Strandercare?'

Dan looked puzzled for a moment then raised the mug in a toast and replied, 'Strandercare. Cheers.'

Helga made up a bed on the sofa as he sipped the drink.

'This is for me,' she told him. 'I will be sleeping here. You are too long for this and the other rooms are not ready for sleeping in.' She paused, then said, 'My brother's room is full of wood from the sea. I save the best bits for carving and the rest for the stove – sometimes it is better than the turf. The other room . . .'

'You have a brother?' Dan asked.

'He is now dead for many years. And my father and my mother as well. You can sleep in *my* bed. It is quite comfortable, but it is old. You won't mind that?'

'No, I won't mind that,' Dan replied, grinning to himself, and following Helga as she lit a candle and went into a small room leading directly off the main one.

The room had a wardrobe, a dressing table with a mirror, and a bed in a similar style to the furniture in the living room. On the wall was a poster-sized picture of a Viking warrior standing in the prow of a longship, his black hair and beard blowing sideways in a strong wind.

'Who's that fellow?' Dan asked and Helga blushed.

'He is Sven Forkbeard. He has always been a hero to me.' Pride was evident in her voice when she added, 'We of Faroyar are descended from the Vikings you know.'

'Was he a real man?'

'He has been to me,' Helga replied. 'Ever since I was a little girl. Here is your bed for this night. I have changed the sheets for you. I hope that you will be comfortable.' She glanced around, smiled a 'good-night' and left the room.

Dan took the candle over to the poster. The man, the Viking hero of this woman, was a giant compared to the other warriors lightly sketched in behind him. His beard, from which he had obviously acquired his

49

name, was about nine inches long and forked in a dramatic and unusual way and his eyes gleamed with anticipation of some unseen pleasure ahead.

Dan drew himself up and saluted the hero, then stripped to his vest and jockey shorts, got into the bed and waited, sure the blonde would soon come padding in.

He lay there enjoying the smooth sheets and the soft pillow – so different from the night before. The smell of a recent hot iron on the cotton took him back to the security of Mrs Gaskell's flat. She often used to do her ironing as she had chatted to him, keeping him in the flat until his mother was alone again.

The candle burned lower and lower but Helga did not come. Perhaps *she* was waiting for *him.*

The wick fell sideways in a pool of melted wax and the flame died. Dan swung his bare legs from under the blankets and crossed the room, feeling along the wall for the door.

It opened noiselessly and he steered across the room towards the sofa, found it, knelt on the floor, lifted the corner of the blankets and slid his hand over the warm body. He could feel that she was lying with her back to him.

She's pretending to be asleep, he thought, as she restlessly turned towards him murmuring sleepily. He felt for her breast through the thick soft material she was wearing.

'Sven?' her voice said softly, then, 'No, no, NO!'

Dan felt her body arch and the bedclothes were thrown back, covering his head. A picture of the sheath knife flashed through his mind and he rolled away. As he disentangled himself from the blankets he heard the outer door slam shut.

I was wrong about her then, the silly bitch, he thought as he went back into her room and, thinking of the knife, pushed the dressing table across the door and got into her bed again.

The morning came and Dan, rising early, put on his clothes and moved the dressing table quietly back to where it had been.

Helga was not on the sofa and her blankets lay where he had left them. He crossed the room, opened the black-tarred door and looked out. The sun had cleared the horizon and he could see the woman hunched on the rocks at the water's edge. She must be fishing, he thought momentarily, then seeing she was still in her night clothes with what might have been a horse-blanket wrapped around her, he swore quietly and walked down to apologise.

Helga stood up stiffly, gave Dan a contemptuous look, walked past him and went back to the house, re-emerging a few minutes later, dressed as before in a man's clothes, the knife prominent in her belt. She was dragging his Bergen roughly along the ground.

'I will take you in the boat over to the village,' she said formally. 'Then you will go away.'

Returning across the fjord after dropping the man at the quayside, Helga felt a dull empty ache in her belly. It was as bad as when the hen's egg she had once carried so carefully between her breasts had broken and the sticky mess in her bra told her that the egg had not even germinated, let alone been ready to hatch.

The old car tyres hanging around the sides of her little harbour looked like the mouths of giants, mocking her. She stumbled up the steps, tears streaming down her face.

Dan leant on the stern-rail of the ferry as it left the terminal at Torshavn and turned southwards. He had wheeled his motorbike aboard as he had done in Aberdeen and with the help of a crew member, lashed it upright to one of the many stanchions on the car deck.

Clouds were forming around the higher hilltops behind the town and he thought of the woman at the farm trying to gather up the hay before the rain swept down over the black cliff face. He'd enjoyed the day he had spent with her even if it was overshadowed by the fiasco in the night, and despite having achieved his objective of recovering his Bergen, he felt empty and dissatisfied. He went down to the light and warmth of the saloon bar and ordered a beer.

In the evening, in the ferry's cafeteria, he bought a hot meal and took his tray into a quiet corner to eat without the risk and bother of having to compare sightings with any of the returning birdwatchers. Hardly had he started eating when a man whom he had watched coiling ropes on the foredeck as the ferry left harbour, came in surreptitiously and sat at the other side of his table.

Dan kept his eyes on his meal. He did not want to talk.

'I know what you are,' the crewman hissed at him in English. 'You are a spy who comes from England to tell us what we can and can't do in our own islands. I live in Eysthavn and I saw Helga Jacobsen take your rucksack when you ran away from her at the hval-kill. Pah! You English have a nerve. I have seen the films of your people all dressed up, riding the horses, going berserker and chasing the foxes and you do not even *eat* the foxes. We *do* eat our whales.' The man jabbed his finger at Dan's chest. 'And it is *you* people who are poisoning the seas with the mercuries and the PCBs. Soon our hvals will not be fit to eat.'

The man paused, watching Dan's face, hoping for a reaction. Dan forked a boiled potato into his mouth and took a drink from his glass. His 'interrogation' training came in useful and here he did not even have to give his rank, name, and number.

The man tried again. 'I saw you come over from the Jacobsen's farm in the boat in the morning after the hval-kill. What did you do over there, I am asking myself. She is a well-built woman, our Helga, is she not?'

Dan resisted the urge to punch the man's nose but farted noisily instead and felt better for it. He ate another potato, waiting for the man to go away but he stayed, glancing at the door now and then. Dan finished his meal in silence and was drinking the last of his beer when another crew member came in carrying a cardboard box. He put the box on the table before leaning towards Dan and saying, 'We thought you might like to have something to remember your fine motorbike by.'

The first man rose from the table and the two walked towards the door, chuckling. Dan pulled the box towards him and looked cautiously inside. It contained Bonny's headlamp, dents in the chrome-plated sides indicating that it had been roughly levered off. The glass had been smashed – even the bulb was broken.

The men were watching from the doorway. He would not give them the satisfaction of seeing how angry he was. Nor was he going to be fool enough to go down to the car deck where others might be waiting for him in the darkness. His bike was on the bottom of sea, he was sure of that. He left the headlamp in the carton and went to buy a mug of tea. It would be wise to stay in the brightly-lit cafeteria through the night.

The ferry docked on time in Aberdeen. Dan was waiting at the embarkation doorway, recalling the layout of the Ferry Terminal building. Concrete and glass, two storeys, flat roof with a viewing platform, built parallel to the dockside.

He walked down the wide gangplank and across the bare tarmac between the quayside and the building. As he had expected, the two men from the night before were leaning on the ferry's rail smoking cigarettes, watching him. One jerked his finger vertically upwards while the other made a V sign in Dan's direction. Dan pretended not to notice, strolled casually into the building then ran up the stairs, two at a time and out onto the empty roof. The men were still on deck, watching the door he had just entered. One of the men, his antagonist from the cafeteria, had his left foot up on the lower rail, the blue cloth of his trouser leg stretched tight across his kneecap.

Dan crouched, took out his catapult and two ball bearings, popped one onto his mouth and shot the other, full force, at the bent knee.

The cigarette fell from the man's lips and dropped into the water near the ring of ripples made by the rebounding ball. The man crumpled to the deck and lay there groaning. As the other man bent over his friend, Dan spat the ball bearing from his mouth into the leather pouch and shot it at the bare skin of that man's elbow. The ball struck home, dropped to the sloping deck and ran like quicksilver across the steel plates and out through the scuppers before making its own little splash in the water between the ferry and the quay.

Dan whistled to attract the attention of the injured men, held up two fingers against the sky then strolled back downstairs to pass through the immigration office and out into the road beyond. The men wouldn't dare make a complaint, he was sure of that. Even so, he found a lying up place in a clump of Japanese knotweed on a railway embankment and stayed hidden amongst the tall maroon stems until dark, reviewing what he had learned on his reconnaissance run. There was no chance of taking *The Warrior* to the Faeroes and hiding amongst the islands as he had once hoped. All but two of the islands were inhabited and the English build of the trawler would be very noticeable. Besides which the killing was done on beaches and the whales were driven ashore by dozens of small boats. Little scope there for dramatic 'on camera' intervention. Perhaps he should consider Norway. But no, he owed it to Bonny if not the whales, to tackle the Faeroese.

At nightfall he easily found a lift on a lorry heading south. He would replenish his stock of ball bearings when he got back to Poole.

# CHAPTER NINE

Dan thanked the lorry driver and dropped down from the cab. Only six lifts from Aberdeen to the Poole bypass. It was now three o'clock in the afternoon – not a bad run. He swung his Bergen up onto his back and started to walk towards the town, was tempted by a passing taxi, waved it down and travelled in comfort to Smith's Boatyard.

The man who rowed him out to *The Warrior* asked about his motorbike.

'She met with a bit of an accident up north,' Dan replied and something in the tone of his voice killed any more questions.

*The Warrior* was as he had left her, moored out in the open harbour with the new Zodiac inflatable stowed on deck. The man from the boatyard helped Dan with the net-hoist as he swung the Zodiac over the side and moored it at the stern, then pocketed the proffered fiver. He shoved off in his dinghy and rowed towards the shore as Dan unlocked the companion-way hatch and went below.

Although it had been several years since *The Warrior* had caught and carried fish, the odour of long-gone cod still lingered in the rooms that had been built into the fish-hold. From the tiny galley in the centre, doors led to two cabins, each with a pair of bunks, and a storeroom with a workbench along one side. A very narrow door opened into the cramped 'heads' which was fitted with a lever-operated flush toilet. Skipper Jack had never been one for 'bucket and chuck it.'

Dan opened the storm-proof portholes that had been fitted into the sides of the boat and let fresh air move through the cabins and the galley. He was hungry and searched the lockers for a quick meal.

When he had first gone below, after inheriting *The Warrior* a year before, he had found that long-range fuel tanks had been installed under the foredeck, but in the cabin area only studding frames for the partitions were in position. The ceilings had been fitted though, and the wiring was complete. He was glad of the latter. Trying to plot the routes between the generator, the batteries, the lights and the switches would have been a bore.

The money in Skipper Jack's bank account had not been as much as he had expected. Perhaps a boat did cost nearly as much as a house – or maybe there had been a mortgage to pay off. As a consequence Dan had done most of the fitting out himself with only a little help and much advice from the boatyard staff. The 'security' job he had taken at the headquarters of a national bank in the town left him ample time to finish fitting out *The Warrior*. The day job was boring and undemanding but the pay was sufficient now that he lived aboard and no longer had to find rent for the flat and the garage in Bristol.

He ran his hand over one of the plywood locker doors he had varnished himself and grimaced. The surface felt more like coarse sand than the proverbial baby's bottom. He would give it a rub down with some fine glass-paper when he had nothing else to do. Even he would have to admit that much of the work had been fairly crudely done, but then he was an amateur and *The Warrior* was a working boat, not a rich man's yacht.

On deck again he sat on the gunwale, eating cold baked beans out of a tin with a fork, and tried to make plans for the future. Plan A *had* to be a return run to the Faeroes to try and draw the attention of the world's media to the horrific slaughtering of the whales. There might be time *this* year if he could get a crew together quickly.

He was still in touch with some ex-squadron men. He started to make a list, certain they would all be keen on some real action, but unsure how many would be able get away for long enough. He would need three men to make up his crew. In the meantime, he would provision the boat for a long voyage and finish off the myriad of small jobs that would make *The Warrior* ready for the task Skipper Jack had bequeathed him.

Helga Jacobsen sat in the front row of the wooden church, staring at the grey-coloured pinewood screen full of intricately cut holes, but seeing nothing. Her mother's coffin rested on trestles near the altar.

She had been surprised that so many of the villagers had turned out for the burial service. If she had wondered why, she would probably have thought it was idle curiosity that had drawn them there. Few would remember the last time Annette Jacobsen had come across the water from her house. For most, it was a spontaneous gesture of support for Helga – the loving and dutiful daughter who had given up her chance of marriage to stay at home after Lars Jacobsen and his old father had been lost at sea and her brother Christian killed netting the lundi.

Some may have been there in the hope of finding out more about the tall, bearded man she had brought across the fjord in her boat – the man with the backpack, who had walked rapidly away along the fjordside road. If they were, they would be disappointed.

After the coffin had been lowered into the shallow soil enclosed by the wooden fence around the church, Helga's uncle asked her what she planned to do.

'I want to get away, Uncle Roi. See more of the world than sea and cliffs and sheep and more sea and cliffs and more sheep.'

Her uncle nodded. He had felt the same when he was younger, but after circling the world several times in the Danish Marine Service he had been glad to come back to sea, sheep and cliffs. Especially now that there was electricity and television and a good bus service all over the islands *and* now that fresh fruit and all the other tasty items of which he was so fond, were flown in and sold in the supermarket in Torshavn.

'Where do you want to go? Danmark?'

'Perhaps. I always wanted to go to England but now I'm not so sure.'

Her uncle raised an eyebrow but Helga ignored it.

'If you want to go, your aunt and I will look after the farm. I can go over twice each day to milk the cow, and the sheep can look after themselves well enough. England is a fine place. Have you read their writer, William Shakespeare? When I was in England one time I went to the place where he was born. He is a very famous man. He said in one of his stories, "There is a tide in the affairs of men . . .", but you do not want to hear of that now, Helga, my dear. Do you have any money?'

'Very little, Uncle Roi. You know . . .'

'I know. But if you really want to go, there may be a way.' He drew her to one side and glanced around.

'After the hval-kill there was one grindhval saved, a white one, and a dolphinhval. They are in the Old Harbour behind nets. An Englishman wants them in England and is paying good money, but the Government must not know. A boat is going to take them soon. I *could* arrange for you to go on that.' He was watching Helga's face. 'But it may be an uncomfortable journey.'

'Uncle Roi! I know all about boats and discomfort. I *would* like to go.'

*All* Englishmen would not be like the one who had come to her house, any more than all Faeroese men were as kind and as understanding as her Uncle Roi.

'You should really have a passport but there will not be time for that,' he was saying. 'However you will be going in by the back door, so to speak, and in England they do not ask you for your passport in the street if your skin is white.'

'What about when I come back?'

'Just speak to the officials at Torshavn in Faeroese and there will be no problem. No one would have learned our language just to come to these islands.'

The boat that was to take Helga to England was a fishing vessel, high at the bow and stern, low amidships to make it easier to haul in the nets.

With the many problems affecting the island fisheries, the owner had decided that a run to England, paid for in advance by the rich Englishman, would earn much more than going after ever more evasive cod.

When the trawler finally came past the sea-cliffs and into the fjord, it was towing a hulk – a wooden sailing ship dismasted in a storm many years before. It had been quietly rotting, unwanted, in a corner of Torshavn harbour, though refusing to sink. The harbour authorities were pleased to allow it to be towed away and wise enough not to ask any questions. It was enough just to be rid of it at no cost to the Harbour Board.

The villagers all knew what was being planned but had not spoken of it 'outside'. The older children, bussed to school in the town, knew it as a village secret and often visited the Old Harbour to look at the dolphinhval and the white grindhval before going home to a meal of grindflesk from the deepfreezes in the basement of every house.

The hulk was moored near the harbour, and the villagers used power-saws and axes to cut away most of the deck. They created a plastic-sheet-lined pool inside, using the remnants of last year's hay from the barns to pad between the black sheeting and any sharp projections within the hull.

As a diesel-driven pump, fitted inside a large packing case secured on its side aft, was used to fill the pool, the hulk settled deep in the water. Experienced sailors shook their heads and prayed the journey south would be through calm seas. The trawler skipper was unconcerned.

'If it sinks, it sinks. We cut the towrope and we sail back again. The hvals can swim away and none of us will be on board it in a storm. The damn-fool Englishman has paid me most of the money in advance and he would not dare try to get his money back. So . . . who cares?' He shrugged and spat into the harbour.

Helga carrying a small suitcase and her accordion in its box, came over from the farm, left her boat in Uncle Roi's care and walked around to the Old Harbour where the hulk was now moored to the outer side of the stone quay. She smelt the familiar odours – dead fish and dank seaweed – and thought of the days when she and Christian had waited for their boat to come and take them home from school. She had always hoped it would be her grandfather who came. In those distant days she would climb up the base of one of the harbour lights and wave and wave as soon as she saw the boat set out from the rocks below the farm. That was all before . . . before . . .

There must be a brighter, less sad world out there over the horizon waiting for her. She turned and looked down into the water of the harbour.

The white whale, Nordstar, was skulking in the depths, rising only to breathe and sinking again at once, trying to lose the sight of the upstarts who had killed her family and all her friends, and worst of all, who were now prolonging the agony of anticipation of her own death. Having witnessed the horror at first hand, the white whale was even more scared of the pain and suffering which she believed must soon be hers.

The dolphine, Grace of FairIsle, was taking a different attitude. She was sure now that her mother and aunt had escaped, though they were unlikely to come to find her. They would be convinced that she must be with the crabs, or whatever the equivalent was on the Land, and would have swum back to their homewaters, mourning her as lost to them forever.

She circled the tiny harbour again, trying to ignore the spot of intense pain from the pebble of ice in her lung. The harbour was large enough for only a few boats though there were none moored in it now and the entrance was closed off with a heavy net. She pushed at it with her nose but there was no way out. The humans – she nearly used the starwhales' word 'upstarts' – had done a good job. Boulders on the seabed, and poles jammed across the opening, held the net firmly. She eyed the other net hung across the opening above the water. That net was held up by a rope stretched between the lightbrackets at the end of each stone quay. The shipstone from which these were made was red with rust, but they were evidently still strong enough to hold the top edge of the net high and taut.

FairIsle sank to the bottom of the harbour, positioned herself and shot to the surface, leapt at the net but failed to clear it. She fell back with a splash, her skin scratched by the harsh twisted fibres that formed the meshes.

'Hope swims with dolphins.'

She tried another leap, and another.

'It is of no use,' Nordstar's voice came through the water to her. 'We will be killed here together.'

'Jetsam!' said FairIsle. 'I don't give up that easily.'

She tried another equally unsuccessful jump, then rested in the water to think of alternative plans. She eyed the human female who stood watching her from the smooth-stone of the harbour-side. She was the same one who had made the sad sounds on the rocks across the channel. The human's long white hair hung behind her head like a land-mammal's tail though patterned in a pleasing, interwoven way and secured at the lower end with a knot of something the colour of the sky on a summer's day.

Only the ~yegods~ knew why this human and the white stargazer had as yet been spared from making their sacrifices. What was to be her own role in the impending drama? It was as exciting as one of the ancient dream-stories that all dolphins learned and retold to themselves and *others during wakeful nights or on boring days when little could be made to happen. Somehow she, Grace of FairIsle, would influence the outcome and swim free – perhaps even take the white stargazer with her. Would the mysterious ~yegods~ appear at the end to save the day as they did in all the best stories? 'Hope swims with dolphins.'*

Uncle Roi watched with Helga as the dolphin and the grindhval were netted and lifted out of the waters of the Old Harbour by a Hiab crane mounted on a truck, hoisted over the harbour wall and lowered into the flooded hold of the hulk moored alongside the outer wall.

'This was your grandmother's.' Uncle Roi took a small gold cross and chain from his pocket and held it out towards Helga. 'Your aunt and I thought you should have it. If you would like it, that is. I am not sure how you feel about . . .' He gestured vaguely in the direction of the church behind the village.

Helga held out her hand. 'Uncle Roi. I would like to have it very much but I am myself not sure how I feel about . . .' She repeated Uncle Roi's gesture and he smiled.

'There can be no harm in wearing it then,' he said. 'Your aunt and I will be pleased if you do.'

Helga rubbed her fingers across the smooth surface of the cross. 'Then I shall wear it all the time. Will you do up the catch, please?'

Uncle Roi kissed his niece goodbye, gave her some money and watched her step easily across from the quay onto the deck of the towing boat. He had never had a daughter of his own.

When the two vessels had disappeared around the far cliffs he went in his own boat across to the farm to check the livestock and see that all was in order. In his sister's room he saw the corner of a pillow lying on the floor under the bed and retrieved it to put away in a cupboard. The pillow smelt of old tobacco smoke. It was not the sort of thing Annette would have had in her room – she hated smokers.

He held it up to his nose and sniffed it again, turned it over in his hands thoughtfully, then took the pillow outside and carried it down to the edge of the rocks.

With his clasp knife, he cut a hole in one corner of the coarse fabric and forced loose stones through the slit before dropping the pillow into the sea. He knelt on the rocks and watched as it floated for a while, drifting slowly out to sea, then sank rapidly, sliding down into the depths looking just like one of the many octopuses he had often seen gliding around tropical reefs searching for prey.

He stood up, put his knife away, dusted his hands and walked slowly back to the house.

# CHAPTER TEN

*FairIsle was feeling queasy. The motion of the hulk caused the water in which she was trapped to slosh from side to side and before long she vomited out the fish that the white-haired human had fed her in the morning. Bits of half-digested cod swilled past her head. She swam forward to clearer water and forgetting to scan, bumped against the flaccid body of Nordstar.*

*FairIsle bubbled an apology, but Nordstar, herself feeling sick, did not respond She had not fed since before that last Starwatch many nights before. The night when she had seen the shooting stars follow the sky-streak, knowing as she saw them that she was doomed. 'Let me die, just let me die,' she pleaded through the surging water.*

*FairIsle ignored her. She again concentrated her thoughts on finding a way to escape. After her first futile attempts to leap over the side had been seen – leaps frustrated by a lack of launching depth within the hulk – human males from the fishing boat had come aboard and stretched a net across the opening in the deck. She had no wish to drown beneath that. Her chance would come. Keep grinning. 'Hope swims . . .' But the hulk was as secure as usual and the sagging net made further leaping impossible.*

*She forced the queasiness and the pain from the ice-pebble out of her mind and projected a story into the water. The scenes ran well enough, though they faded at times if her concentration weakened. Hours passed and the hulk moved steadily southwards. FairIsle chose the happy ending and closed the story.*

*'How did you do that?' Nordstar's voice came through the water from behind her.*

*'Do what?'*

*'Show me that story.'*

*'Did you see it then?' asked FairIsle, not having suspected that a Stargazer could read.*

*'Some bits were faint, but I followed most of it. Do you know anymore?'*

*'Many, many more,' said FairIsle. 'Would you like to share another. I love to regale. I just never thought that stargazers . . .'*

60

'You were probably born under the constellation of the Seal, they are the entertainers,' said Nordstar. 'I was born under the stars of the Crab – the scavengers of death. You might have guessed.'

When Grace of FairIsle had finished the legend of the 'Sea Mountain and the Caves of Crystal', choosing the happiest of the endings, Nordstar told her of the starwhales' knowledge of the movements of the planets and how they affected all living things.

'Starwhales have known these things for a million years,' she told FairIsle proudly. 'But even so, we learn more each year, though some knowledge gets lost when a whole constellation of us dies at the same time. As with each chapter of the Great Whales, every constellation of starwhales holds knowledge unique to it alone. I weep for what was lost in the Channel of Sacrifice in the Eighteen Islands. Only I have this knowledge now and I will never have the chance to pass it on.'

'Will you sing me your song, the one you sang with your uncle that day?' FairIsle asked, floating alongside the white whale and allowing the movement of the water in the wallowing hulk to make her flipper casually caress the other's flank.

'It is a sad song, as mine always have been, but it is My Truth, and a starwhale's song is the Truth as each of us perceives it to be. There are many different Truths under the Stars.'

'Surely there is only one real Truth?' FairIsle asked. 'One Whole Truth.'

'The Great Whales believe so,' replied Nordstar, 'or so Aldebaren told me. He heard a lonely whale sing once. A song of the ~Prime Yegod~, the Great Spirit, the all-encompassing Love of Life and living creatures, but Aldebaren said he could only grasp a little of what the Great Whale was singing, and he was more comfortable with his own smaller personal Truth. I think I am too. Shall I sing my song now?'

As she rose to breathe there was a sudden change in the movement of the hulk. The frayed end of the towline flew backwards and lay on the net over the pool as the vessel slowly turned sideways on to the seas.

Nordstar inhaled deeply, sank back to the plastic bottom of the pool and sang a song of such sadness and longing that FairIsle could see the stars with their planets circling endlessly and hear the roar and whisper of Space going out and away forever.

A second song seemed to join in, and then a third and a fourth, fainter than Nordstar's, each penetrating the soggy timbers of the hulk as a constellation of starwhales, hearing a stranger's song, swam alongside the drifting vessel and joined their songs to hers.

Eventually, the other whales' songs faded and were gone, to be replaced by the throb of the trawler's engines after her crew had reeled in the broken line and circled back to pick up the tow again.

When the rope had parted the skipper had wanted to leave the hulk adrift and turn for home. The journey was proving so slow there would be no profit on this trip. Helga had argued with him as he undid the halyard from the cleat ready to lower the black metal 'towing' signal from the masthead.

'The grindhval and the dolphinhval will die,' she had said, 'trapped under the net.' Then, seeing what little effect this had on him, added, 'And the hulk will be a danger to shipping. Your son is at sea somewhere? Suppose it was *his* boat that hit into it and sank.'

The diamond-shaped signal was hauled up again as the trawler came alongside the hulk, frightening away the pod of grindhvals that was swimming nearby. Timing his movements carefully, a man leapt onto the hulk with a light line attached to a new hawser, pulled the heavy rope aboard, secured it, and the towing recommenced.

On every day of reasonable weather, Helga was taken aboard the hulk by one of the crewmen in the trawler's Zodiac inflatable boat and she fed the dolphine with fish that she had earlier caught herself with a line over the side of the trawler. The grindhval refused to eat, evidently living off its reserves of blubber.

Helga learned how to start the pump and change the water in the pool with fresh seawater each day. She was more concerned than the men to see the dolphine and the whale swimming in their own body wastes.

The skipper liked Helga to be the one to do this work, it enabled him and his male crew to force the tow onwards at maximum speed.

He had chosen the western route to the English south-coast town of Dormouth where his cargo was to be delivered. The Shetland Islands passed, familiar waters to him, and then he navigated through the Minch and into the Irish Sea. In a day or so, weather permitting, they would be ready to cut between the Scilly Isles and the tip of Cornwall.

He avoided other shipping wherever possible, not only because it was difficult to manoeuvre with such an unwieldy tow, but he did not want unwelcome publicity, nor investigation by a British Fishery Protection Vessel.

The storm came in the Irish Sea, east of Dublin.

At home Helga would not have called it a storm, merely a severe blow, but when you are on a deep-laden hulk and the tow line breaks, as it did for a second time, it certainly feels like a storm.

She had been fishing since early morning, glad to be out of the mess-cabin she had to share with the crew, relieved to be out of the overpowering smell of mens' sweaty bodies, and away from the coarse language and crude jokes, many of which were at her expense. She had caught three good-sized fish, certainly enough for the dolphinhval. The white grindhval was still not eating.

In the afternoon, Helga, dressed in a stiff yellow waterproof jacket and a pair of similar trousers, had been taken back to the hulk in the Zodiac, its outboard motor buzzing her along beside the towline to the wallowing vessel in less than a minute. Here she waited for a wave to lift the inflatable nearly to deck level when she jumped agilely from one of the rubber sponson tubes onto the hulk's deck as it rolled towards her, boarding through the gap that had been crudely hacked in its high wooden gunwale for just this purpose.

The Zodiac buzzed back to the trawler. It had been tacitly accepted that the price of her passage to England was her complete care of the two 'hvals'. The boatman would come back for her in an hour.

Helga crouched down and fed the dolphine, passing the dead fish through the netting. The dolphinhval did not seem to fear her and eagerly took each fish from her hand and swallowed it whole. Helga looked into the knowing eye trying to find a name for her new friend who poised there, with its head above the water, as she reached through the coarse mesh and gently rubbed the soft silky-smooth skin. The dolphinhval was looking straight at her, seeming to be reading her mind.

A vision of a cliff-girt island appeared, blurring the net and the dolphinhval's head below. Helga remembered the one time her father had taken her on a long sea voyage as a little girl. He had some business on a remote British island between home and Scotland but she had no idea what the business could have been even now, though the memory of the first sight of the Fair Isle appearing through the mist had stayed with her always.

'*FairIsle* is your name,' she said as the net came back into focus. 'That is a good name for a dolphinhval. I will always call you that.'

Helga stood up and walked along the swaying deck to start the pump, snug and dry in the open-sided wooden packing case that was lashed to the deck and sheeted down with heavy canvas. She unlaced one side of the sheet, turned on the fuel and swung the heavy handle, an awkward task in the confines of the case. The engine coughed asthmatically, then settled down to a steady rhythm, the exhaust gases venting towards the sky where a hole had been made in the canvas for the sooty-black pipe.

Spray slashed across her face as a wave struck the side of the hulk, part of it rushing through the gap in the gunwale and draining into the pool. Helga opened the suction valve on the heavy flexible tube that ran from the pump-house across the deck and down into the lowest part of the pool. The engine note dropped as the load came on and water gushed from the outlet pipe and spewed over the side. As Helga watched, she noted that most of the waves around the cumbersome hulk were now white-capped and she could taste the salt from the spray that splashed against her face and rattled on her oilskins.

A seagull circled down from the overcast sky and perched precariously on the gunwale, looking at her with cold yellow eyes. Another joined it and then several more, all perched in a row facing into the wind and balancing with an occasional fluttering of grey wings.

The water in the pool dropped slowly but before it reached the marker that Helga used as a signal to change over the inlet and outlet pipes she felt the hulk judder. The towline jerked tight and the bow veered away downwind as the line broke again.

Helga was thrown sideways and fell onto four stubby projecting bolts that had once secured a deck winch. The heavy vessel turned broadside to the wind, and waves broke hard against the black wooden side. Water sloshed through the gap and into the pool. Helga staggered to her feet on the heaving deck, her hip aching from the violent contact with the bolts, slipped and fell again, the bolts jabbing into her thigh.

Clenching her teeth against the pain she gave up trying to stand and crawled along the deck, ducked into the shelter of the tarpaulin covering the wooden case and pushed the throttle of the pump to 'Maximum'. It would be a race between her and the unthinking but malevolent sea. Her task being to keep the water level in the pool as low as she could, while the sea did its furious, hissing best to fill it and drag the hulk under.

Helga lifted the corner of the tarpaulin and looked out. Near darkness, hastened by the heavy clouds, surrounded her. She stared through the gloom. The gulls had gone, blown away into the storm and she felt desperately, frighteningly alone. She searched for the lights of the trawler but could not see them in any direction. The wind whistled and moaned through the remains of the cut-away rigging. Spray showered over her again and again, pouring in rivulets from her waterproof hat and clothing. She turned back to the pump. Was there enough fuel to see them through the night?

Kneeling in the darkness, the stiff oilskins awkward in the confined space, she fumbled around the top of the thudding engine, found the fuel tank, unscrewed the lid and poked her finger down through the hole. By wiggling her fingertip she was sure she could feel the liquid move against her skin but she held her finger close up to her nose just to be sure. The tank was well filled, thank God, though the smell of diesel oil made her feel nauseous.

She decided not to go below deck into what remained of the old cabins. These, she knew, stank of rat droppings and decay. If she was going to die she would have a clean drowning, like her father and grandfather, rather than being caught below in such squalor.

The thought of being trapped turned her attention to FairIsle and the white grindhval.

The waves broke over the side and surged along the remains of the deck as she crawled forward to the netting and pulled at the ties in the darkness. When her fingers were too numb to feel the knots any more, she hacked and cut at the net with the knife from the sheath on her belt until she had made a hole in the corner big enough for the grindhval and the dolphinhval to swim through if the hulk should sink. Crouching behind the gunwale she blew on her hands and rubbed them together until she was able to tie the loose netting back from the opening.

Kneeling on the lurching deck she pushed her hand down through the hole and waved it about to sense the level of the water. It was well down. If only the pump can keep it at that level, we all have a chance, she thought.

A smooth nose nuzzled at her hand and she patted it reassuringly, her loneliness dissipating like the banks of bubbles blowing across the deck, sea foam torn from the wave-tops by the wind.

'We will be all right,' she said to the dolphin. 'We will *all* be all right.' She patted the nose again then crawled aft to the pump-house.

The engine was running steadily and she lifted the corner of the sheet and wriggled into the packing case, keeping well clear of the spinning flywheel. She tried to pray, remembering that Uncle Roi had once told her that there were no atheists on a sinking ship. But the words would not come and she felt hypocritical calling on a god whom she had ignored since her brother had died. She'd done her duty by her mother and there had been little chance of other misconduct, at least until the Englishman had come. Her behaviour then had been, she was sure, above reproach. She undid the top of her oilskin jacket and reached down inside her jersey for the gold crucifix. It felt warm and comforting and she held it as she dozed and shivered through the night, trying to ignore the pain that gnawed and pulled at her hip and thigh like crabs attacking a dead conger eel.

The thought of her mother made her uneasy in her mind but she could not focus on why and the physical pain was more than enough to try and control. She gripped the crucifix and shut the nagging, half-suppressed memory out of her consciousness.

*FairIsle sought out Nordstar, who was floating listlessly in her usual place, breathing infrequently.*

*'The human female has tied back the net,' the dolphine announced. 'Be ready to swim through the space if this boat goes to the sea-bed.'*

*'I may as well stay here and drown,' Nordstar replied. 'My life is
forfeit in any event. My fate is to die.'*

*'That is the fate of all living creatures, but I've got a lot of living to do
before the crabs have me. Hope swims with dolphins . . . and starwhales,
if you will let it. Would you like me to show you a story.'*

*Nordstar signalled an unenthusiastic 'yes' and FairIsle began.*

*'Long ago the ~yegods~ were angry. Whales and dolphins were not
following the ~yegod's~ edicts and many offenders had to suffer a belly-
tusking before the Order of the Deep could be re-established. One young
dolphine had a friend who was a starwhale . . .'*

Helga woke as the dawn light showed her that the weather had eased.
She could see the trawler positioned to windward, protecting the hulk
from the worst of the seas. As it moved alongside, Helga crawled from
under the sheeting and two of the crew leapt aboard, pleased to see she
was safe. They helped her to stand and stayed with her while she made
sure that the grindhval and the dolphinhval were unharmed.

She went back to the trawler with the men, leaving the corner of the
net tied back and it remained like that for the rest of the voyage. The
jokes at her expense from the crew ceased after this incident. This pleased
Helga but, no matter how hard she tried at night, she could never recreate
the magical dreams she had experienced while she had dozed next to the
pump. She must have been 'high' on leaking exhaust fumes, she thought,
and fortunate not to have died there in the packing case.

In the dreams *she* had been a grindhval, weightless in the water,
swimming effortlessly through undersea passages of brilliantly coloured
crystal and corals, pursued by huge black and white killer whales with
towering fins, such as she had sometimes seen cruise past the entrance of
the fjord near her home. In the underwater distance she had glimpsed the
outlines of a pair of ivory-tusked narhvals but they seemed only to be
there as observers, playing no active part in the pursuit. It was odd that,
although all the excitement of a chase was there, she knew as she swam
that she would not be caught and neither would her companion, the
graceful dolphine FairIsle.

The ferry from Wales to Ireland passed astern that evening, having altered
course to starboard when the captain saw the three white lights at the
trawler's masthead indicating that the vessel behind was in tow.

Most of the ferry's passengers were comfortably below in the warmth
and security of the lounges or bars, a few watched a cartoon film in the
ship's cinema. On the almost deserted stern-deck a pale-faced young
woman with shoulder-length brown hair leant over the rail to stare at the
trawler as it passed with its awkward tow. The woman was wearing slacks

tucked into white ankle socks, and a loosely knitted jumper. A bum-bag was buckled tightly around her waist and she clutched this with one hand and held onto the rail with the other. She was thinking of going below to get her anorak but the way the black vessel with the broken-off mast-stumps pitched and rolled in the long troughs between the waves fascinated her. There was a figure on the deck of the hulk, wearing a man's clothes but unmistakably a woman.

Something in her stance struck a chord in the mind of the woman on the high deck and she waved self-consciously. The woman on the hulk, evidently seeing the movement against the grey sky, waved back.

The sister ferry coming towards them from Ireland moaned a greeting and the ship shuddered as its own foghorn bellowed out a mournful reply. The pale-faced woman looked apprehensively around the now empty deck, fearful of seeing movements in the shadows, then scurried below for a hot meal in the brightly lit cafeteria, the tic in her left eye pulling savagely and the scar on the back of her head thudding from her exertion. The thudding pulse beat out the rhythm she had become used to over the last two months, 'There is . . . no God. There is . . . no God. There is . . . no God.'

She slumped on the shiny artificial-leather seat and waited for this terrifying message to fade away. Soon she would be swimming with Fungie. Soon, soon.

*FairIsle felt the vibrations of the foghorns judder the water in the hold in which she was resting and rose to view the giant vessels as they passed. On the stern deck of the one heading west she caught a glimpse of a human figure hurrying towards an opening in the shipstone wall. The slightest trace of a familiar aura illuminated it for a fraction of a second but the figure had disappeared into the opening before she could shimmer it. Even so she was sure that it was the female human who had play-shared with her three years before near the Land of the Dragon somewhere to the west of where they were now.*

Helga felt less alone after she had waved to the woman at the rail of the huge ferry. There was at least one other woman in this great empty world even if she did not know who the woman was and would never see her again. What was it that Uncle Roi used to call such things? Ships that pass in the night. The lights of this one were nearly out of sight already.

Back aboard the trawler she carried a bowl of hot water into her tiny cabin, bolted the door and stripped to wash herself. Down her left hip and her thigh were eight round yellow and purple marks in two neat rows. The only thing that could have made such marks was an octopus. So there *had* been a real octopus. Anything she might have had to do to get rid of it had been justified – but she could not remember what it was that she might have done. Whenever she tried to think of her home it was as though a November fog had rolled it from the sea and hidden it from memory but, even in the fog, she knew now that the constraining horror had gone and she could sleep undisturbed.

In the English Channel south of Lyme Regis, the trawler skipper radioed the obscure message given to him by the Englishman who owned his cargo, then towed the hulk through a dense summer sea mist past Portland Bill. He kept well to seaward of that great rock, an island in name and spirit but joined to the mainland by one of the most dangerous lee shores in the world, the notorious Chesil Bank. Twenty miles of unforgiving pebbles, the graveyard of many larger ships than his. The skipper steered by his satellite navigation system, glad of its pinpoint accuracy, which largely made redundant the giant foghorn on the Bill lighthouse. The sound of the horn came regularly, tearing through the mist like the roar of a dying bull.

In the shelter of Dormouth Bay he anchored, sounding his own much smaller horn, until another radio message told him that a crane lorry would be waiting at the end of Dormouth Quay at high tide late that night. The hulk was winched alongside and secured against the trawler, most of the water pumped out of the plastic-lined pool and the two vessels came nosing in together on the top of the tide to moor with the hulk between the trawler and the dock. Practised operators secured the whale and the dolphine in nets and used the lorry's crane to lift them onto old mattresses on the flatbed behind the cab. The vehicle twisted through the deserted back streets to a disused swimming pool.

Here the crane swiftly and efficiently lifted the creatures, swung them off the lorry, over a wall and into the water to join a young male dolphin. Notes changed hands, and the lorry sped away.

A long-haired man in his late teens or early twenties stood in a doorway of the high wall surrounding the pool, looking at the blonde woman dressed in a man's clothes. She carried a suitcase and a funny shaped box.

'Who are you then?' he asked. 'Did you come with them?' He jerked his thumb over his shoulder towards the pool behind him and peered at the woman in the yellow glow of a streetlight.

Helga nodded, the ground swaying gently under her feet.

'I'm Kenny,' the young man said, shaking her hand awkwardly when the woman held it out towards him. 'I look after the dolphins for old man Cartwright. We'd better go in the side door and see that the new ones are OK.'

He followed her through the door, wondering why she had a large sheath knife on her belt.

# CHAPTER ELEVEN

Kenny Palliser had always wanted to work with dolphins. As a small boy he had been taken to the Windsor Safari Park with the other children from his Home. There he had sat in the very front row shrieking with pleasure when a shower of water had splashed over him as a dolphin, after leaping high in the air, dropped back sideways into the water. His housefather, also soaked, was not so amused.

'It's time we went,' he told the group, and Kenny was dragged away protesting that he wanted, 'More doffins, please, more doffins, please.' The vision of the dolphins, though overlaid by the smell of Billy Tranter being sick in the minibus, had stayed with him as the most important thing to have happened in his life.

In the years that followed, Kenny built up scrapbooks of dolphin pictures and dolphin articles from comics and magazines. *His* small personal space on the wall of the communal bedroom at the Home was filled with a plastic-coated picture of four dolphins swimming towards him, coming, as he used to tell himself, to take him to live with them in their watery world.

The two big ones at the front were his mother and his father, Mummy D and Daddy D, the two smaller ones his imagined brother and sister, Flipper and Flapper.

Kenny might have been as useless as everyone told him he was, but in his dreams he was a Super-dolphin who could not only swim, but fly as well. Kenny the Super-Dolphin.

Perhaps he really was useless. No GCSEs on leaving school, a year on the dole and a string of failed work experiences and temporary placements had left him believing that he was no good at anything.

Now, at the age of twenty-one, even Super-Dolphin seemed to have flown out of his life leaving him spotty-faced and depressed.

The dolphin he looked after, Rockall, was the centre of his existence but even *he* was a disappointment.

The advertisement in the local paper had asked for a Dolphin Trainer, right here in his own home town of Dormouth. Kenny hadn't even known there were any dolphins in Dormouth. He had asked John who ran the

Arcade to help him write his letter of application and was thrilled when he learned after the interview that he had got the job. He might have been slightly less pleased had he known he was the only local applicant. The first person, from Brighton, who had been recommended for the job, had walked out when he had seen conditions at the pool, leaving the dolphin's owner, Mr Cartwright in a quandary. His advertisement in the Dormouth Echo had produced just one reply.

Mr Cartwright had been impressed by the young man's keenness and apparent knowledge of dolphins and had overlooked the paucity of entries under 'Previous Positions Held' on his application. He was even prepared to ignore Kenny's long hair and single earring. The kid would have to do until he could find someone more qualified.

The huge 1930s open-air swimming pool, once the pride of Dormouth, had been an embarrassment to the Town Council for years. Far bigger than most pools, it had at one time catered for all those holidaymakers who did not enjoy the sea with its real waves and the danger of touching a jellyfish or treading on something nasty. But nowadays no one wanted to swim in a pool of unheated seawater. The windowless, echoing, chlorine-scented but heated Super-Pool with the Wave Machine was all the rage now, though its owners were concerned that even this was likely to be overtaken in popularity next year when their rivals opened the new Aqua-Centre with Giant Slides and Bubble Experiences.

Mr Cartwright's offer to take on the maintenance of the open-air pool for a peppercorn rent was a good way to cut costs and, as he had pointed out to the Borough Treasurer, the town would still own the freehold if ever the rundown mess of narrow streets and derelict buildings surrounding it, should be considered 'ripe for development'.

There had been only one dolphin for Kenny to train, a young male who had been caught accidentally by a French fishing boat off Brittany and shipped to Dormouth at Mr Cartwright's expense.

At first it was called 'the dolphin', then the name 'Rockall' seemed to come into Kenny's mind when he was watching 'the dolphin' swim round the pool. He told his friend John that he had given it that name because it would do 'rock all' for him but John had not picked up on the joke.

Kenny's first row with Mr Cartwright had been about the dolphin's food.

'He needs *fresh* fish, Mr Cartwright, some of this is old and it stinks. I don't wonder he won't eat it.'

'*You* feed it what *I* get it,' Kenny had been told, but the next delivery from the market was notably fresher and the dolphin ate a little each day. Kenny knew that it could live on its blubber reserves for some time and was not too worried. He was sure it would start to eat a full ration soon – when it had learned to trust him.

He tried to teach Rockall tricks. He waved his arms in high circles as he had seen real trainers do in films. In the cinema the dolphins had leapt like the ones at Windsor, but Rockall just swam slowly round and round the pool ignoring him.

Now Mr Cartwright had told him another dolphin and a white pilot whale were on their way to join Rockall from somewhere up near Iceland.

'Perhaps he'll do better with some company,' Mr Cartwright told Kenny. 'If not, I may be advertising again.'

*Elegance of Rockall circled the pool again – and again – and again – there was nothing else to do. Soon the human would come to feed him with stale dead fish. Rockall defecated. He was eating as little as he could and had held back as long as he was able. He hated fouling the pool and having to swim through his own dung until the filters eventually cleared the water. Most days the filter pump was silent.*

*Rockall thought of the open sea somewhere to the south of him. He could sense it in that direction. Sense it in his very being as the tides surged up the Channel chasing the moon, and then fell back again, twice every day, forever and always, as the tides had flowed since his first four-legged dolphin ancestor had tired of the land and slipped back thankfully into the comfort of Mother Sea.*

*Imagine living on the land, he thought, where your body would feel as heavy as a waterlogged tree trunk and it would be an effort to lift your tail. Apart from joyleaps, when he had been living in the sea, he had only been right out of water twice, once after the humans' net had captured him and he had been towed to a boat nearly drowning in the rushing water, and again when he had been carried from the boat to this tiny rock pool. He recalled the lifting and the lowering, the humans splashing water over his skin when he lay helpless and heavy surrounded by the empty air, with the hardness beneath him hurting his belly. More lifting, more lowering, more splashing – the places the water splashes had missed were searing hot – and finally the relief of being lowered into the cool water here, only to find there was no channel out.*

*Humans had done that to him. Humans who he had always believed were the dolphins' friends.*

*He longed to escape, to dive and leap in the open sea, to chase the lively fish and ride the tide-race of Portland where the currents rushed past the end of that great rock, creating endless opportunities for play. Then to swim leisurely up the back-currents and launch himself into the* race again with his parents, Elegance of Malin and Grace of Lundy, the three of them swimming in joy together through the bubbling waves.

Where were his parents now?

He had been caught up in the net on his first adventure away from them. Would they have given him up for lost when he had not returned? Did they think he was dead and with the crabs?

Rockall swam round and round, watching the sun climb higher over the humans' squarestones – the ugly sharp-edged cliffs with the blind cold eyes in rows along their sides. They were regular and uniform, not in pleasing weatherworn patterns like sea cliffs, and he could not swim away from their ugliness. One, not so quite so ugly, rose to a high rock tower and the blind eyes along its side were the shape of humans' boats standing on their tails. He had no idea why this squarestone was different and he did not care. He was beginning to hate them all, forever staring down at him, and hate was a strange and unpleasant feeling. It twisted his guts. It wouldn't take much more to make him hate the humans too, although he knew dolphins were supposed to love and to help them.

The young human would come soon. He didn't really hate him, he wasn't worth hating – a mere sprat – a little fish hardly worth bothering about, except that the Sprat fed him.

That other human now, the hairless-headed one, he could hate him. He was a shark – grab first, then see if what he had caught was worth eating. Yes, it would be easy to hate the Shark.

The day dragged on. The Sprat came, fed him and waved his arms about. Elegance of Rockall knew, not just from the crude actions but from the subtleties of stance and the whispers of mindwaves, what the Sprat wanted him to do. He wanted him to joyleap. As if one could do that when joy was as far away as the Island of Blue Trees. He might as well ask him to fly or to dive through the bottom of the pool.

Rockall ate a little of the dead fish, yearning for the sweet juices of a fresh salmon crushed in his jaws, then swam round the pool. Once more he circled, lashing with his tail-flukes as he turned each corner until water was slopping out over the paved surround. He went faster and faster, building up a wave and watching the Sprat jumping back to avoid getting his feet wet. Rockall slowed to a halt and bobbed his head out of the water to watch the Sprat's body slump in disappointment. Joyleap indeed! Not him.

Long after the Sprat had left the poolside, night-time came, darkness creeping up the surrounding buildings until all were shadowed and only the sky glowed with a yellow light from the streetlamps outside the pool *enclosure, washing out the stars. Rockall tried to recall a story and project it from his memory but the residue of his anger made the images ripple and distort. It was as though he was viewing it through wind-riffled water. He relaxed and the images faded away. He swam round the pool again. Let something happen, he pleaded to no one. Let someTHING happen. Let ANYTHING happen!*

*Maybe the strange vibrations in the water would come again today as they had the day before – he hoped so. Anything to provide a change from this endless circling and the stale fish.*

*The harsh yellow glow in the sky had faded a little when he heard the sound of an engine outside the pool-compound come nearer, then change note. Rockall lifted his head above the water as the Sprat came through the side door and the dolphin watched as a metal arm rose above the smooth-stone barrier surrounding the pool and a netted bundle was swung over and lowered into the water. A wave of dolphin-presence engulfed him and he backed into a corner. Humans were pulling at the bundle and, as the metal arm lifted again, he heard the unmistakable sound of another dolphin exhaling and drawing in air.*

*Another, bigger bundle swung slowly through the air and was lowered into the pool, the Sprat's hushed voice directing what was going on. Humans pulled at the second bundle, then the engine note changed again. Rockall gave his whistle softly and a dolphine's whistle answered.*

*He swam slowly towards the sound. He whistled again, 'I am the dolphin, Elegance of Rockall of thirteen years, son of Elegance of Malin and Grace of Lundy.'*

*A whistle returned, I am the dolphine, Grace of FairIsle, also of thirteen years, the daughter of Elegance of Moray and Grace of Tyne. How are your seas?'*

*'Calm enough. And in your swim?'*

*'I would say "Favourable currents" as is the custom, but this water feels dead, though it tastes of the sea.'*

*'It is dead and confined,' Rockall replied. 'Who comes with you?'*

*'A stargazer by name of Nordstar, saved from sacrifice, though we do not know why. She starves herself and is unhappy.'*

*Rockall whistled a greeting to the starwhale but it provoked no response, though the whale-presence was strong in the pool. A white light came on above the pool and the dolphins sank to ease their eyes. Two human shapes were peering down at them.*

*'The male one – I call him the Sprat – holds me here in confinement,' Rockall grunted. 'The other, the female, is a stranger.'*

73

'She came with the stargazer and me,' FairIsle told him. 'She is the white-haired one who was to die with Nordstar, but she too was saved.'

'The stargazers call humans "upstarts", the dolphine added.

'I can think of many names for them,' Rockall said, rising rapidly to breathe, then sinking again. 'Upstarts would be the kindest.'

'Elegance of Rockall!' FairIsle chided. 'Dolphins are to love and to help humans. The ~yegods~ have decreed that.'

'Then they don't know how the humans treat us,' said Rockall with a sharp snap of his jaw.

'I am sure they do and it is part of some plan of which we are unaware. Like with the Orca.'

Rockall shuddered at the word. 'What about them?'

'Surely you know that the ~yegods~ set the Orca the task of keeping Whalekind alert? When the Great Sea Lizards died out, all whalekind grew lazy and let their brains degenerate. It was to keep brain and body development moving forward that the ~yegods~ set the Orca to their dreadful task.'

Rockall signalled, 'Explain more.'

'Orca must hunt and try to kill every whale or dolphin they find. Naturally it is the Laggards – the old, the weak or, more usually the dullest – who are killed. This leaves the fittest, fastest and the most able to survive and breed. Thus the miracle of evolution progresses. They say that the Orca hate their task, but it has kept Whalekind advancing. The ~yegods~ are wise and must be obeyed. Would you care to have a tusk through your belly?'

'Do the ~yegods~ really exist?' Rockall asked. 'I only half-believed in them. They are in all the legends, but I have never met a 'phin who has seen one.'

'Neither have I, but I'm taking no risks. Love and help the humans – whatever they do.'

Kenny was pointing into the pool, directing Helga's view. 'There's Rockall, so *that* one must be yours. The pilot whale has been down a long time. If she's not OK, Mr Cartwright will have something to say in the morning. Where are you staying?'

'I am wanting to spend some time in England. Is there a hotel near here that is not an expensive one? I have only a little English money and a bit more Danish.'

'Is that all your gear?' Kenny asked.

'Gear?'

'Kit, baggage, clobber.'

'You mean *this*?' Helga held up the case and the box holding the accordion. 'Yes this is all my gear, kit, baggage and – what did you say – clubber?'

'It's a bit late to find a hotel.' Kenny looked at his Mickey Mouse watch, faithful servant of many years, then at Helga's unconventional clothes. 'We can try. Follow me.'

Helga picked up her suitcase and the box and followed Kenny out into the empty street. If this was England it was crumbly. That did not seem to be the right word. She searched her memory and found the word she was looking for – crummy. English was a language with a word for everything.

As they came out of the back streets and neared the sea front her spirits lifted. Rows of smart hotels lined the road, quite unlike anything in Torshavn but she was afraid they would be terribly expensive.

She need not have worried. Most of the doors were locked and, at the few that were still showing lights, Kenny's request for a 'room for this lady' was brusquely refused.

After the third such refusal Helga said, 'It is of no matter. There is a beach over across the road. I can sleep there tonight.'

'You can't sleep on the beach,' Kenny said, feeling responsible for almost the first time in his life. He wondered if he could sneak her into his room but knew that Mrs Scrimshaw, his landlady, would find out and he would be out on his ear in the morning.

'Can I not stay with the dolphins?' Helga asked, sensing Kenny's embarrassment.

'There's nowhere to lie down.' He wondered what Mr Cartwright would say if he knew that a strange woman had spent the night at the pool.

'At home I would often sit up at night on the rocks fishing. It is of no matter.'

It seemed the only solution and they walked back to the pool.

'Are you sure you will be all right here?' Kenny asked as he showed her into a room with the fading word 'CAFE' over the door. 'I'll lock the door onto the road when I go out. There's a bog over there.' He pointed towards the lavatory door at the far end of the pool.

'A bog, here?' Helga looked in the direction Kenny was pointing, knowing that she must have misheard him yet hoping in her heart for a glimpse of tussocky moorland with white tufts of cotton grass tossing in the wind. She could almost hear the curlews calling but Kenny had realised his mistake.

'Loo, toilet.' Kenny was embarrassed again.

'I am understanding now. Thank you. I will be all right here now. You will come again in the morning?'

75

Out in the misty darkness of the English Channel the hulk was stripped of anything that might identify its origin. With the pump, plastic sheeting and netting removed and stored in the fish-hold of the trawler, the waterlogged vessel was cast adrift in the mist to the north-west of Portland. A sea-mile off Deadman's Bay with the distant foghorn on the Bill unknowingly lamenting the passing of a once-graceful craft, the skipper of the trawler, after studying the charts, had sent a man in the Zodiac to free the tow rope and let the sodden hulk drift away towards the lee shore.

At dawn, the coastguards were examining the remains of an obsolete form of Baltic sailing vessel grounded on the Chesil Bank and were trying to work out how it could have drifted so far unreported. A week later it had been broken up and ground to pieces by the smashing waves and rolling pebbles. What little remained on the sea bed became the home of conger eels and the ever-scavenging crabs.

Helga woke early, stood up and stretched before going out to the poolside. FairIsle and the white grindhval were there and though she told herself that there was nowhere else that they could be, somehow it seemed important to know they were near. FairIsle swam to her and nuzzled her hand as the white hval rose to breathe at the far end of the pool then sank again.

Helga explored. There was an air of neglect, almost of despair in the high-walled enclosure. It felt as she imagined a run-down prison would feel. She shuddered. Then, feeling grubby and stale in the clothes she had slept in, she showered in cold water where bathers had once been encouraged to wash themselves before entering the pool, towelled herself dry as the sun struck the top of the church tower beyond the pool walls and dressed in the best blouse and skirt she had brought with her. She was in 'England' now, even if she had not yet seen any of the thatched white cottages nor the tall, red-coated soldiers with the big furry hats that she associated with the name.

As the sunlight moved down the tower she brushed out her hair and replaited it before going back to kneel at the side of the pool to rub the top of FairIsle's head.

Helga heard Kenny unlock the side door and come in from the road. He held out a carrier bag to her. 'I brought you some breakfast,' he said.

Helga took the bag and peered inside. In the bottom, unwrapped, were two slices of cold toast and a stale-looking doughnut.

'Thank you for this,' she said. 'You are very kind to me.'

Kenny blushed and turned away. No woman had ever spoken to him in quite such a way.

'I'd better check that I locked the door. Mr Cartwright goes mad if he finds it unlocked. He's likely to come down any time now to inspect his property.'

Helga took the breakfast gift and the apparent warmth in his voice to be an invitation to stay, and walked round the galvanised-pipe railings as Kenny went and checked the door before coming to stand next to her beneath the frames of the high diving boards.

She nibbled at a slice of toast.

Kenny had spent a sleepless night. He had always been uncomfortable with girls and women and this one with her foreign accent, who the night before had been wearing a man's clothes and a big sheath knife, was even more disturbing. He was not sure what Mr Cartwright would say if he found out that she had spent the night at the pool. She had moved a step or two away from him into a patch of sunlight and was eating the toast he had brought for her.

He looked at her and was moved in a way no woman or girl had ever moved him before. His knees felt weak and he leant back against the frame that had once supported the springboard.

She was older than he was but that was no matter. He admired her fair hair, neat in a plait down her back and tied with a bright blue ribbon. She was tall – he had always preferred tall women – and she had good boobs, as Billy Tranter had always called them, filling the front of her white long-sleeved blouse.

He glanced surreptitiously at her legs, strong but white and untanned below her dark skirt, and his knees wavered again. Then he could not keep his eyes from the tightness of the fabric across her breasts.

She was talking to him again, he realised.

'Sorry, I wasn't listening,' he said.

The two dolphins were circling together at the shallow end, their dorsal fins out of water. The white whale was motionless at the bottom of the deep end.

'She is not happy,' Helga said, bending over the water.

'I hope she's OK, not sick like. Mr Cartwright goes bananas about vets' bills.'

'Bananas?'

'Sorry, I forgot you're foreign. It means 'goes crazy', you know, mad, bonkers.'

'Bonkers?'

'Forget it.'

FairIsle swam towards Helga, lifted her head out of the water and waited to have her nose rubbed. Kenny watched jealously as Helga petted her, talking in some strange language.

77

'Can *I* do that?' he asked.

'If she'll let you.'

'Is it definitely a she?'

'I don't know for sure,' Helga said. 'I've always thought of them both as hers – females. How can you tell?'

Kenny's face coloured.

'Only the vet can tell – unless they get excited. Fancy one another or something like that. The males' things – you know – are hidden away for streamlining. In what the books call a genital slit. Males and females both have one of those.'

'I understand,' said Helga. 'Yours is a male?'

Kenny looked down as though he had been told his zip was undone, then laughed.

'Oh, my *dolphin*! Yes, he's a male all right. He was caught near the coast of France. His name's Rockall. I'm trying to train him to jump but he's an uncooperative sod.'

'Sod?'

'Dolphin. I'm going to feed him now. Do you want to stay?'

'Ja – yes please. I have nothing other to do.'

Kenny fetched some fish from a rust-spotted refrigerator in the room with the drab 'CAFE' sign over the door. Helga looked at the food in disgust and picked up a sorry-looking mackerel, its dead eyes dull and the once-bright skin, grey and soft. It was limp in her hand.

'If this is what you feed him, I have no wonder that he will not jump for you. If you fed this to me I would not jump for you either.'

The angry look in Helga's eyes when she looked up wiped the smile from Kenny's face.

'This is all Mr Cartwright lets me buy.'

'I will talk to this Mr Cartwright. Did you say that he was coming today?'

'He should be here soon to see these two.' Kenny waved his hand towards the water.

'He likes to surprise me by coming in quietly – he's got his own key. You can't hear his car either, it's a Roller.'

'Roller?'

'You've got a lot to learn about England if you're planning to stay here.'

Mr Cartwright was impressed with Helga's affinity with the new dolphin. This gave him an alternative option, in case young Kenny continued to fail with the training. He could employ her and sack the kid. He agreed to an increased budget to buy better fish and offered her a small retainer if she 'stayed around until the new ones settle in'.

Helga was less impressed with Mr Cartwright. After he had left she asked Kenny, 'What does he want the dolphinhval and the grindhval for?'

'To make him money. I don't know what he paid for them but you can be sure he's expecting a big profit somewhere.'

'I think he is a creepy man. I do not like him at all.'

'Why did you agree to stay here then and work for him?'

'I did not want to leave my friend the dolphinhval here. I do not know yet if *you* will look after her properly.'

Kenny looked downcast.

'What do you do here when it is time to eat?' Helga asked. 'Soon I must find a more comfortable place to stay.'

Kenny took her to a chip shop for lunch and then to see his landlady, Mrs Scrimshaw. To his barely concealed delight there *was* a bedsit vacant, the one next to his. She had just given immediate notice to 'that gawky Welshman who can't read very well. He's weeks behind with his rent and uses his room as a workshop. Wires and things all over the place. I'm not going to have *that* going on. I'll be in trouble with the Council for sure. Always snooping about, they are. Nosy parkers.'

Mrs Scrimshaw took Helga's money-in-advance and told her, 'Come back later, my dear. If Taffy-boy's not taken all his stuff by then, he'll find it in boxes out the back. About five o'clock would be fine.'

*'I've seen that human before,' FairIsle told Rockall. 'The one you call the Shark. I remember him by his head. It is as bare of hair as yours or mine. He saved my life in the Faroff Islands. Why is he here?'*

*'That is the knowledge of the ~yegods~, not of me,' Rockall grunted. 'He is a Shark and I hate him.'*

*'Dolphins are to love and help all . . .' FairIsle started to say but Rockall had swum away, slapping the water with his tail-flukes.*

# CHAPTER TWELVE

Mary O'Connor leant against the slender stone pillar that stood on the grassy mound of Slea Head on the western coast of Ireland. She was panting from the exertion of the climb and was afraid the throbbing in her head would start again – the tic in her eye was bad enough. She forced herself to breathe slowly and deeply.

As her heartbeat slowed she was sure the stone against her back was vibrating. She stepped away and turned to look at it. The surface was mellow with orange and grey lichen and it had evidently been there for a long time – perhaps a thousand years or more. Half hidden by the lichen were patterns of lines that crossed the vertical corners of the stone but the lines signified nothing to her. She reached out and touched one of the corners where the marks joined but there were no vibrations now. They must have been in been her imagination.

None of the other cyclists had followed her up to the stone. Most had walked down to the tiny beach and a few had stayed sitting on the walls of the car park to finish their sandwiches.

She looked out over the now uninhabited Blasket Islands, trying to imagine the hardships of surviving on those rugged and windswept rocks. Imagination was something she had in plenty – some said in excess. She tried to picture the islander's canvas-skinned currachs braving the waves but the picture that came to mind was of a wallowing black hulk being towed through the dusk by a fishing vessel with three lights at its masthead. From the deck of the hulk a woman looked up and waved to her.

She leant back against the stone and once more it seemed to be vibrating. It was like hearing a distant phone ringing and not being sure if it was your phone or your neighbour's. She stepped forward and the vibrating stopped.

The memory of the two boats was lost. She saw only a windswept sea and the lonely desolate islands that had once been home to several families.

Mary shivered and walked down to her bicycle. It was the only one in the car park now and she peddled hard in an attempt to catch up with the others. They must be well ahead so she eased back and cruised, once more afraid that the dreadful throbbing in her head might return. She dared not let it come to taunt her with its terrifying beat, 'There is . . . no

God. There is . . . no God.' She must stop putting things off. Tomorrow she would go to swim with Fungie. Tomorrow – definitely tomorrow.

When Mary was not smiling no one ever noticed her. A plain pale face, shoulder-length mousey-coloured hair and an undistinguished figure made her seem like any one of a thousand young women one would pass in the street without a second glance. But when she smiled . . . Then you noticed her.

It was not just her mouth that smiled, nor even her whole face. Somehow, her whole body smiled and became radiant. It was this quality that had endeared her to the succession of priests at the Roman Catholic church in South London that she had attended with her mother from the time she was a tiny girl. Regular customers in the shoe shop where she had worked since leaving school would wait to be served by her, studying the shoes on display and ignoring the other assistants until they could see that Mary was free, then jostling with other similar-minded customers rushing for the fitting chair.

But few people had seen her smile since the mugging.

The young man who had struck her from behind and run off with her bag, had stolen more than the week's pay packet and the pink-beaded rosary she had carried with her since her First Communion. He had taken her smile and thrown it away with the navy-blue bag, the emptied purse and the string of worthless beads with the cross on the end.

A week in hospital and a month off work while her head wound healed had not made her feel much better and the doctor had advised a holiday.

'Get away from it all – a change of scene. Get out of London – try and forget what happened. I can sign you off for another couple of weeks.'

Mary had grimaced – a painful caricature of her smile.

'I'll think about it. Right now I don't even feel like going out of doors.'

'Why don't you go to Ireland,' her mother had said. 'It's different there.'

'It's different all right,' her father had spoken over his shoulder, turning away briefly from the television. 'All priests and no work.'

'Don't you be listening to him,' her mother had added. 'Go to County Kerry, it's where my family came from. You'll love it there. I was reading in the paper about a dolphin at Dingle who lets people swim with him. Remember the dolphins *you* swam with in Wales?'

As if Mary could ever forget.

Mary would have been the first to admit she had been a fool to hire a bicycle from the hostel near Dingle when she hadn't ridden one for years but, persuaded by other young people that it was an easy ride out to Slea Head, she had succumbed and joined their party. Most of them had brought their own bikes to Ireland and were used to riding every day. Now, they were somewhere on the road ahead of her. They might even be back at the hostel cooking their evening meal.

If Mary had been totally honest with herself she would have seen that the cycle ride was delaying tactic. She had come to Ireland to swim with a dolphin again in the hope that it would put things right for her but ever since getting off the ferry at Rosslare she had found a hundred ways of delaying it.

She was freewheeling alone down towards Ventry Bay. To her left, a few yards into a field, was an intriguing gorse-covered circular bank. There was no painted sign such as those advertising the prehistoric beehive huts or cliff-top duns, yet she sensed that this earthwork was as old as any of the huts or forts. And it was clearly free of visitors with their cars and their chatter.

Mary stopped and leant her bicycle against the bank. There was no need to lock it up – she was quite alone and would see if anybody approached. She pulled off her scrunchy band and shook her hair free.

The ugly grey galvanised-metal gate was tied with blue plastic twine – visitors were obviously not expected. She glanced round, then climbed stiffly over the gate and walked through the long grass to the earth ring-mound. There was a gap on the side facing towards the sea, and through this gap a path, paved with irregular slabs of stone, led into the enclosure.

This path has been here for probably three thousand years, she thought, treading delicately from one stone to the next through the enclosing ring. Three thousand years! Inside the ring the ground felt hallowed and she crossed herself instinctively then, fearing a recurrence of the dreadful life-emptying doubt she said out loud, 'There is a God. There is a God,' but her words sounded weak and unconvincing. Her eyes were moist and the left one twitched frantically as she knelt in the centre of the circle, feeling the warm south-westerly wind in her hair and on her face. Through her tears, she watched the light of the setting sun glow on the mountains beyond Dingle Bay. A vanilla scent from the gorse flowers filled the hollow and a voice from deep, deep within her was saying, 'This is your home, here are your roots. Stay here – here you are safe. You don't have to go back.'

Mary had been hearing *this* voice for several days. It had grown louder and more insistent the further west she had come and with the voice she had felt the fear and tension draining from her mind and body, even though the dreadful doubt remained. Now the beguiling voice was singing in her head as sweetly and insistently as the songs her mother used to sing to her when she was little. Songs that had stayed with her long after she had been tucked up in her bed in the tiny terraced house in Battersea. But it was *not* the voice she wanted to hear. She wanted to hear *God* speaking to her – God confirming that He *did* exist. God telling her what He wanted of her and *this* voice was surely not His. This voice made no demands on her. She was waiting for a message as clear, as precise and as compelling as her elder brother had said that he had heard when he had been called to the priesthood – only *that* could give a meaning to her life. Father Sean (how odd to call your brother, 'Father') was in New Zealand, as out of reach as if he had been on another planet.

Slowly, her crying stopped and she sat back on one of the flat stones, feeling the warmth of it through the seat of her jeans. She wrapped her arms around her knees and stared out through the gap in the ring over the green grass and the blue water beyond. The head wound may have healed but the greater hurt remained. Why, when she had been actually praying as she walked through Morley Park, had God not protected her? Why had he made her . . . let her suffer so?

It was not for her to question His will. How many times had she been told that?

She stood up, looked around, then knelt and bowed her head.

Kneeling on the stones, surrounded by the gorse-covered earth bank and with a skylark singing far above her head, she prayed for forgiveness and guidance, though missing the familiar feel of the rosary beads between her fingers. 'Hail Mary, full of grace, the Lord is with thee . . .'

A scruffy looking seagull's feather floated down to land on the grass at her side. When she had finished praying she picked it up and ran her fingers along its length. As she did so, the filaments locked together and the raggedy quill was suddenly neat and efficient looking. She held it nearer to her eyes and saw how tiny hooks linked each filament to the next. She separated several and reunited then with a stroke of her fingers. God had clearly designed these – there was no way such elegant complexities could have merely *evolved*.


The run down to Ventry, with the blood-coloured fuchsia hedges tall on either side of the road, was pure joy spoilt only by the pull and tug of the tic in her eye. That was still there but Fungie would get rid of it – she was sure now. Tomorrow.

She swept though the tiny village, peddled furiously along the coast road, ignoring the pain from the chafing saddle, through Ballymore and over the ridge to where Dingle Harbour was spread out ahead of her. Not far to the hostel. It was getting late.

She passed a cottage with a sign offering 'Wet Suits for Hire', then at Milltown Bridge she turned left for the hostel.

She put her bicycle in the shed and walked stiffly through the back door. The smell of fried onions, curry, and pot-noodles engulfed her as she entered the combined kitchen and dining room. Her companions had cooked far more curry and rice than they needed and she could help herself from the communal cookpot. As she ate she kept hearing one word again and again from the tables around her – *Dolphin, dolphin, dolphin*.

The hostellers were discussing the dolphin that had appeared in Dingle Bay some fourteen years before and had stayed there alone, becoming more and more ready to swim and sport in the water with humans. Boats left the town quay frequently each day taking sightseers and swimmers to the harbour-mouth. Here the dolphin, known to the townspeople of Dingle as Fungie, would entertain them by diving and leaping around the boats. Those who were adventurous enough to don wet suits were sometimes allowed by the dolphin to stroke and pet him, though Fungie was quite wild and free and fed himself.

'Let's swim with the dolphin tomorrow,' an Australian girl said, sipping coffee and looking round the table. 'I seem to have *lived* on that goddamn bike since I came to Europe. Who's game? What about you, Mary O'C from England?'

This was the moment of truth. Mary had only one, possibly two more days in Ireland and she knew she had been putting off the meeting with the dolphin. Was it because she was afraid the magic would not be there this time and the fear and her twitching eyelid would be with her for the rest of her life? She thought of the gull's feather. 'Count me in,' she said.

*The dolphin, Elegance of Kerry, floated uneasily in the deep-water cave at the harbour mouth, counting days. Fourteen cycles of the planet round the sun and four more days. A third of his expected life spent here merely in obedient waiting and trying to give the 'message' from the ~yegods~ to any human who had the ability to listen. Only once had he felt he was getting through but that man had swum ashore and climbed out onto the rocks, his teeth chattering with cold, and had not returned.*

*It was as if there was a hidden barrier of incomprehension and disbelief in humans that a dolphin would have something important to say. Yet he dared not leave, even if for the past few years he had spent more time frolicking in the water with the humans than in trying to penetrate the barrier.*

*Supposing the ~yegods~ had gone to the crabs. He could wait here for another ten years or more before he too joined them. Grace of Valentia had come again the previous night, pleading with him to leave station and join her joy, to raise a family together but again he had caressed her smooth flank with the 'I'd love to but can't' gesture that needed no sounds to elaborate it. Once more she had accepted his decision and had swum sadly away to rejoin her companions across the bay.*

*He was not tired, so he replayed some of his favourite sea legends, projecting the mental sounds and pictures into the darkness of the cave, enjoying the subtleties of the light and the whispering echoes. He had been well taught in the legends of the Dolphins of Old, had been an active pupil and his retention had always been good.*

*He kept 'Valentia and the Orcas' until last. It was permitted to use the name of one's favourite as The Blessed One – it heightened the tension, especially when one also used one's own name for the Hero.*

*When he had finished the chase through the volcanic labyrinth and he and Valentia had been saved from certain death at the jaws of the Orca Pack by the intervention of the ~yegods~, he felt quite exhausted and he dozed, relaxing in the gentle lift and fall of the water in the cave.*

*In this somnolent state he only half-consciously controlled his flotation and breathing and moved his flukes just enough to keep his body clear of the limpet-encrusted rock walls.*


*The ~yegods~ came at dawn as the first fronds of light reached into the cave. As before, there were two of them and in his sleepy state he thought the tusked ones were an unlearned extension of the story. But, when their deep voices filled the cave, each sentence emphasised by the movement of the tips of their tusks which described circles and jabbing movements in the water and the air, he shook himself fully awake and listened with the respect due to these Conductors of the Sea.*

*He knew ~yegods~ did not have individual names, and even now, with two of them actually sharing his cave, he wondered again if they really existed outside of his imagination and the legends. In the ancient stories they not only appeared at the critical moment to save the dolphin heroes but in his favourite tales they frequently sacrificed themselves for the good of Whalekind.*

*The dolphin hung in the water, trembling slightly. Had they come to release him from his task? He hoped so. Fourteen years of frustration was more than enough to expect of any active 'phin.*

*He waited apprehensively. The legends also told how ~yegods~ punished the irreverent and the disobedient with a tusk through the belly. Little shudders rippled down his body as he thought how he had neglected his task recently.*

*After a pause that seemed to take a whole tide, the nearest of the ~yegods~ spoke.*

**~Elegance of Kerry. You have kept station loyally as directed, though the humans have been blind to our purpose and we, on behalf of all Whalekind, thank you. Learn carefully what we are about to teach you. It is a new message of great importance and your role is vital.~**

*The sun had lifted over the horizon and light from the sea outside filled the cave, reflections from the ripples making bright patterns flicker and dance on the cave roof. Fungie watched the ~yegods~ as they used their spiralled tusks to scratch row after row of lines on the green algae exposed on the cave wall by the falling tide.*

*Tracks made in the algae during the night by grazing limpets circled from their resting places, each track looping back to its starting point. The limpets were sleeping now and the ~yegods~ seemed to take care not to disturb them as their ivory tusk-tips scratched the lines on the rock face.*

*The ~yegods~ finished their task and one said enigmatically, ~**Take this message to the humans. Perhaps they may read this where they have failed to understand our earlier messages.**~*

*Both simultaneously blew a 'Farewell' snort that echoed in the hollows of the cave, clashed tusks with each other, sank, and were gone, leaving only a slight disturbance in the water and the lines on the cave wall to show that they had ever been there. The dolphin studied the lines, committing them to memory and wondering how he could show them to the humans. It was typical of the ~yegods~ in the stories that they left such details to other, lesser creatures who then had to exercise their own ingenuity. Today, he would have to miss the morning games with the humans that he had come to enjoy and which had helped him pass the waiting years. The grazing limpets would all but obliterate the lines in a few tides.*

*What strange patterns these scratches made – each one straight but all crossing or touching vertical centre lines at two different angles. The all-wise ~yegods~ may know what the lines meant but he, an ordinary 'phin, was none the wiser.*

With the others from the hostel, Mary hired a wet suit at the cottage, hoping it would not leave her sore anywhere. Her behind was still complaining about the bicycle saddle.

While waiting to be fitted with a suit in the barn next to the cottage, she studied the dolphin and whale posters on the walls and smiled at an extract from *The Hitch Hiker's Guide to the Galaxy*. It had been painstakingly copied out and was now pinned to a notice board alongside a tide-table for Dingle Bay.

It is an important and popular fact that things are not always what they seem. For instance on the planet Earth, man had always assumed he was more intelligent than dolphins because he had achieved so much – the wheel, New York, wars and so on – while all the dolphins had ever done was muck about in the water having a good time. But conversely, the dolphins had always believed they were far more intelligent than man – for precisely the same reasons.

'You'll be next?'

Mary turned towards the voice. A slender girl wearing ethnic clothes and many strings of coloured beads was smiling at her. Dolphin earrings danced from her earlobes but the green Wellington boots she wore seemed incongruous.

'I'm Shelagh,' she said. 'Are you ready for your fitting? I think you're the last this morning.'

Mary had no difficulty in finding a suit to fit her and she chose one with red legs and a black top, put it on in one of the brightly painted changing rooms then, carrying a mask, a snorkel and a pair of fins, walked awkwardly to the mini-bus outside.

The boat chugged down the channel towards the harbour-mouth. Gulls flying alongside called for food to be thrown for them but all the passengers were staring ahead hoping for a glimpse of the dolphin.

Another boat, its decks crowded with onlookers, was anchored in the narrows and the skipper of Mary's boat called to it, 'Is he about then?'

'Not seen him as of now.'

Mary waited until the other swimmers had gone over the side, apprehensive as she had never swum in a wet suit before, then dropped into the water. She shivered with the coldness of it splashing around her face and penetrating the suit. Within a minute, much sooner than she had expected, she felt comfortably warm and found that she floated easily, buoyed up by the air trapped within the neoprene of the suit.

She pulled the mask down over her eyes, wriggled the mouthpiece of the snorkel tube into her mouth just as Shelagh had shown her and turned face down, breathing noisily.

The sea bed was clearly visible though she could not judge how far below her it was. The tide was moving sand and loose pieces of weed from the sea towards the harbour but she was disappointed to find the water was not as full of fish as it always had been in the underwater wildlife films she had seen. Wet suits, snorkels and a myriad of brightly coloured fish seemed to go together. Nor was there any sign of the dolphin. She lifted her head and floated vertically.

Another swimmer called to her, 'See anything?'

She shook her head and turned face down again.

Mary sat uncomfortably in the boat taking her and the other disappointed swimmers back to the quay at Dingle from where they had set out, full of excited anticipation, two hours before. The wet suit was clammy on her back, the tic was still pulling her eyelid and she was looking forward to getting into warm clothing again.

The boatman was apologising. 'I don't understand it,' he said. 'Fungie has always come to meet the boats. Always. Never let us down before. You'll all be getting your money back for sure.'

There was a silence, then, 'I hope he's not hurt or anything. I hope it's not that.'

Mary and the others returned to the cottage in the minibus, showered, and handed back their wet suits. Most of them returned to the hostel but Mary stayed in the information room to ask Shelagh about Fungie.

'Where do you think he's gone?' she asked.

'Probably just gone fishing,' said Shelagh. 'He's a free agent. He can come and go as he wishes but he usually likes to play with the swimmers. Are you going to stay around and try again?'

'I'm not sure,' Mary replied, her doubts overwhelming her again. What if Fungie didn't come back? What if he didn't have the same healing, calming magic as the 'Welsh' dolphins? But she had nothing to lose. 'I'll stay another day or so, Dingle's a lovely place.'

'I love it here,' Shelagh said. 'Can't think where I'd rather be.'

'Were you born here?' Mary asked.

'In Kerry, yes – near Killarney, but my father got himself a fancy government job in Dublin and I didn't want to go there so I came to Dingle. Would you like a coffee? It'll warm you up.'

When they had finished their coffee, Shelagh had to see to a couple who had come just in. Mary called, 'Thank you and goodbye,' to her and began to walk the half-mile into the town. She would stay for one more day and, if the dolphin returned, book another trip to swim with it. Beyond that she had no plans. God would guide her – if there was . . . She thought of the gull's feather. God *would* guide her.

Her walk took her along the side of the harbour. The tide was well in now, the mudflats that had been exposed earlier were covered in water and the oystercatchers and other birds that had been feeding there were resting at the tide-line waiting for the turn. A curlew called mournfully across the bay. The birds near her seemed not to be frightened by her presence and she realised that she too felt less afraid and was now not glancing over her shoulder every few paces. The breeze was fresh and smelt of the sea. Her step lightened.

The first building of the town on the Waterside was a jewellery workshop with display windows facing the road. Mary peered through the glass at the shelves of gold and silver brooches and earrings, admiring the delicate workmanship in the Celtic designs, then went inside to browse. Perhaps a tiny pair of earrings as a memento? Maybe in the shape of dolphins like Shelagh's. Even if she had not seen Fungie, his presence permeated the atmosphere of the town. Perhaps if she bought some dolphin earrings, it would bring him back to help her.

There were surprisingly few dolphin items and she waited by the till for a shop assistant to appear, thinking as she did so that to leave a shop like this unattended in England was unimaginable. Her own shop manager had constantly reminded the staff, 'Never, ever leave the shop unattended. Watch the till all the time – ALL the time.'

She picked up a green leaflet from the counter, titled 'The Ogham Collection'. It had a picture of a standing stone on one side with lines crossing the corners, just like the one at Slea Head that she had leant against the day before. It might even be the same stone.

Mary turned the leaflet over. There was a diagram of the Ogham Alphabet and a text. She read, 'The name Ogham is derived from the Celtic God of eloquence or fine speech.' Mary smiled. Only the Irish would have a God of Eloquence.

'Use of Ogham in Ireland probably dates to the third century AD. The Alphabet consists of groups of lines from one to five, set across a vertical stem line. Each group represents a different letter. It was used mainly for commemorative inscriptions.

'Using the Ogham Alphabet we can engrave your name on sterling silver or gold.'

A woman had come from the back of the shop and was waiting patiently as Mary read the leaflet. 'Can I be helping you?' she asked.

'How much are silver earrings like this?'

'Those are eighteen pounds, only.'

Mary did a mental calculation. Ireland was not costing her anything like as much as she had expected and she had more than five hundred pounds as a reserve in her building society account.

'How long does it take to write the names?'

'Just a few minutes. You can watch if you wish.'

Mary followed her through a back hall into a workshop where a young man asked what the engraving was to be.

'I can't do your name M A R Y the English way,' he told her. 'There's no Y in the Irish alphabet. Can I write M A I R E the way we spell it here?'

'I'd like that. Yes please.'

Mary watched as the young man inscribed the lines reading MAIRE on to each of the delicate silver wafers.

She was silent at first, not wanting to interrupt the man's concentration. He finished one earring, passed it to her and said, 'My grandfather was the local expert in this writing. He said it came from trees or something like that. He showed me how to cut the letters onto sticks, and my brother and I used to send each other messages. We pretended we were chiefs or druids and say, "Come quickly, the Vikings are in the bay." Things like that.'

He smiled up at Mary who smiled back, encouraging him to continue. The soft lilt in his voice reminded her of the Irish nuns who had taught her at her first school.

'What else?' she asked, as he started the lettering on the second sliver of silver.

'Oh. "Can I marry your daughter?" Or, "Barbecue on Monday night, all are welcome".'

They laughed together as he worked. She laid the first of the delicate silver pendants in the palm of her left hand and ran her fingers across the lines, to read 'M A I R E'.

'How did you know which end to start from?' she asked. 'It could mean something quite different if you read it from the wrong end. Talk about getting hold of the wrong end of the stick!'

'That could be where the expression came from,' the young man said, handing her the other earring. 'I'd never thought of that.'

Mary thanked him, carried the earrings through into the shop and gave them to the assistant who hooked them inside a little green box and slid that almost reverentially into a coloured paper bag. Mary paid the eighteen pounds, took the bag and stepped out into brilliant sunshine. Then, unable to resist the urge, opened the bag and examined the box. Tiny flecks of gold in the green plastic lid sparkled in the sun, mirroring the sparkle of the waters beyond the shop. She opened the box, lifted out the earrings, put her gold studs in the box, and hooked the thin wires through her ear lobes. The slivers of silver swung in the breeze and sang 'Maire' in her imagination. She walked lightly along the road, past the shops and past the quay where another boatload of visitors was about to leave in the hope of seeing the dolphin. Without knowing or caring why, and feeling quite safe from any kind of attack, she took the shore path out towards the disused lighthouse.

The tide was falling now and sea birds were exploring the uncovered seaweed and sand, looking for a meal. Plastic bottles and yellowing pieces of polystyrene littered the high tide mark, but Mary did not see them. The stone folly on the high ground ahead and the red and white lighthouse building beyond were drawing her irresistibly towards them as though she herself was floating buoyantly on some invisible tide.

She passed the folly, then a beach where more hopefuls in bathing costumes or wet suits stood waiting for Fungie to appear, before taking the cliff path towards the old lighthouse with its view out over the vastness of Dingle Bay to the distant mountains beyond. She looked down on to the flat blue sea. Silvery-grey lines like the half-remembered stretchmarks on her mother's stomach showed where currents flowed. Gulls circled and called below her as she took a seat on a broken-down wall near the cliff top. A fishing boat was coming in, its wake drawing a line on the sea, bubbles lingering white in the water long after the boat had passed.

Something black appeared in the wake and then disappeared again. The dolphin?

Mary watched the black speck behind the boat. It *was* a dolphin, leaping clear out of the water each time it completed a pass through the boat's wake. She knew that dolphins loved to swim and play in the wake of boats or even ride their bow waves. But there was something more positive about this dolphin's actions as he swam back and forth through the line of bubbling water behind the fishing boat. It was just like the action of the young jeweller as he had inscribed the Ogham letters on her earrings. Mary put her hand up, felt the silken surface of the silver and traced the horizontal and diagonal lines. They were *just* like the lines the dolphin was making through the wake.

Could it be . . .? No. That was absurd. Her stupid imagination again! A dolphin writing Ogham in the sea? No way.

Even so, she reached into her bum-bag to get the leaflet with the alphabet but it wasn't there. In her excitement at getting the earrings and her eagerness to try them on, she had left it in the shop. She looked for a pencil to record the apparent line pattern but that too was missing. She almost uttered a profane word, stifled it and tried to memorise the pattern, but it was no use. Barely had she concentrated on one pattern than the dolphin was swimming another. Now she was *sure* that there was some kind of message there. There was a directness in the lines and they were in groups of up to five, never more. Also there were some groups in each of the four Ogham patterns she had seen in the leaflet – right angled lines on either side of the wake and right-angled and diagonal lines cutting across it.

The fishing boat had passed the sea-caves in the cliff opposite and had reached the narrows where Fungie usually entertained the visitors – where, a couple of hours before, Mary had been swimming and waiting in vain. The dolphin leapt and she could see the viewing boats list as the passengers crowded onto the side nearest to him. He leapt again as Mary turned and hurried back towards the jewellers to collect an Ogham leaflet.

Her mind was busy as she walked down past the folly. Ogham was a very ancient form of writing; could a *dolphin* know how to use it? She had seen herself how the lines had been cut on standing stones to display messages of some kind through the centuries, and the man at the shop had told her about writing messages on sticks. But no, it was all too crazy, just her wild imagination. The excitement brought on the dull throbbing in her head and the tic quickened again. She forced herself to slow down as she reached the quay and, seeing a café over the road, crossed to have a cup of tea and take an aspirin. She was tempted by the smell of fish and chips to have her lunch there whilst waiting for rational thought to return. Then, when it didn't, she bought a notepad and two pencils in a gift shop before collecting a leaflet and returning to the cliff top. The dolphin was still there, entertaining the afternoon boatloads. Away to her right a fishing vessel was leaving the quay and steering its way between the red and green buoys that marked the deep water channel, just as her boat had done that morning.

Was it really only that morning? She fingered one of her new earrings. It seemed at least a week ago.

A young man she had met at the hostel was sitting near the lighthouse where she had been earlier. He wore glasses, looked serious and was from Dublin. She tried to remember his name. Michael – that was it.

'Hello, Michael,' she said. 'Mary, from the hostel, remember?' How different from the fear-haunted streets of London.

Michael smiled and gestured for her to sit near him. 'Have you seen Fungie?' he asked, pointing down to where the dolphin's fin showed intermittently around the boats anchored below.

Mary nodded, wondering how she could record any repeat message without appearing to be out of her mind. She took out the notebook and sketched the cliffs opposite. Michael chatted easily about the weather, the view, the dolphin and Ireland, then shut up and sat in silence when he realised that Mary was trying to concentrate on her drawing.

Suddenly, the dolphin broke away from the viewing boats and followed the fishing boat out to sea, swimming back and forth through the wake as he had done that morning. Mary recorded the lines as best she could, pretending she was still sketching the seascape, hiding the page from Michael's view. A line of Ogham script grew down the page. She drew another line, then another.

The dolphin was clearly showing his back above water for the extent of each line, then diving, leaping and diving again to reappear at the start of the next line. Mary's excitement grew with each stroke of her pencil. Then the dolphin dived, to reappear a long way out to sea. He leapt, then swam back, with a sequence of leaps and dives towards the cluster of small boats. Mary surreptitiously reached into her bag for the leaflet. Michael was standing now, his back to her, watching the dolphin playing around the boats.

Mary translated, letter by letter. TA TEACHTAIREACHT AGAMSA A DTUGANN NA DAOINE FUNGIE AIR I MBA AN DAINGIN DO DHUINE A BHFUIL AN MEANMA ANN LEAMH TUISCINT AGUS GNIOMHU, she wrote. TEIGH GO SASANA AIMSIGH ANSIN TRIUR CHINE NA MIOLTA MORA I LINN CHEARNOGACH TAOBH O THUAIDH DEN CHARRAIG MHOR AGUS DEN DUIRLING AGUS TABHAIR LEAT A NAMHRAN GO DOMHAN NA NDAOINE . . . It was a meaningless jumble of letters. Her heart sank. Had she just imagined it all? Got hold of the wrong end of the stick?

She picked up the notepad again and tried reading it from the other end. ENIOADN AN NAHMOD . . . It was just as meaningless that way. She dropped the pad in disgust as Michael turned towards her.

'Chocolate?' he offered, bending over to give her a piece, then added, 'You didn't tell me you knew Irish. I thought you were from London.'

'Irish?'

Michael picked up the pad and translated. 'THERE IS A MESSAGE WITH ME WHOM PEOPLE CALL FUNGIE OF DINGLE BAY FOR PEOPLE WHO HAVE THE HEART TO READ UNDERSTAND AND ACT.' He paused, took a deep breath and continued. 'GO TO ENGLAND FIND THERE THREE OF THE RACE OF WHALES IN A SQUARE POOL TO THE NORTH OF THE GREAT ROCK AND THE PEBBLEBANK AND TAKE THEIR SONG TO THE WORLD OF PEOPLE.'

'You made this up,' he said accusingly, 'You made this up.'

By the next day Mary had persuaded Michael to write the Irish for I HAVE READ YOUR MESSAGE AND WILL DO ALL I CAN TO DO WHAT YOU HAVE ASKED OF ME, and she had scratched the translation in Ogham on a piece of driftwood and booked another trip to swim with the dolphin.

'By God, it takes all sorts. . . .' said the boatman as she dropped over the side in her wet suit clutching the stick. 'Don't you be hurting our dolphin with that, now.'

Mary bit onto the mouthpiece and turned face down, blowing the water out of the tube as she did so. Below her was an enormous black shape just as she remembered from Wales. The dark shape cruised effortlessly below her and vanished into the cloudy distance, then reappeared from another angle and swam slowly towards her, turned slightly away and hung in the water watching her with a huge knowing eye. She felt a warmth flowing towards her and held out the stick, taking care to present it the right way round. Fungie moved forward slowly, eyeing the stick intently. He's reading it, she thought and shivered with excitement. He's really reading my stick and understanding the message. She could see comprehension and gratitude in that great eye as the dolphin slid towards her and she reached out to touch the smooth skin of its flank. He allowed a brief caress then dived, twisted in the water and shot through the surface, leaping over Mary as she turned face-up to watch.

A minute later the dolphin was joyously racing out to sea, leaping high in the air as he did so. Mary was the only swimmer not to be disappointed when he did not return. Her tic had gone.

*Elegance of Kerry had not expected a result so soon. This human who had dropped into his world carried a stick with marks on it similar to those the ~yegods~ had scratched on the wall of his cave. He studied the patterns on the stick but they were as incomprehensible as the scratch-marks had been.*

*This did not matter. The mind-waves emanating from the human were clear to him. They told him of understanding and impending action and that was enough. He was free of his 'waiting' duty. He swam forward to signal a 'thank you and power in your task' message, felt a brief touch of a soft hand on his side then flicked round and did an involuntary leap of joy.*

*'Valentia, I come.'*

Mary returned the wet suit, and was tempted to tell Shelagh about the 'miracle' of the dolphin's message. But, no, it was all too new and too incredible to share. She had not yet come to terms with it herself.

She thought of her parents in London – a card was due or they would begin worrying about her. She went into the town and bought a postcard, choosing one with a picture on it of Fungie leaping over a rubber dinghy.

*Dear Mum,*
*Ireland is all I had dreamed it would be and I am feeling much better*
*as you said I would. I have met someone who wants me to go back to*
*England urgently. If I do I will write again from there. Don't worry, I*
*won't do anything stupid.*
*Love Mary.*


She felt uncomfortable about referring to Fungie as 'someone' but
with his picture on the card it seemed acceptable.

Drawn by an urge she had almost forgotten, she walked up the hill
to the Catholic church, the card unposted in the pocket of her anorak.
Inside the church it was as not as quiet and as peaceful as in others she
could recall. People were coming and going and some just came in,
looked at the high ceiling supported by incongruous black-painted
steel girders and went out again. The familiar Stations of the Cross
were spaced around the wall and the statues of a sad-eyed Jesus and a
compassionate-looking Mary were familiar and comforting. She knelt
and prayed, addressing herself to the Virgin with whom she had always
felt a special bond.

'Hail Mary, full of grace, the Lord is . . .' The words rose effortlessly
like bubbles in a pond.

When she had finished the prayer she thanked the Holy Mother for
bringing her and the dolphin together and asked for guidance, in the way
she had done when, as a little girl the choices had been about which
dress to wear for a party, or whether she should ask for a doll or a puppy
for a Christmas. Then, the answer had always seemed to come easily to
her.

Now, when she asked if she should follow the dolphin's instructions,
no answer came whispering into her mind.

A black-robed priest strode into the church, looked at her expectantly
and she rose, smiled and said a polite, 'Good Morning, Father,' as she
went out. It had been priests who told her God would protect her from
harm if she prayed. Now she knew *that* wasn't true – even if there was a
God. Anyway, she had already decided what to do about the message.
She posted the card and headed back to the hostel for her bags.

*God moves in a mysterious way*
  *His wonders to perform . . .*

She sang the words of the old hymn quietly to herself as she walked
along the harbourside.

# CHAPTER THIRTEEN

The day before the arrival of the dolphine and the pilot whale at Dormouth, the Reverend David Thomas had fumbled with the heavy iron key as he tried to open the door of the Church of Saint Peter the Fisherman. The tower of the church, virtually rebuilt in the Victorian orgy of church reconstruction and restoration, looked down on the rippling water of the 1930s swimming pool in the walled enclosure alongside.

Arthritis and age had stiffened the fingers of the Reverend Thomas' right hand and he dropped the key to the ground as he pushed the studded oak door open and the musty smell of disuse enveloped him. He sniffed at the combination of scents – candle-grease, old wood, stale air and mice, then bent to pick up the key but a twinge in his lower back stopped him. He could get it on his way out. It would be safe there. Since Old Joe had gone to his maker no one but him ever came to the empty church.

He shuffled up the nave, noting the dust on the pews. He flicked at the back of one with his handkerchief, then coughed as a cloud of airborne particles swirled about his head and hung as glowing multi-coloured motes in the shafts of sunlight streaming through the stained-glass windows. Beautiful, he thought, even dust can be beautiful.

His eyes followed the sunbeams up to the glass, the panes of this window depicting a ship in distress and a lifeboat riding the waves towards it. The painted lifeboat was clearly Dormouth's old boat, now preserved in the museum on the quay, but the other ship was portrayed as an old-fashioned galley, the sort of vessel Saint Paul would probably have been in when he had been wrecked on the island of Malta, nearly two thousand years before. Artist's licence, he mused, the actual ship that had almost come to grief in Dormouth Bay had been a rich man's yacht, and the Portland Bill lighthouse with its lantern and projecting foghorn had been grossly exaggerated by whoever had designed the window.

The stained-glass window and the replacement organ had been a thank-you gift from the grateful yacht owner to the lifeboatmen sometime in the thirties, a time when the church had been more closely associated with the soul of the town. That had been a long time ago, even before he had come to Dormouth.

The old man stood and watched the floating specks in the sunbeams for a minute or so until a sparrow flew in through a dolphin-shaped hole where a piece of glass was missing from the ornate border surrounding the main picture. The dust specks swirled violently in the draught from the bird's wings, making a kaleidoscope of colour, and the bird's twittering filled the empty church. As suddenly as it had come, the sparrow flew out again through the same opening and all was silent again.

I must get someone to come and fix that glass, he thought, knowing he never would. He continued slowly up the aisle to the organ and seated himself at the console, the one place in the church free of dust. As he reached for the switch to start the electric blower and heard the familiar hum of the motor, he again wondered why no one had ever come to the disused church to turn off the mains power supply. A computer error at the Electricity Board, he supposed. The Rev. Thomas might once have attributed it to 'God's will', but in *these* modern and confusing days, all unexpected and inexplicable things he blamed on computer errors. God would surely have bigger things on his mind.

The old man depressed an ivory key and held it down, as a long echo of sound reverberated through the empty building. He pressed another key, then another, the fingers of his right hand stiff and painful. He held one note for several seconds, paused for several seconds, then played the same note again.

*In the pool beyond the church wall the dolphin, Elegance of Rockall – named by his parents for his birthplace near a tiny rocky islet in the Atlantic to the north of Ireland – stopped his restless circling, raised his head above the water then submerged it again, sensing the strange and exciting vibrations through his lower jaw. As on the rare occasions when these sounds had come before, the dolphin turned his head to locate their direction. The tingling waves were once more coming from the grey squarestone with the rock tower above it. He swam forward slowly, listening until the vibrations suddenly stopped.*

In the street outside, Hywel Jones had paused and turned his head towards the sound of the organ. It was coming from that disused church. Surely there could be no one in there. Brambles and rosebay willowherb grew in profusion over the few grubby gravestones and from the cracks between the paving slabs around the base of the tall square tower. A sign, with faded gilt letters, was leaning at a crazy angle as one of the posts had rotted away at the base. He read with difficulty the words on it.

Hywel Jones was dressed in an odd mixture of clothes. His shoes were of highly polished black leather and his trousers were also black with a sharp crease fore and aft and a glossy ribbon down the side seams. In contrast, and as a concession to the heat of the day, he was wearing a white brag shirt several sizes too large. On the front and faded by many hand-washings, the boast of 'Triple Crown Winners' was just legible beneath the Prince of Wales' three-feathered crest. On the back of the shirt a single upraised finger was surrounded by an English rose, a Scottish thistle and the shamrock of Ireland.

Slowly, Hywel made out each word on the painted sign saying them aloud as he did so.

THE . . . CHURCH . . . OF . . . ST PETER THE . . . FISHERMAN

THE . . . PARISH OF . . . DORMOUTH

He paused. The list of Times of Services was indecipherable so he moved on to the easy words.

ALL ARE WELCOME.

Below this he could just make out:

THE REV. D. P. THOMAS – VICAR.

The sound of another organ note, long and clear, came through the open door. Hywel recognised a quality in the tone that was inconsistent with such a neglected-looking church. Intrigued, he picked his way through the litter of discarded cigarette packets and polystyrene chip-boxes on the path leading to the porch and peered into the interior. Another deep note reached into his guts and he suddenly yearned to play such an instrument again, even though he thought he had walked away from all that religious nonsense long ago.

He tiptoed in and called, 'Hello,' in a quiet voice so as not to startle whoever was there.

The fragmented playing stopped and a frail looking, elderly man in a yellowing clerical collar shuffled out from behind the pulpit and stood blinking in a shaft of sunlight. His white hair glowed in a halo around his head.

'Who's there?' the old man called, his voice tremulous.

Hywel stepped forward and walked quietly up the aisle.

'I heard you playing, and came in. I'm sorry if I disturbed you.'

'All are welcome,' said the old man, smiling his relief. 'Though it must be fifteen . . . No, twenty years since anyone but me or Old Joe came here. I hope you don't want to hear a real hymn, my fingers aren't nimble enough any more.' He smiled again.

'Not into hymns me, now,' said Hywel, wondering why he had come in. 'I used to play the organ in the chapel at home, that's all.'

He peered up at the bank of pipes, each decorated with a pseudo-mediaeval pattern of twisted vines. 'This one's rather large for this church, isn't it?' he asked, noting the old vicar's crumpled clothes and the food stains down the front. The man must have retired long ago. What brought him back to this dusty old place?

'Yes, much too big, but very beautiful, even if the world has forgotten it's here. Thank God.' The Reverend David nodded respectfully towards the bare altar.

'It was a gift to the church by some people who were saved from drowning in a storm once,' he continued. 'Did you notice the stained-glass window?'

Hywel shook his head.

'Never mind. Coming here and playing the organ is about my only pleasure nowadays. Did you say *you* played?' His eyes gleamed.

'The organist in Chapel taught me when I was a boy in Wales. I was never very good but Mam liked to hear me play.'

He moved past the old man and stroked the keys fondly. He touched a few of the stops, the familiar names chiming in his memory. He had no difficulty in reading these. VOIX CELESTES: Voices of Heaven. DULCIANA: Very sweetly.

'Who tunes it?' he asked.

'A friend of mine – Old Joe – used to come in now and then. He died last month, bless him, so it won't be long before it's unplayable. He was the last of my generation but for me. It's fine to outlive your enemies but sad when you outlive all your friends too.'

Once more a smile lit up the thin face and Hywel warmed to him.

'I'd like it if you would play something for me,' the old man said. 'Please do.'

'I'm very rusty.' Hywel seated himself. 'Is there anything special you'd like?'

'Can you play *Eternal Father*?'

Hywel nodded, tested a few keys, then surprised himself with the way his memory, seemingly in his fingertips, retrieved the notes. The organ's plea, 'For those in peril on the sea,' rolled round the empty nave, disturbing a pair of pigeons on the grey slate roof. They clattered away across the old swimming pool where Elegance of Rockall poised motionless, feeling the water-borne vibrations thrill through his skin. Memories of storms at sea filled his mind and he leapt and plunged joyously through the windswept waves until, as the vibrations faded away, the sea calmed and he found he was back in the pool, angry and alone.

When Hywel had finished playing the hymn he turned on the stool. 'Do you ever have services here?' he asked.

'Not now. It's a pity. I *prefer* this place to the new wood and glass box up on the hill. I shouldn't really be saying that but I sometimes feel that when they built the new church, God stayed down here. I can't say I blame him.' He smiled again.

God had died for Hywel in Second Form at school when he had decided to be a scientist. Despite that decision he had continued to attend Chapel for another two years to please Mam. Dyslexia had killed his hope of a place at university to study electronics and this disappointment had finally convinced Hywel that Life *was* an accident on a minor planet and that evolution made mistakes. His own learning disorder was just a tiny and totally insignificant one of these. Even so he liked the way this old man spoke of God as though he were a personal friend. A friend with human tastes for architecture and ambience. He waited for the vicar to continue.

'I'll be able to ask Him soon. It can't be long before *I'm* called.'

A cloud seemed to cross the papery white face.

'Of course I may be wrong,' he went on. 'There may be no God after all. Even some of the bishops argue about that nowadays. If I get up there and find there isn't, I'm going to be more than a little disappointed. Cheated in fact.'

Hywel felt it was time to change the subject and turned to look back down the nave. There was a small door set in the wall near the pulpit.

'Can I go up the tower?' he asked.

'The tower door's not locked any more. I'll come with you if I can. I haven't been up there for years. You go on, it'll take me quite a bit longer.'

Hywel opened the arch-topped wooden door, found a light switch and climbed the circular stone stairs. He could hear the vicar puffing and blowing far below him and wondered if he should go down to help, but didn't. Some people resented being helped, it emphasised their weaknesses.

The door at the top would not open, yet there was no sign of a keyhole. He rattled the big metal latch and pushed the door hard with his shoulder. It moved a little. He pushed harder until there was a gap wide enough for him to squeeze through and he stepped out into a tiny meadow of grass and wild flowers surrounded by a castellated stone wall.

Where the door had opened, a carpet of turf had wrinkled up. Hywel stooped and turned the mat of roots and grass blades back on itself, like the corner of a rug, to allow the door to swing free. The underside of the turf was a woven mass of white rootlets flattened by contact with the grey lead sheeting that covered the roof.

Behind him the Reverend Thomas stepped out into the sunlight.

'Dear God,' he puffed, 'the drain must have blocked again. It did that once before back in . . . in . . . Anyway, it was a long time ago.'

Hywel did not know any of the plants by name except the sweet-smelling purple and brown wallflowers, which grew out of cracks in the lichened stone parapet. Similar plants had grown wild in the cracks in the wall behind his parents' terraced cottage in Inkerman Street, back home in Cwm Glas. The seeds must have blown up here or have been carried by birds, but where the soil had come from he did not know.

There was a superb view over the roofs of the derelict warehouses towards the white cliffs beyond Dormouth Bay. He remembered having been told that wartime radar scanners had been sited there to warn of the approach of enemy bombers but there was no sign of any such sites now. His eyes followed the undulations of the cliff tops until they disappeared in the distant haze, then he turned the other way, hoping for a sight of Portland. It was on this 'almost' island that Mam's grandfather had lived before being drawn from the quarries to work in the mines of South Wales, but the massive rock was hidden by the houses on the hill beyond the warehouses and the masts of the boats in the Inner Harbour.

Hywel walked across the square of grass and leant on the parapet, avoiding the moist seagull droppings on the coping stones. The old man, his white face now veined with red lines, joined him there.

'I love it here. Closer to God, I used to think. I'd often come up after a service and apologise to Him because so few people had been there. I used to think it was my fault, boring sermons or something, but now I see it was just the way people are. They don't *need* a God now. Television and supermarkets provide all their wants. They don't starve any more, and watching the telly saves them having to think. Now I'm boring you. Sorry.'

Hywel was silent. There was no God, he knew that for sure, but there was no point in upsetting the old fellow.

The vicar was leaning over the parapet and looking down. Hywel followed his gaze. There was a pool of water between the warehouses and the church, showing bright blue. He could see white lines running along its length. He'd lived in Dormouth for years without knowing there was an open-air pool there. It was big, at least twice the size of any other pool he had seen. Something dark was swimming listlessly along the far side.

'Are my eyes playing tricks on me, or is that a shark in the water?' the old man asked.

'It's a dolphin,' Hywel replied, as surprised as the vicar. 'How did it get *there?*'

'God knows,' replied the old man. 'I'll ask Him when I get up yonder. I love dolphins. I was a missionary once, you know, in the Far East, as my father had been. I was born at sea – on the *SS Polaris*. My mother gave me Polaris as a middle name. The dolphins used to come and meet the boats in the Bay of Biscay and they'd swim alongside, looking up and grinning at us as though they knew something we didn't. If God gave any other creatures a soul, I'm sure it would be dolphins. Maybe elephants too, but definitely dolphins. If there's any truth in the idea of reincarnation, I'd like to come back as one of those. If I've been good enough, that is.'

The dark shape in the water was circling aimlessly.

'That one doesn't seem too happy,' Hywel remarked. 'I wonder why anyone would want to keep it in that pool.'

The vicar quoted, 'And God said, "Let us make man in our image, after our likeness and let him have dominion over the fish of the sea, and over the fowl of the air, and over cattle and over every creeping thing that creepeth upon the earth." Man has a lot to answer for, I'm sure God meant us to cherish His creatures, not exploit them.'

The warm wind from the sea was blowing the old man's hair about and Hywel was reminded of a Sunday school picture of a biblical prophet declaiming in the desert. It was only then that he noticed that the vicar had no fingers on his left hand. He wondered whether to comment.

'You're looking at my hand,' the old man said. 'Don't be embarrassed. I find it easier for people if I talk about it than if I pretend my hand is normal.'

'Was it an accident?' Hywel asked, remembering his Uncle Dai's arm mangled by the machinery at the mine.

'Oh, no. I was born like this. No one seems to know why. I like to think that God wanted to give me a handicap to make me work harder at serving Him, but to be honest it hasn't been much of a problem. I had to learn a different way to play the organ and I have to get someone else to change light bulbs for me, but otherwise I hardly ever notice. I sometimes say it means I have to do God's work single-handed.' He smiled at the oft-repeated joke he had used to dispel parishioners' embarrassment.

'Perhaps we should go down now,' Hywel said, thinking that he ought really be looking for new digs. He'd evidently pushed his landlady's patience too far this time.

He *did* have to help with the descent. The vicar, coming down close behind him, rested his hands on the young man's shoulders, the fingerless left one pressing down hard.

'I expect that'll be the last time *I'll* ever go up there,' the old man said sadly, as they reached the door into the nave. 'Lots of the things I do now are *for the last time*. I must go home and lie down,' he said as they walked along the aisle. There was a hint of distress in his voice.

'Is it far?'

'No. I've got my car outside.'

'Are you OK to drive?' Hywel asked, listening to the old man's laboured breathing, his thin frame shaking as though with a fever.

'If you could drive me it would be better. Would you have the time?'

Hywel was embarrassed. 'I would, but I never learned to drive, me. Is there someone I could telephone?'

'No, thank you. But you could lock up here if you would. I dropped the key by the door on the way in. I can get a bus from the front. The car'll be safe enough.' He breathed harshly between each sentence.

'Of course. I'll lock up and walk with you.'

Hywel picked up the heavy key with the ornate cast handle and turned to shut the door as the vicar shuffled down the litter-strewn path. The door was stiff on its hinges and he fumbled with the unfamiliar lock. When he was sure all was secure, he went out into the road, the key in his hand.

Fifty yards away, in the direction of the sea front, the old man had collapsed on the pavement. Hywel ran to him, sensing by the way he was lying that it was too late for first aid. He looked up and down the road but there was no one else to help. He knelt by the body, fumbled for the wrist to feel for a pulse, then realised there was little he could do even if he found one. He stood up, looked around again but the street was still empty of people. He ran to find a phone box.

Hywel was kneeling protectively by the body in the empty backstreet when the ambulance arrived. The medic swung down out of the cab and looked at the smile on the man's face as the driver went to the back of the vehicle for the stretcher.

'I'd say he knew something we don't know,' he remarked. 'Are you a relative?'

'No. I don't really know him.'

'Thanks for calling us, anyway.'

The medic turned to his colleague. 'DOA. for sure,' Hywel heard him say as he walked away. DOA meant 'Dead on arrival'. The key was heavy in his pocket.

# CHAPTER FOURTEEN

Mary O'Connor had expected to have difficulty following Fungie's instructions. The dolphin's message had told her to find THE GREAT ROCK AND THE PEBBLEBANK somewhere in England and then find A SQUARE POOL TO THE NORTH OF IT. That could take her months, she thought.

She took the bus to Cork, not now questioning her mission. She had been told *what* to do, even if she could not yet make sense of it. A message from a wild dolphin . . . She was thrilled to be the one chosen. God was clearly behind this as He was behind everything. Much better than being called to be a nun. How could she ever have doubted His existence?

On the overnight ferry to Swansea, she shared a table in the cafeteria with an English student who had been at the hostel. They sat and faced one another across a table in the lounge, drank apple juice and talked about Ireland. When the conversation died Mary, trying to sound casual, said, 'If I asked you where there was a great rock and a bank of pebbles somewhere in England, what would you say?'

The man thought for a moment. 'Easy one. I'd say it was Portland in Dorset. We used to go to Dormouth near there on holiday when I was little. Nice sandy beach. And Portland is joined to the mainland by a ridge of pebbles called the Chesil Bank. Why do you ask?'

'Just curious, that's all. Someone asked me and I didn't know.' Her conscience wriggled a little, but it was only a tiny lie and could hurt no one.

Mary shared a taxi from the ferry terminal to Swansea railway station with the student and asked there about trains to Portland.

The clerk smiled indulgently. 'You'll be lucky,' he said. 'That line closed before I was born. I can get you as far as Dormouth. I expect there'll be a bus to Portland from there.'

She took the next train to Cardiff, changed for Bristol and finally got a connection to Dormouth. She dozed in the hot carriage, watching the countryside roll past the window. A herd of cows were standing up to their udders in a river and she recalled something she had once read about dolphin evolution. Some scientist had claimed that dolphins were descended from a cow-like creature that had taken to the seas millions of years ago.

It was all nonsense of course. God had created dolphins, whales and cows just as they are – and now a God-inspired dolphin had given her a message. She hugged herself with excitement. She was the only person in the world, apart from a sceptical Michael, who knew what she knew.

Suddenly, she wanted to stand up and declare it to the other passengers but who would believe her? So she slept, her left arm through the handles of the blue holdall on the seat beside her and her right hand clutching her bum-bag.

Mary arrived at Dormouth in the late afternoon. She left the station, smelling the wet sand of the beach on the warm easterly wind as she walked up the road towards the sea front. She had no idea how long her 'mission' would take and her ready cash was running low.

Looking for a sign to direct her to a tourist information office where she could ask about hostel accommodation, she saw a cardboard notice in a hotel window, 'Staff Wanted – Live In.'

Hywel had got 'home' to his bedsit to find a note from his landlady saying unless he moved 'all that rubbish' out of his room by lunch time the next day, *and* paid the arrears of his rent, he would find it in boxes in the yard and he would have to live elsewhere.

He sat on the edge of the narrow bed slowly reading the note. He was on 'lates' at the hotel that day and 'earlies' the next morning. No time to move anything now. He painstakingly composed a reply, apologising for the rent position and promising to move the offending things the next afternoon. He would put the note out for Mrs Scrimshaw in the morning. He said nothing about having spent the rent money on some computer equipment he had desperately needed.

He washed in the tiny basin, and set out for the hotel where he worked as a waiter. His cutaway black jacket, starched shirts and clip-on bow tie would be ready for him in the locker of the staff rest room.

Mary started her duties at the same hotel at 7 a.m. the next day, making up the trays of morning tea and taking them with the newspapers to each room. The hotel prided itself on its old-fashioned service.

'None of this business of kettles in the bedrooms,' the proprietor's wife had told her. 'The guests are here on their holidays, remember that.'

When this work was complete Mary went to the rest room for her breakfast before starting the round of bed making and room cleaning. The proprietor's wife showed her what she had to do in each room and left her to get on with the work alone.

When she had cleaned several of the rooms and made up the beds she went down to the rest room to see if she could get a cup of tea for herself. Here she found a young waiter who had finished serving the guests' breakfast and was himself drinking tea, his jacket hanging on the back of his chair. He looked up as she came in.

Mary thought he looked suave and darkly handsome in the crisp white shirt with the black bow tie. His hair and eyes were also dark. Perhaps he was Italian – or possibly Spanish. The name Manuel flashed across her mind and she half-smiled waiting for him to introduce himself. When he didn't, she said, 'I'm Mary. Mary O'Connor. I've just come from Ireland. My first morning here.' She smiled again, a little hesitantly, wondering if the waiter's English was good enough for him to understand her.

'I'm Hy-wel. I'm from Wa-les,' he said with an exaggerated accent. 'Is Ireland your home?'

Mary was relieved, no language barrier to try and overcome. 'Not really. My family live in London and I grew up there. I've been on holiday in Ireland and I've just got back.'

'Why Dormouth?'

Mary hesitated. 'There's a job here.' It wasn't a lie, even if it was an evasive truth.

'That's something nowadays.'

Hywel stood up and carried his cup and saucer through the door into the kitchen. He called back over his shoulder, 'If you want a cuppa, stick your head in here and ask.' He came back, pulled off his tie and put it with the jacket into a tall locker in the corner. 'Me, I'm finished now until this evening. See you later. Happy bed-making.'

Mary smiled a thank you.


She worked all morning, making the guests' beds, dusting, hoovering, emptying the wastebaskets and cleaning the bathrooms. She finished just before one o'clock and went up to her room to change, rubbing her aching back.

After lunch she caught a bus for Portland, paid the fare and climbed to the upper deck. From there, as the bus travelled along the road between Dormouth and Wyke Regis she could see, between the elegant houses, out over the waters of the harbour to where Portland crouched like a sleeping lion. A yellow tongue of land joined this great rock mass to the mainland.

The bus trundled down the road, lined by rows of between-the-wars bungalows and villas, stopping frequently. As it crossed over a bridge Mary could see that the tongue of land was in fact a bank of pebbles. This *must* be the PEBBLEBANK in Fungie's message.

On the harbour side to her left the sea was a kaleidoscope of twisting colours as dozens of wind surfers sped backwards and forwards over the shallow waters.

The bus stopped and she and several other people got off to cross the main road to a car park with an Information Centre, a snack bar and toilets. She would call in at the Information Centre on her way back. Right now she wanted to see over the bank behind it. The pebbles were about the size of pigeon's eggs and rolled uncomfortably under her feet as she climbed to the top.

The view took her breath away. To her right the pebble bank stretched away in a vast arc until it faded into a mist of distance and spray. Just a mile or so to her left, the bank ran into the foot of the Portland cliffs, ending in what appeared to be a jumble of fallen rocks.

As far as she could see, great rollers tumbled in and rushed up the pebbles, roaring as they surged hungrily towards her and causing an agony of grinding sounds as they retreated, each dying wave overcome by the next towering giant.

Overnight, the wind had moved round to the southwest and gusts of warm sea-scented air snatched at her hair. The dry pebbles above the reach of the waves shimmered in a haze of reflected heat under a cloudless sky of the palest blue. Her mission was momentarily forgotten. She stood entranced, taking in the salty air and mentally floating like one of the gulls that cruised over the waves beyond the white-crested breakers.

Mary watched for a few minutes, her mind bemused by the immensity of it all, then turned and ran back down the silent, sheltered side of the bank to the clumps of sea campion and tufts of thrift, tossing her head and wanting to shout for joy. She had found the GREAT ROCK AND THE PEBBLEBANK of Fungie's message.

'Sober up, girl,' she told herself. 'People will think you're out of your mind.'

Perhaps I am, she reflected. Coming all this way on the fancied instructions of a dolphin.

She stopped running and stood still as a terrible thought struck her. Suppose Michael had played a trick on her near the lighthouse at Dingle? He had accused *her* of making up the message, but it had been *he* who had translated it for her. She had no way of knowing if what he had told her was true. He might have made the message up *himself.*

She sat down abruptly on a mass of tight-packed thin leaves from which some late sea-pink flowerheads protruded. Portland was real *and* it had a bank of pebbles – but Michael could easily have known that. The square pool could just be a tease and singing whales equally so. Had she been tricked? If she had, Michael must have laughed at her naivety all the way home to Dublin.

Mary waited despondently on the roadside for a returning bus and slumped in her seat on the way back to Dormouth. She would have to tell the hotel owner that 'something had come up and she had to go home to London.' It was not the whole truth but near enough to satisfy her stupid conscience. The nuns at her primary school would not have allowed it, she thought, smiling grimly to herself and listening to the soft Irish voice of Sister Mary Columba speaking to her through the years since then.

'Mary dear, you must learn always to speak the real truth. Jesus will know if you are lying.'

The girls had been treated more gently than the boys. The boys' misdemeanours had been punished by having to kneel in the corner of the classroom to say five 'Our Fathers' and ten 'Hail Marys' with the coarse fibres of the coconut matting pressing into their bare knees. Her brother swore that he bore the imprints to this day – a kind of stigmata or symbol of God-fearing schooldays. Still it hadn't stopped him from being called to the priesthood. He'd had a *real* call!

How stupid she had been to believe that Michael's trick had been God's message for her! That must still be to come. Would he want her to be a nun after all?

By the time the bus reached Dormouth, Mary had accepted her stupidity as her own fault. She got off at the harbour-side stop, thinking that as she had come so far she might as well see something of the town before checking on the times of trains to London. She stood on the lifting bridge and looked down on the double line of trawlers moored against the quay.

Below her the Welsh waiter from the hotel was pushing a loaded supermarket trolley along the quayside with a television set balanced precariously on the top of a stack of boxes. The set slipped sideways and nearly fell off. The man was no longer the suave, confident waiter she had seen that morning. Now, he was wearing a white T-shirt with some kind of emblem on it and tattered jeans. He looked harassed and cross as he reached out with one arm to steady the load. Mary hesitated for a moment then went down the steps to offer help.

Hywel saw her, smiled and stopped pushing. 'These things have a mind of their own,' he said kicking the nearest wheel. 'Hello.'

'Are you taking this to the dump?' she asked.

'I know at least one person who thinks I should,' he replied. 'No. Would you believe I'm taking it to church?'

He studied the face of the girl by his side and decided he could trust her.

'Me, I've been kicked out of my digs. I've got the key to an old church here and I'm taking these things there. I can't think of anywhere else.' He moved a Walkman headset to a more secure position on the trolley as he waited for a reaction.

The girl was looking at the knee of his jeans where he had mended a tear with loops of fine wire the day before.

'Can you take all this stuff *there*? Have you got permission?' Mary asked.

'Not as such,' Hywel replied. 'But the old vicar's dead and it's just an empty place. There haven't been any services for years.'

'Can I come with you?' Mary asked. 'I like churches and old places.'

'Yes, of course. But I'm a bit slow with this thing.'

They rounded the corner, Mary holding one side of the trolley to help guide it. Even so it seemed determined to run into every wall and every shuttered and padlocked warehouse they passed. At the church, Hywel hauled the trolley awkwardly up the path, unlocked the door and pushed it inside.

Mary followed him in and sniffed. 'There's mice in here,' she whispered.

'Don't mind a few mice. Be company, like.'

'Company?'

Hywel looked at her. 'Don't tell anyone, but I'm going to sleep here for a while. Until I find a place with a bit of a workshop, that is.'

'Sleep here – in a church?' Mary asked, her face showing her disapproval.

'Why not? No one else uses it.'

'But it's . . . it's a church,' she protested.

'So? I don't believe in ghosties and things like that. I'll be OK.'

'No. I meant it isn't right, not – well – respectful,' she replied.

Hywel was pushing the trolley up the aisle. A few magazines slid off and fell under a pew. He knelt, reached down and retrieved them. Mary hung back for a moment then followed. He turned towards the vestry and opened the door as she caught up with him.

'This should do me for a while. You won't tell anyone,' he pleaded. 'I don't know where else to go with these things.'

Mary shook her head.

'This was the last load,' he told her as he saw her looking at the pile of boxes, coils of cable, and the black bin-liner that she guessed held his clothes. On a wooden chair was a sleeping bag. She turned to leave.

'Please stay.'

'I'm sorry, it's really none of my business but . . . I'll go now.'

'Please don't. I've got a camping-gas stove here and a bottle of water. I was going to make coffee. Stay and have some?'

Mary looked around her again.

'You're still going to be a waiter and all that?' she asked.

'Oh yes. Got to earn some money to eat, but I can live here rent-free until I'm found out. I can do my *real* work here.' He lit the stove and stood an aluminium kettle on it.

'Real work?'

'I'm a frustrated inventor, scientist, electronics buff – call it what you will. I love making things that work in new ways but . . . I'm dyslexic,' he added, as though it was something shameful. 'You know, difficulty with reading and all that.'

'There are lots of dyslexic people. They're supposed to be highly intelligent,' Mary said.

'So I've heard, but that didn't get me a place at university, nor a job in electronics. Bloody waiting at tables, that's all I'm good for.'

'What are you making . . . inventing?'

'Always been fascinated by sound. Perhaps because I played the organ when I was a kid. That was something I *could* do. I'm working on new ways of recording certain types of sound. This is all my gear.' He spooned instant coffee into two mugs, poured on boiling water, stirred it, dropped the teaspoon and swore quietly.

'Sorry,' he said, retrieving it from under the trolley. 'Now, where did I put the milk?'

He searched in several boxes, found a carton, tore off a corner and passed the carton to Mary. 'Oh Lord. I hope you don't take sugar.'

'No. It's OK, I don't.'

They sat in silence, sipping the coffee in the vestry, Mary was still feeling uncomfortable. Suddenly, she stood up.

'Look, I'm not happy about this. I must go.'

She looked round for somewhere to put the half-empty mug, chose the least vulnerable looking of the piles of boxes and hurried out into the nave. A sparrow was chirping loudly as it fluttered from the back of a pew up to a hole in a window.

'God sees every little sparrow, my dear,' a nun's voice reached her from somewhere in her memory and she stopped to watch. The bird pitched its tiny body through the hole and all was silent again. The hole was shaped like a dolphin.

Hywel's voice from behind her said, 'Please, don't go. Come up the tower, there's something I'd like to show you.'

There was a naivety about the appeal that touched Mary – a hint of loneliness perhaps. Possibly a desire to have someone share his wrong-doing in taking possession of the church. She turned and smiled.

'As long as it's not bats.'

'Not bats, I promise. Something much nicer. Please.'

The smile that flitted across Mary's face was gone as suddenly as the sparrow. 'Have you got *that* key too?'

'It's not locked, but it's a bit of a climb.'

Mary followed Hywel up the spiral staircase, feeling somewhat less of an intruder in the unfamiliar surroundings than she had in the nave below.

She was as surprised as he had been at the greenery on the roof.

'Trust a buddleia to get up here!' she exclaimed, a flash-smile of pleasure lighting her face. 'Complete with butterflies – and wallflowers and knapweed.' She slipped off her shoes and walked barefoot across the grass to the parapet. 'Kipling said a man who walks barefoot thinks with his whole body. I know exactly what he meant. Do you?'

Hywel was standing in the doorway watching her. 'Never really tried, me,' he replied as he knelt on one knee and undid the laces of his trainers.

Barefoot, he joined her to look out over the town and sea. 'I like it, sort of connects you with the earth, no insulation in between,' he said.

Mary was gripping the parapet and staring down, her eyes wide. Below her a man and a woman were standing together on the edge of a square, blue pool feeding two dolphins with what looked like fish. A larger, light-coloured, dolphin-shaped creature was submerged at the other end of the pool but was clearly visible from above.

. . . THREE OF THE RACE OF WHALES IN A SQUARE POOL TO THE NORTH OF THE GREAT ROCK . . .

So Michael had *not* lied to her.

'Thank you, God,' she breathed.

'Did you say something?' Hywel asked, peering down and not waiting for an answer. 'That's strange. There was only one dolphin there yesterday.'

'Who do they belong to?' Mary asked, her voice a whisper.

'No idea. That feller lives in the room next to mine, but I never see much of him. I thought he was a girl at first with his long hair. I don't think I've seen the woman before but it's hard to tell at this distance. Maybe *they* own them. The old vicar, the one who gave me the key, didn't know. He thought dolphins had souls!'

. . . THREE OF THE RACE OF WHALES IN A SQUARE POOL TO THE NORTH OF THE GREAT ROCK . . .

'Sorry. What were you saying?'

'The old vicar thought dolphins had souls.'

'I thought you said he was dead?'

'He is.'

'Then how did he give you the key? Oh never mind.'

Mary was studying the creatures in the pool below. Two were swimming slowly round side by side. The bigger, grey looking one was resting on the bottom. THREE OF THE RACE OF WHALES . . . She watched the grey one rise sluggishly to breathe, then sink again.

'Dolphins should be in the sea, not in pools,' she said. 'I swam with one in Ireland a couple of days ago.'

She felt a great urge to tell Hywel about Fungie and the Message, to share her wonderful secret with someone else. She opened her mouth to tell him how she had seen the Ogham Writing when Hywel spoke. 'Lot of bloody hoo-ha talked about dolphins. Like they were sea-going humans or something – souls indeed. Not even humans have those, whatever the old vicar thought.'

'You don't believe in God?'

'I told you, I'm a scientist – or trying to be.'

'Some scientists believe in God.'

'God knows how! Scientists are supposed to be intelligent, rational people.'

Mary decided not to tell about Fungie to this man who she had started to like but who was now blatantly showing himself to be Godless. She was tempted to change the subject to something bland and non-controversial, then recalled Saint Peter denying that he knew Jesus and the cock crowing thrice as he did so.

'*I* believe in God,' she declared.

'That explains you being so touchy about me being in the church, then.'

'Well, yes.' Mary looked down at the dolphins. If the message had really been from God about THREE OF THE RACE OF WHALES, then He had obviously guided her here – so it must be all right. But now was not the time to try and explain. She had to work out what was meant by AND TAKE THEIR SONG TO THE WORLD OF PEOPLE. She felt overwhelmed – the task was too big for her.

'I really must go now,' she said slipping her shoes on.

'Will you come again?' Hywel asked. 'I didn't mean to upset you. I would like it if you would.'

'Maybe. It depends.'

'On what?'

'God,' said Mary and flashed him a smile that disappeared almost before it had registered.

*FairIsle had seen the movement on the top of the square-stone tower. Humans were up there looking down. Were they there to help her escape, mere onlookers, or a part of other humans' plans to keep her here in captivity for reasons she could not guess at? One paused in a gap between the square cut stones and stared down at her in the pool. FairIsle knew that aura. It was the female who had play-shared with her so long ago and who she had sensed briefly on the deck of a boat near the Land of the Dragon. Of that she was sure.*

*She swallowed the fish that the white-headed human had given her. It was dead and flabby but she would need all the strength she could get to find a way out of this featureless pool. She swam alongside Rockall, the sullen pain in her lungs making her breathing uncomfortable.*

*'There are humans up there,' she said. 'Is that usual?'*

*Rockall followed her gaze and saw the heads outlined against the sky.*

*'There were two there for a short time yesterday but none before that,' he replied. 'It's bad enough to be trapped here without being watched all the time.'*

*'They have gone now,' FairIsle said. 'So it is not all the time.'*

*Rockall snorted, turned about and swam in the other direction.*

# CHAPTER FIFTEEN

*Nordstar lay in the deep end of the pool as night crept over the sky, hardly moving except to rise sluggishly to breathe. Grace of FairIsle glided up and lay beside her, caressing the whale's flabby flank with her fin.*

*'We'll get out of here,' she said confidently. In the absence of a reply, she scanned Nordstar's body to assess her blubber reserves. She'll not die of starvation yet, she thought.*

*'We **will** get out of here,' she promised again.*

*Rockall cruised past on one of his many circuits.*

*'If there was a way out, do you think **I'd** still be here?' he said.*

*FairIsle ignored him.*

*'Will you sing me your star-song,' she asked Nordstar.*

*The whale shuddered the length of her body.*

*'It died with my constellation in the Eighteen Islands.'*

*'It didn't. You sang it to me when we were coming here in the floating pool. Sing it now for Rockall and me.'*

*'Why would two Grinners want to hear my song?'*

*'To see if you still touch Truth,' FairIsle replied.*

*'The Truth is that I should have died to save all other starwhales. You were told of the prophecy. I've failed – that's the **Truth**.'*

*'Jetsam,' said FairIsle. 'In the history of this planet of Water, many, many, unexpected things have happened to those who don't give up. Hope swims with dolphins.'*

*'I'm not a dolphin.'*

*'I am – share my hope.'*

*There was a silence between them. As Rockall swam past, Nordstar was saying, 'What I fear is not dying, that is my destiny. My fear is to die alone.'*

*'I'll not leave you to that,' the dolphine said.*

*'You promise?'*

*'My word. While the Moon pulls and the Sea surges, I will stay with you whilst you live.'*

*Waves of gratitude washed around FairIsle.*

*Rockall swam past and flicked his tail scornfully as he turned the corner nearest the rock-tower.*

*'Will you sing for me now?' the dolphine asked Nordstar.*

*'I must find a new Truth and a new song to express it. I will talk with the stars.'*

*The white whale rose slowly to the surface and raised her head above the water, unable to achieve the true starwatch pose as her tail-flukes were bent backwards uncomfortably by the bottom of the pool. The sky was obscured by the yellow glow of surrounding lights and the stars were not bright enough to penetrate the glow.*

*'There is a poison of lights in the sky,' Nordstar declared and sank again.*

Hywel had finished his late shift and walked back to the church. An old Morris Minor was still parked by the kerb under one of the streetlights and he realised it must be the dead vicar's car. Perhaps he should tell the police. That might lead them to ask awkward questions though. He had half expected some kind of visit from church officials, if there were such beings. A vicar doesn't drop dead after visiting a disused church and no one comes nosing round, surely? He'd be rumbled soon, one way or another.

Leave it, he decided. Make the most of the time he had there to experiment with his recording systems.

Inside the church he felt curiously unfocused. He seemed to be just making slight improvements to existing systems and he yearned for some new challenge, something really original. Something that would – he fumbled for the expression that his childhood mentor, Mr Williams, had once used – 'Push forward the frontiers of Science'. Or was it, 'push back'? He felt inadequate again. What was he, a dyslexic valleys boy, going to discover that was not already known in the laboratories of Oxford, Cambridge and Manchester?

He did not go into the vestry but sat at the organ console and put on the tiny light above the keyboard. He wanted to play to see if there was any inspiration in music, his recent playing for the old vicar having reawakened dormant feelings. He turned off the light, afraid that playing so late at night would alert someone to the church being unlawfully occupied. He sat there for a minute indecisively, then turned on the light and the electric blower, feeling the pleasure of anticipation as the low hum increased and stabilised. He touched a key and the picture of a girl's smiling face floated before his eyes. Mary – from Ireland.

When he had been fifteen the Cwm Glas Male Voice Choir had given a concert to celebrate St Patrick's Day. 'Just for a change, like,' the choirmaster had said.

Could he remember the songs? He tried *Danny Boy* and the haunting Irish tune flowed out of his fingertips, through the organ and into the darkness. He followed this with *When Irish Eyes are Smiling,* and finished on *The Rose of Tralee*, singing to himself, 'Mary, my Mary, the Rose of Tralee.'

*'Can you feel that?' Rockall asked FairIsle as the notes from the organ vibrated through the water of the pool.*

*'What is it? Has it happened before?' FairIsle asked.*

*'Only a few times while I've been here. What sings those songs? Can it be a Great Land Whale?'*

*'If there were such a creature we'd have known of it. It cannot be that. A human is making those sounds somehow. There is a human female's face hidden in them.'*

*The dolphins listened intently until Nordstar stirred from her lethargy and joined them.*

*'Who sings?' she asked as the music faded and died.*

Hywel switched off the bellows and the light, and fumbled his way across the echoing emptiness of the church, the girl's face still filling his mind.

'Don't be so daft, boy. Girls like that are not for the likes of you,' he told himself.

# CHAPTER SIXTEEN

Kenny and Helga stood in the shade under the diving platforms watching the white pilot whale swimming slowly round the pool. The dolphins were also swimming the circuit, noticeably more lively than before and frequently overtaking the whale as they swam. Helga fetched some fish from the café room.

The water was dirtier than the day before. She asked Kenny about the filters and why the water was so murky.

'There's a big pump to draw clean water from the harbour and another pump that sucks the stale water down that grid in the bottom and back to the sea somewhere. Mr Cartwright only lets me run the pumps once a week. He says it uses too much electricity to run them often.'

'Switch on the pumps now,' said Helga. 'If Mr Cartwright does not like it, I will tell him – how would *he* like to swim in his own muck? We will do the pumps every day.'

Kenny grinned and went to the filter room next to the café-room. He stood on two blocks of wood, kept in there for the purpose, reached up to the power box in the corner and pulled the metal switch-arm down. A low whine came from an electric motor mounted in the centre of the floor. He moved the blocks and repeated the action on another power box.

Outside again, he watched Helga at the far end of the pool trying to tempt the pilot whale to feed with the dolphins but she was being ignored. She was crouching and holding out a fish when he heard a key turn, saw the street door open and Mr Cartwright come in. Kenny tried to signal to Helga but she was absorbed in her efforts to get the whale to feed. Mr Cartwright walked up behind her and spoke. 'Are they all feeding?'

Helga stood up and turned on the man. 'It is a bad thing to creep at me like that,' she said angrily as Kenny came round the poolside to join them.

Kenny cringed. He had never heard anyone speak to his boss that way.

'Sorry,' Mr Cartwright replied with no hint of apology in the tone. 'Are they *all* feeding?'

'No, the white hval is still not eating. But she *is* swimming about the pool now,' Helga said.

Mr Cartwright turned to Kenny.

'Have you got them jumping yet?'

'Not quite, but we will soon.'

'Better had,' the older man said. 'You damned well better had.' He turned and went out again. Kenny breathed a sigh of relief. Mr Cartwright had not noticed the sound of the pumps.

'Is there a shop for the hair dressing in this town?' Helga asked Kenny.

'Yes, do you want to get yours done?'

He looked at the immaculate blond plait. Don't change that, he pleaded silently. It reminded him of one of the few housemothers who appeared to have been genuinely interested in him when he was a boy.

'No, for *you*, I meant. Why do you have it long like a girl's? I don't like it any more than Mr Creepy Cartwright does. I saw how he was looking at you. And I think that the earrings are for girls too. You are not wanting to be a girl are you?'


When Kenny came back to try some dolphin training after his curry and chips lunch, his hair was short and the earring was not to be seen.

Helga stood back and looked at him.

'That is better. Now you look like a man.'

Kenny's heart grew so big it was tight in his chest and pounded like the payout-clunking of a fruit machine in The Arcade. He stammered a response.

'I . . . I . . . went to that p . . . place near the front—' then stopped when he realised that Helga was laughing at him.

'Now you are being like a silly boy again,' she said and turned towards the pool. 'I will see if I can get the dolphinhvals to do the jumps.'

She crouched down at the edge of the water and held out a fish for FairIsle. When the dolphine came to her and lifted her head out of the water Helga put her hand under the smooth jaw, looked straight into her eyes and spoke slowly in a language that Kenny did not know.

FairIsle slid backwards, swam to the deep end of the pool, following the shelving bottom, turned and surged to the surface, breaking through and leaping to the height of the second diving board before curving over and re-entering the water with scarcely a ripple.

Helga clapped her hands.

'What did you *say*?' asked the awe-struck Kenny.

'I just said I wanted her to show me that she could jump out of the water,' Helga replied.

'Can you speak Dolphinese?' Kenny asked, remembering Super-Dolphin.

'*This* dolphinhval speaks Faeroese,' Helga said, trying to keep a straight face.

'Really?'

'No, I am pulling the leg, I think you say. But I think they can know what you want them to do.'

She walked to the deep end and made a rising circle with her arm. FairIsle leapt again, higher this time, droplets of water falling from her body and sparkling in the bright sunlight.

'We will have something to show that shiny-headed Mr Creeper when he comes again, will we not?'

*Rockall was swimming at FairIsle's side.*

*'Why do you do what the little fishes want?' he asked.*

*'Little fishes?'*

*'The Sprat and the She-salmon.'*

*'Have you anything better to do?'*

*'No, but it is stupid. How can you do a Joy-leap when there is no joy?'*

*'I like the She-salmon, as you call her. She does not care to see us here and soon she will pine for her home where the sea is real and the cliffs are not all square. Maybe when she goes, she will take me too.'*

*'Remember your promise.' Nordstar's voice flowed weakly through the water.*

*Grace of FairIsle swam to her.*

*'While the Moon pulls and the Sea surges. Float gently – be at peace. We leave together or I stay.'*

Helga was pleased with the way the dolphins were responding. Even Rockall had made a rather clumsy leap in the late afternoon. The water was now clear and cool so she told Kenny to switch off the pumps. She gave the dolphins extra fish and joined him in the café room.

'Is there a shop for mending things in this town?' she asked.

Kenny looked round suspiciously.

'For mending what?'

'For my accordion. It is old and is now broken. I would like to play it again.'

'*I'm* good at fixing things. I've got a tube of superglue. Bring it in to my room this evening.'

'OK, yes, I will do that. At seven of the clock.'

'Seven of the clock will be OK,' Kenny replied, his heart doing the payout-clunking again.

After serving lunch at the hotel, Hywel returned to the church. He had seen Mary briefly in the morning break and invited her to meet him at the church in the afternoon. She had said she *might*.

119

As he walked up the aisle the sun was striking through the stained glass, throwing beams of colour across the pews and onto the dusty floor. He picked up one of his technical magazines lying almost out of sight under a seat. If only I could read these damned things more easily, I might be better at my job, he thought, then mentally added, 'my real job.'

He flicked through the magazine, each page illustrated with wiring diagrams and photographs, the pages bright from the sunbeams passing through the stained glass. One article he had not noticed before was glowing orange as a ray of light shone through Portland's lighthouse in the ship-in-distress window.

Where the coloured light lit the page, the words were not jumping about as they usually did. Hywel moved the page from colour beam to colour beam, but only the orange light glued the words to the page. Trembling slightly, he read the article. It was headed:


## FISH IN THE EAR PROJECT DEFEATS INVENTORS.


Hywel read on, faster and more easily than he had ever read before.

> Many readers of this journal will be familiar with Douglas Adams' book *The Hitch Hiker's Guide to the Galaxy*, in which the hero, Arthur Dent, has a Babel Fish inserted in his ear and can then understand any language spoken to him. The concept of a universal translation device has appealed to inventors for centuries and, with the advent of computers, many language experts hoped to be able to create such a program. Tales are still told of the first attempt by a machine to translate 'The spirit is willing but the flesh is weak,' into Russian. The translation is reported to have printed out as, 'The vodka is co-operative but the meat is rotten.'

Hywel turned the page and moved the magazine back into the orange light.

> Fame and fortune await the inventor of a working Babel Fish or its equivalent, and research continues in America and many other parts of the world. The increasing acceptance of English as the international language may eventually eliminate the need. That is, until we want to communicate with aliens from other planets. However, they may come equipped with Babel Fish of their own.

120

Hywel turned the pages and found he could read all the articles more easily in the orange light but the one on the Babel Fish had caught his imagination. He closed the magazine and walked quickly up the aisle and into the vestry, changed from his waiter's trousers into his worn-out jeans and crossed the room to where his half-completed recording device lay on a bench made of boards between two chairs. He picked up a notepad and sketched a diagram involving a pattern of microchips connected to a computer memory in a way that he thought was unique. The memory would have to contain all the words in each of the languages between which interchanges would be needed.

The obvious weaknesses in his design and the vastness of the memory required, shouted to him that this was not the solution. If it had been *that* easy, other people would already have done it. What he had to do was tackle the problem from some completely new and original angle. He pocketed the pad and climbed the spiral staircase to his tower-top garden to think.

He blinked as he came out from the cool darkness into the intense sunlight, relishing the gentle breeze from the sea and the pale washed-out blue of the sky. One renegade cloud drifted aimlessly to the south of him, somewhere over the Isle of Portland that was hidden by the houses and the hill beyond the harbour. The pungent scent from the buddleia was all about him and red, brown and black winged butterflies flitted from flower to flower.

He leant against the parapet and took off his shoes and socks before looking down into the pool. The man and the woman there were evidently trying to teach the dolphins to leap from the water. The dolphins could do with a Babel Fish in their ears, he thought. There was obviously a communication barrier between them and the humans on the poolside.

Then he noticed a woman hurrying along the street between the tall buildings. She seemed nervous and kept glancing over her shoulder as she walked. Only then did he remember he had promised to meet Mary at the door.

He ran down the stairs barefoot, as fast as he dared, intensely aware of the coldness of the stone under the soles of his feet. He sprinted through the aisle and unlocked the heavy door.

'Hello – sorry,' he gasped, 'I was up on the tower.'

He was about to add, 'I forgot you were coming,' but decided this would be tactless.

'Sorry,' he said again. 'My fault. Glad you could come.'

Mary was looking at the grey dust on his bare feet and flashed him a smile. 'Mind you don't tread on anything nasty,' she said.

They climbed the steep tower steps, Mary leading, while Hywel admired the bare legs now at his eye level.

'If this grass was clipped,' Mary said at the top, slipping off her shoes, 'it would make a lawn fit for an angel. It's like the Garden of Eden in miniature.'

She walked to the parapet and looked down at THREE OF THE RACE OF WHALES. How did they sing? And how would she know it if they did?

The afternoon passed slowly. Hywel and Mary moved from the open sunlight into the shade at the top of the steps and back into the sun's warmth as they felt too hot or too cold. Mary frequently stood up to look over the wall and down into the pool.

'Do you ever go back to Wales?' she asked Hywel as they sat side by side on the top step, enjoying the coolness of the draught flowing up the tower stairway, even though the air smelt musty and dank like an abandoned well.

'Only at Christmas – to see Mam. Nothing much else there for me now. Not like it was.'

'How was that?'

'We had a pit in the village then – Cwm Glas Colliery. Plenty of work for those who wanted it. Money to spend in the shops, a choir and the mountains for when you needed to get away from it all. Lovely up there with the skylarks and the curlews.'

Mary thought of the terraced houses around her home in South London. She had thought Morley Park was lovely when she had been a little girl but there were no skylarks or curlews there. Now she knew that much of the world was beautiful, especially Ireland, though much more was like her home and had to be put up with by ordinary people like herself.

'You said you were dyslexic. Is there a cure for that?' she asked gently, feeling that she might now be treading on dangerous ground.

'Yesterday I'd have said "No" – but today . . .'

Hywel told Mary about the orange light and what he had read about the Babel Fish. His excitement was obvious and catching.

She again wanted to tell him about Fungie and the message in Ogham but checked herself, still not sure that he would understand. If he didn't believe in God he was unlikely to believe in dolphins writing messages in the sea. She stayed with a slightly less sensitive subject.

'If you've always been dyslexic, how did you get to know about electronics?'

'My mother used to clean house for a man called Mr Williams. He lived at Ty Mawr – that's "Big House" in Welsh. In the school holidays I'd go with her and play in the gardens while she was working. Mr Williams

122

wasn't married – no children of his own, see. I think he liked it when I went there.

'Ty Mawr was built by the old colliery owners, right at the top end of the valley – high walls and laurel bushes all around to keep it private like. A different world from outside – all run-down though.'

Hywel stretched himself and yawned.

'Mr Williams had made his money from miners lamps – told me his company was once the biggest maker of those in the world. He was passionate about electricity – had a workshop in the stable block. I used to hang around and watch him working. Of course he was retired then, living on savings or shares in the company, I suppose. It was Mr Williams who taught me to solder and how currents flowed and what resistors were for – all that sort of thing. It was the one-to-one showing that worked for me – not like in school. Physics masters there came and went. None of them wanted to stay long in a crummy comprehensive in a dying valley. Can't say I blame them.'

Mary tried to picture the old man and the eager young boy working side by side in an old stable.

'Mr Williams was just learning about electronics himself,' Hywel continued. 'He used to read aloud out of technical journals – then we would make things together. Learned a lot from him I did.'

'Is he still alive?' Mary asked.

'Oh yes. I phone him about once a year – nice to speak to the old fellow again. Bit sad really – his money ran out I think – had to sell up and go and live in an old folks home down at Abergavenny.'

'What happened to Ty Mawr?'

Hywel pulled a face.

'Ty Mawr? That's a home for the elderly now. Bit ironic really, him being in Abergavenny in a different one, but Mr Williams said he couldn't stay at Ty Mawr with a couple of dozen old codgers when he'd lived there most of his life on his own.'

'I can understand that,' said Mary, standing up to look down into the pool again, then coming back to sit in the shade. The dolphins were not swimming about and she could not see the man and the woman.

'What happened to the workshop?' she asked.

'He gave *me* all his equipment and instruments. Said I must do something worthy with them – whatever that means. Most of the things I've got in the vestry were his. I can't help feeling I've let him down in some way.'

'How?' Mary asked quietly but Hywel was clearly not wanting to continue the conversation. He was sketching something on a pad.

Mary shivered and moved out into the sunshine again, closed her eyes against the glare and listened to the hum of bees working around the flowers growing in the wall. She was thinking of dolphins singing. Whales sang, she had heard a recording of strange semi-musical wailings recorded underwater near Hawaii but as far as she knew dolphins only made clicking and grunting noises.

Hywel stood up, took off his shirt and sat down in the sun with the pad on his knee, staring into space.

'I must get some shorts,' he said unexpectedly, pulling at the tight legs of his jeans, the wire that held the tear together pressing into his knees.

'I could cut the legs off those,' said Mary, instantly regretting what she had said. He might take them off and she was not ready yet to be alone with a man in just his underpants.

'Would you?' he asked. 'Have you got any scissors?'

Mary nearly said, 'No,' but it would have been a lie.

'I've got nail scissors in my bag,' she admitted. 'Stand up and keep still.'

She knelt at Hywel's side, cut upwards a few inches from a hole in the left knee then snipped around his leg, feeling strangely excited as her hand moved against the hairs on his thigh.

He shook his leg and the tube of cloth slipped down to his ankle. He kicked it off over his bare foot. She did the same with the other leg of the jeans and he kicked that trouser-leg clear as well, then walked across the roof and back to where Mary was still kneeling on the grass.

'Could you take a bit more off?' he asked. 'These look like Bermuda shorts – neither fish nor fowl.'

Her heart beating even faster, Mary clipped off a further three inches.

'That'll have to do,' she said giving him a flash of a smile. 'Any more and you'll be arrested. And me as an accomplice.'


A seagull flew over Dormouth church tower on its way to scavenge for an evening meal, to poke around amongst the remains of bathers' picnics on the beach. It squawked when it saw the humans so close.

'God,' said Hywel suddenly, snapping out of a reverie where Mary's smile mixed inexplicably with unlikely 'Fish in the Ear' circuit diagrams. 'I'd forgotten I'm on lates as well today. I must go down and change.' He stood up quickly.

Mary stood too, her head swimming from the sudden exertion. She leant on the parapet – below her the dolphins were unhurriedly circling the pool. A whole afternoon gone and she was no nearer to finding out how dolphins might sing.

'Will you come again tomorrow?' Hywel asked.

'Yes,' she said and it was as though the word had spoken itself.

# CHAPTER SEVENTEEN

Kenny leant out of the window in the airless room that was his entire home, and stared down into the yard. He would rather have had one of the rooms that faced towards the sea, even if it was three roads away, but Mrs Scrimshaw charged more for those and on what old Carters paid him, there was no chance.

He could hear Helga moving about in the next room, beyond the plaster-board partition that had made two ugly rooms out of a single elegant Edwardian one, then her door opening and closing, followed by a gentle tap on his door. His heart leapt. He opened the door and invited Helga into his room, which was tidier than usual, and asked her to sit down. She glanced from the bed to the single upright chair and chose the chair, putting the battered hexagonal box carefully on the floor beside her.

Kenny stood awkwardly, then perched himself on the edge of the bed.

'It's in the box?' he asked, knowing it was a stupid question as he said it.

'Ja – yes, it is in the box. I will get it out for you to see.'

Kenny took the instrument from her and studied the tear in the fabric. 'I can mend that easily, but it really needs new material all over. I don't think *I* could do that.'

Kenny opened a small cupboard beside his bed and took out his best shirt, keeping his body between what he was doing and Helga. He tore a strip off the tail. The pattern was not unlike that on the concertina.

Using a pair of cheap scissors and a tube of instant glue he expertly patched the split with a piece of the shirt-tail. He had to use three layers of cloth, each stiffened with glue, before the patch was sufficiently airtight.

'You are clever young man and I thank you,' Helga said.

'I used to make models,' Kenny replied, 'but the other children used to break them up.'

Helga did not ask who the other children might be and Kenny continued.

'This superglue dries in a few seconds, you'll be able to play it soon.'

'Thank you, Ken-ney. I am looking forward to playing it again – but not here, I think.' She stood up. 'Can we go to the hval's pool? It will be not so hot there and the hvals like to hear the music, I think.'

'Sure,' said Kenny, feeling in his pocket for the key to the pool enclosure.

He put the scissors back in the drawer next to the mouth organ he had never learned to play and the tiny ship with the hinged masts which would not quite go through the neck of the bottle for which it had been made.

Helga slipped off her shoes, sat on the edge of the pool with her feet in the water and prepared to play.

The dolphins and the white whale circled slowly, watching her. Kenny sat on the rails studying Helga's back in the evening light, tapping the key lightly against his pursed lips.

Lamp standards in the street beyond the wall flickered on, each fluted glass bowl turning from orange to a sickly yellow as the sodium gas inside the bulbs ionised.

Helga drew a long note from the instrument, then played softly.

One by one the dolphins and the whale rose to breathe, each gentle hiss seeming loud in the still air of the pool enclosure. Sounds from outside faded to insignificance as the music filled the enclosure and slid over the walls into the unheeding night beyond.

Kenny held the key against his lips and listened in rapture. He knew none of the tunes but he was suddenly Super-Dolphin again, flying through the air, swimming and diving under the sea, invincible and invulnerable.

*FairIsle floated at ease, drifting towards Helga's feet in the tiny residual current from their earlier swimming. The dolphine's head touched against bare toes and she stayed there, moving very gently, reading the pictures in the music both through the water and the body contact with the woman. She projected her own mind-pictures towards the humans and noted the music change to match the mood of her own thoughts. Rockall drifted to her side and rubbed his head against Helga's other foot and his flank against FairIsle's side. Only Nordstar held back, excluding herself from the intimate triangle.*

Kenny's alter ego circled overhead or swam and leapt and dived silently in the salty water of the pool.

The distant whine of a police car's siren eventually broke the spell as the vehicle sped along the sea front on some unknown mission.

Helga clipped the hooks that held the accordion closed and returned it to the case. The dolphins backed away and Kenny stepped down from the railing, rubbing his stiff buttocks.

Hywel had finished his shift earlier than usual and had climbed the dark staircase of the tower to look down on the magical scene below. Now, as the music ended, he wriggled his shoulders and rubbed his knees to relieve the tingle of near sunburn and watched as the two people left the pool, locking the door behind them. A Latin phrase engraved on the panel of an old organ he had once seen, floated up out of his memory. *IN MUSICA EST VERITAS.* He had asked and been told it meant 'in music there is truth', but had not really understood at the time. Yet somehow the music and the dolphins seemed to go together and make a vague sort of sense of the phrase. *In musica est veritas.* He'd stayed too long in the sun.

'We will go home now?' said Helga in the quiet street outside the pool.

Kenny kicked gently at the front tyre of the old Morris that had been parked there for the last few days. He wanted the night to last forever.

'The Arcade will still be open,' he said. 'Let's go there.'

Helga screwed up her eyes at the glaring lights of the amusement arcade on the sea front as she followed Kenny inside. Holidaymakers in garish T shirts and gaudy Bermuda shorts jostled her, their breath smelling of beer and chips. Her ears were assaulted by shrieks, thumping sounds and electronic squawking noises. The distinctive five-note recognition signal from *Close Encounters* was played again and again by some unseen music machine. Men and women stood in rows staring intently at the fruit machines as the pictures of cherries, pears and pineapples spun before their glazed eyes and clicked to juddering halts, then spun again at the push of a frenzied fist on a glowing button. Through all the electronic noise came the rattle and clatter of falling coins.

Kenny turned to her, grinning, and shouted something she could not hear above the din. It was like being in the midst of a disturbed cliff-top colony of sea birds. She imagined them pecking and spitting at her, looked about frantically and ran back through the arcade and into the street.

*The experiences of the evening left FairIsle restless during the night. She swam round the shadowy pool and was soon joined by Nordstar who glided at her side. Rockall moved to the centre of the pool and rested, floating at ease and half listening to the females' conversation as they circled.*

*'The She-salmon makes moving sounds,' said Nordstar. 'It is almost as if she speaks to us.'*

*'I could sense her spirit and see word-pictures in the sounds,' FairIsle replied.*

*'I once heard a Great Whale sing,' said Nordstar. 'It was before . . . before . . .' She shuddered.*

*'Could you understand its song?' FairIsle asked.*

127

'Mostly, but I was overwhelmed by fear of my destiny at the time and did not do justice to the privilege.'

'What did it sing?' asked FairIsle eagerly, as they circled in the darkness.

'It seemed that this whale was the last of her Chapter to be alive and she held knowledge known to no other whale. Knowledge of what she called the Wishful Mixing of Life.'

'Could you understand her meanings?'

'A little. I had swum away from my constellation to be on my own and meditate, and this whale was seemingly desperate to tell some other creature of what it was that she alone knew. She sang, and I listened as best I knew how.

'She told me how all creatures pass on their body shapes and their instincts to the next generations as patterns in their seeds.'

'Patterns?' asked FairIsle.

'Patterns like ripples down the edges of kelpweed was how this whale tried to describe it to me. I found it hard to follow. She said that females have one pattern in their seeds and males another pattern in theirs. When the seeds combine at Joy-sharing it is as though a whirlpool had twisted the kelp-strands together and somehow merged them. The combined ripples direct the making of the new-life which has in it some of each parent.'

'How did she know that?' FairIsle asked.

'She did not say. The intellects of the great whales are far superior to ours. Perhaps it was just speculation – mere fancy.'

'Even so, it is a wonderful idea,' said FairIsle. 'All whalekind should know of that.'

'That was the concern of the Great Whale. But she told me much more.'

'More? Tell me.'

'She said that she believed a female's mind can alter the patterns, but only before the joyning of her seed with the male's. If she desires something enough – like being able to swim faster, dive deeper or understand more clearly – and wishes it for the future, then the power of her mind can alter the patterns, but only a little. It takes many generations of similar desires before the effects are visible.'

'Only the females can do this?'

'She did not say. Perhaps the males can do the same with their seed.'

'That's extraordinary,' said FairIsle. 'The whale told you all of this?'

'And more that I have forgotten, or did not understand. I hope she has found others of her kind to whom she can pass it on. When knowledge is held by only a few, it is fearfully vulnerable to loss.'

'Humans record things outside of their minds,' broke in Rockall. 'That's why they have hands.' He slapped his tail on the water, pleased that he knew something the females didn't.

'That's extraordinary,' said FairIsle for the second time.

'There are more mysteries in the Sea and Sky than even dolphins dream of,' said Rockall, slapping the water again.

FairIsle circled the pool, enjoying the fresh water that surged in at a hole in the side of the pool when the pump was running, though the hard spot in her lungs irritated her.

As she swam past Rockall she asked, 'Will you deep-scan my body and tell me what you see?'

She felt, as well as heard, the probing ripples penetrate her flesh as Rockall scanned her from head to tail.

'There is a spot of hardness in your lungs, as big as a codfish's eye and of a perfect roundness. It is hard enough be made of shipstone.'

'It entered my lungs in the place of death in the Faroff Islands when I was about to be killed. It hurts when I breathe.'

'Swim belly up and it may be pulled out by the Earthsuck.'

'I have tried that but it will not move.'

'Try again and I will shimmer it as you swim.'

FairIsle drew in a deep breath, turned her belly to the sky and swam the length of the pool slowly as Rockall, swimming towards her at an angle, directed the most powerful of vibrations at the spot in her lungs.

The pain intensified as the ice-pebble vibrated and started to move back along and down the tubules, slowly at first then faster as it reached the larger airways. Suddenly, it was gone.

FairIsle turned over and rose to breathe.

'Thank you,' she said weakly.

Rockall was nosing a small silver ball along the floor of the pool.

'I have never seen the like,' he swam up and told her. 'It is smooth and round and shines like a full moon. It must be a starbit that fell from the sky to save your life.'

'Where is it now?' FairIsle asked.

'It is resting on the bars across the hole where the foul water is drawn away at the deepest part of the pool,' Rockall told her. 'Come and see it.'

Helga had tried to wipe the unnerving experience of the Arcade from her mind and concentrate on the magic of her communion with the dolphins. She did not go to the pool early the next morning to feed them with Kenny and wondered how much he would miss her. Too much, she thought, and walked aimlessly around the town looking in the shop windows before buying a sandwich for her lunch and sitting in the sunshine on a bench overlooking the sands.

Families were streaming down from the Promenade and settling in groups, each a fixed distance from the next. Helga was reminded again of the way gulls nested at home, each preserving a space around its nest just a pecking distance from its neighbour.

The children dashed down to the water's edge and, after splashing in the shallow water, ran back shrieking to their parents. Youngsters were making friends with children they had never met before and, after that holiday, were unlikely ever to meet again. It was all so different from home where she had known everybody on her island virtually from birth. At times the sheer size of England and the number of people frightened her, but these *did* all seem to be enjoying themselves on the sands.

Helga slipped off her shoes and walked down the steps to the beach, wincing slightly at the heat of the concrete. The sand felt cooler and the fine grains tickled between her toes. So that's what sand feels like, she thought, remembering the hard sea-rounded rocks and the coarse shingle beaches at home.

She walked to the water's edge and paddled, feeling clumsy in her long skirt, then suddenly she turned and marched purposefully up the beach towards the shops. She had seen a store called Marks & something next to the little shop where you could watch a man cutting new keys or mending shoes while his customers waited.

She found the store and went into the cool interior. She was sure they would have a clothing department for women.

Half an hour later she left, swinging a green carrier bag containing a short skirt, a pair of denim shorts and, to her own surprise, a two-piece yellow swimming costume similar to several she had seen women of her age wearing on the beach. She went to her room at Mrs Scrimshaw's and tried on every item, feeling very daring in each.

She walked back to the beach, wearing the shorts but leaving the bikini lying on her bed. One experience at a time.

The beach was even more crowded and she stayed away from the busiest part, watching to see if anyone was looking at her. It felt as though she was parading naked and, when a middle-aged man leered at her while his wife was looking the other way, she turned and fled, then sat on a bench calling herself a fool.

She hurried back to her room, it was too hot to be in the open. Kenny would have to look after the dolphins by himself that day. She slept until six, then washed and ventured out again onto the sands. The tide was out now and she wandered along the water's edge feeling the sandy ripples firm beneath her bare feet. There were fewer people about now.

A couple passed her, walking close together and carrying their shoes as she was. The girl was looking happy. Helga smiled at her and the girl smiled back, a smile like sunshine on a sparkling northern sea. Helga yearned to be home.

'I think that's the woman who feeds the dolphins,' said Mary. 'I'm sure it is.'

Hywel looked over his shoulder.

'She's got the same plait and she's blond,' he said. 'It could be.'

Mary thought of calling after the woman but that might mean having to explain about Fungie to Hywel and she wasn't ready to do that yet.

Hywel had stopped and was digging his finger into the sand. He winkled out a half-buried yellow coin. 'Look what I've found,' he said.

Mary looked at the coin. 'A pound for the poor box,' she said.

'The *poor box?*'

The nuns taught me that if you found money that didn't belong to you, you must put it in the poor box. It *does* sound a bit old-fashioned now but I still do it.'

'I'll buy you an ice-cream with it,' Hywel said, laughing, and raced up the beach, Mary running along behind him.

'I'd choke on it,' she called. 'Don't you dare.'

They put their shoes on and walked past the shops and Amusement Arcades facing the Promenade. One shop had a sign advertising the National Lottery.

'It could be YOU,' Hywel pointed at Mary then, tossing the coin in the air teasingly, went in. Mary stayed on the pavement until he came out. In his hand was an Instant Lottery card.

'Will you rub the silver off, or shall I?' he asked.

'I'm having nothing to do with it,' she said and turned away.

'Wow!'

Mary turned to see Hywel grinning. 'Just won fifty quid,' he said.

'Good for you,' replied Mary coldly.

'No, we'll share it.'

'Fifty-fifty,' said Mary. 'I'll take half.'

'That's more like it,' said Hywel and went back into the shop to claim his winnings.

He gave twenty-five pounds to Mary, who held the notes in her hand as they walked along the front towards the King's Statue. A Salvation Army man with a collecting box stood there, in his usual place, looking hot and sweaty in his uniform and peaked cap. Mary crossed the road and with some difficulty pushed the folded notes into his collecting box.

'Thank you, Miss,' he said. 'Would you like one of our magazines?' He held out a copy of *War Cry*.

'No thank you,' she replied and turned back towards the hotel giving the slightest of formal waves in Hywel's direction.

# CHAPTER EIGHTEEN

At Poole, Dan was on the deck of *The Warrior* doing his early morning exercises. Soon he would change from his tracksuit into his black uniform and go ashore for the day shift at the bank His work there consisted mostly of checking visitors' passes.

He had been disappointed with the responses of his ex-squadron mates to his invitation to join him on a trip to the Faeroes. Some were afraid to give up their jobs in case they might not find new work when the show was over. Others were now family men 'with responsibilities'. All would have been 'keen to come' and all wished him 'the best of luck'.

A heavy wooden rowing boat was pulling out of the mass of shipping moored between *The Warrior* and the shore and heading towards his isolated mooring. An old man in a blue fisherman's jersey was rowing with long easy strokes, his back towards *The Warrior*. Though unable to see the trawler ahead, he seemed to know exactly where it was, pulled more heavily on one oar and came up alongside.

'Marrning,' he said. 'Can ah come aboarrd? Ar've somethin' here youm might like.'

Dan had not seen the man before but reached over for the dinghy's mooring rope and made it fast. The man climbed stiffly over the gunwale, carrying a small sack in which some animal was squirming about. A faint mewing came from inside the sack.

'Ah was going to 'ave to drown this liddle feller,' the man said. 'Then ah thought as how youm might like 'um vor a ship's cat. He looked at Dan enquiringly.

Dan made a 'No way,' gesture. A cat would only be a nuisance.

''Tis no matter if youm don't. Ah can drop 'um over the side on uz way back.'

'Don't do that,' Dan found himself saying. 'Some other boat will take him I'm sure.'

''Tis possible,' the man replied stepping back over the gunwale. 'Youm *sure* as youm don't want 'um?'

Dan thought of cat crap on the deck and the problems of feeding the animal when he was on shift and said a positive, 'Yes, I'm sure.'

The man stepped down into his boat, put the sack on the bottom boards between his feet and rowed away. Dan watched him go.

When the boat was halfway between *The Warrior* and the other vessels the man stopped rowing, bent forward, picked up the sack and dropped it over the side. The sack floated, twisting in the water as though it was itself alive.

Dan pulled off his tracksuit top and dived over the side. He reached the wriggling bag and held it above water as he swam on his back to where the Zodiac was moored astern of *The Warrior.* He hauled himself aboard and opened the sack. Inside was a miniature edition of old Mrs Gaskell's cat, the one he had murdered as a nine-year-old boy.

The rowing boat had gone.

Next morning Dan awoke to find the kitten sitting on his chest kneading him with its paws. He reached out and smoothed its fur. The kitten rubbed its head against his hand and purred.

'We must think of a name for you,' Dan told it.

Several days after his scratch-card win Hywel came back to the church from his early shift during which he had served breakfast to an exceptionally demanding roomful of guests. There were not enough tables if they all came down at once, which they frequently did on fine days, eager to make the most of their holiday time.

Mary had not come to the church again and seemed to be avoiding him. He could not concentrate on his work in the vestry although he had been able to set up his equipment, test the soldering iron and organise the materials. But he could not focus on anything other than the most routine and uninspired tasks. This was not what he had hoped for. He climbed the tower stairs and looked down at the dolphins and the whale in the pool, his mind elsewhere.

Mary was making beds. She did not mind doing this sort of work. It was as good as any other short-term job to provide her with food and shelter while she thought out what she should be doing next.

In Ireland it had all seemed simple. There her agitation and nervousness had been receding, she had been sure that a message would come to her and all she would have to do to was to follow what it said. Her greatest concern then had been that it might have directed her to become a nun. Of course if it had been that, she would have had no choice but to comply as her brother had done with his Calling, but the dramatic message from the dolphin had brought her to Dormouth. Now she was here, and had found the 'three of the race of whales', she did not know what to do.

Also, there was Hywel . . . the atheist. And she liked him. Perhaps if she tried hard enough she could . . . but her mother's voice came to her from the past, 'Don't think you can change a man. If you can't live with them the way they are, stay away. Look at your Dad . . .' Mary smiled. For all his faults and shaky beliefs she loved her father. It was time she wrote home again.

She tipped the contents of an ashtray into the black plastic bin-bag that she carried with her from room to room, wrinkling her nose as she wiped the glass dish with a damp rag, then she couldn't remember if she had emptied the wastepaper basket in the last room, and went back to check. She had.

It was time she did something more to 'take the whale's song to the world of humans' – whatever that meant. She had found the three in the pool next to the church. If she was going to fulfil her mission she would have to go back there, and Hywel had the key. She would have to swallow her pride.

Hywel was prowling about on the tower-top, unsure what to do next. The day before, he had borrowed a pair of garden shears from the hotel and had crawled across the tangled grass in his cut-off shorts, clipping it so that it was more like a lawn than an ungrazed mountain meadow. The pile of grass in the corner was drying in the sun and a nostalgic smell of new-mown hay hung in the hollow within the stone castellations. It reminded him of boyhood summer walks over the few sparsely cultivated fields between the terraced cottages of home and the bracken-covered mountainside. He gulped down the *hiraeth* that rose to choke him. There was nothing for him back there, only unemployment and more disappointments. He looked over the wall and down at the dolphins. The young man *and* the girl were there now. Some days he had seen only the man, feeding the dolphins or listlessly brushing the paving before sluicing the hot slabs with water from a hose pipe. Today he seemed more perky. Even the dolphins appeared to be livelier.

Hywel knew he would have to go down into the chill vestry and start some work soon. His experimentation with the sound system was held up by lack of will, not the usual lack of funds. The twenty-five pounds from the lottery win had gone immediately as a part-payment on the arrears for his last batch of microchips, but not having to find rent money each week helped. Even so, he stayed on the tower leaning on the wall and looking down.

A woman was coming along the street towards the church – Mary. She looked up and he waved a little hesitantly. She responded with an unmistakable signal for him to come down and unlock the door.

'I'm glad you've come again,' he said simply, as she stepped into the dimly lit nave.

'I couldn't stay away,' she replied though something in her tone warned Hywel that she had not come just to be with him.

'The dolphins are still there,' he said and her smile told him that his guess had been correct.


At midday Helga borrowed the side door key from Kenny and slipped out from the pool compound to buy some sandwiches for them both. On impulse she went to her bedsit and put on the yellow bikini under her blouse and shorts. Kenny looked up anxiously as she came back in through the side door.

When they had eaten, Helga said, 'Now that the water is always clean I am going to swim with the hvals . . . the dolphins.'

'Can you *swim*?' he asked, in the same tone of voice that he might have used for, 'Can you fly?'

'Yes, a little. At home I would swim in a pool under a waterfall, but I was a small girl then. Can you?'

'No,' replied Kenny, as though admitting to being unable to dress himself or do up his shoelaces.

'Then I will have to teach you, Ken-ney. I do not think the dolphins will mind us sharing their pool.'

She was undressing as she said this. She knew Kenny was watching her, though he was pretending to be looking at the dolphins that circled very slowly, their heads turned towards her. Nordstar was in her usual position at the bottom of the deep end, rising to breathe at long intervals.

'I haven't got any bathers,' Kenny said.

Helga shrugged her shoulders, sat down on the edge of the paving and slipped into the water where it was about waist deep, watching for the reactions of the dolphins. She wondered whether she should have taken off the gold chain and the little cross but before she could decide FairIsle swam up nudged her with his nose whilst making unintelligible clicking and whistling noises. Helga reached into the water and rubbed the smooth black skin of the animal's head then turned to see Kenny, in a pair of slightly grey underpants, hesitantly climbing backwards down the worn wooden steps in the corner. He grinned at her over his shoulder. 'Hope you don't mind,' he said.


FairIsle, Helga and Kenny splashed and played in the water for an hour and, by three o'clock, Helga could easily swim across the pool and Kenny could manage half a width 'doggie-paddle'. He kept bumping into Helga but each time she just said, 'Ken-ney,' with no trace of annoyance in her voice. Rockall stayed with Nordstar while FairIsle played with the humans.

'We will burn ourselves if we stay in the water for a longer time,' Helga declared and climbed out. Kenny followed her. They sat in the shadow of the diving boards and let the air dry them.

Rockall surfaced and slapped the water with his tail. A moment later Mr Cartwright came in through the side door.

'I pay you to train the dolphins, not to sunbathe,' he said, looking at Kenny's sagging underpants then, more appreciatively, at Helga's bikini.

Kenny stammered, unable to reply until Helga, now standing, said, 'We have been in the water with the hvals. I am sure that you know that is the best way for the training. If we stay in too long we will be burned by the sun. You see I have a white skin that will burn easily?'

Mr Cartwright nodded grudgingly. 'How's it going?'

'You must not be impatient. They have to know us and to trust us. You too. Soon we will show you what they can do. But do not ask today. We must now stay in the shade.'

'In a week?'

'I cannot say, these are animals, not machines.'

Mr Cartwright looked at the woman, her breasts rounded and firm in the bikini top and her thighs showing just the tiniest puckering of the skin near to the tightly stretched yellow material. He mentally valued the cross and the gold chain around her neck.

A good woman wasted, he thought. I bet she drives that little twerp frantic. He turned abruptly and left.

*'What did the She-salmon have around her neck?' Rockall asked FairIsle. 'I shimmered it and it was made of soft yellow shipstone.'*

*'I did the same. The shimaura showed a man fastened to it – a sad man – but my eyes could not see him. The shipstone itself was smooth.'*

*'It was smooth though I thought that I sensed the same,' Rockall said. 'But I believed I was mistaken. It is truly said that there are more mysteries in the Sea and Sky than even dolphins dream of.'*

Kenny and Helga swam again later in the afternoon, dried in the warm air, dressed and walked back together to Mrs Scrimshaw's to lie pleasantly tired on their beds in the adjoining rooms.

*Rockall had felt a special excitement in the water throughout the afternoon and, as soon as the Sprat and the She-salmon had left, he swam up to FairIsle and nudged her in a more than friendly way. She, also moved by the unseen vibrations responded, and they swam slowly together round*

*and round until Nordstar surfaced and joined them. As a huge harvest
moon rose behind the warehouses, Nordstar left the pair and returned to
the deep end where she feigned sleep.*

On the tower Mary leant against the parapet and looked down, watching
the dolphins. The afternoon had passed quickly, Hywel, at first reluctantly
then with greater enthusiasm, telling her more about his life in the valley
and how the soul had gone from the town with the closing of the mine
and the consequent demise of the male voice choir.

'Why did you leave?' she asked.

'Nothing for me there. No jobs, no future – no spirit like.'

'But why Dormouth?'

'Used to come here on holidays. Paradise this place, to little boys.
Seems different now though. What was it like in *London?*' The word
held a kind of awe.

'Streets and parks, school and Saint Mary's church.'

Hywel's mind tried to superimpose these on visions of Buckingham
Palace, the Houses of Parliament and the lights of Piccadilly Circus but
Mary's words did not say '*London*' to him.

'Have you been to London?' Mary asked.

'Only the one time. Glad to get back to the valley after.'

They swapped more childhood memories as the sun dipped towards
the horizon, the smell of hay growing stronger as the air cooled.

Hywel, standing close beside her, slipped an arm around Mary's
shoulders. She did not shake it away but moved slightly towards the
warmth of his body.

A nearly-full harvest moon rose above the line of cliffs across the bay,
the great ball a gleaming yellow in the scented evening air.

*Below, in the fading light, the pair of dolphins circled. For the first time
since he had been in captivity, Elegance of Rockall felt his joyner swell
and emerge from the slot at the rear end of his belly. He enjoyed the
smooth flow of water past the sensitive skin and moved so that it would
touch against FairIsle as she swam beside and slightly below him. It
always seemed that when his joyner was out, his whole body was extra-
sensitive, as though a layer of skin had been peeled away all over him.*

*Grace of FairIsle responded to the compliment, moving closer and
enjoying the special tickle that it gave. She recalled the group-plays
when she was younger when the young males had displayed in front of
the dolphines of their own age groups, each with their gracefully curved
joyners extended to the maximum as though saying, 'Look at me – I'm
the biggest.' Foolish creatures, she had thought then, that was the least*

137

*important attribute she would look for in a mate. But it was the custom and life had been all fun in those days.*

*FairIsle was about to present her belly to joyn with Rockall when she realised that if a new-life was created by their joyning, the young one might be born here in captivity and she did not want that to happen. Should she make the traditional, 'It is magnificent, it would be wonderful, the Sea is calm, but it is not to be today,' signal? Her spirit rose. Somehow I, and Elegance of Rockall, will be free long before any new-life is ready to slip, she told herself, and turned her belly to his.*

*'Is this your first joyning?' she asked.*

*Rockall's tail flicked the small 'yes', and FairIsle rose to take a deep, deep breath before turning dorsal-down beneath Rockall. It was always the most experienced who should take the lower position – drowning in ecstasy would be no joke to a first-joyned dolphin.*

*She rose beneath him, timing her swimming speed to match his as they swam so, so, slowly in the confines of the pool. Rockall felt as though it was his whole body that had entered this lovely and graceful dolphine and had become one with her.*

*Nordstar watched surreptitiously. Such experience had been, and would always be, denied her. All she could expect was death. She tried not to let her envy leak out to spoil the others' pleasure.*

Kenny lay on his battered wooden bed, wearing only his T-shirt and fiddling with a lace-trimmed handkerchief. When his last 'comfort-blanky' had been taken from him by a long-forgotten housemother, he had got in the habit of sneaking into one of the girls' rooms and taking a handkerchief as a substitute. This was the last one he had.

Billy Tranter had been much more adventurous and had frequently got into trouble for it. Handkerchiefs though, even ones with embroidered initials, had seldom been missed.

He rocked the ageing bed back and forth, the dry wooden joints creaking like trees in a windstorm, then turned his head into his pillow and cried.

On the other side of the partition Helga dozed restlessly in the oppressive heat, wearing only a thin slip and hearing the rhythmic creaking of the longship's oars as it rowed up the inlet towards the rocky promontory where she waited apprehensively. She could see Sven Forkbeard standing in the bow staring at her. Any moment now he would leap ashore and ravish her as he had done so many times before. The sound of the oars stopped, he was bending over her, he was . . . 'Sven, Sven, SVEN, Sven . . .'

Kenny heard Helga's cry and tapped lightly on the partition to let her know he was there but there was no response.

On the tower top Hywel and Mary watched the vague shapes of the dolphins in the dark water. Mary said, 'I think I should go now.'

Hywel took his hand from her shoulder, debated with himself as to whether he should kiss her and decided not to rush things.

'Of course. I'll walk you back to the hotel.'

Once there he again decided to hold back, his rebuffs from the valleys' girls still raw in his mind, said, 'Good-night' then returned alone to the echoing emptiness of the church.

He collected his sleeping bag from the vestry and climbed the spiral stairway to the tower top. Here, high above the lights of the town, he arranged the hay into a bed and lay awake watching the stars as the silver moon, far smaller now than it had appeared earlier, sailed smoothly across the vastness of the sky.

When Helga arrived at the pool the following morning, Kenny was self-consciously wearing a new pair of Bermuda shorts with multi-coloured legs reaching nearly to his knees. She tried not to laugh and he asked, defensively, 'Is something the matter.'

'It is what you are wearing. It is not right for you.'

'What's not right? *Everybody's* wearing these.'

'Only the young boys and the silly men. You go to the sand beach. You will see that the real men are wearing short things for bathing. Like the bottom part of my bikini. Though not quite so short, perhaps.'

Helga went into the café room where she had left her bikini and changed. Kenny was not in the enclosure when she came out, and ten minutes later he returned breathless, went into the café room and emerged wearing a narrow, bright red pair of trunks. Helga looked at him and said, 'Kenney, soon we will be making a real grown-up man of you.'

Kenny blushed and grinned back, wondering exactly what she meant, and jumped into the pool still wearing his Mickey Mouse watch.

'Your watch is drowned?' Helga asked, seeing him take it off, hold it to his ear, shake it and listen again.

'Yes,' he said. 'The bloody thing is drowned. Mickey and all.'

'It is time you had a man's watch. Put your Mickey away in the drawer with the other things of being a boy.'

The afternoon was spent playing in the water with the dolphins and, by the time they had finished, both Helga and Kenny could comfortably swim two widths. FairIsle and Rockall were cooperating by jumping in unison to a signalled command.

At five, Kenny locked the door and together the woman and the young man walked back to their lodgings, meeting Mrs Scrimshaw on the steps.

'I'm glad I've seen you, Miss Jacobsen, only there's a programme on the telly this evening about whales and your country. It said in the paper about it being in the Faeroes and all. That is your home, isn't it?'

'Ja, yes, that is my home.'

'If you would like to see it, come down to my flat at seven.'

'Thank you, Mrs Scrimshaw. May Ken-ney come too?'

Kenny spent the next hour, and £7.80, fishing with a miniature grab-crane in the arcade until he was successful in extracting a digital watch similar to those on sale in most of the garages in Dormouth for £1.50.

Mrs Scrimshaw bustled about her flat, making tea and plumping up cushions as they waited for the programme to start. If a Mr Scrimshaw had ever existed, there was no sign of him.

The film started with shots of pilot whales in the Canary Islands, with much underwater photography showing the graceful way in which the creatures swam and the endearing role the matriarchs played in organising the 'baby-sitting' roles so that each adult could dive deeply for squid. Then the scene changed to views of towering black cliffs topped by brilliantly green grass. Tiny coloured houses clustered at the edge of the sea, some with green turf roofs.

'Look, look. That is my home island,' Helga said excitedly.

The music changed and the camera moved in closer. Shouting men ran down banks and waded into the sea with pointed hooks and long knives to slice at the necks of whales that had been driven ashore by a cordon of small boats.

'Is this what they do in *your* country?' Mrs Scrimshaw asked, her voice a whisper.

Helga nodded, unable to speak.

# CHAPTER NINETEEN

Mary was late finishing her work. On Sundays the guests tended to get up later than on other days. Hywel was waiting in the rest room, wearing casual clothes rather than his formal waiter's uniform.

'It's your day off,' she said.

He looked disappointed. 'I hoped you'd come to the church again – up to the tower.'

Mary read the look and balanced the danger of becoming too involved with someone who her mother would classify as 'unsuitable' because of his lack of belief, with her needs and desires to find out more about the dolphins. How did they sing? Her mission was to 'take their song to the world of people' and from the tower she could at least see them if not yet hear any songs. Inspiration would come.

She flashed a smile at him.

'I'd like that,' she said. 'Shall we buy some picnic food to take up with us?'

When they reached the tower top they leant on the familiar stone parapet and looked down into the pool, watching the man and the woman who were swimming in the water with the two dolphins and the sluggish white creature. This one, though more or less the same shape as the dolphins was much larger and seemed to lack the vitality of the other two. It spent the entire time at the deep end of the pool while the dolphins circled, leapt and splashed about with the humans.

Hywel slid his arm tentatively around her shoulders.

'We were being watched,' Elegance of Rockall said, after the Sprat and the She-salmon had left. 'I saw the humans on the rock-tower. A male and a female. I think they were more interested in each other than in us. Did you see how close together they were? They must have been touching. Humans usually stay apart, not like we 'phins.' Rockall moved closer to Fairlsle and caressed her flank. Nordstar rose and expelled her breath noisily, inhaled and sank again.

Fairlsle ignored her.

141

*'The Sprat tries to touch the She-salmon but pretends he doesn't mean to. She speaks, "Ken-ney," and he stops, but I don't think she really minds. Soon she will be going home – I have been filling her mind with pictures of the Faroff Islands. Soon too, we must find our way to the sea.'*

*Nordstar rose slowly from the bottom of the pool, turned and swam to join them. 'Remember your promise,' she urged FairIsle.*

*FairIsle replied, 'When we go, you will come too. If you can't go, I will stay. That is still my promise. While the moon pulls and the sea surges.'*

*'You can go when I am dead. It is only while I live that I am fearful.'*

*FairIsle swam on one side of the starwhale and Rockall on the other.*

*'If FairIsle stays, I stay too,' he told Nordstar. 'You will not be alone.'*

*After three circuits Nordstar glided down into the deepest part of the pool. 'I would like to be apart a little now, my friends,' she said. 'You forget that I am here. I will pretend to be a rock.'*

Once the sun was near the horizon, the breeze on the tower top turned chilly and Hywel and Mary went down into the vestry. 'Will you play me something on the organ, please,' Mary asked.

'What sort of thing?'

'Anything. You choose.'

'Anything?'

Hywel switched on the electric blower and sat on the console seat. Mary stood behind him, he could sense her closeness even though they were not touching. He pressed a few keys wondering what to play. Perhaps a hymn tune – she might object to anything secular in a church. Then he considered the Irish tunes he had played before but rejected those – she might find those patronising in some way. While he pondered he played a sequence of notes that Mr Williams had taught him in the old days at Ty Mawr. The notes had always seemed to have an almost magical significance. He played three of the sequences then paused to get a reaction from Mary.

'What are those pieces?' she asked. 'I don't think I've heard them before.'

'There was a sixteenth-century mathematician and astronomer named Kepler – Johann Kepler – who was the first man to work out the orbits of the planets around the sun. He set the mathematics of the orbits to music so that ordinary people might be able to visualise them. I think they're rather beautiful in themselves, don't you? I played *Mars*, *Venus* and *Saturn* – they're my favourites. I'll see if I can remember any more.'

He started to play *Earth*.

Mary's hand was resting on his shoulder.

*FairIsle and Rockall had been swimming, joyned in ecstasy, when the mysterious and wonderful vibrations had tingled through the water. Nordstar lay in the deep end trying to ignore their joy, but she twitched and her brain became instantly alert and attentive as the soul-stirring vibrations reached her. She swished her tail-flukes and surged around the pool disturbing the dolphins who drifted apart.*

*'Listen,' she called them. 'Listen. The Planets are singing. Listen – there's the song of the Dead Planet – how sad it is. Now the White One sings – and now the Great Ringed One. How beautiful their songs. They are singing to me, to me, to me.'*

*She glided from one side of the pool to the other and turned as she heard the song of her own Planet begin, only to fade away before it had really started.*

On the far side of Dormouth an operator, working late on the town's new sewage system, moved a giant crane forward in the dusk. The flash as the jib struck a power line could be seen as far away as Portland and the lights in a large part of the town flickered once and died.

The electronic machines in the arcades stopped immediately, traffic lights failed and motorists hooted as the more impatient drivers edged forward and blocked exit roads. The sound of the organ in The Church of Saint Peter the Fisherman faded away on the fifth note of Kepler's expression of the orbit of the Earth around the Sun.

Hywel flicked the blower switch up and down again, saw that all the streetlights outside had gone off as well, and said, 'It must be a power cut. Let's go and find something to eat.'

He led Mary by the hand down the aisle of the empty nave and out into the darkness of the street.

*Nordstar rose to breathe, lifted her head above the water and looked up. The stars were clear in the sky above. The sickly-yellow light that had hidden them for so long was gone and they hung above her head as bright spots in a vast black dome. She moved to the deepest part of the pool to enable her stance to be most upright, checked each of the constellations and located the brighter planets, plotting their positions on the sky-map she held in her head.*

*The Great Eel was there, its head pointing everlastingly towards the North Star, the Star of Hope, after which she had been named. Energy flowed from the stars into her body and she slipped back into a horizontal position and swam joyously around the pool, hardly noticing her two friends.*

*Unseen, the ball bearing on the grid, disturbed by the sweep of her tail-flukes, rolled around the bottom of the pool and ran back down to the grating, dropping though a gap where a bar had corroded and broken. It rolled along the pipe, checked briefly against an engagement ring lost by a swimmer sixty years before, then rolled on down until it came to rest between the end of the pipe and the eroded aluminium vanes of the impeller at the end of the vertical shaft from the pump room above.*

*Soon FairIsle and Rockall were swimming with Nordstar – it was easier than being jostled as she passed. Whale-bond held them in unison, all turning and rising to breathe at the same time, their minds working together in the way that makes the shared thought greater than the thoughts of the individuals. Escape to the sea was the common subject and every remotely possible and many totally impossible ideas were worked through until finally, having exhausted all the schemes they could devise, an overwhelming sense of futility sank them. The whale-bond disintegrated, Nordstar drifted to the bottom at the deep end, Rockall cruised listlessly around and even FairIsle felt deflated, as though her blubber had melted away.*

*The lights outside flickered and came on again and the stars vanished once more behind the sky-glow. In the distance a machine played cold metallic notes. Nordstar rose, took a breath and sank again.*

Hywel was working the early shift and only occasionally seeing Mary as she brought the morning trays from the rooms into the hotel kitchen. Her smile lit the dark hillside inside Hywel's mind – he could hear the skylarks singing in the clear sky above the heather, rushes and cotton-grass of Waun Fawr.

In the first room to be cleaned, Mary made the bed, dusted the tops of the furniture and took a Sunday paper out of the waste bin. It was folded at a page with a report about the latest European Union directive on water pollution and comments on the purity of water at bathing beaches. 'Dormouth' jumped out at her from a list of seaside resorts.

She stood, duster tucked under her arm, and read the article, noting that although Dormouth was already well rated, a new sewage system was shortly to be brought into operation. She dropped the paper into the bin bag – there was too much to be done to spend time reading. And she still had no idea about how dolphins sang. Perhaps Hywel would know. She was almost sure now that he wouldn't laugh at her when she explained about her mission. She would ask him when the time seemed right.

Kenny had arrived at the pool before Helga and switched on the two pumps as usual. A grinding, crunching sound came from the extractor pump down the well in the floor. Suddenly, the motor raced and he knew that whatever moved the water through the pipes, must have broken or become detached. He jumped back onto the wooden blocks and threw the switch to 'Off'.

A few minutes later he tried again but the motor would not start at all. What would he tell Mr Cartwright? It would have to be fixed or the water would be foul in a few days.

Helga knocked at the side door. He let her in and told her about the pump.

'We will have to tell Mr Creeper-man when he comes next,' she said, 'but now I am going to have a swim with the dolphin-hvals. Are you swimming too?'

They were both in the pool just before lunchtime when Rockall slapped the water with his tail. Mr Cartwright came in the side door and walked across to the railings as the two climbed out, Helga squeezing water from her plait.

'I think I've got a buyer for the dolphins,' Mr Cartwright told them. 'But God knows what I'm going to do with *that* useless hunk of cat-meat . . .' He indicated the shape of Nordstar lying on the bottom at the deep end. 'Bloody waste of money she was. Still, can't win them all.'

He shrugged. 'Can you have the dolphins ready to show off in three days time? I've got a Froggie coming over from Paris who's interested. Oh, yes. And I've had a letter from the council about the drains. The old sewerage system runs under here somewhere and takes the waste water from the pool. The new system runs the other way and they don't want hundreds of gallons of seawater in it. I'm going to have to close this place.'

He swept his hand around the pool. 'All a bit of a loss, anyway. You'd better think of finding another job, Kenny-boy. And you too, Miss . . . Miss . . .'

'Jacobsen,' said Helga as he turned to leave.

'Ready in three days, remember. And the whole goddamned operation to close in a week. Whatever happens,' he called back over his shoulder.

Kenny thought there was no point trying to mention the pump now and Helga had evidently made the same decision. He stuck one finger in the air as he heard Mr Cartwright lock the door.

'Tonight I think I will play some music to the hvals,' she said. 'Can I have the key?'

'Can't I be here?' Kenny asked.

'Of course you can. I thought that you might prefer to be at the Arcades.'

'I'd rather be here with you . . . and the dolphins. Mr Cartwright wouldn't like it if I let anyone else have the key. He was very strict about that when he gave me the job.'

'OK, Ken-ney. I will be here at seven of the clock. There are some other things I must do first.'

Helga went looking for small presents to take home. She called in at a travel agent and asked the cost of a train ticket to Aberdeen and the ferry from there to Torshavn. It did not leave her much money unless Mr Cartwright was more generous than he had been so far.

She bought a Swiss Army knife for her Uncle Roi and a blue Poole Pottery jug for her aunt. Then she went to Marks & Spencers and bought some special things for herself, slithery, silky things that she had always wanted. After this she treated herself to a Big Mac and ate it on a bench on the sea front before going back to the bedsit to try on her new underwear. Later, at a quarter to seven, she took her accordion and walked to the pool.

Kenny was already there. He let her in and locked the door again.

Helga sat on the poolside, her bare feet in the water. Kenny took off his trainers and sat beside her, hoping to share the foot-stroking experience with the dolphins.

Helga started to play.

On the tower top Hywel was plucking up courage to kiss Mary as they sat on the pile of hay. He had been telling her about his hopes of finding some new way of recording certain sounds but knew she wasn't following the technical detail. Once or twice she had started to say something, then had seemed to think better of it.

Now he was afraid that if he kissed her, she would walk away as Rhian Morgan had done when he had kissed her on the mountainside. He hesitated, then turned his head to sense where the unexpected music was coming from. He stood up and looked over the parapet. Below him the couple who cared for the dolphins were sitting side by side on the edge of the pool with two dolphins nuzzling at their toes.

'Come and look at this,' he called softly to Mary who was already getting to her feet.

They watched for an hour, oblivious to anything else, seeing the dolphins communing with the woman through the music, and the bigger dolphin or whale coming ever nearer to listen. The young man, sitting with his feet in the water, kept moving closer to the woman until it was obvious that he was restricting the movement of her left arm as she played.

At last the music faded and stopped. The woman stood up and put the instrument into a box, then reached into the water and petted the heads of the dolphins. She had started to turn away when the white whale rose near her and breathed out with a sound that Hywel and Mary could hear from the top of the tower. The woman reached down again and stroked the head of the whale which lingered for nearly a minute before submerging and gliding down to the deep end.

They watched the man and the woman lock up and leave together, then went down the spiral stairs to the vestry where Hywel showed Mary how to solder tiny wires onto printed circuit boards while they discussed what they had seen. Mary was sure she would soon hear the dolphins sing though she still held back and did not talk to Hywel about her Message.

After working together for the next hour and a half Mary looked at her watch and said, 'My eyes are aching, can we leave it now?'

'Of course,' Hywel replied. 'Thanks for the help. I'll walk you back to the hotel.'

On the way Mary stopped as they were passing the window of a bookshop and pointed to a large poster printed in a regular pattern of coloured waves and ripples. 'Can *you* see anything in these?' she asked Hywel. 'I can't.'

He stepped back on the pavement. 'They're called Magic Eye posters,' he said. 'But they're not really magic. It's a trick to deceive the brain. Your brain is always trying to make sense of what your eyes are seeing and your ears are hearing – these things fool it. Try doing this.'

He stepped up to the glass of the window and then walked slowly backwards. 'There you are, *I* can see it now. You try. Keep your eyes focused just as they are. Don't let them refocus as you step back. What can you see now?'

'Nothing,' said Mary. 'No more than I could see before.'

'Try again, there's another picture that you can't see – but it *is* there when you know how.'

Mary tried four times before an unmistakable picture of the Statue of Liberty appeared in the pattern. 'I can see it,' she cried excitedly.

'Now, keep your eyes as they are and move your head sideways.'

'I can see behind it . . . Oh – it's gone now.'

'Start again.'

Eventually, the 'magic' palled and they walked on towards the hotel.

# CHAPTER TWENTY

*FairIsle and Rockall were playing Cube Three in the dark water, keeping the shimmering mind-cube between them as FairIsle tried to decide whether to slip a crab or a shrimp into the next space to counter-balance and distract Rockall's eel. Nordstar swam up behind them.*

*'The ~yegods~ moot tonight,' she announced unexpectedly as the full moon rose above the square-stones surrounding the pool enclosure.*

*The mind-cube faded and vanished as FairIsle signalled, 'Tell us more.'*

*'Every full moon the ~yegods~ moot in a cave on the eastern side of the Island of Fire and Ice to read the future,' Nordstar told the dolphins as they circled the pool together.*

*'How?' signalled Rockall, the angle of his fins clearly indicating a high measure of disbelief and annoyance. He had been ahead of FairIsle in the game for the first time that day.*

*Nordstar rolled sideways to turn a corner. 'When the moon is full it pulls the future backward in the same way as it pulls the tides twice each day. The ~yegods~ read the pictures in the reflected ripples on the walls of the cave.'*

*'Have you seen the pictures?' Rockall asked.*

*'Look over there,' said Nordstar. 'There are the reflected moon-ripples on the walls and on the boat-end-shaped eyes of the square-stone with the rocktower. Can you see pictures in the ripples? We starwhales can read the stars but not the moon. Each to their own. Dolphins tell stories. Great whales think and remember. Minke whales play with numbers. Only the Nowhales – the ~yegods~ of the North, can interpret the patterns made when the moon-ripples live and die. It takes a special kind of brain to do that. Tonight they moot. I wonder what they are seeing.'*

*'Is that a Truth?' Rockall asked.*

*'We starwhales believe it to be so,' Nordstar replied. 'How else would they know where to be when they are most needed?'*

*'I thought that was only in our stories,' FairIsle said.*

*'Dolphins still have much to learn,' Nordstar replied. '**That** is a Truth.' She glided away to the far end of the pool.*

*Rockall tried to restart the game but the mind-cube wouldn't form. FairIsle's thoughts were elsewhere.*

Lying in his sleeping bag in the vestry, Hywel could not sleep. Though it was great having Mary coming to the church so often, she seemed more interested in the dolphins than in him. He tossed and turned far into the night then lay awake, cross with himself for his inability to design and make whatever it was he felt he should be making. He didn't even know what that was, and this made him even more angry. He would go up onto the tower for a while – maybe he would be able to sleep when he came down again.

An unfamiliar noise came from the nave. He could have sworn someone coughed. The hairs on the back of his neck rose and he sat up quietly, unzipped his sleeping bag and got up from the bed he had made out of kneeling-hassocks pushed together on the floor in a small alcove.

He tiptoed to the doorway and peeped out into the nave, now lit by bright moonlight streaming in through the windows on one side. A figure stood halfway down the aisle, a fingerless left arm raised towards the lifeboat window. Hywel peered at the apparition, his heart beating wildly.

There are no such things as ghosts, he told himself. Then, as the figure moved towards him, his confidence evaporated and he ducked back into the vestry and eased the door closed. There was no key in the lock so he leant against the door wondering what to do next.

'Bloody coward, you boy,' he said under his breath, and forced himself to turn and open the door a little and look out. The nave was empty.

He stepped forward, heard the unmistakable rising sound of the organ blower, and froze, sweat cold on his forehead. A long note filled the church, just like the one that had first attracted his attention in the street outside. The note ceased and he heard the hollow cough again.

There are no such things as ghosts, he told himself again and moved to where he could see the dimly lit keyboard. The dead vicar was seated there, his right hand poised above the keys. Hywel crossed himself as he had seen Mary do before the empty altar, feeling theatrical and self-conscious as he made the gesture. The apparition remained, one hand on the keyboard.

Another note echoed down the aisle, then another. Hywel moved a little closer and the ghostly organist turned.

'Who's there?' the old vicar's voice called towards him.

It couldn't be a ghost. Ghosts don't have voices.

'It's me – Hywel Jones,' Hywel called back, his voice sounding stupidly squeaky. 'I played the organ for you the day you . . . the day you . . . What did happen?'

'You thought I'd died, did you?' There was amusement in the thin voice. 'So did those young fellows in that ambulance. God wasn't ready for me yet. He must have something he still wants me to do. What are *you* doing in here at this time of night?'

Hywel ignored the question. 'How did *you* get in? *I've* got the key!'

'You've got *one* of the keys. When I persuaded the doctor to let me out of hospital I went to see Old Joe's daughter. She still had *his* key.'

Hywel's heart was not beating quite as fast. He steeled himself for a lecture on the misuse of a church and realised that in the morning he would be looking for digs again.

The old vicar rose from the organ seat, walked past him into the vestry and turned on the main light. In its glare the workbench, the piles of boxes and the makeshift bed all looked hideously out of place.

'I think you'd better tell me what's going on, my boy,' the old man said in a voice that reminded Hywel of Mr William's when he had found him in the potting shed at Ty Mawr.

'Would you like a coffee?' Hywel asked, his voice still squeaky. He cleared his throat and asked again.

'All mod cons, eh,' said the vicar. 'I always said we should serve coffee and tea in here after the service but there were always those who disagreed with me. Yes, please. Strong and black. *Whatever* the doctors say.'

Hywel boiled the water as the old man wandered around the vestry in an absent-minded way.

'Please sit down,' he said, pouring the boiling water onto the granules in the mug. He stirred it with a teaspoon before passing the mug to the old man who took it with a hand that shook slightly, put it on a box beside him then reached into a pocket of his shabby jacket. He took out a leather-covered hip flask, unscrewed the lid and poured a generous amount into the mug.

'A long-time failing,' he apologised. 'I started on this stuff when my wife and daughter died in India and somehow . . . You don't want to hear all that though. Forgive my ramblings. Do you want a splash?' He held out the flask.

Hywel took it and poured a small amount into his own mug.

The old vicar sipped at his coffee. 'What are you doing here? It all looks fascinating.'

Hywel tried to explain without mentioning Mary. The vicar listened, leaning forward as though wanting to be a part of whatever was going on.

When Hywel finished the old man said, 'I'm glad you came here. I hate to think of this lovely building standing idle all the time. I'm sure God will bless and guide you in whatever you do here.' He stood up as though to leave.

Hywel stood as well and asked him why he had come to the church in the middle of the night.

'Night and day seem the same to me now. I'm living on borrowed time, as they say. I can't work out why God has spared me. I hoped the answer would be here. That's why I was going to try the organ for inspiration.'

'Will you come again?' Hywel asked as they walked down the moonlit aisle side by side.

'If you don't mind.'

'It's *your* church. I was afraid you'd turn *me* out.'

'Like Christ with the moneylenders in the Temple? No, son, not me. "Judge not, that ye be not judged." As far as *I'm* concerned you can stay as long as you like.'

They reached the door and the old man held out his hand. Hywel took it in his. The skin was as smooth and dry as an old silk purse but the hand felt frail as if it might easily collapse into a bag of loose bones. He covered it with his own left hand, held it gently for a few seconds then released it.

'I'll lock the door after you've gone,' he said. 'By the way, is that your car outside?'

'The Moggie? That *is* mine. I've had it since the fifties. I daren't drive it now, not after . . . Is it in anyone's way? I'll arrange for the garage to take it away if it is.'

'It's no bother to me,' Hywel replied. 'Can I walk you home?'

'Thank you – no. I'll go up on the sea front and sit there for a bit. The police won't bother me. I'm one of their local characters – a harmless old buffer . . . Good-night, son. God bless you.' He shuffled away.

Hywel watched him until he was out of sight, went back to the vestry and turned off the light. Other people, the police perhaps, might not be as easy-going as the old man. Now he was wide awake. The adrenaline rush, the laced coffee, and his relief at not being turned out, combined to make him even more restless. He walked back into the moonlit nave and looked up at the window. What had the old man been pointing at?

The picture in the window appeared to be rippling. Moonlight, reflecting from the pool, was making the shapes distort and change. As he watched, the effect died away. If it had been the dolphins disturbing the water they must now be floating quietly or resting on the bottom.

In the cold silvery light all the colours of the glass had turned to shades of grey, and the monochrome image Hywel now saw was transformed into something other than the familiar picture.

An ocean current, showing as a dark curved line, swept from near the head of one of the dolphins in the border and across the bay to the white cliffs where he had been told wartime radar-scanners had once stood. Suddenly, the scanners were visible, two dark-grey discs, then they were

151

gone again. From there the current curved back, via the galley and the lifeboat, to end up below the lighthouse with its exaggerated foghorn.

Hywel hadn't noticed the line of the current before, and saw in the monochrome design how the artist had used the sweep and flow of it to connect all the features of the picture together. But there was something more . . .

He let his eyes unfocus. The images changed. Not into the deep three-dimensional effect of the Magic Eye posters, but into an illusion of a printed circuit board. The cames, the strips of lead between the panes, appeared to straighten and took on the characteristic parallel lines and sharp changes of angle of a printed circuit board. The lifeboat, with a row of projecting oars on either side appeared to have changed into a microchip and Hywel was sure he could read the Series and Identifying numbers printed on it. But as he focused on them they blurred and moved about as writing and numbers usually did for him.

He unfocused and they came swimming back to flicker and tease him. He tricked them by catching each letter or number one at a time and forcing them into his memory before flicking his eyes onto the next. The numbers and letters read 85/12/71WR and, as the last number on the chip was captured, the illusion faded and the window once more contained merely a picture.

Hywel went back into the vestry and lay down, wondering what the old vicar kept in his hip flask. A few minutes later he got up to write down the string of numbers and letters and to make notes on what he had seen. He boiled the kettle and made another mug of coffee. His head ached. All this was absurd.

Finally, he gathered up his sleeping bag and the bundle of clothes he used for a pillow and went up to the tower top. Across the bay the chalk faces of the cliffs gleamed white in the light of the full moon.

Who had told him of the wartime radar receivers having been there? He could not remember, but if the pattern that was imprinted on his mind was to make any sense at all they had to represent some sort of listening device – perhaps a microphone.

'Diawl,' how his head ached.

Next morning, despite what felt like a hangover out of all proportion to the dash of spirit from the old man's flask, Hywel worked through the notes he had made. In the *Radio Spares* catalogue, he looked up the reference number he had written on his notepad the night before. A chip with that number did exist and was listed, though it was new and not in a category that he would ever have thought of using in connection with sound recording. He circled the item and turned down the corner of the page before walking along the aisle to look at the stained-glass window in the daylight. It was just as it had always been, a coloured, highly dramatic picture of a rescue at sea.

Telling himself he was being stupid, he taped a new sheet of paper to his portable drawing board and sketched the line of the current he had seen in the night. It flowed from the border dolphin's mouth to the site of the radar receiving dishes and from there swept round to the lifeboat before curving in the direction of the galley, then on to the lighthouse with its giant foghorn. He drew a microphone in the place of the radar dishes and a speaker instead of the foghorn, enjoying this interpretation of his dream or whatever it had been. He was sure Mary would have called it a 'vision'.

He replaced the lifeboat with the microchip but if it *had* been some kind of vision, and he was loath to believe that, the galley had to represent some other unit. He went out into the church again and studied the window. A pennant at the galley's masthead was shaped by the apparent wind into the form of a treble clef and the billowing sail below reminded him of a bass clef. The heads of the rowers, showing as black dots above the gunwales, looked for all the world like a line of musical notes.

Was the clue in music? If it was, what was the connection between a near-shipwreck and music?

He remembered the old vicar sitting at the organ when they had first met. He had said the window and the organ had been given to the church as a gift by some people who had been saved from drowning. He tried a different routing.

A signal leaves a dolphin's mouth, is captured by a microphone, passes through the microchip, through an organ or other musical instrument and is transmitted by a foghorn or a similar speaker. That *felt* right. Mr Williams often used to tell him to follow his feelings even if doing so sometimes seemed illogical.

Hywel went out into the nave and across to the organ, switched on the power and played softly, sensing each key with his fingers. How delicately he could introduce feeling and passion into each note. An instrument like this had . . . had . . . there was only one word for it – soul. He played on, not caring if it was heard outside, lost in the joy of drawing silent air out of the empty church and making it sing for him.

'Look at the hvals, Ken-ney,' Helga said, as the first notes of the organ reached into the pool. 'How they love the music.'

'It's coming from the church,' Kenny replied. 'I've never heard it before. I thought the place was all shut up.'

'Someone is there now,' said Helga. 'See how the hvals listen.'

153

'That is the Great Wind Song Maker calling to us again,' said Elegance of Rockall. 'I thought it was going to sing in the night but it changed its mind.'

'How grand it is,' Grace of FairIsle replied. 'It reaches my innermost depths.'

Nordstar had turned towards the church and was sensing the vibrations through the water.

Suddenly, she was singing a new version of her Song – one very different from the one she had sung when she had swum with her uncle into the Inlet of Sacrifice.

> Out of the Northern Sea I swam
> To satisfy an age-old prophecy
> My life a sacrifice. I am
> The last sad sorry tale of the Sea
> 'Why did I fail?' I cry –
> Soon I must die.
>
> Out of the Northern Sea I swam
> The hope of life for all my kin and kind
> I failed in my task. I am
> To die, and I will never find
> What it was I did wrong.
> How sad my song.
>
> Into the Endless Night I swim
> A failure, dying in this place of shame
> And as I die, and stars grow dim,
> The distant echoes fade.
> 'Am I to blame?' I cry, to no avail
> Why did I fail?
> Why did I fail?

Rockall and FairIsle listened in awe to the song, as it wove in and out of the sounds coming through the water from the Great Wind Song Maker.

They moved across to lie one each side of Nordstar, caressing her flanks. They could find nothing of comfort to say. As the music faded, FairIsle asked her gently, 'That is your song now?'

'That is my True Song,' Nordstar replied, swished round and glided to the deepest part of the pool.

Kenny went round and tried the door of the church. It was locked.

'There was no one there,' he told Helga, breathlessly. 'Whoever was playing has gone now.'

*'We must give Nordstar a new song,' Grace of FairIsle said to Elegance of Rockall. 'That was a song without any currents of hope. Let us each compose a song of hope for ourselves and for her.'*

Hywel went to the hotel for his 'middle and lates' shift, cornered Mary in the rest room and tried to tell her what had happened in the night. She was behind with her own work and, her mind on the tasks ahead, she could not fully absorb what he was saying.

'Did you follow all that?' Hywel asked, after he had told her about the old man and the mystical way the window had seemed to change into something else. As he was telling her, the latter part sounded silly and unbelievable.

'If I'm honest – no,' Mary replied, holding a tray and trying to get past Hywel to the kitchen. 'You'll have to tell me later when we're finished here.'

'That's not until nine this evening,' he said.

'If you let me have the key I'll wait for you on the tower. I'll be quite safe there,' she added. 'I can watch the dolphins while I'm waiting.'

'But it'll be dark by then.'

'Only just, I'm not afraid in a church – anyway I'll be locked inside!'

Hywel reached into his pocket and gave Mary the big key.

'OK? See you soon after nine,' he said. 'On the tower.'

Mary put the key in the bum-bag hanging in her locker and after eating lunch in the rest room, she tied the bag round her waist and walked to the church, glad of the chance to study the dolphins without any distractions. On the way she bought a salad sandwich and a can of drink. It would be a long time before Hywel came.

Alone in the church for the first time, she knelt before the bare wooden altar and prayed, though missing the familiar symbols of her faith about her and, most of all, the little rosary that her grandmother had given her.

'Hail Mary, full of grace . . .' Her fingertips ached for the feel of the tiny beads.

When the formal prayer was finished, she asked for guidance in her task of 'taking the song of the dolphins to the world of people'.

No obvious answer came and, her knees aching, she stood up and climbed the stairs to the tower top.

All afternoon she watched the couple feeding the dolphins and encouraging them to jump. She stayed on into the evening after the people had gone, noting every movement the dolphins made, hoping for some pattern that might be Ogham Writing that she could record and translate. The two smaller dolphins swam anti-clockwise, sometimes joined by the larger one, but nothing suggested a signal for her nor anything that might be a song. At seven, she sat on the hay, ate the sandwich and sipped her drink, then lay back hoping inspiration would come. Here at least she was safe. Beautifully, totally, wonderfully safe.

The moon woke her as it rose above the parapet and shone on her face. She held up her wrist and tried to make out the time on her watch – it was nearly ten o'clock. She shivered as she slipped on her shoes, turned on the lights of the spiral stairway and hurried down and along the nave, dimly lit from the streetlights and the moon through the windows. The key seemed not to want to open the door at first and when it did she saw Hywel seated on a gravestone.

He stood up. 'I wondered where you were. I went back to the hotel to see if you were still there. Then came back here.'

'I'm sorry,' she said, 'I fell asleep – up there. I had a very funny dream about this church. Shall we have some coffee?'

'Yes, let's go in. It's a bit cold. I was beginning to shiver.'

'Sorry,' Mary said again. 'Coffee will warm us both up.'

She gave him a smile that contained far more than an apology.

In the vestry, under a now-shaded light, he asked about her dream.

'Before I tell you that, there's something else I must tell you. I haven't dared to until now, in case you thought I was barmy.'

Hywel held the hot mug between his hands, waiting, his head slightly tilted.

'When I was in Ireland I swam with a dolphin called Fungie,' Mary began.

'You told me that,' he said softly.

'Well Fungie gave me a message – something I had to do.'

Hywel raised his eyebrows and Mary continued.

'I had to come to England, find three of the race of whales – that was the way Fungie put it – in a square pool to the north of a great rock – I'm sure that's Portland – and a bank of pebbles, and take their *song* to the world of people.'

'How did the dolphin tell you all this?'

Mary had expected to sense scepticism in his voice but it wasn't there. She explained Ogham writing and how Fungie had written a message in the sea.

156

'Mary, you weren't listening this morning when I tried to tell you what happened here, but after the old vicar came in the night I went out into the nave . . .'

Hywel told her what he believed he had seen. How the window had become something else – a circuit-drawing complete with a microchip and how he would not have thought to look at it had he not seen the old man raise his fingerless hand towards it.

'The man in my dream had no fingers on his hand!' Mary told Hywel. 'His left hand. The other one was OK. It didn't seem to bother him though. He was up on the tower with me and looked down into the swimming pool. He told me to put the past behind me and follow my heart until the world hears the dolphins sing. But now I'm wondering if it *was* a dream – or did he come up the tower and really speak to me.'

'If he did come to the church tonight I don't think he'd have climbed the stairs. It was doing that which nearly killed him the first time we met.'

'It *was* a vision then,' Mary said and smiled. 'All I've got to do is put the past behind me and follow my heart – whatever that means – until the world hears the dolphins sing.' Mary crossed herself.

Hywel recalled crossing himself the previous night – a theatrical, defensive act, and compared it to Mary's gesture, so obviously one of thanks. 'Follow your heart,' might be good news for him. *None* of this made cold, logical, scientific sense and Mr Williams would probably have pooh-pooh'd it all. Maybe not though. Anyway, Mr Williams wasn't here in this silent echoey church, and the girl who had the most beautiful smile of anyone in the world *was* here with him – her face glowing. To hell with science.

'We've been chosen,' Mary said.

'Chosen?'

'God does that. Chooses people to work His will for Him.'

'You know I don't believe in God.' Hywel could not let go.

'That didn't stop *Him* choosing *you*.' Mary smiled at Hywel and he felt he could cheerfully abandon a lifetime of science and scepticism for another smile like that. What justification was there in pure logic, anyway? He stood up, bent and kissed her forehead.

'Another coffee?'

'Yes please. Then make a list of the things you'll need if we're going to make the device you saw in the window last night.

'One problem,' said Hywel. 'The usual – no cash.'

'How much will we need?' Mary asked.

'A ton and a half would cover it.'

'A hundred and fifty pounds.' Mary paused for a moment then said, 'I've got more than that in my building society book. I'll give it to you tomorrow.'

'Lend – not give.'

'We can talk about that another time – we're in this together. Will you walk me back to the hotel when I've finished my drink?'

The next afternoon they ordered the microchip and a small microphone from Hywel's friend at the computer shop and bought several other things that Hywel thought he would need, as well as 100 metres of fine insulated two-core wire. Then Hywel, grinning like a dolphin, led Mary into a fishing tackle shop and bought a twelve-foot fibreglass beach-casting rod and a multiplier reel, together with 300 metres of braided-wire fishing line and a six ounce wired lead.

'Always wanted one of these, me,' he said. 'My uncle used to take me to Porthcawl fishing. One of the reasons I came to Dormouth – chance of a bit of fishing – but I could never afford the gear, after.'

## CHAPTER TWENTY-ONE

Kenny and Helga sat in the shade of the diving platforms. They were both wearing their bathing costumes even though the water was getting murky from lack of filtration and they did not like the idea of swimming in it. Helga was fidgeting with a short piece of rope, twisting it around her fingers.

Kenny was surreptitiously admiring her legs and the way the tight material of her bikini-top bulged tantalisingly over her nipples.

'I am not used to be doing nothing,' Helga said. 'At home I would be knitting or carving woods when there was nothing else to be doing.'

'Can you carve wood?' Kenny asked in the same tone of voice he had once asked, 'Can you swim?'

'My grandfather taught me to carve,' she replied, reaching into her bag and taking out the knife Kenny had not seen since her arrival. 'Where can I get some wood to carve into.'

'There are some blocks in the pump room. Would one of those do?' He was already on his feet.

'Show me and I will tell you,' Helga replied, smiling heart-thumpingly at the young man. Kenny ran to the pump room and returned with a rectangular block the size of Helga's accordion case.

'Will this do?' he asked eagerly.

She took it from him, turned it over and over and weighed it in her hands.

'It is a good wood inside – heavy and without any knots to spoil it. The outside has oil on it but it will not go far into the wood, I think.'

She turned the block round slowly, studying each side.

'There are two dolphins in there, waiting for me to cut them out.'

'Where?' asked Kenny peering at the block.

'*You* will not see them yet. You have to be much practised as a carver before you can see them. I will cut them out of the wood for you.'

'For me?' said Kenny. 'You'll carve dolphins for me?'

Helga smiled again. 'If you would like that, I will carve them for *you*. They will remind you of me when I have gone back to Faroyar.'

Kenny's face fell.

'When are you going?' he asked.

'I do not know, but soon I think. The man from France will come and take the hvals away and the pool here will be emptied of water and there will be no more jobs for you and for me.'

As she spoke she rubbed the blade of the sheath knife with a little flat stone from her bag, pared a sliver of wood off the corner of the block and examined the grain.

'Yes, it is a good wood for the carving. Now the dolphins in there are calling to me to let them out.'

The knife moved quickly, the rough wood falling away until the outside of the block was smooth and clean.

Kenny watched Helga as she worked.

'How do you know where to cut?' he asked as she confidently carved deep bites out of the corners.

She looked up, her eyes twinkling. 'That is easy. I cut off all the pieces that are not parts of the dolphins and that is it.'

Kenny's eyes narrowed. 'It can't be as easy as that.'

'You watch and you will see. But it will take several days of carving before they will be done – then my dolphins will be out of the wood for you.'

In the sunshine on the tower top, Hywel and Mary were waiting for the couple who looked after the dolphins to leave the pool but they seemed to be in no hurry, they were sitting half hidden under the diving platforms.

Hywel had threaded the fishing line through the rings on the rod, and had tied the weight, with its backward-pointing projecting wires, to the line as Mary watched.

'You're not trying to hook the dolphins, are you?' Concern was evident in Mary's voice.

'Good God – no.' He laughed.

Mary liked his laugh, it was the first time in all these weeks that she had heard it.

'I'm going to try and cast it right across the pool and then, when the microphone comes, we'll use the line to carry that until I can drop it into the water.'

'Won't anyone notice it?' Mary asked.

'From below it'll be almost invisible and people don't look up much anyway.'

He was standing, holding the rod and fingering the reel, impatiently waiting until he could cast across the pool.

'A watched pot . . .' said Mary and flashed him a smile, but he had rested the rod against the parapet and was looking over.

'Hang on, they're packing up now. Give them a few minutes.'

When the dolphin keepers had gone, Hywel took up the rod and swung it to cast the weight across the pool. The shiny torpedo-shaped lead weight with the stiff projecting wires snagged in the buddleia bush growing out of the wall behind him.

'Hell's bells! I *used* to be good at this. I spent days as a boy with Uncle Dai casting for cod and conger off the rocks,' he told Mary. 'I never caught much, but the practice should come in useful – if I can only disentangle it.'

After several unsuccessful attempts at casting he put the rod down, sat on the hay pile, took a tattered box of Hamlet cigars from his pocket, put one in his mouth and made as if he was going to light it.

Mary said, 'I didn't know you smoked,' at the same time as the familiar *Air for the G String* music from the old cigar advertisement came as from nowhere. She looked around. Hywel was laughing again as he put the dummy cigar back in the box and handed the shabby brown packet to her.

'Used to have a lot of fun with that,' he said. 'Mr Williams made it for me when I was a kid. I'd forgotten I still had it. I found it again when I moved my stuff to the church.'

Mary examined the box. There was only room for one cigar and that one was made of wood – the rest of the space inside was filled by a metal box.

'How does it work?' she asked, pleased to have discovered a less serious side to his character.

'Inside the box is a tiny tape player with a motor and a battery. When I push this button a loop of tape goes round and plays. We recorded it on a proper recorder, then cut up the tape and made it into a loop.'

Mary pressed the button and the Hamlet music played until she pressed the button again.

'What are *these* ones for?' she asked.

'Try them.'

Mary pressed another button and a brass band played *Colonel Bogy*.

'Did *that* track for Uncle Dai,' said Hywel. 'He was always telling me about when he was in the army. Whenever he came the old soldier with me I played that. It used to tickle him pink. Of course I never take it out of my pocket except when I'm doing the Hamlet gag. That way no one knows where the music is coming from.'

Mary pressed the third button and an exquisitely sad-sounding violin played *Hearts and Flowers*.

'Got to be careful when you play that one,' Hywel said. 'Effective though, when you hit it right.'

Mary pressed the last button and gales of contagious laughter burst out of the tiny box. She pressed it again and smiled as the laughter stopped abruptly.

'How did you get all that in there?' she asked.

'Simple really. Ordinary stereo-tape has four tracks. Mr Williams and I recorded one thing on each of them. The four buttons move the head to the right track and start it playing. If I made one now it wouldn't need the tape – it'd all be recorded on microchips. I call it my spoof-box.'

He put it back in his pocket, got up and again untangled the line from the bush.

At the fifth attempt the weight flew through the air, arcing across the pool to catch in something out of sight in the disused yard beyond the far wall. Hywel tugged the line. 'Well and truly hooked, I think,' he said, jerking the line several more times before tying it to the thick stem of the buddleia and cutting it from the rod with a pair of pliers.

He looked at his watch. 'Hell! There's a do on tonight at the hotel – I'm going to be late. We'll have to leave this for now.'

*FairIsle asked Nordstar about Songs.*

*'They just come,' Nordstar told her.*

*'No. There must be rules about how they are made.'*

*'If there are, I was never taught them. They just come.'*

*FairIsle was insistent. 'If it was as simple as that, any 'phin or whale could devise one easily. Your Song was beautiful. Sad, but beautiful.'*

*Nordstar rose to breathe. 'The most important thing is that they tell the Truth as you see it. We spoke of this before, in the dead boat on the way here from the Eighteen Islands.'*

*'Tell me again,' FairIsle asked. 'I would like Rockall to hear. We would like to make a Song of our Truths.'*

*'Then it will be two Songs, and two Truths. No whale ever sees the same Truth. First you must find what your Truth is. When you think you have found it, surround it with a shoal of words and see which ones fit. Sometimes the words change, sometimes the Truth changes, but eventually they all swim together. Then you must sing the Song and see if it floats through the surface of the sea towards the stars. If it does not, you must work on it again and again until it does.'*

*'What if it never does?' Rockall asked.*

*'Let it sink – it is not a True Song.'*

*By midnight Rockall had found his Truth and had the first part of a Song in his mind.*

> *When I was born the sunlit sparkling Sea*
> *Patterned the seabed, light delighting me.*
> *Sun, Sea, companionship and joy were mine*

> *Grace, beauty, love and peace would intertwine*
> *As kelpweed in a swirling current's flow.*
> *Now – what is the life I know?*

Pictures, words and emotions jostled in his head like fleeing herring, twisting and turning elusively. Every now and then one would be caught by the power of his anger at being in captivity, or netted by his yearning to be free. He swallowed it into his Song, then pursued more ideas, hardly noticing that he was surging around the pool as he did so.

'Swim slowly,' FairIsle called to him. 'You are disturbing our body waste from the pool-bed and the water tastes foul again now that the humans no longer clean it.'

Rockall ignored her call and swam on, anger close behind his tail.

FairIsle had been surprised when her Truth had surfaced. She had no idea she had been thinking like that. Her Song, only bubbled to herself as yet, said:

> *I, FairIsle, call to Thinking Men –*
> *See us for what we are.*
>
> *Not competition for your fish*
> *Not fools to entertain your young*
> *Not handy hulks of oil and flesh*
> *But creatures of intelligence*
> *Deserving something better from our land-based friends*
> *Who occupy dry portions of the planet humans will call Earth*
> *But which is mostly Sea.*

FairIsle captured her Truths while floating in the centre of the pool, now oblivious to Rockall's violent circling.

Nordstar lay on the bottom at the deep end, rolling slightly in the currents Rockall was creating and keeping her mouth closed against the swirling filth. Her thoughts were elsewhere.

As dawn lightened the sky beyond the streetlights, Rockall asked FairIsle to sing her Song.

Nordstar intervened. 'Songs must not be sung until they are complete and True,' she said.

'There seem to be a lot of rules for something that has no rules,' FairIsle said and floated motionless, waiting for the whole of her Truth to surface within her brain.

# CHAPTER TWENTY-TWO

Helga and Kenny were sitting out of the sun where the diving boards cast a shadow on the paving slabs.

'The water is getting really shitty,' Kenny said. 'What can we do about it?'

'It is for Mr Creeper-man to have the pump mended but we know it won't be done if the hvals are going away in a few days.'

Kenny flicked at a fly that had landed on his knee. 'He said nothing about the pilot whale. If the dolphins go to France he'll probably have her put down – killed. Shot.'

'He is a bad man, our Mr Creeper. I think he is the one who should be shot.'

'I don't want any of them to go to France, or be shot,' Kenny said. 'But either way it's the end of my job. The only one I've enjoyed. The only *real* one I ever had. You're going soon anyway, I think.'

'Ja, yes. I will be going soon. I want to be back in Faroyar before the winter comes – there will be much for me to do at home.'

'You remember old Carters said something about the drains being changed. Well, it's true. There's a new sewage system starting soon and the water and the gaga from the town is all going to be treated before going into the sea. I pretended that I was old man Carter's personal assistant and went to the Council Offices to find out about it. They had a posh bloke from the Water Board to answer questions and he explained it all to me.'

Helga did not ask what 'gaga' and 'posh' meant. Kenny's explanations usually left her more confused, and most times she could guess.

'What did he say, this 'posh' man?'

'He said that we must not put seawater from the pool into the drains after the end of next week, the seventh. The old outlets are being closed off and the outfall pipes removed.'

Helga had to ask. 'Outfall?'

'The big pipes that go out into the bay for the sewage to be taken away by the tides.'

'So after the seventh day we must not change the water even if any of the hvals are here and the pump was working?'

164

'That's what he said.'

'So all the hvals must be gone by then. What would Old Carters do if the man from France does not want them?'

'He'd probably shoot them all and swear to the insurance man that they died of natural causes.'

'Ken-ney. He would not do that?'

'Don't you believe it.'

Helga was not sure if this was a statement or a question. She stood up. 'Come. We must teach the hvals to be better at the jumping. To go to France will be better than being shot.'

*Grace of FairIsle was intrigued at the way the Truth emerged from the hidden depths of her mind – like an eel from a hole in a rock. It had to be coaxed out gently, with promises of pretty words and rhythms until, when it was exposed for all to see, she would capture it in her Song.*

*The She-salmon and the Sprat were signalling for Rockall and her to jump, but she was reluctant to cooperate, wanting more than anything to tease out the last of the Truth that she felt she was so near to securing.*

*Rockall had stopped his circling and now seemed immersed in thought.*

After trying unsuccessfully to get the 'hvals to do the jumping', Helga gave up and went into the coolness of the café room. Here she carved at the wooden block while Kenny dozed in the sunshine outside, wearing an old straw hat that he had found on a high shelf with the invitation KISS ME QUICK on the band. He sat with his back to a wall like a Mexican peasant in a shrunken sombrero.

Rockall's tail slap alerted him and he was on his feet even before the side door opened.

'Are they jumping yet?' Mr Cartwright asked abruptly, looking at but ignoring Kenny's hat. 'If they don't please the Frenchman, they'll end up feeding the foxhounds at the Dorchester Hunt kennels. All three of them. I've had a letter. We've got to close this place up on the seventh, whatever happens.'

'Couldn't we just put them back in the sea and let them swim away?' Kenny asked.

'Have you learned nothing about business? God, I despair about your generation sometimes. Get those bloody things jumping – soon!'

He glanced around the pool and asked, 'Where's the foreign girl? Taking more time off, I suppose.'

He turned and slammed the door behind him as he went out.

Hywel was eager to see if the items he had ordered had come in.

'They won't be here yet,' Mary said. 'It was only yesterday you ordered them.'

'They will be – if they were in stock. Electronics suppliers send things out for next-day delivery. Things go obsolete fast in this business!'

The slim microphone and the chip *had* arrived and Hywel paid for them and went outside.

'There's something else I need,' he said. 'I won't be a minute.'

Mary watched him cross the road to a chemist's shop and re-emerge a minute later grinning and patting his pocket.

A thought crossed Mary's mind but she dismissed it as unworthy.

Together they walked to the church and up the litter-strewn path.

'I could sweep this up,' Mary said.

'Don't do that. We're not supposed to be here, remember. Mustn't draw attention to ourselves. Specially now.'

He unlocked the door, then reached into his pocket and brought out a similar key, only this one had a heart-shaped loop at the top end.

'I made this for you,' he said handing it to Mary. 'More use than a love-spoon.' He was watching her reaction. Would she know the significance Welsh people gave to the gift of a love-spoon?

She felt the polished metal. A great deal of work had gone into making it. When had he done that?

'Does it work?' she asked.

'Of course it works. Try it.'

She tried the key in the lock of the open door, feeling the resistance of the tumblers give as she turned it. The tongue of the lock protruded then retracted as she turned the key back again.

'Now you can come and go without waiting for me,' Hywel said.

Mary smiled but her conscience was starting to nag again. Having her own key made her an undisputed accomplice in the misuse of the church. But then she remembered that the old vicar had given Hywel his blessing. And then there was her dream – her vision. Did that make it all right? Surely it did?

Hywel collected a bag of equipment from the vestry and almost ran up the stairs to the top of the tower with Mary not far behind.

He put down the bag, took a packet of condoms from his pocket and held them up. 'A man's best friend,' he said.

Mary blushed and stepped backwards. 'If you think . . .'

Hywel turned towards her. 'Oops. Sorry, I forgot . . . I mean . . . Look, these are for . . . Wait. I can explain . . . Mary . . .' he was calling down the stairs. 'These are to stop the water getting into the microphone,' he shouted. 'Not for . . . Mary – Mary – wait.'

When he had persuaded her to come back up the stairs, he connected the microphone onto the end of the wire and unrolled the thin rubber protective sheath over the shiny stainless-steel instrument.

'Improvisation speeds invention,' Hywel told her as he bound the neck of the condom securely with insulating tape. 'I'm sorry if . . .'

'Leave it, please,' Mary said, her face still flushed. 'It doesn't matter. Only me being old-fashioned or something.'

It was the first time she had seen a condom other than the used ones lying in the long grass of Morley Park where she had played as a girl. Seen close up it looked incredibly flimsy. 'The Devil's life traps', her mother had called them when Mary had asked her what they were, then had refused to tell her more.

Hywel prepared to slide the microphone down the taut fishing line, the wire of the 'mike' threaded through a series of brass rings that he had borrowed from a curtain in the vestry.

*Rockall's song had progressed. He repeated the newest part to himself again and again, committing it firmly to memory.*

> *All I possess is here within my brain*
> *I have no hands to grasp and hold and claim.*
> *But human hands once cast a subtle net*
> *Unseen, unheard, unechoing – and yet*
> *Strong to ensnare, to capture and enslave*
> *This spirit born for Sea-life, wind and wave.*

*FairIsle would have been surprised had she known how near to Rockall's Song parts of her Truth were. She was singing her Song to herself, wondering why it seemed to be directing itself towards humans.*

*Thoughts and ideas that were new even to her, were channelling themselves through her brain and into her Song.*

> *We have no hands, we need no hands,*
> *Our culture, art, philosophy*
> *Is carried in our brains*
> *And then sung down from age to age*
> *Mother to calf, Wise One to acolyte.*

*Consider when you kill a dolphin or a whale*
*Ten million years of history is gone.*
*Philosophy and knowledge on a scale*
*Beyond your present comprehension, dies,*
*Becoming just a hulk of oil and meat*
*To be consumed and lost.*

*Where had these images of whale-death come from? Nordstar, she supposed. She didn't care for these thoughts – they might be Truths but they were not the Truths that she felt really belonged in her song. She let them float away.*

*A metal object the size of a half-grown herring came slowly down from overhead and into the water, and hung there, suspended with most of it just under the surface. FairIsle circled around it suspiciously then called to Rockall.*

*'What is this that looks like a fish with a smooth skin but is made of shipstone and hangs by its tail?' she asked.*

Hywel passed the headphones that he had adapted from his old Walkman to Mary who was still thinking of the offensive rubber things.

'Listen to the dolphins,' he said.

High-pitched crackles and squeaks filled her ears and her mind, followed by whistles. She thought of Fungie far away in Ireland and his message to her. FIND THREE OF THE RACE OF WHALES . . . AND TAKE THEIR SONG TO THE WORLD OF PEOPLE. This must be their song but it was like no song that she had heard before.

Hywel had an oscilloscope connected to the wire.

'Look at the range of frequencies,' he said. 'They go from under 100 to over 150,000 Hertz!'

'What does that mean – in English?' There was an unusual sharpness to her voice.

'Sorry. It means the dolphins' voices range from quite slow sounds to unbelievably fast and high-pitched ones. Far beyond what *we* can hear – like the sounds that bats make.'

He switched off the oscilloscope.

'Tomorrow, I'll try recording it then slowing down the tape to see if I can make sense of it then, but I'm sure many other people will have tried that. It'd be too much to expect dolphins to speak in English. They may be clever but . . .'

'Fungie knew Irish,' said Mary putting the headphones down.

'I'll sort out the recorder tonight and tape them in the morning,' Hywel said. 'Maybe one of them speaks Welsh.'

'You can joke, you think you know it all.' She turned on him, eyes blazing, the scar on her head throbbing again. 'If you *can't* explain it then it *didn't* happen. That's all you scientific people think.' She was at the top of the stairs again.

'Wait . . . I . . . Mary – please . . .'

Mary was well down the stairs and did not hear the rest of the sentence. She let herself out of the church and walked rapidly back to the hotel.

## CHAPTER TWENTY-THREE

A few days after Dan had received the final refusal from his hoped for crew, a letter arrived addressed to Mr Jackson, c/o Smiths Boatyard, Poole, Dorset.

Dan sat on the gunwale of *The Warrior* and opened the envelope. The writing was elegant but the single sheet of paper was undated and there was no address at the head.

*Dear Jack,*

*I have heard there has been a delivery of a pilot whale and a dolphin to a disused swimming pool in Dormouth recently. The person who told me said he thought there was another dolphin in the pool already. I know you hate dolphins being in captivity and may be able to do something about it.*

*Yours,*
*Bill.*

Who was Bill? The envelope had a London postmark – that didn't help much.

Dan looked out towards the harbour mouth. Dormouth was only twenty or so miles down the coast to the west. Here was a chance to be doing something active that Skipper Jack would approve of while he worked out a new plan for crewing *The Warrior.*

Without Bonny to ride and with a kitten to look after, he would have to take the boat along the coast to act as a base. His mind started planning the operation. Since coming back from the Faeroes he had already done several runs around Brownsea Island and back to his moorings and knew that he could handle the trawler on his own for short distances. All necessary provisions were aboard and he had used some of the residue of Skipper Jack's money to have the fuel tanks filled.

He had just finished the last of a 'pattern' of shifts at the Bank head-quarters – he had five clear days before he was due back. He could take two days for the run down to Dormouth if need be. Lulworth Cove would make a safe stopover place for the night.

He looked at his watch – five-thirty. What the hell, he could be in Lulworth before dark on a such a warm, clear summer evening.

He shut Lucky in the storeroom with Skipper Jack's boxes of books. The kitten immediately crept into one of the boxes and curled up in a corner. He often slept there. Dan closed the door and went on deck. He used the net hoist and the hand winch to lift the Zodiac aboard then started the trawler's engine, left it in neutral, lowered the black ball from the stubby mast then slipped the chain that passed through the loop on the top of the buoy. The boat drifted backwards on the tide as he did this. One day he would have a crew so that it could all be done in a more seaman-like fashion.

*The Warrior* rode out on the falling tide, Dan steering to pass well behind the car ferry at the harbour-mouth before setting a course that would take him clear of Handfast Point and the Old Harry Rock.

It was dusk when he nosed in between the cliffs guarding the entrance to Lulworth Cove and dropped the anchor in thirty feet of water, safe in the enclosed bay.

Lying on his back on the top bunk in the starboard cabin, stroking a purring Lucky, he listened to the sounds of a party on a yacht nearby. Above him was a small hatch in the plywood ceiling. It was only about twelve inches square and was held in place by four screws. Probably an access panel for the lighting wires, he thought, then, as it seemed to be in the wrong place for that, he could not resist undoing the screws to find out. There were no wires visible through the opening and he reached into the space and felt about.

The box he withdrew held ten detonators, each as thin as a pencil and about four inches long. Otherwise the space was empty.

He found a similar panel in the port cabin concealing three MK 7 Variable Timers, and a panel in the ceiling over the 'heads' hid a five-kilogram pack of Plastic Explosive and two long bar-magnets. What had Skipper Jack been planning? At least he had stored the P E and the detonators separately as per the training manual.

Dan sniffed the pack. The distinctive smell took him back to his last operation. The carousing from the yacht across the bay was like the sounds that had come from the concrete blockhouse, except that there the voices had been calling to one another in Arabic. He smelt the pack again then put it away in the ceiling hatch in the heads and screwed it shut. One never knew . . .

So *that* was what the Skipper had meant in his letter when he had written, 'check the overheads and dispose of any unwanted gear'. Over *heads*. He'd completely missed the message. But it didn't matter now. Cunning old sod!

Later, sometime well past midnight, he went up on deck planning to sleep there as the heat in the cabin was oppressive. He spread out the tarpaulin that he kept folded on the winch housing to make a crude mattress and lay on that waiting for the hubbub from the yacht to stop. Loud voices continued to hold futile arguments punctuated by silly laughter in high-pitched voices.

Dan thought of the explosives below and worked out the exact amount that would be needed to sink the yacht without harming the occupants, before dismissing the idea with a grin. The voices continued, one suggesting a 'midnight swim'.

'*Such* fun in the nuddy, you know.'

Dan walked back to the wheelhouse, reached down the loud-hailer and spoke into it.

'For Gawd's sake shut up and go to bed. Damn you all.'

The sound in the enclosed bay had an unusually powerful resonance. The voices stopped and after a few minutes the lights on the yacht went out one at a time.

Dan took *The Warrior* across Dormouth Bay in the morning, decided not to head for the town basin but to pass through Portland Harbour and moor in the Fleet Lagoon at Ferrybridge near the Army's Bridging Camp which he had once visited as an observer. The mooring fees would be less there and he would not have to try and explain his boat's current role to the crews of active trawlers who used Dormouth Quay to unload their catches.

Here at Ferrybridge more than a century before, an iron bridge had replaced a wooden one. That bridge had itself replaced the ferryboat that once carried cattle and foot passengers across the narrow gap between the mainland and the Chesil Bank. Now, even the iron bridge had gone and the gap was spanned by a modern concrete arch. He came in under the bridge without mishap, noting that there was little clearance above the mast – it would probably foul at high tide. He selected a buoy that appeared not to have been used for some time and moored to that. It was time to listen to the shipping forecast on Skipper Jack's radio/cassette player, though the previous night's forecast had been for continuing high pressure. The forecast for sea-area Portland was for winds Force 3 to 4, south-westerly.

Helga seemed to have transmitted some of her concern about their future to the dolphins and they were jumping well to her waved commands. She was trying to project a mental picture of just what it was that she wanted them to do, and was pleased to find that she could now get FairIsle and Rockall to jump simultaneously. Nordstar obligingly moved up to the shallow end to be out of their way.

The water was noticeably murkier than the day before.

*'Our leaping seems to please the She-salmon,' FairIsle said to Rockall.*

*'A waste of energy' he replied.*

*'What would you do with that energy otherwise?' FairIsle asked. They leapt again, curved through the air and slid into the water with scarcely a splash, angling their fins to steer their bodies to the surface again.*

*'Let's surprise her. Can you do the imitation of their walking?'*

*'Show me.'*

*FairIsle drove hard with her tail, reared her body from the water and, by flicking her tail-flukes alternately, she 'walked' the length of the pool on the surface.*

*Helga clapped her hands in delight.*

*'Wow! Make her do that again,' Kenny asked.*

*Rockall was fishing a memory from deep, deep in his brain.*

*'I've seen that done before,' he told FairIsle. 'When I was calf. A Joy of Messengers came by with news from the other side of the Northern Ocean. They told us about 'phins in captivity and about other 'phins who had been taught by humans to take and hide dangerous things under other humans' boats. I didn't believe all they said because some of their stories were only for entertainment.*

*'One of those Messengers would pretend to be a human and walk on the water like that, to amuse us calves. But I knew even then that humans could never walk on water.'*

*'There are more mysteries in the Sea and Sky than even Dolphins dream of,' FairIsle replied. 'You told me that.'*

Dan lunched on cold baked beans eaten from the tin with a fork as he sat on the gunwale, with Lucky playing around his feet. The sun was bright and only a light breeze riffled the waters of the lagoon, sheltered as it was by the Chesil Bank to seaward. Below the landward side of the boat he could see a shoal of small fish darting about in the clear green water.

They were almost translucent. A larger fish with a big open mouth cruised by and the little ones scattered, flashing silver as they turned.

The tide was falling, exposing acres of flat sand where men in Wellington boots were digging with spades, leaving sharp-sided mounds that soon crumbled into low grey hummocks. Occasionally, one of the diggers would stoop, pick something up and drop it into a tin nearby.

Some kind of sand worms for bait, Dan thought. He might have a go at catching a fish or two, they'd make a change from baked beans. He walked across the deck to look towards the Chesil Bank. Cars were turning off the road beyond the bridge and parking on the gravelled area near the Information Centre and little groups of people were struggling up the pebble bank beyond. A vast area of flat sand was being exposed by the falling tide on that side. He could even see the edge of the tide-scoured channel where the sandbank fell steeply into deep water. Nasty spot if anyone stepped over the edge – the current would be fast there at half-tides.

He took the kitten below, locked the companionway door and swung the Zodiac out over the side using the net-hoist. With the hand winch, he lowered it into the water then ran up the engine. He would go into Dormouth and see if he could find out anything about dolphins in a disused pool.

He cast off and steered the inflatable under the centre of the low concrete arch of the new bridge as the tide was at its lowest and, when in the open space of Portland Harbour and clear of the swarming wind-surfers, he wove a zigzag course across the harbour, circling around the lonely warship buoys and frightening the gulls perched on them. The birds tilted forward, wings spread, squawked their annoyance, sprayed another layer of white onto the caked covering of guano and dipped towards the water, to ride the up-currents of air from the small waves.

Out into Dormouth Bay the boat sped, Dan standing at the controls, drawing wide circles of foaming wake in the dark surface of the sea. He imagined himself once again at the helm of an assault boat full of eager marines all keen to put their training into practice.

Dan circled again and again, making the circles smaller each time. Hey ho for the hachi-pachi bird!

The wind had risen a little. He looked at the sea's surface, 'small waves, becoming longer, fairly frequent white horses. Force 4 – a moderate breeze'.

The breeze tugged at his hair and beard and he felt more alive than he had since being in the Faeroes. How long ago was that? It didn't matter. All that mattered now was the rush of the wind and the thrub, thrub, thrub of the waves under the bow of the boat. He made a final wide sweep away from land, then swung in past the old fort on the point, throttling back as he approached the first of the ships moored against the quay. He passed trawlers, crab boats and pleasure yachts and slowed right down as he steered astern of the ferry that carried passengers from one side of the harbour to the other. Gulls called overhead and groups of holidaymakers peered down at him as he passed them. Some waved and he waved back, sensing the holiday atmosphere. He was a little disappointed to see no naval vessels.

Once under the lifting bridge Dan looked for a place to tie up, found one and locked the boat carefully, using a heavy padlock and chain, making sure that the chain secured the outboard motor as well.


Helga had needed some new canvas shoes – she thought there might be some in the shop on the quay where they sold all things for boats and boat people. She left the pool, walked to the shop and into a treasure house of interesting and exciting objects. She wandered about, looking at everything from yacht pennants to life jackets. She picked up a pair of galvanised rowlocks, interested in the way the metal arms curved round to hold the oar, so unlike the way a boat's oars were secured with cords for rowing at home.

A gallery, reached by a central flight of open wooden steps, encircled the upper floor, and up there she could see the shelves of paint cans, racks of plastic fenders and shelf after shelf of maps and charts. Under the stairs was a display of weatherproof clothing and footwear. She tried on a bright yellow sou'wester and turned to look for a mirror.


After securing the Zodiac, Dan climbed the steps, crossed the railway lines set deep in the tarmac of the road, and strode along the quay wondering how to find a local person who might know the whereabouts of a disused swimming pool. He stopped outside a ship chandler's shop and looked at the displays in the windows on either side of the central door. One window was devoted to scuba diving gear and modern electronic equipment for navigation, while the other window, evidently planned for contrast, was displaying old sextants and a rubber diving suit with a heavy brass helmet. He went in to ask about a disused pool and was fascinated by the displays of brightly coloured fenders, sails, clothing and ropes and by the shining brass fittings. A sign pointing up a flight of steps to the gallery read, NAVIGATION CHARTS FOR MOST EUROPEAN AND CARIBBEAN WATERS.

The assistant was busy so he went up the stairs to see what charts they had for the Faeroe Islands and the coast of Norway.

Through the open steps Helga could see the bulky shape of a man who had just come into the shop. His figure seemed familiar. She stared hard at him as he stood in the light from the door – his black beard was fuller, but there was no doubt that it was the man who had been watching the hval-kill and who had then come to her house.

He had not seen her and she slowly took off the hat, put it back on the shelf and watched, keeping out of sight under the stairs. The man looked round, paused for a moment by the counter then came towards her. Helga lowered her head as the wooden treads creaked from his weight as he went up, then she tiptoed towards the door, nodding apologetically at the shop assistant behind the counter. Once outside she ran along the quay, dodging the holidaymakers, found the silent street with the pool and knocked frantically on the side door.

'God,' said Kenny. 'You frightened me, I thought it was old man Carters gone bonkers. You look as if you've seen a ghost.'

Dan had turned at the top of the steps and seen a woman with a blond plait stealthily leaving the shop. What was *she* doing in Dormouth – in England even? He bounded back down the stairs and out onto the quayside. He looked left and right but there was no sign of her so he walked to the edge of the quay and looked down at the moored boats. If she was in one of those she would be hiding below decks. He would just be wasting his time and she meant nothing to him anyway. 'Ships that pass in the night' as Skipper Jack would have said. He went back to the shop, found the charts he needed and asked about a disused swimming pool.

Rockall tail-slapped the water and Kenny, hosing down the paving stones, and Helga by the café-room, both automatically turned to look at the side door, expecting to see Mr Cartwright. The door rattled again and Kenny took the key from the pocket of his trousers hanging over the rail and walked cautiously across the concrete paving to open it. A bearded man in jeans and a tartan shirt was standing in the doorway looking past him.

Kenny asked sharply, 'What do you want?'

'Sorry, I didn't know there was anyone here,' the man said. Then, seeing a dolphin's fin projecting from the water, and a woman on the far side of the pool, added, 'I'm interested in dolphins. I didn't know there were any in Dormouth.'

'This is private,' Kenny said. 'It's not open to visitors.'

Dan stepped back. So it *was* the blonde from the lonely farm.

'Sorry to have bothered you,' he said as the door was shut in his face.

Had Helga seen him? He thought she had but, if so, it was too late now. What was *she* doing there? Did it matter anyway?

Helga felt restless after Dan had left. It *was* the man who had betrayed the Strandercare tradition at home. What was *he* doing here? Kenny was obviously uneasy too. She would be glad when the hvals had gone and were no longer her responsibility.

Hywel had been watching from the tower top. After he had seen Helga and Kenny leave in the late afternoon, he went to the hotel to apologise to Mary and ask her to come and help him with his recording session.

'I'm really sorry about the . . . you-know-whats, and I *wasn't* making fun of you about Fungie. I spoke without thinking. I want to know how the dolphins react when I play the organ. They should be able to hear it in the pool but it will need someone to watch them from the tower. Will you come? Please.'

Mary looked at his eager face, recalled herself saying, 'We're in this together,' and agreed. Neither of them raised the matter of dolphins knowing human languages.

Hywel set up the recording equipment on the tower and went down to the organ.

Mary switched on the tape recorder as Hywel had shown her, put on the headphones and waited, hearing only indecipherable dolphin sounds. She leant against the parapet looking down into the pool, wondering what Hywel would play. She heard the music start – strangely muffled, though with a curious echo to it. The dolphin sounds died away for a while as she recognised the hymn-tune *Cwm Rhondda* coming through the water and into the submerged microphone – slightly distorted. The dolphin voices came again, at first sounding discordant – random whistles, clicks and grunts which then converged with the waves of sound. Soon it was as if the dolphins were singing some mysterious tune of their own that wove and twisted melodiously through that of the hymn.

The two dolphins themselves were lying horizontally in the water, facing towards the church and she saw the big white one rise from the deep end of the pool and swim between them. A new, deeper and sadder note joined the others.

After a few minutes the music faded and stopped and the dolphins swam together round the pool. Mary took off the headset and could hear Hywel's footsteps as he ran up the stairs.

'What happened?' he asked breathlessly. Mary was trembling.

'The two dolphins were singing,' she said. 'Really singing in time with your music. The sounds they made were all mixed up but they were singing, I'm sure of that. I think the big white one was too.'


*When the vibrations in the water ceased, Nordstar swam back to submerge herself again at the deep end of the pool.*

*FairIsle floated next to Rockall, their fins touching. 'You were singing strange words,' she said.*

*'So were you – and Nordstar.'*

*'The spirit moved me and I sang, but it was not **my** song of Truth. I think it was the song of the Great Wind Song maker who hides below the rock tower. The song was telling of a journey through dry lands to the bank of a river and in the song I saw the man who hangs on the She-salmon's shipstone neck thing. He was guiding the traveller.'*

*'I saw a pillar of fire and cloud – and water flowing from a rock. You were hearing a different song,' said Rockall.*

*'There are more mysteries in the Sea and Sky than . . .'*

*'I should never have told you that.' Rockall slapped the water with his tail and swam off to join Nordstar.*


At 11 p.m. Dan, wearing a dark jersey and a navy blue knitted hat, walked quietly along the empty street towards the old swimming pool. He tried the door, then took a twisted wire from his pocket, inserted it into the lock and moved it slowly round, sensing for the tumblers. This one was going to be easy. The door opened and he stepped through, closing it quietly behind him. He went over to look into the dark water. Two dolphins rose and eyed him, followed a moment later by a larger grey-white creature that came slowly to the surface and exhaled. He recognised it as a pilot whale by the shape of its fin.

Whoever the guy Bill was, who had written the letter, he had got it right.

Dan examined the walls of the pool enclosure. He tried the main doors under the arched nameplate, rattling them slightly, then opened the door of the café room and shone a torch around the inside. He did the same with the pump room before kneeling by the overflow outlet in the side of the pool and listening. He dipped his finger into the water and licked it. It tasted of salt – seawater.

He walked about, looking down at the paving until he stopped over a round black metal disc the size of a dustbin lid, set level with the slabs. He lay on the ground and put his ear to it. Below him he could hear running water.

A dolphin exhaled noisily behind him and he swung round, knelt by the pool and stared down. By the light of a street lamp outside he could see a dolphin's head just below the surface.

Dan stared back at the unblinking eye that appeared to be seeing deep into his head. 'Get me out of here,' the eye was pleading. 'Get me out of here.'

*'What did you make of that?' Rockall asked FairIsle when the human had gone.*

*'He was here to help us, I could read that in his mind. I have sensed his presence before but I don't know where.'*

*'He's an Orca,' Rockall declared. 'He wants others to think he is fierce but really he is gentle and warm inside. Even so, I think he could be bad to run foul of on a stormy night.'*

*'You do make quick judgements, don't you.'*

# CHAPTER TWENTY-FOUR

The next afternoon in the vestry Hywel played the tape again and again, Mary at his side listening, her previous excitement replaced by disappointment. The coordination of the dolphin voices and the music was still inspiring and beautiful but she could not make any sense of the sounds. If this was the 'song' she was supposed to take to the world of people, she at least, could not understand it. Perhaps other more intelligent people could.

'They've got a real sense of rhythm,' Hywel remarked. 'It's almost as if they knew music.'

'If they've had bigger brains than us for millions of years longer, I'd be surprised if they hadn't discovered . . . invented, no – discovered, music,' Mary replied.

'If they had hands like us, I could teach them to play the organ,' Hywel said.

'That old vicar could play with one hand, you said.'

'Yes, but he had fingers on that one and he wasn't trying to do it underwater.'

Hywel walked to the vestry door and looked across towards the organ.

'If I made a board to go across the keys of the organ, with relays and solenoids to hold the keys down as long as a signal held, I could activate each one from a narrow range of c.p.s. – cycles per second.'

He started searching through his boxes. Perhaps some of that old Telecom junk would come in useful after all.

*Rockall swam alongside FairIsle.*

*'I've finished my song. Will you hear it?'*

*'Mine too is almost complete, but I would hear yours.'*

*Rockall swam slowly, a little self-consciously – singing something so personal made him feel immensely vulnerable.*

> *When I was born the sunlit sparkling Sea*
> *Patterned the seabed, light delighting me.*
> *Sun, Sea, companionship and joy were mine*
> *Grace, beauty, love and peace would intertwine*
> *As kelpweed in a swirling current's flow.*
> *Now – what is the life I know?*

*All I possess is here within my brain*
*I have no hands to grasp and hold and claim.*
*But human hands once cast a subtle net*
*Unseen, unheard, unechoing – and yet*
*Strong to ensnare, to capture and enslave*
*This spirit born for Sea-life, wind and wave.*

*For I was taught that Dolphins love all Men*
*And Men love us, but now I wonder when*
*Their arrogance and greed this concept killed –*
*Still whales and dolphins die. My soul is filled*
*With alien emotions. Fear and hate*
*Pollute my mind – a toxic stream in spate.*
*I am a symbol of all whales' plight*
*Captured or killed, not knowing how to fight.*

*Trapped here, I swim in circles and a hatred grows*
*I yearn for freedom where the Sea wind blows*
*Don't let a hate for Mankind poison me*
*~Yegods~ and little fishes – set me free.*

'I didn't know that you were as bitter as that,' FairIsle commented at last.

'Neither did I, but I feel better now the Song has drawn it out of my guts,' he replied.

Nordstar had swum up to join them.

'That is quite a Song,' she said. 'You dolphins don't know your capabilities. I'm looking forward to hearing yours, Grace of FairIsle.'

'It's not ready yet, but it is surprising even me.'

Nordstar swam to the centre of the pool as the She-salmon and the Sprat came in at the side door.

Dan had bought a wet suit, a pair of fins, a mask and a snorkel from the ships chandlers. He was used to a made-to-measure suit but there was no time for that. At this time of year having one specially made could take up to six weeks. He also bought a large bag to put all the gear in before calling in at the pool to sound out the young man and Helga. He heard the slap of a tail-fluke on the water when he rattled the side door. This was unlocked by the same young man as before. He was wearing red bathing trunks and a straw hat with KISS ME QUICK on the hat-band. Dan could see Helga over the young man's shoulder. She was backing away, then stopped, facing him. He pushed his way in and closed the door behind him.

'I told you before – this is private,' the young man spluttered. 'It's not open to visitors.'

Dan looked at him. He had seen many such before – hopefuls trying to join the marines. Skipper Jack had had a saying which described most of them – 'having delusions of adequacy'. But he had often been wrong. Many had surprised even Dan when they had a chance to show their true selves.

'This is private,' the young man said again.

'Shut up, Ken-ney,' said Helga, who had come forward. 'I know this man. We have met before.' She turned to Dan. 'You have come here wanting something?' Her voice was cold.

Dan nodded, looked around the pool enclosure then told Kenny to lock the door. He obeyed meekly.

They went to the café room and Helga made coffees for them all from a kettle that had just boiled.

Dan watched her. She was obviously waiting for him to tell her why he was there. Her earlier tone of voice indicated that she was still sore about that night at her house. Should he apologise? No – get straight to the point.

'Do you think these dolphins should be kept here in captivity?' he asked her.

This was clearly not what she expected. She passed him a mug and then one to the young man who, taking his cue from her, said nothing.

Dan waited.

Then Helga asked, 'Why have you come to this place? I am not happy to see you again. The dolphin-hvals are leaving here soon. They are going to France. To answer your question – yes, I would rather all the hvals were free and in the sea.'

Dan looked at Kenny. 'What about you?'

'When they go, I haven't got a job anyway. But I don't want them to go to France.'

'Would you help me release them?' Dan asked. 'I think I could fix it.'

'How?' asked Kenny, leaning forward.

Dan sipped his coffee. 'Explosives.'

'You'd kill them,' said Kenny.

Dan scowled at him. 'Listen son, if I didn't know better than that, I wouldn't be here.'

There was another silence, then Helga asked, 'Could you really get the hvals to the sea? How would you do it?'

'Come outside. Have you got the lifting handles for that manhole cover?' he asked Kenny.

'T shaped things with flat lumps at the end?'

'Sounds right.'

'There are two hanging up in the pump room.'

'Good lad. Would you get them please? Has anyone else got a key for the street-door?'

'Only Mr Cartwright – he owns this place.'

'Put *your* key in the lock and give it half a turn. If he comes he won't be able to get in so he'll shout over the wall. That'll give you time to square up and for me to disappear.'

Kenny went into the pump room and found the manhole keys. He left his hat on an old crate upended in a corner. He had suddenly felt stupid wearing it.

Using the keys Dan and Kenny lifted the heavy metal lid and a gust of foetid air came from the black hole. Helga wrinkled her nose and stepped back. Below they could hear the sound of running water. Dan took an electric torch from the bag and shone it downwards. The light showed a square brick chamber with projecting metal steps built into the brick-work. At the bottom of the chamber, through an arched brick-lined tunnel, a spate of filthy water rushed seawards. Brown and dirty-white objects floated in the greyness. Helga was sure she could hear the squeals of invisible rats.

Dan was assessing the angle of the flow-channel to the side of the dolphins' pool.

'Just what I hoped, this sewer runs out to sea through a big pipe. With the right amount of P E, I could take the bottom out of the pool here and the dolphins could swim free.'

'P E?'

'Plastic explosive.'

'That would kill the dolphins.' Kenny was persistent.

'They'd have to be clear of the water when it went off. We can sort that out later.'

'How do you know there's no barrier at the end of the pipe?' Kenny was not going to be put off.

'With all that muck going through, and the speed it's moving, any screen or barrier would foul up in hours. It's *got* to be a clear run out.'

'Where would you get the explosives?'

'That's my business.'

He sent Kenny to fetch the long-handled broom used for brushing the bottom of the pool and upended it in the sewer to test for depth.

'There's enough water down there for them to swim in,' he said. 'It'd taste foul, but they can swim for miles on one breath and I'm sure they know how to keep their mouths closed underwater. Now I want to go down the manhole and check the layout.'

Dan stripped to his underpants and worked his body into the wet suit. Kenny watched intently – he had seen frogmen in many films but had never been this near to a living one. This was James Bond stuff – but for real.

Dan sat on the edge of the hole, feet dangling.

'Don't you want these?' Kenny asked, holding out the fins.

'Not yet. This is only a recce – standing up I hope.' Dan lowered himself down the hole and into the filthy water below.

As the broom handle had indicated, the level was waist height. He held onto a looped metal step and peered along the tunnel then climbed up, reached for the torch and climbed down again. He examined the walls of the chamber in great detail.

Dan climbed out again and asked Kenny to hose down the wet suit before he peeled it off, underpants and all.

'Now wash me off – gently,' he said. 'What's the matter, son, never seen a man before?'

Helga went into the café room.

Dan, standing naked on the poolside, looked at the water in the pool which was relatively clean as the dolphins had not been circling and much of the muck had settled. He called to Kenny, 'Do you swim with these?'

'Yes,' said Kenny, 'before the pumps . . .'

Dan dived expertly into the pool and swam a length underwater, seeing the grey back of the pilot whale below him. When he surfaced there was a dolphin on either side of him. He turned and swam back between his two escorts then trod water and looked into their eyes. 'I'm going to get you out of here,' he said aloud in English and the dolphins slapped the water with their tails as he swam to the poolside and hauled himself out.

'There's a lot of shit on the bottom,' he said to Kenny. 'Don't you clean it?'

'The filter pumps have packed up. I tried to tell you,' Kenny replied. 'It used to be nice and clean.'

'Have you got a towel?'

Kenny went and got one. Dan showered at the end of the pool, dried himself and dressed. Helga came and joined them.

'What are you going to do with the hvals?' she asked.

'They should be in the *sea*,' Dan said. 'Will you two help me release them?'

Kenny looked at Helga. His whole world was collapsing. Helga would be going back to the islands that she had come from and the dolphins and the whale were going to France or would be killed on the orders of Mr Cartwright. He'd be back on the dole with only the Arcade for entertainment. If this man planned to use explosives and it went wrong he could end up in prison like Billy Tranter. Everything was going pearshaped. Helga appeared to be waiting for him to say something. He didn't want the dolphins killed.

'Why don't you just ring the R S P C A?' he asked.

'It's not illegal to keep dolphins in captivity. All over the world people are trying to get captive ones freed. My way, these two could be back in the sea in a couple of days.'

'What about the whale? Could she get through the pipes?'

'She might, but if not and she was still here, we could ring the R S P C A then. They'd *have* to put her straight into the sea – with all the water gone there'd be nowhere else. Are you game?'

'*I've* got nothing to lose,' said Kenny. He suddenly liked this big man who acted so decisively and it would be fun to see the look on Mr Cartwright's face the following morning. Even prison might not be too bad – he might get to share a cell with Billy. It would be like old times at the home. 'Count me in,' he said.

Dan looked at Helga. 'I expect you will want to keep out of the way,' he said.

'Why do you say that?' she responded. 'These hvals are my friends. I would like to help them to go free. I know what it is like to be not free. You can *count me in* as well.'

'Have you got a phone here if I need to ring you?' Dan asked.

Kenny laughed. 'Not one that works. That'd cost money and old man Cartwright wouldn't trust me with a mobile.'

'I need twenty-four hours to work out a plan. I'll come back at the same time tomorrow.'

While returning in the Zodiac to *The Warrior*, Dan was estimating the charge needed for the job. He'd said at the pool that he could do it without harming the dolphins and the whale, so he'd have to find some way of getting them out of the water at the time of the explosion, or the boy would be right, the shock waves would kill them for sure. He'd think of something. At least the lad and Helga seemed to be willing to go along with his ideas.

*When Helga and Kenny had left the pool, FairIsle told Rockall that her Song was ready. Nordstar immediately swam up beside her. The dolphine sang:*

*I, FairIsle, call to Thinking Men –*
*See us for what we are.*

*Not competition for your fish*
*Not fools to entertain your young*
*Not handy hulks of oil and flesh*
*But creatures of intelligence*
*Deserving something better from our land-based friends*
*Who occupy dry portions of this planet, humans will call Earth*
*But which is mostly Sea.*

*We know that you have eyes to see*
*And ears to hear.*
*We know that you have brains to think.*
*We know imagination flourishes in men.*
*We hope that you have souls to feel compassion too.*
*Please, use your hands to signal*
*STOP*
*And let us live.*

*See us for what we are*
*A peaceful, gentle, cultured people of the Sea.*

'Why have you directed your Song at humans?' Nordstar asked.
'That's how it came to me,' FairIsle replied.
'I like it,' Rockall said. 'It is better than mine.'
'No one Song is better than another, as long as it is your True Song, but each will be different,' Nordstar said and swam away again.

Inside the church, Mary was helping Hywel manoeuvre a heavy wooden plank across the lower of the two keyboards on the organ. Another board, also fitted with a double-row of precisely spaced solenoid actuators, leant against the wall. Wires came from each bronze-coloured coil and these were neatly bundled together where they led away from the ends of the boards down into a black box standing next to a car battery on the floor. Under Hywel's guidance, Mary had spent the afternoon drilling into the end of the soft-iron core on each actuator and inserting short wooden dowels into the holes she had made.

When the first plank was in position they lifted the second one onto the upper keyboard.

Hywel studied them for a minute, went out into the churchyard and came back carrying four old bricks. He put one on each end of the two planks.

'What are you laughing at?' he asked Mary.

She pointed to the bricks.

'All this high-tech stuff and you need those to make it work!'

'Let's trust it does, bricks or no bricks.'

He switched on the blower and checked the connection of the solenoids to the battery and to the wire that led across the floor of the nave and up the steps of the tower.

'Race you upstairs.'

Mary refused to run in the church and, by the time she had got to the top of the tower, Hywel was sliding the microphone down the line and lowering it into the water. One of the dolphins swam over at once and inspected it.

An organ note came from within the church far below them, then another.

They saw the dolphin back away, then swim forward again. More random notes echoed up the stairway.

'It works,' Hywel said, hugging a startled and breathless Mary. 'It bloody-well works. The dolphins are playing the organ!'

*'Are you sure?' Rockall said to FairIsle and the distant organ echoed the pattern of his speech.*

*'Try it yourself.' More notes reached them.*

*Rockall tried a rising scale of squeaks and a similar scale vibrated through the water.*

*'You are making the Great Wind Song Maker sing for you!' FairIsle said incredulously. 'Let me try.'*

*Nordstar had joined them, and the three took it in turns to practise, finding exactly which of their sounds awoke which note from beyond the wall. By the time the sun had dropped behind the buildings, each could get the Great Wind Song Maker to respond at will. Eventually it stopped and no matter what they did, it remained silent.*

'This has been the most exciting day of my life,' Hywel said as he switched off the blower. 'Tomorrow I'll put a speaker into the pool, with another 'mike' here near the organ to feed back the notes directly into the water. Then, if I can finish the black-box with that new chip in it, I'll wire that in as well.'

# CHAPTER TWENTY-FIVE

Back on *The Warrior* Dan lay awake planning. He could do a small diversionary explosion in an electrical transformer beforehand. That would have the added benefit of putting the lights out in the area of operations. The main charge would be in the pool on the side next to the sewer. That would blow a hole through the pool wall and the dolphins could ride out on the backwash and the flow of the pool water down the hole. All he had to do was get them out of the water at the *exact* time of the explosion. But, even if they could be hauled out onto the side, the shock waves through the ground might cause internal injuries. Perhaps they could be lifted out in nets slung under the diving boards . . . but then the water would be all gone before they could be lowered back . . .

He woke at dawn as the trawler turned on its anchor chain to face the tide flooding in under the concrete bridge to fill the Fleet Lagoon – the water surging in from the east as it had done twice each day since the great pebble bank that protected the inland sea from the ocean had formed thousands of years before.

He fed Lucky, dressed, then climbed the narrow wooden steps to the deck and watched the sun rise through the thin summer mist. The deck and rail were chill and damp with dew as he leant there, smelling the unique scent of a sea dawn.

A pair of cormorants swam past on the tide, their black necks snake-like above the water. Dan watched them as they dived for young flatfish and bass. Fork-tailed terns hovered and dipped into the water, to rise with small fish in their beaks.

Hywel had been up much of the night building his 'vision' device in the vestry-workshop. The special microchip he had bought was soldered into place on an old printed circuit board from which he had removed or isolated unwanted components.

He slept for a few hours, glad that the next day was his day off and at dawn, burning with impatience, he connected the black-box into the wires between the microphone and the organ. On the tower he slid that and the new speaker, protected by two polythene bags – having proved too big to fit inside a condom – down the wire until they were suspended ready to be lowered into the water. He had already switched on the blower of the organ but made himself wait until Mary came before he turned on the microphone.

She had told him that she would join him early in the morning but had not given an exact time. This was the one day each week when the hotel owner's wife did the morning teas herself, but Mary had told Hywel that she would have to go back to make the beds and clean the rooms later.

He prowled around the tower top frequently looking over, either at the dolphins or along the street where Mary would be walking.

When she came in sight he waved to her and she waved back with the key in her hand. Hywel waited until she arrived breathless at the tower door and stepped out onto the grass before he lowered the microphone and the speaker into the water and switched on the tape recorder.

*FairIsle inspected the two offerings.*

*'We've got a jellyfish as well as a shipstone herring today,' she said and jumped backwards as the voice of the Great Wind Song Maker sang at her from inside the jellyfish.*

*She swam forwards carefully and tried some of the sounds that had produced results the night before. The jellyfish reacted at once, singing the expected notes right in the water with her.*

*Nordstar swam up and sang the first line of her new and as yet unsung Song –*

>   *Out of the Northern Sea I swam . . .*

*The jellyfish mimicked it perfectly, sounding every word.*
*Nordstar started again –*

>   *Out of the Northern Sea I swam*
>   *To satisfy an age-old prophecy*
>   *My life a sacrifice. I am*
>   *Part of the everlasting saga of the Sea*
>   *'I did not fail,' I cry -*
>   *Though I must die.*
>   *Out of the Northern Sea I swam*
>   *The hope of life for all my kin and kind*
>   *The Times and Tides were not right then*
>   *Now hear our Songs of Hope for all Whalekind*
>   *So though I dread the coming pain*
>   *Let it not be in vain.*

189

*Hope fills my heart for all Whalekind*
*Though soon into the endless night I'll swim*
*And echoes fade and stars grow dim for me*
*I trust Mankind will hear our plea*
*Sung from this place of shame*
*'Let whales swim free again*
*Let whales swim free again'.*

Hywel turned to Mary who was leaning on the wall, still breathless from climbing the spiral stairs.

'Check the tape recorder's on?' he urged her.

She bent over the machine, 'It is.'

'You won't believe this . . .' he said, almost as breathless as she was. He held up his hand and settled the headphones over his ears again. 'Shuss.'

Below them in the early morning light he saw the big white creature back away from the microphone, and one of the black dolphins swim forward in its place.

Through the headphones, each word as clear as before, came a song so beautiful that Hywel cried unashamedly while Mary looked on in astonishment. She thought she could hear someone singing far down in the church below and moved across the grass to stand near the top of the stairs straining her ears to make out the words.

Hywel heard Rockall's Song of longing and pleading, starting with:

*When I was born the sun-lit sparkling Sea . . .*

through to:

*I yearn for freedom where the Sea wind blows*
*Don't let a hate for Mankind poison me*
*~Yegods~ and little fishes – set me free.*

Hywel turned to Mary. Her cheeks were as damp as his.

'No,' she said, 'I *don't* believe it.'

The sound of a different singer came up the stairway, backed by the sweetest of organ music and Mary cupped her hand to her ear. Hywel glanced at the tape recorder to make sure that it was still running, then peered down into the patch of grey water below, the surface flicking sparkles of light as it caught the first of the sun between the stark buildings. A female voice was singing:

*I, Grace of FairIsle, call to Thinking Men –*
*See us for what we are . . .*
*Not competition for your fish . . .*
*But creatures of intelligence . . .*

*See us for what we are*
*A peaceful, gentle, cultured people of the Sea*

The voice faded away and only unrelated notes of the organ played intermittently.

'Did I really hear what I think I did?' Hywel asked, reaching out and squeezing Mary's hand before hauling the microphone and speaker out of the pool and back up to the tower. 'I must make a copy of this tape, just in case.'

Hywel carried the tape recorder down the stairs, trying to remember which box held his duplicating deck. Someone was knocking loudly at the door of the church.

Mary looked at Hywel quizzically. He shrugged.

'I'm not expecting anybody,' he said, and passed her the tape cassette. 'It's only just gone eight o'clock anyway. Look after this, I'll go back up the tower and see who it is. Don't open the door.'

Mary slipped the cassette into her skirt-pocket, patting the bulge to make sure it was secure. The knocking had ceased but she could hear men's voices outside. A ladder was being placed against an outside wall, and through the stained glass of the window she could see the shape of a man climbing the ladder, carrying a tool bag of some kind. He reached up and the tiny light above the organ keyboard went out and the low hum of the organ's blower died away.

Hywel came down the tower. 'Bloody electricity men. Their van's out in the street. Come to cut off the power now, of all times. The old vicar said it had been on for thirty years. Sod it.'

'Hywel! This is still a church, remember.'

'Sorry. We may have been rumbled. They've gone now but I'd better stay here for a bit in case anyone else comes. Take the cassette back to the hotel and I'll join you later with the gear to duplicate it.'

Mary walked back through the streets, just beginning to fill with people on their way to work and with holidaymakers taking a stroll in the early sunshine. She was thinking, 'I've got the *song* in my pocket, I've actually got the *song* in my pocket. All I have to do is to *take it to the world of people*. But how? She prayed silently for guidance.

She was hungry. Then, remembering Fungie and talking to Michael in far-away Ireland she said to herself, 'The hunger is upon me.' She could go back to the hotel and have her breakfast there, but the smell of frying bacon drifted out of a café door and on impulse she stopped and went in, ordered a bacon sandwich and a mug of tea then sat at a corner table watching the other people eating and drinking. She was not due back at the hotel for at least an hour. She took the tape cassette from her skirt pocket to put it in her bum-bag but the zip on the bag had jammed and wouldn't open. It dawned on her that if the bag wouldn't open she couldn't pay for her sandwich. She couldn't go out without paying and she could hear the sizzle of the bacon frying in the pan behind the counter. A man there was spreading butter on her bread. She looked around in a panic.

In the opposite corner a white-haired, elderly man in a clerical collar was sipping tea from a cup held in his right hand. His fingerless left hand was resting on the check tablecloth. He saw Mary looking at him and smiled a greeting.

Mary got up and went across to his table.

'You don't know me . . .' she started but the old man cut her short.

'Won't you join me?' he asked. 'I hate eating alone. Have you ordered?'

Mary blushed. '*That's* my problem. My bag won't open and I won't be able to pay for it.' She suddenly felt like a silly schoolgirl.

'Be my guest,' the old man said, standing up and moving a chair so that Mary could sit down.

Seeing her hesitation, he continued. 'Please do, I get very lonely sometimes. I would welcome your company. I think *this* frightens some people away.' He fingered his collar.

Mary sat down. 'I wouldn't have bothered you but I think you know my friend – Hywel.'

'The young man who's turned my church into a workshop? He's a friend of yours, is he? Lucky fellow.'

Mary blushed again.

A man in a white apron came around the counter with her sandwich and a mug of tea on a tray.

'Over here, George.' The vicar beckoned, then reached into his pocket for some change. 'I'm treating this young lady today.'

Mary started to thank him but he was asking her, 'Have you known Hywel a long time?'

She tried to work out how long it was, could not decide and replied, 'We work together at the same hotel. He's a waiter – I'm a chambermaid.'

'Do you go to the church with him?'

The atmosphere in the corner where they sat was like it used to be in the confessional when she was a girl, admitting to minor sins and omissions, this present congregation of breakfast eaters and tea drinkers just out of earshot. She found she was telling the vicar about her first visit to the church with Hywel when he was taking the trolley load of equipment there. Then, as a sort of justification, she told him the whole story. She told him about being mugged, having her rosary stolen, going to Ireland, and the message Fungie had written in the sea, the old man encouraging her silently as she talked. She started to tell him about her dream but that sounded far too silly with him sitting across the table from her.

Instead, she told him what had happened the evening before and how she and Hywel had recorded the dolphin's songs that morning before the power had been cut off.

'Oh. They've got round to that at last, have they?' the old man said as George, following what was clearly an established routine, brought another cup of tea for him. George asked Mary if *she* wanted another cup and she shook her head.

When he had gone the vicar poured something from a hip flask into the cup. 'A long-time failing,' he said apologetically. 'I started on this stuff when my wife and daughter died in India and somehow . . . You don't want to hear all that though. Forgive my ramblings.' He screwed on the lid and put the flask back in his pocket.

'Where's the tape now?' he asked. 'I'd *love* to hear that. Dolphins singing in English. Well I never!'

Mary took the tape from her pocket and passed it across to him – it seemed to make everything she had said a little more believable.

'Hywel wants to make a copy of it but the power's gone now. He's bringing the tape-machine to the hotel. I'm sure he'll let you hear it when he's done that.' She paused. 'I don't know where we will do the copying though, I'm not allowed to have men come up to my room.'

'And very proper, too,' the old man said, his eyes twinkling. 'Bring it round to my house, if you like. The power's on there and I can act as chaperone, though no one seems to bother about things like that nowadays. Here's the address. I'll have a little present for you if you do come,' he added.

He put the tape on the table, wrote an address on a paper napkin and gave it to Mary, took a sip from his cup and coughed, his face going very red. He coughed again, holding the cup in his right hand and pressing his chest with the fingerless end of his left arm.

Mary took the cup from him as George came over. The old man was sitting back, his eyes streaming.

193

'Are you OK, Reverend?' George asked.

'Will be soon. Could you get me a taxi, please? I need to go home and lie down.'

'I'll get one,' Mary volunteered. There was a taxi rank only a few yards along the street.

George and Mary helped the old man into the taxi and she gave the driver the address from the napkin.

When the taxi had gone she felt in her pocket for the tape cassette. It was not there. She must have left it on the table. She ran back but it was gone.

'Are you looking for the music tape, Miss?' George asked, seeing her searching under the table. 'I slipped it in the Reverend's pocket. I thought it was his.'

Mary went to the taxi rank – she would take a taxi to follow the other, then remembered she could not open her bag. Her watch told her she was overdue at the hotel – there were all the beds to make still.

The tape would be safe until Hywel came, she tried to reassure herself. Vicars don't steal things. Hywel could go to his house, make the copy and come back with it to the hotel. It would give the old man a chance to hear the dolphins as well. Everything would be all right. Please God! Everything would be all right.


Dan went round to Dormouth again and knocked on the side door of the pool. The parts of the road in direct sunlight shimmered in the heat and the tarmac surface at his feet was bubbling up in little black blisters. Kenny opened the door.

Helga was wearing a bikini again and seemed quite pleased to see him. The kid was positively friendly and greeted him enthusiastically.

'Hi. I was afraid you wouldn't come,' he said. 'I've been thinking about getting the dolphins out of the water. Helga can make them jump together.'

'All three of them?'

Kenny's face fell. 'No. Only the dolphins. The whale's never jumped.'

Dan looked at the diving board.

'Perhaps we could lift the whale out in a net under here while the others jump.'

He climbed the rotting wooden steps to the highest board to see if the structure was likely to carry the weight of a pilot whale. From there he could see over the wall and froze as he saw a Rolls Royce glide round the corner and stop in the shadow of a grimy warehouse opposite the pool entrance.

194

Two men got out as Dan slowly lowered himself to lie prone on the hot black-ridged rubber matting. Rockall slapped the water with his tail. Helga and Kenny looked round fearfully but Dan was out of sight.

The side door opened and Mr Cartwright came in, followed by a smaller man wearing a dark suit despite the heat.

Mr Cartwright introduced the man to Helga and Kenny with a wave of his hand.

'This is Mr Lefarve, he's here sooner than I expected.'

Helga did not like the way the man held on to her hand and stared at her bikini top with his bulgy eyes. She pulled her hand free.

Monsieur Lefarve ignored Kenny and walked to the edge of the pool.

'Will you make them jump, if you please?' he asked Helga.

She made the circular motion with her arms.

*'The She-salmon is asking us to jump, said Rockall.*

*'I know,' FairIsle replied. 'Do you want to?'*

*'No,' replied Rockall, 'Not for that lobster.'*

*FairIsle grinned. The little man looked just like a lobster, especially now he was waving his claws in the air. The two dolphins rose for air then glided down to join Nordstar.*

'Make them jump,' Mr Cartwright snapped.

'I am asking them. Sometimes they do not want to jump,' Helga replied.

Kenny tried to intervene. 'It's true Mr Cartwright. Sometimes they will not jump – even for Helga.'

'Shut up, you.' Mr Cartwright glowered at Kenny as he turned to Helga.

'Try again please,' he hissed. 'Mr Lefarve has come a long way to see them.'

Helga made circles with her arms. The dolphins swam by, contempt for the visitors clear in their every movement, the swishing of their tail-flukes stirring up the sediment from the bottom of the pool.

'I should have sent you all to Japan,' Mr Cartwright shouted at the dolphins. 'In deep-frozen blocks. That's all you're goddamned good for.'

He turned on Helga. 'You're fired,' he said. 'You told me they were jumping.'

'I don't know what *you're* grinning at,' he shouted at Kenny. 'You're out of a job by the end of the week as well. Why haven't you run the pumps? Every day, like I told you. This water is filthy.'

Mr Cartwright turned to the little man in the dark suit. 'I'm sorry, Mr Lefarve, they told me the dolphins were ready.'

'I will take them,' the Frenchman said. 'But not at the price you have been asking. Something much more less.'

The door slammed shut as the two men went out. Dan lifted his head enough to see the black car roll out of sight round the corner before he came carefully down the steps.

'I can be ready tonight. Are you still game?'

'*I'll* be here,' said Kenny, looking at Helga.

'Me . . . I too will be here.'

'Can you get hold of a net big enough to lift the whale out of the water?'

'There's one in the pump room. It came with Rockall.'

'What about reduction pulleys?'

Kenny looked blank. Dan explained how they were used to enable very heavy weights to be lifted by one or two people only. Kenny had never heard of such things.

'I'll get a set from the chandlers,' Dan said. 'Rope?'

Kenny shook his head.

'I'll get some of that too. Is Mr Cartwright likely to come back?'

'I doubt it, but I'll keep the key in the lock like you said. Knock three times.'

Nothing Super-Dolphin had ever done had been as exciting as this.


The Reverend David Thomas, one-time vicar of The Church of Saint Peter the Fisherman, Dormouth, got out of the car and as he turned to pay the driver the taxi moved off, back towards the town centre.

No one in the town seemed to want to take his money nowadays. George, at the café, always tried to convince him that he had already paid though he was sure on most occasions that he hadn't.

The coughing fit had left him feeling very weak. He went into the house, climbed the stairs slowly so as not to bring on the coughing again and lay on his bed, dozing fitfully and sipping sometimes from the leather-covered flask. After a while he remembered that he had promised to give the young lady a present when she came to the house, and got up from the bed to find it.

The tin trunk in the spare room contained his mementoes of India. Carved ebony elephants, ivory figurines and what remained of gaudy pictures painted on skeleton leaves, lay between brightly coloured silk scarves. In a corner of the trunk was a small wooden box, crudely inlaid with mother-of-pearl and inside, wrapped in a delicate silk handkerchief was a tiny rosary made from the hard black seeds of some tropical plant. The cross and the figure of Christ Crucified were carved out of ebony, the projections of the body worn smooth by countless hours of handling.

196

The old man took a long pull from the flask, put it back in his pocket and fingered the rosary.

'I want you to take this, it's all I have,' the dying Eurasian woman in the dak bungalow had told him and he had argued with her in the candle-light.

'You are going to get better,' he had lied to her, the stink of dysentery filling the room. 'You'll need it then.'

But the woman had insisted. 'Someone would like to have it,' and he had thought, as he boiled the rosary in an old tin can on his spirit stove after burying her, that he *should* have put it in her grave with the body. But she had been *so* insistent . . .

One of the silver links that held the beads together was broken. He would take the rosary into town and see if he could get it mended before the girl and her young man came for . . . whatever it was they were coming for. Perhaps they were coming for their pre-wedding talk? He would remember soon – they would know, even if *he* had forgotten.

He shook the flask. It was empty so he unscrewed the top and filled it from an expensive-looking triangular bottle. If one was going to indulge a vice one might as well make a proper job of it. He went out, got as far as the porch then went back for the rosary.

# CHAPTER TWENTY-SIX

Hywel, realising that Mary would not be free until one o'clock, spent the rest of the morning tidying up the vestry, unable to do any electrical work in the absence of a power supply. At ten minutes to one he put the tape player and his duplicating deck into a tattered holdall and went out, the bright sunlight hurting his eyes. He strode through the busy streets, eager to hear again the incredible recording they had made together, or to confirm that it had been all an illusion. He was almost sure now that the tape would prove to be blank or at most a recording of dolphin-created organ music.

Mary was waiting on the steps of the hotel looking a little apprehensive. Her smile of greeting wavered as he asked, 'You've got the tape? I can't wait to hear it.'

'Well,' she said, forcing the truth out. 'I met the old vicar and he was coughing and I got a taxi for him and somehow . . .'

She was crying and Hywel put his arm around her and held her.

'Calm down,' he said. 'We'll sit over there and you can tell me what happened.'

They crossed the road to the Promenade and sat on a bench facing the sea. The beach was busy with holidaymakers but the two were oblivious to them.

Mary, between sniffs, told Hywel about the incident in the café.

'Why are you so upset?' he asked. 'All we've got to do is go to his house and ask for the tape. You've got the address?'

Mary took the napkin from her pocket and handed it to Hywel.

'That's not too far away, we can walk there in no time.'

'Can you fix this?' Mary asked, unbuckling her bum-bag. The zip's stuck.'

Hywel took it from her and examined it. 'There's a thread caught in the zipper. Have you got your nail scissors?'

'Yes – but they're in the bag,' she said and they both laughed.

Hywel jiggled at the zip fastener, teasing out the thread with his fingers and teeth until it opened, handed it back to Mary, stood up and said, 'Come on then. We're off to see the vicar, the wonderful vicar of . . . Dormouth.'

As they walked along the promenade hand in hand, a smile played around the corners of Mary's mouth like distant lightning around the edges of a storm cloud.

Hywel was grinning like a dolphin.


The address on the napkin was that of a shabby Victorian house with an open porch glowing with stained-glass panels, several of which were missing. The door badly needed repainting and a mass of green and cream variegated ivy rambled over the porch roof and the walls of the house. Hywel pressed the bell but heard no sound from inside. He banged the heavy brass knocker and they waited.

'There's no one in,' he said.

'How can you tell?' Mary asked. 'He may be asleep, or in the . . . the toilet.'

'You can always tell when there's no one in. The knocking sounds different.'

'Are you having me on,' she asked.

'No, honestly. I don't have a proper scientific explanation but that's how it is. I used to collect pools coupons at Cwm Glas. The knocking sort of echoes more when there's no one in.'

'What do we do now – wait?'

'Either that, or go and look for him. If we don't find him we can come back later. I'll check the garden first.'

Hywel walked round the side of the house and through a sagging wooden gate into the garden behind. The air was heavy with the smell of early apples ripening in the sun. It was like Ty Mawr in the days before Mr Williams had left to go into the Home at Abergavenny. The grass had not been cut for at least a year and the white discs of last year's honesty plants in the weed-filled borders stared at him blindly. He ignored them and, shading his eyes, peered in at the kitchen window. Unwashed dishes stood on the wooden draining board but, as he expected, there was no sign of the old man.

'He must be out somewhere,' he told Mary who was waiting by the front porch.


Dan came back from the chandlers and knocked three times. The door was immediately opened by Kenny.

Dan walked round the pool and dropped the heavy bundle from his shoulder. He turned to Helga who was standing in the door of the café room.

'Have you got anything to eat in there? I'm starving.'

199

The three sat round an unstable metal table, eating cream crackers and cheese in an atmosphere charged with conspiracy.

'We must look like baddies planning to rob a bank,' Kenny remarked.

Dan scowled and Helga asked, 'You have seen the *real* bank robbers?'

'Only in films,' Kenny replied. 'I used to go to the pictures a lot before . . . before you came.' He blushed.

There was another silence before Dan said, 'The problem's going to be timing the explosion for when the dolphins are both in the air – I'll need to get that exactly right. Then we'll have to lower the white whale before all the water runs out or it'll be lying on the bottom of the pool like a . . . a . . . like a stranded whale. But it's the dolphins that are going to be the main problem . . .'

He got up and went out to the poolside, followed by the others. He had written off the white whale in his mind. He could save two out of three. Two out of three wasn't bad. Tough decisions were necessary to achieve one's main objectives sometimes. The whale looked pretty sick anyway.

'The dolphins'll have to be *exactly* together, both well clear of the water, at the precise moment I press the button,' he said. 'One slip, one tiny miscalculation and they're dead.'

'What we need to do is have the button where the *dolphins* can press it themselves as they jump,' said Kenny, remembering some such scene from a half-forgotten film. 'I saw Lassie do that once.'

Dan raised his eyebrows and looked at Kenny with a new respect.

'But there are two dolphins,' he objected.

'Two buttons then,' said Kenny, remembering another war film he had seen on television. 'Joined together. Neither goes off unless they're both pressed at the same time.'

'Good lad,' said Dan. 'Is there an electrical whatsit shop near here. I could make that rig.'

The afternoon was spent with Dan and Kenny fixing two connecting push-buttons onto long poles that reached out from the diving boards and with Helga teaching the dolphins to jump for them. This they seemed happy to do for her now, though the constant disturbance turned the water into a brown soup.

At five o'clock Dan took the Zodiac round to Ferrybridge to collect the explosives from *The Warrior*. Kenny had asked to come with him. At first Dan had refused on the need-to-know principle but he had taken a liking to the lad. *He* was going to need somewhere to hide up for a bit and there were spare bunks on *The Warrior* but he would not tell Kenny this until the time came then, being aboard, at least he would be under his control.

Helga had told Dan quietly that she planned to take the first train to London in the morning and then on to Aberdeen for the ferry and home.

Now, as they left Dormouth Harbour, Kenny was intent on watching how Dan used the controls on the inflatable.

*FairIsle matched her swimming speed to Rockall's and they circled the pool together.*

*'The humans are planning something,' she said. 'I can sense it. Maybe they have heard our songs and the thing-with-wheels will come and take us back to the sea.'*

*Rockall replied, 'Maybe whales can fly.'*

*'Hope swims with dolphins,' FairIsle responded. 'Never forget that.'*

*'I know – any moment now the ~yegods~ will come, like they do in your stories and set us free with a wave of their tusks!'*

*FairIsle smacked Rockall's side with her tail-flukes.*

*'They'd probably leave you here for the lobster-man if you speak of them disrespectfully.'*

*'~Yegods~ don't exist,' Rockall said. 'We're here for the rest of our lives – and don't say, 'Hope swims with dolphins' again or I'll bring back this morning's mackerel.'*

The Reverend David Thomas sat on his favourite seat on the promenade, wondering why he had come out. Perhaps, like most days, there was no reason. It just made a change from being in the house alone.

On the beach in front of him a young woman was sitting on a deck chair while her daughter played in the soft sand. The woman's back was to him and something in the way she sat reminded him of his wife as she had been on the boat to India. His own little girl would then have been about the age of the one playing there on the sands.

He wondered, not for the first time, if Joan would be grown up when he joined them in Heaven or would she still be a child. He hoped she would be just as he remembered her. Dear God, take me soon! He unscrewed the lid of his flask.

When the woman and the child left the beach, he too got up and wandered off towards the town quay to watch the fishing boats leave on the evening tide and to savour the scents that had been such a part of his life since he had come to Dormouth. He was sure he should be doing something else but could not remember what it was. It would come back to him soon. It usually did.

Mary and Hywel returned to the house twice but each time their knocking was as unproductive as before.

'He might have had to go to hospital,' Hywel said. 'He wasn't a well man. Was the coughing bad?'

They rang Dormouth Infirmary from a phone box and asked if a Reverend Thomas had been admitted but were told, 'No'.

'Excuse me,' Hywel said to Mary, 'I must make another call – a private one.'

Hywel made his call while she waited outside.

'Hywel Jones here,' he told the proprietor of the hotel. 'I've got a stomach bug. I don't think I can come in this evening. Sorry it's such short notice. I thought it would go away, but . . .'

'Spare me the details. We can cover for you tonight. If you're fit enough, ring me in the morning and tell me how you are. We don't want the guests catching it and blaming us. Go and lie down.'

Mary looked quizzically at him as left the phone box but he offered her no explanation.

'Let's go to the church and see the dolphins. We can check at the house later. He should be back by then.'

'What *is* going on down in the pool?' Hywel asked Mary when they had reached the tower-top and looked over the parapet. 'Keep your head low. It all looks odd to me. Best if we're not spotted.'

They watched the two familiar figures, the blonde woman and the young man, together with a bearded man that they had not seen before, moving around the pool and in and out of the room in the corner until, at about eight, the three of them all left together by the side door.

'I wonder if *they'd* let me run a cable from a power-point in the place that says Café around the pool to the church,' Hywel said. 'I could tell them I only needed it for a day or so. I could say I was working on the organ – that wouldn't be far from the truth. If they're there again tomorrow, I'll ask.'

Mary was walking around the tiny lawn, stretching her arms and yawning. 'It's time we cut this grass again,' she said

'Do you have to go back to the hotel?' Hywel asked.

'Do you mean *now* or *tonight at all*?'

'Either.'

Mary looked at him in the rapidly fading light. If she couldn't trust *him* she would never trust anyone again.

'No one's waiting for me,' she said and Hywel went down the stairs to reappear breathlessly with a blanket, a packet of biscuits, two bananas and a can of Coca-Cola.

As it got darker the last shrieks of the swifts flying over and around the tower were replaced by the squeaks of bats, their echolocation systems replicating those of the dolphins in the pool below.

Mary leant back against the warmth and comfort of Hywel's chest. God wouldn't have let the tape of the dolphin's songs go away with the vicar unless He had intended it. There was nothing else she could do now. Her responsibility was over. She slept.

# CHAPTER TWENTY-SEVEN

Dan let Kenny take the wheel of the Zodiac on the way back from Ferrybridge to Dormouth Harbour. The lad was keen to learn and quickly picked up the uses of the controls and the jargon, though Dan saw him glance at his left and right hands whenever his directions included the words port or starboard. Kenny had eagerly explored *The Warrior* and had obviously been disappointed when Dan had sent him up on deck while he prepared the charges.

When they had moored in the Inner Harbour Dan sent Kenny back to the pool while he found the nearest electricity transformer box and dropped a small parcel down behind it. It landed with a rustle on the litter of cigarette packets, chewing gum wrappers and chip papers that had accumulated between the green metal casing and the wall behind.

In the parcel was a timer, set for 0100 hours, a detonator and just enough P E to knock the transformer out but not enough to cause danger to anyone passing. Give them a bit of a fright though, Dan thought as he strolled casually away. I wouldn't want to be the one who had to wash *their* underpants in the morning.

He went back to the Zodiac and checked that everything was in order should he want to make a quick get away later. Then he walked through the empty streets to the pool. It was midnight. He knocked three times and Kenny opened the side door.

Helga had packed her few belongings and taken them with her to the pool. Kenny carried her case and she had the accordion in one hand and a green plastic Marks & Spencer bag in the other.

'You're not coming back?' he had asked her as she counted out the rent that was due and left it on the dressing table with a note for Mrs Scrimshaw.

'No, I am not coming back, Ken-ney. I have always wanted to come to England but now I want to go back to Faroyar – to my own island. Tonight the hvals will be free, and so will I. I will get a train to Aberdeen and the boat will take me home from there. Soon we will be saying goodbyes.'

Kenny had gone into his room to find some little gift for Helga. He rummaged through his drawer until he found a little box with a bluestone dolphin set in the lid. It had been given to him by the nice housemother who had found it in a junk shop somewhere. Helga would like that.

He was about to close the drawer when he saw the mouth organ and he slipped that in his pocket with the box. He would have another go at learning to play it. This time there wouldn't be shouts of, 'Aw – shut it, Kenny,' when he needed to practise.

There was an hour before the transformer would blow and the three sat in the darkness of the café room drinking coffee.

'Why do your people kill the pilot whales?' Kenny asked Helga.

'We say it is to eat, but that is not the whole truth. To understand you must know about the history, about the past of the Islands. For a long time we were treated by Danmark as a part of them and then, when the Nazis invaded there, the British Navy sent warships and men to stop the Nazi sailors from using the islands for their U-boats to hide in. The British guns are still to be seen near the harbour at Torshavn.'

Dan looked up at the mention of guns but before he could say anything Helga was speaking again.

'The British were not interested in the government so the islanders ran their own affairs and we had a flag of our own for the first time. Then, after the war the British went away and the Faeroese expected to go on being a country of our own. Danmark did not want that.'

A distant bleep-bleep, bleep-bleep from a police car reached them and Dan looked at his watch in the light filtering in through the window. It was not time yet.

'Go on,' he said to Helga.

'In the Islands some people did not want to be a part of Danmark again and some others did. There was much arguing. In the end it came to be that Danmark was to deal with what they call 'external affairs' and to provide the police and the big laws. In the Islands we can do other things and make small laws through our own parliament.

'Danmark would like us to stop killing the hvals. They like the rest of the world to see them as "Green" people. But that would be doing something that Danmark wants us to do, so we do *not* stop the killing. It is like a boy who wants to be grown-up – he stays out late because his parents say he must come home early. Soon I hope my country will be really grown up.'

Helga stood. 'Is it not time to get the white hval into the net? I hope that she will want to go there.'

Dan changed into his wet suit and Helga and Ken into their bathing costumes, both of them shivering slightly in the cool night air. Helga went back inside and came out again wearing a T-shirt over her bikini.

'The Orca is plotting something with the She-salmon and the Sprat,' said Rockall.

'I told you that the humans were planning things,' FairIsle replied. 'But I think your Sprat is turning into a Mackerel. Something out of the ordinary is due tonight. I dare to think that they plan to return us to the Sea. Could it be that they have heard our songs?'

The two dolphins discussed the possibilities, Rockall noticeably less sceptical than before. Nordstar swam over to remind FairIsle of her promise not to go if she could not go with them.

'I promised,' said FairIsle. 'While the moon pulls and the Sea surges. I will not go without you.' As if in confirmation of the seriousness of her promise, what seemed to the dolphins to be an earth tremor, shook the ground around the pool. The lights beyond the wall went out and the stars showed, their images twinkling and dancing above them as the water vibrated with the shock waves.

Nordstar rose and lifted her head above the surface.

'I can see the stars again,' she said, joy in her voice. 'I can see my stars.'

A minute later an asteroid, hurtling through space at an unimaginable speed was deflected briefly from its course by the pull of the Earth's gravity and touched the outer edge of the atmosphere high above the point where a great rock in the sea was joined to the mainland by a bank of pebbles. In less than a second the asteroid glowed to white heat, shed a trail of incandescent fragments and skipped back into Space like a stone from the surface of a pond, cooling to invisible blackness again in the intense cold as it continued on its everlasting journey.

As Nordstar stared skywards, reading the portents as best she could, a silvery ball flashed across the sky from west to east, glowing with such intensity that it left a residual trail of light. In its wake tiny silver spots twisted and sparkled. She drew in a deep breath and sank. Tonight she was to die. She called to FairIsle who swam to meet her.

Voice low, she said, 'You are released from your promise. My time has really come. Tonight, I and the white-headed one die together as was prophesied. The creatures of the sea will eat the white-headed one and I will be consumed by the creatures of the land. My kind will soon be free of the Death-duty. I have no fear now.'

FairIsle swam beside her friend, their flippers touching.

'I need to ask another vow from you,' the starwhale said.

'Ask,' FairIsle replied.

*'When you are free, will you swim north and tell all the starwhales of their freedom. Otherwise they will not know and my gift will have been in vain.'*

*'While the Moon pulls and the Sea surges,' swore FairIsle, watching Helga on the side of the pool, sad that she was to lose a human friend and a whale friend, even if she was to gain her freedom.*

The distant explosion from the transformer woke Mary where she lay on the hay pile, asleep in Hywel's arms. She sat up. Hywel was struggling to stand.

'Did you hear anything?' he asked. 'All the street lights have just gone out.'

He leant over the parapet and looked down. 'Come and see this,' he called softly over his shoulder.

Mary joined him, still half asleep. As she peered into the darkness the sky was lit by a flash of light that shot across the sky and disappeared beyond the far cliffs, leaving in its wake twinkling spots of intense white light. These went out one by one and, although the moon was up over the sea, the darkness below seemed even more intense. Whatever Hywel had seen below was invisible to her.

The Reverend David Thomas sat on a sea front bench, the moonlight shining on his silvery hair, a night-time breeze from the sea making him shiver. He felt in his pocket for the flask, even though he knew it was now empty again. It felt comforting and he wrapped his fingers around it before becoming vaguely aware that there was something else in the pocket – a small flattish box feeling as though it was made of plastic. He took it out and held it up. He just had time to recognise it as the one containing the tape cassette the girl had shown him in the café that morning. Then the streetlights went out.

How had the box got into his flask pocket? Nothing else ever went in there. The girl would be worrying about it. She had told him how important it was. He would return it at once – if he knew where she was staying. Try as he would, if she *had* told him the name of the hotel where she worked and lived, he could not remember it now. He *did* know where her friend lived though – in his own beloved church. He stumbled to his feet and shuffled off, the light from the moon sufficient for him to see the way.

A bright light flashed in his head. Nothing unusual in that. His head often seemed to fill with lights since the night the ambulance had taken him to the Infirmary.

At the church he felt for the key, checking even the flask pocket but he knew he had not brought it. In another pocket he found the rosary, wondered why he had brought *that* with him and dropped it back into the pocket again. That wouldn't open the door.

There were sounds coming from inside the pool enclosure next door – muffled voices and splashing noises. He went back down the path into the street to where his old Morris was still parked. He tried to remember if he had asked the garage to move it but it seemed unimportant now. He leant against his car listening to the voices.

There were at least three different ones. He shuffled over to the door and knocked, once for each voice. There was a silence then the door opened, and closed again quickly.

On the other side a young man said, quite audibly, 'He's wearing a dog-collar. It's the old vicar-man. I've seen him a lot around town.'

More, now indistinct, voices followed before a bearded man in a black rubber suit opened the door and said, 'Come in and say nothing or you'll end up in the pool with the man-eating sharks.'

The Reverend David Thomas followed the bearded man around the pool to a door. By the moonlight he could see the sign, CAFE. He was propelled inside and the man said to someone he could not see, 'I think he's harmless – he's been on the piss – but keep him in here until the job's done. OK?'

The door closed again and he felt around for somewhere to sit down. There would have to be chairs in a café.

Dan went back to checking the ropes holding the whale in the net above the level of the water. This was the weakest part of the plan. Out of the water the pilot whale looked enormous. He was *sure* now that it would never go through the sewer, especially if, as he suspected was the case, the passage got smaller when the brick-built section joined onto a metal outfall pipe.

The sound of a police car's siren reached them from the direction of the transformer box.

'That little bang should keep *them* quiet for a bit,' said Dan, as he pulled on each rope in turn. They all moved easily through the pulley blocks.

Super-Dolphin grinned at him. 'Are you ready?' he asked the wet-suited hero.

'Perhaps we should get the whale up a few more feet, her belly's touching the water again.'

Nordstar had floated into the net without the slightest trouble, to the surprise of all concerned who had regarded this as a potential problem.

Dan had wondered if it would not be kinder to let her be killed by the shock waves. It would be a quick and painless death at least but the others would expect him to have a plan to release her as well as the dolphins.

Now, she hung flabbily in a net suspended from the diving platforms by the two sets of reduction pulleys.

Dan went to one set and Kenny to the other. 'Your end first,' he said.

Kenny undid the highwayman's hitch that Dan had taught him to tie, and swung on the rope, enjoying the power he felt when the pulleys lifted a weight far greater than he could have managed unaided. Super-Dolphin in real action at last. He tied the knot again, checking that the end was free so that, when the explosion came, one pull would drop the whale into the water before it all ran out.

Dan did the same at his end, then lowered a plastic wrapped parcel on a thin wire to the bottom of the pool. Kenny was watching intently.

'Is that the charge?' he asked as Dan uncoiled the wire round the side of the pool towards the diving platforms where the two trigger-sticks were silhouetted against the lighter sky above.

Not getting a reply and realising that it must be, he asked, 'Why put it in the pool and not in the sewer?'

Dan was climbing up the ladder to the triggers. He paused. 'Didn't you see *The Dam Busters*? The water holds the force of the charge against the wall. If it works OK it blows a hole right through. Pass me up the tool-bag.'

Kenny, shivering with cold and excitement, could hear Dan working above his head. When he had connected the wires together Dan swung down from the top platform and dropped agilely to the ground.

'You ready?' he asked. 'Get Helga out here to signal to the dolphins. Leave the old fellow – he's pissed as a newt. Try and get him to sit down away from the windows. You'll need to be out here to shine the torch on Helga, or the dolphins might not be able to see her. I've got to be ready to jump in, to guide them through the hole. You too if need be.'

Helga came out. 'Are you sure that you are doing all the things right?' she asked and sensed rather than saw the scowl on Dan's face as a cloud drifted across the moon.

'Stay down at the end, both of you. Are you ready? . . . Now!'

Helga circled her arms in the light of the torch Kenny was holding, the beam quivering slightly as Super-Dolphin's hand shook.

*'The She-salmon wants us to jump in the dark,' Rockall said. 'Should we?'*

*'I think we have to trust her,' FairIsle replied. 'We'll go together when she next signals . . . Now!'*

*Two dark bodies rose from the water, past the dull grey shape of Nordstar, hanging motionless in the net, up to the height of the highest board and then down into the water again. Nothing unusual happened.*

*'Did you touch the thing on the stick?' FairIsle asked.*

*'I couldn't see it clearly, could you?'*

*'No,' said FairIsle, 'but I am sure that is what she wants us to do, try again.'*

The dolphins jumped unprompted every half minute. Super-Dolphin's imagination leaping with them until he suddenly said, 'They can't see the targets. I'll shine the torch up there.'

He turned the light upwards as the dolphins leapt again. As they did so, the white-haired man staggered from the café room shouting, 'Don't do it – they'll be killed. They can sing. I've got a tape . . .'

He lurched towards the pool as Kenny turned the beam of the torch onto him. The man snatched at a hanging rope-end to stop himself from falling in. Helga ran towards him and tried to grab his jacket.

'Don't do . . .' The knot jerked loose and the old man and the whale in the net, splashed down into the pool. At that exact moment the ground shook, a fountain of water shot upwards and a wave sloshed over the sides.

There was a crash and a tinkle of falling glass from the church next door, the dong of a bell from the tower, a metallic thud as the manhole cover fell back onto the paving, a brief silence, then a deep gurgling sound.

Dan jumped into the rapidly falling water and pushed FairIsle towards the gaping hole in the side. She swam towards it and disappeared, followed a moment later by Rockall and Dan together.

Kenny jumped down into the pool, the water now only to his knees. Almost immediately it was all gone apart from a few shallow puddles and a salty low-tide and sewage smell.

Helga swung the beam of the torch around. The whale was hanging, tail up, in the net, its head on the pool-bottom. There was no doubt *she* was dead. Beside the whale's body lay that of the old man. He was lying in the same unnatural position as Christian's body had been in at the foot of the Lundi-cliff ten years before. She collapsed to her knees and was sick into the empty pool.

The streetlights outside flickered on again and bathed the whole area in a dull orange glow that, after a few seconds, turned yellow. Kenny knelt beside the vicar to feel for his pulse, as he had seen doctors and nurses do in a hundred films, then dropped the limp arm quickly. There were no fingers on the hand he was holding – they must have been blown off in the blast. He got up, looked at the whale, shook his head and splashed through the remaining puddles of water and muck to peer down into the jagged-edged hole. Dan had gone down there with the two dolphins. Kenny reached up over the edge of the paving and picked up the torch Helga had dropped. He shone it into the hole. Dan was there with a dolphin either side of him.

'Where's the water gone?' he called down, his voice echoing in the empty tunnel.

'Bloody night-time. There's only a trickle coming through the sewer. We've made a right cock of this. My leg's stuck between these sodding dolphins.'

Kenny directed the beam at Dan's legs. The dolphins were jammed side by side in the narrow channel with Dan astride one of them and his right leg out of sight between the two black bodies. The dolphins were breathing loudly and flapping their tail flukes intermittently.

'Hang on down there,' he called into the hole. 'I'll get the hose connected. We must keep the dolphins' skins wet.'

'Never mind that,' Dan's voice came back. 'Find a way to get my bloody leg free. I can't move it.'

'I'm working on that.'

A hose came snaking down the hole with water running out of the end.

'I'll be gone for a couple of minutes.'

Kenny dressed quickly, pulling on his jeans over his wet bathing costume and fighting his way into a T-shirt that stuck to his damp skin. He went over to Helga, carrying her clothes. She was kneeling at the side of the pool, retching.

'Put these on,' he said, laying the bundle in a dry spot next to her, 'and wait here. I'll be back soon.' He put his hand on her shoulder. She was shaking but there were other things to be done than try and comfort her. 'Let me in when I knock three times.'

Super-Dolphin's brain was working fast. There was this film he had once seen . . .

Once in the street Kenny hurried towards the transformer that had been blown. He could see regular blue flashes flicking on the sides of buildings ahead – lights from a police car. He peeped round a corner and saw a group of men near the shattered metal box. A policeman was crouched down in front of the transformer and another, holding a notebook, was talking to three other men. The patrol car, parked just in front of Kenny, was unattended.

Super-Dolphin approached it from the side away from the group, opened the door and slid into the driving seat. Billy Tranter had told him that if a police car's blue light was on, the keys had to be in the ignition.

Billy Tranter, who had taught Kenny to drive in 'borrowed' cars, knew all sorts of things like that. How he would laugh if he knew that Useless Kenny was planning to nick a police car.

Whether Billy's information was right or not, the keys *were* still in the ignition.

Kenny crouched low, started the car and drove it slowly forward. The two policemen and the other men did not even look up until Kenny was nearly round the corner. 'Yes,' he shouted, spinning the wheel with his left hand and punching the air with his right, 'Yes. Yes. YES!'

Two streets away he stopped and turned off the blue light then drove up the hill towards the nearest posh residential area, stopped the car again and searched for the switch to operate the loud-hailer.

'Attention. Attention.' His voice echoed round the empty streets of the sleeping town. 'This is a police message. This is a police message.' He turned on the interior light and glanced at his new watch. 02:15.

'This is a police message. This is a police message. There has been a chemical spillage in the town drains. There is no danger, but all people . . .' – that didn't sound right – 'All householders are requested to flush their toilets and turn on all their taps at two-thirty precisely. Two-thirty precisely. That is the end of the police message.'

He drove to another street and repeated the message, then into the next, watching his rear mirror anxiously. He was afraid he might see the blue light of another police car behind him though Billy Tranter had always held that only one car patrolled Dormouth at night. Billy was not *always* right, he thought. It was less than six months since he had been sent down for two years.

Cyril Cartwright was sure he could hear young Kenny whatshisname's voice in his dream. He woke up and turned over in bed. The voice came again. It was just like that bloody fool Kenny's voice, asking everyone to flush their toilets at two-thirty. Let *them* if they wanted to, it was nothing to do with him. He turned over and tried, unsuccessfully, to sleep.

At 2:27 Kenny drove the car, with all its lights off, down the street past the pool and the old church, and backed it into a loading bay between two of the empty warehouses. He took out a handkerchief and rubbed his fingerprints off the steering wheel, the gear knob, the light switch, the switch for the loud hailer and the door handles, exactly as Billy Tranter would have done. He contemplated throwing the keys into the harbour, decided against it, wiped them clean and left them in the ignition before running back to the pool, his trainers squelching water as he ran.

# CHAPTER TWENTY-EIGHT

Hywel and Mary leant over the parapet of the tower trying to make out what was happening below them. The small explosion that had woken them and put out the streetlights had been followed by human activity around the pool. Indecipherable voices drifted up to them on the still air.

'Should we call the police?' Mary whispered. 'Whatever is going on down there can't be right.'

'If we do, it's the end of me living in the church *and* any chance of recording the dolphins again. Stay quiet and see what happens.'

Shortly afterwards the moon went behind a cloud and a torch flashed down near the diving boards. Hywel picked up the blanket to put around Mary's shoulder as the dolphins started to leap, their dark bodies sinuous in the torchlight.

They leapt at regular intervals for a few minutes until another explosion, nearer and much louder than the last, shook the tower and a bell beneath their feet clanged once. This was followed by the crash and tinkle of glass falling onto stone.

A deep sucking, gurgling sound reached them.

'What the hell is going on?' Hywel whispered, holding Mary tightly against him.

The torch beam flashed around the darkness below, then the street lights flickered on and they could see a dead whale hanging head downwards in an empty pool, on the far side of which a dark hole gaped like an open mouth. What appeared to be a man's body lay sprawled beside the whale's head. Someone else was now shining the torch into the hole.

'What should we do?' Mary whispered.

'Nothing, just watch. There's nothing we can do and we might see something important from here.'

Two figures moved about the pool area. Then a man slipped out through the side door and hurried up the road to where the lights of a police car flicked blue on the sides of buildings.

'Someone's gone for the police,' said Hywel. *'They'll* be here soon.'

A minute or two later the blue light moved away in the opposite direction, then went out.

'Curious,' said Hywel. 'Curiouser and curiouser.'

In the distance, they could hear a public address system giving out an unintelligible message, repeated again and again.

Helga went inside and got dressed, taking her time, glad of the warm clothing over her bikini. Her fingers fumbled with the buttons but the mere act of dressing gave her an illusion of normality and she wanted to make it last. Outside was chaos and she didn't want to have to be part of it. Kenny had gone away without saying where. Dan had disappeared down the hole with the dolphins. In the empty pool were a dead grindhval and a dead man and she, Helga Jacobsen from Eysthavn in Faroyar, was here in a dark room on her own. She walked about irresolutely, wasting time. She fumbled for her suitcase, picked it up and put it down. Then she picked it up again.

She would leave. She would go to the station and get the train for Aberdeen and then the ferry home. She would never leave Eysthavn again. England had not been what she had expected at all. She stepped outside, carrying her suitcase and the accordion in its box. The half-carved dolphins she would leave behind for Kenny.

Kenny! She stopped. Kenny had told her to open the door for him when he came back and knocked three times. She had to be there to do that. No, she didn't. She could just leave the gate unlocked for him to come in.

She took another step towards the side door and heard a flapping noise from the round hole in the paving slabs at the side of the pool. At least one of the hvals must be down there, and not on its way to the sea. The torch was lying on the slabs near her feet. She put down her luggage, picked up the torch and shone it down the hole. Dan was there, his black woollen hat looking like a baby's. He did not look like a bad-man in a film now. His arm was up, shielding his eyes from the sudden light.

'Kenny?' he asked.

'No, it is I, Helga. What are you doing?'

'My sodding leg's stuck between the dolphins. None of us can move. Where's Kenny?'

'I do not know. He went out to the road. Can you not get your leg out of the black rubber?'

'That's hard enough when there are no bloody dolphins squashing it to hell.'

'Ken-ney is coming back. He said to open the door when he knocked.'

'Thank God for that,' Dan called up. 'If you two can fix the pulleys and get a rope around me maybe you can haul me out.'

Helga looked down into the hole again. The dolphins were distressed, flapping their tails, the sounds echoing back up the empty tunnel. Each time they moved their bodies, Dan winced.

Dan, the big man who she had rather feared, was looking up at her like a little boy wanting to be picked up and cuddled.

'I go and see if I can undo the pulleys and bring them to here for when Ken-ney comes back. Wait there for me,' she said, realising as she said it that it was a stupid remark.

'No bloody choice, have I?' Dan's voice came up out of the hole.

Helga climbed up the frame of the diving board and tried to undo the knots holding up one set of pulleys above where the grindhval's head lay. The knots were tight around the framing and she struggled for several minutes. She thought of cutting the ropes with her knife but decided to wait until Kenny came back. Dan was calling from down the hole, his voice faint and echoey.

'Helga. Helga, what's going on?'

Helga climbed down and went across to the hole. 'Ken-ney has not come back and the ropes are tied tight.'

'Can you come down here with a stick – a brush handle or something. We might be able to get my leg free that way?'

Helga fetched the stiff-bristled broom, laid it next to the edge of the round opening in the slabs, dropped the torch to Dan and started to climb down, feeling with her toes for the metal steps. Dan reached up and guided her feet onto each projecting metal loop.

His firm hand on her heels gave her an unexpected confidence and she turned and smiled down at the face below, lit by the torchlight reflected from the glistening tunnel walls. One of the dolphins started to flap its tail wildly. There was a rumble in the distance like thunder in the hills.

'Get out,' Dan shouted, pushing her foot upwards. 'Get out of here. Now.'

Dan shoved at Helga's foot as air rushed towards him like that ahead of a train in a tube-station, then he was hit by a wall of water, which lifted the dolphins and freed his leg. He took as big a breath as he could and pinched his nose with his right hand before the water overwhelmed him.

*FairIsle lay in the brick-lined tunnel, her body pressed tightly against Rockall's, with the Orca-man's leg between them. It was hurting her side but she could not move to free it. The Orca-man had been calling to the She-salmon and now she was coming down into the filth-channel to join them. What was the She-salmon going to do to get them all out?*

*FairIsle became aware of a vibration in the stones beneath her belly. It was like a wave-rush on a stony beach and seemed to be getting closer.*

*Air rushed past her head like storm-wind through a cleft rock and she instinctively filled her lungs as though preparing for a deep dive. She felt*

*Rockall doing the same as the water-wall engulfed them and lifted her body.*

*The Orca-man was free and was swept over her back as the wave carried her forward and pushed them all down the dark tunnel. She drove hard to get in front of Rockall and her head came up against the curled-up body of the man bumping along in front of her. She scanned around and beyond him. The tunnel was narrowing and becoming round and the echoes told her that the stone was ending and the round tunnel ahead was made of corroded shipstone. She sensed the human enter this tube and she knew from the echoes that the tube was not big enough for her body to pass through without damaging her back fin. She could do nothing about that but pulled her underfins in tight to her belly and braced herself for the contact with the rough metal. Rockall's head was overlapping her tail-flukes, restricting her movement and she tried to swim faster, the rasping pain from her back fin excruciating.*

*The human ahead of her was fighting to hold his breath – she could sense the intensity of his mental waves as he tried not to let it go.*

*The rush of water was slowing, held back by the seawater that filled the pipe ahead. FairIsle ignored the pain from her fin and drove forward again, manoeuvring her snout between the human's legs and pushing him onwards, Rockall still close behind.*

*The human's body went limp as she felt the tearing, grinding pain on her back ease. She got her head under the body and swam to the surface.*

*The air felt sweet in her lungs as her back curved out of the water and she drew in a deep breath of freedom.*

Dan floated face up, buoyed by the air trapped in the cells of his wet suit. He could remember the darkness as he was tossed along the tunnel and putting his free hand up to protect his head as he hunched his body into a ball. The dolphins had been behind him and he had a vague memory of rough surfaces tearing at the skin on his hand and at the neoprene covering his back and knees. Then his right arm had caught on something, been twisted round behind his back and, as his breath had given out and he had gulped water, he had felt a push against his backside but after that, nothing until now.

A dolphin blew loudly beside him, then another. Dan felt immensely tired and there was a burning pain in his right shoulder. He lay there coughing, trying to clear the water from his lungs.

Only his face and chest were above the surface and he was aware of the lights of the town moving away from him and knew a current was taking him out to sea. He kicked his legs, wishing he was wearing the fins, but his kicking was feeble, his right leg was numb, all his energy gone in the battering he had taken in the outfall tube.

A smooth body rose below his left side and another below his right, cradling his body as he floated between them. Dan lay still, seeing the stars bright above him, then reached out his left arm and rested it across one dolphin's back as they steered him gently towards the shore.

Kenny knocked three times on the door and Helga opened it.

'Dan has gone down the tunnel with the dolphin-hvals,' she said breathlessly. 'The vicar-man is dead and so too is the white grindhval.'

Kenny shut the door behind him, went over and looked down the hole. 'Where's the torch?' he asked.

'It went with the rushing water,' Helga told him.

Kenny called into the hole. 'Dan. Dan. Can you hear me?'

The only sound was the trickle of water from the channel below. He turned to Helga.

'Dan might be OK if he gets out of the end of the pipe. Do you know where the blow-up boat is?'

'Dan ties it to the wall in the Inner Harbour,' Helga said. 'But it will be locked with the big lock. I have watched when he did not know and he *always* locks it.'

'Try his trousers pocket for the key – he was wearing the wet suit, remember. Can you drive the boat? It's not hard. I watched Dan doing it.'

'Ken-ney! I have lived with boats all my life. We will go and find him.'

'What about all of *this*? We can't leave dead bodies all over the place.'

Kenny recalled the look on Billy Tranter's face when he was sent down – and that was for only two years. Any thoughts of sharing a cell with Billy vanished. Explosives and dead bodies must be worth at least ten years, even if one of the bodies was a whale and not a human.

Helga was talking to him.

'I will go myself and look for Dan. One person will be as good as two in the boat. You stay and do whatever you can here. If I find him I will take him to his trawler boat. If not, I will come back here and we will decide then what to do. So – you understand? – if I am not back in one hour – two hours – no, one hour only – you must be sneaking away from here and go to the trawler boat. Now find for me the keys.'

When she had gone Kenny locked the side door and leant against the wall. What would Super-Dolphin do now?

On the tower Mary moved to get a better view.

'Don't show yourself,' Hywel whispered. 'What we're seeing may be needed as evidence.'

After a minute or so the man below them moved away from the side door and went through the door marked CAFE. Shortly afterwards he came out carrying a bundle of what looked like clothes and a dark block that might have been anything. From outside the door he picked up a suitcase and an oddly shaped box with a handle on one end and carried them around the poolside. He put them down in a heap by the side door, then went and slid a heavy lid back into a round hole in the paving.

Finally he dropped into the empty pool and dragged the man's body to the shallow end. Here he tried unsuccessfully to lift it up and onto the paving. He failed with each attempt until, having dragged it by the feet to the deep end again, he struggled to untie the remaining rope from the net in which the dead creature's tail hung.

The tail flopped down into the pool and he stepped over it, pulled the rope down and looped it under and around the dead man's body.

Hywel and Mary watched as he climbed out and pulled on another rope. The body rose slowly, to hang above the level of the paving. The man reached out and pulled it towards himself, paying out the rope as he did so.

'Reduction pulleys,' said Hywel, 'Clever stuff.'

'Dear God,' said Mary, horror in her voice. 'I'm sure that's the vicar they've killed. *He's* got white hair and wears a jacket like that. Can you see if it's got elbow patches?'

Neither could be sure but Mary was convinced that it was the old man who had inadvertently taken the tape that morning. They saw his body being dragged to the side door of the pool and watched the other man try all the doors of the car in the road outside. None would open so he smashed a window with what looked like a brick before opening the front and then the back door on the driver's side.

'We ought to go down and stop him,' said Hywel but Mary, recalling the blow on her head that had put her in hospital, held his arm.

'You said to watch from here and see what happens.'

The man by the car glanced up and down the street then dragged the body through the side door and by lifting, pushing and shoving, bundled it onto the rear seat of the car. He went back for the other things and one by one these followed the body into the car.

The man shut the pool door, got into the driver's seat, got out again, picked something up from the gutter, got in and closed the car door. Shortly afterwards the engine started, ran for a few seconds then stopped again. The engine started again and the car drove away towards the road to Portland.

After Kenny had cleared up as best he could at the pool, he had humped and shoved the skinny body onto the back seat, finding it easier to move it by gripping the old man's clothes than by pulling the floppy arms. The body was little more than a bag of loose bones but seemed to have a will of its own and was resisting awkwardly.

When the body was in the car Kenny threw Dan's and Helga's gear onto the front passenger seat. The half-carved dolphins followed more carefully before he got in himself, shut the door and searched around for something like a screwdriver – it would be too much to expect to find keys in the ignition switch twice in one night.

There was no screwdriver. The dash-pocket contained a mass of polo-mint wrappers and a small tattered prayer book but nothing to push into the key-slot. He opened the door to get under the bonnet for the push-button, saw an ice-lolly stick in the gutter, split it in half lengthways and tried that in the ignition lock. It turned easily. Good old Billy Tranter – he'd taught him well. Kenny pulled the starter knob and the engine coughed twice. He pulled out the choke and tried again. The engine had not been run for days but eventually it fired and settled to a uniform rattle.

Had it been an hour since Helga had left? He wound down the window, twisted round and held his left arm out into the light from the street lamps. It was more than an hour so, hopefully, Dan was OK.

Kenny gave a quick look over his shoulder, found first gear and headed for the Portland Road.

At the top of the hill he circled the roundabout and came back the way he had come, just in case anyone was following him. There were very few other vehicles about but he took a circuitous route. Billy Tranter used to say, 'Never underestimate the pigs.'

Hywel pressed the backlight button on his watch. It was a little over an hour since the woman had left and there was no point in watching any more.

'What now?' he asked.

'I've been thinking,' Mary said. 'If the tape *was* in that jacket pocket, we must get it back. It's the only one in the world.'

'You're right,' Hywel said, snatching the blanket from Mary's shoulders and throwing it onto the flattened hay. 'Come on.'

They felt their way down the now familiar stairs in the darkness. In the moonlight coming in through the gaping windows on the pool side of the nave Hywel could see that the aisle was littered with pieces of glass from the shattered windows. Not knowing why, he picked up a piece the size and shape of a banana. The edges were slightly rounded, not sharp at all and he slipped it into his pocket as he followed Mary towards the door. More glass scrunched under their feet.

In the road they stood, looking in the direction taken by the car.

'What do we do now?' asked Hywel. 'Find a taxi and say, "Follow that car." I've always wanted to do that.'

Mary was walking towards where they had seen Kenny park the police car. She looked in through the open window. The keys were still in the ignition switch. Hywel was close behind her.

'We're going to have to take this car,' she announced firmly.

'Am I hearing right?' Hywel asked. '*You're* going to steal a police car?'

'Not me – you. Anyway it's not stealing. God left it here for us.'

'It didn't look like God to me. It was the guy who feeds the dolphins.'

'Shut up and get in.' Mary went round to the passenger side.

'I can't drive, me – never learned,' said Hywel lamely.

'Come *this* side then.' Mary flounced crossly round the front of the car. 'Let's get away from here before the police work out what's happening. We *must* get that tape back. The dolphins have gone. We won't be able to make another.' She started the car. 'Will the tape be all right? It's probably wet through.' She was easing the car out of the loading bay.

'If we can dry it out soon enough. Mind that bollard!'

Mary turned the car into the street and fumbled for the switch to put on the headlights.

'Watch out and see if you can spot the vicar's car,' she said.

'It could be anywhere, where do we start?'

'It went off towards the Portland road. I'll drive along there to the Chesil Beach car park – if we haven't seen it by then we'll come back, checking out the side roads. It won't be long before the police are searching for *this* car – if they're not already. We'd best do the main road first.'

'God, you sound like you do this sort of thing every day,' Hywel said. 'You're a dark horse, Mary O'Connor. I've always thought of you as . . .'

'Shut up and watch out for that car.'

# CHAPTER TWENTY-NINE

Helga steered the Zodiac through the outer harbour and into the open sea, going as fast as she dare without drawing undue attention to herself and the boat. What a bucket of guts this whole affair had turned out to be. The drunken priest-man was dead, so was the white grindhval. Dan was either floating about somewhere in the vast darkness of the sea ahead or, more likely, drowned in the sewer somewhere below her, with two dead dolphin-hvals for company.

All she could do now was search for him as best she could. The moon was bright again and this would help.

She had no idea where the sewer pipe would end. It would have to be far enough out to where the currents would sweep the sewage out to sea and not back to pollute the beaches. She opened the throttle and headed away from the harbour-mouth, then slowed again in case she drove over Dan or ran into any flotsam in the dim light.

A familiar whoosh of expired air sounded alongside and FairIsle's fin showed to starboard, then moved ahead and to the right. Helga turned to follow it. After a few hundred metres the fin disappeared. Helga cut the motor.

'Hello. Mayday, Mayday.' Dan's voice was calling from somewhere ahead.

Helga called back, 'Hello, hello. Where are you?'

Dan's voice came out of the darkness. 'Helga? Is that you? I'm here with the dolphins.'

Helga, standing in the boat, saw a raised arm in the moonlight, restarted the engine and steered towards it.

Soon she could see Dan himself, still wearing the black woollen hat, lying between two tattered dorsal fins. The dolphins sank out of the way as she gripped the neck of the wet suit and dragged his heavy body over the pontoon and into the boat. Here he lay on his left side, coughing weakly. The knees and elbows of his wet suit were torn to shreds, there were jagged tears in the black material down the length of his back and his left hand was covered in blood.

'I am taking you to the hospital,' she said.

Dan suppressed the coughing. 'I'm all right. Just take me back to *The Warrior* – the trawler boat – that way.' He waved his left arm towards the entrance to Portland Harbour.

Helga started the motor and headed the inflatable in the direction he had indicated. The cloud had gone and the moon was shining brightly. She could see the bulk of Portland to the south and just make out a gap in the dark ramparts of the breakwater.

*'Grateful creatures, humans,' said Rockall sharply.*

*'It is us who should be grateful to them,' replied FairIsle. 'The Orca-man nearly drowned when he came with us down that filth-tube.'*

*'What do we do now?' Rockall asked. 'My back-fin hurts like a shark-bite.'*

*'Mine too, but they will heal if we stay in clean water. We must swim well clear of the end of that tube.'*

*'Listen . . .'*

*Faint dolphin calls came through the water. FairIsle whistled her signature, followed by Rockall making his.*

*Two whistles came back.*

*'Those are my parents' calls,' Rockall said, disbelief in his tone, 'Grace of Lundy and Elegance of Malin.'*

*He whistled again.*

*'Elegance of Rockall, is it you? Are you free at last?'*

*Two black bodies materialised out of the darkness and swam either side of Rockall, caressing his flanks. FairIsle dropped back until Rockall called her to join them.*

*'This is my friend, Grace of FairIsle, we are newly-joyned and, FairIsle, these are my parents.'*

*'How are your Seas?' FairIsle asked politely.*

*'Calm enough. And in your swim?'*

*'You don't have to go through all that,' Rockall interrupted. 'These are my family.' He turned to Malin. 'How did you know we were here?'*

*'When you were netted last year we followed the boat to this place of humans, so we knew you were alive. We could taste you in the water. At one time we could only taste you once in seven days. More recently it has been every day but then it stopped. We hoped it might mean you would soon be free. We feared the other meaning.'*

*'You tasted the filth every day to see if I was there?'*

*Elegance of Malin signalled the small 'yes' in the darkness, then asked, 'How did you escape?'*

*Rockall described the events of the last evening and night, FairIsle helping out where she could.*

'Where is the Orca-man, now?' Grace of Lundy asked.

'We helped him until he went with the She-salmon in the soft-skinned boat,' Rockall replied.

'Was he badly hurt?'

'I think not, but we did not scan him for broken bones.'

'We must follow and be sure. It will soon be dawn.'

The dolphins turned and followed the boat trail, reading the tiny signs in the water – the persistent bubbles, the tinge of petrol, the traces of exhaust emissions and the many unseen things that dolphins and experienced mariners can read but other humans are blind to.

Kenny, driving the Morris Minor, passed the Ferrybridge pub as the sky started to lighten in the east and he could see the shape of a trawler moored upstream, facing the ebbing tide. He turned into the car park on the far side of the bridge and got out, the light now strong enough for him to see that the inflatable boat was moored alongside the trawler.

Helga *must* have got back, he told himself, having found Dan and taken him with her. Otherwise she wouldn't have known where to come. Thank God for that. Dan would know what to do now.

He stood by the car and called to the boat, 'Ahoy. Ahoy there,' but his voice seemed feeble at that distance and there was no response from the trawler.

Between the car park and the channel where the boat was anchored, was a wide expanse of damp sand. He got back into the Morris and drove it carefully down a ramp onto the flat, wet ground. The surface felt firm under the wheels and he drove cautiously towards the boat, then into the shallows, moving slowly forward until the water was above the wheels and the engine choked, coughed and stopped.

Kenny reached behind him for the carving, got out and waded towards the boat, aware of the cold wetness around his legs. He stopped, thinking he should not leave the body in the car in case the police came, and returned to drag it out into the shallow water. It floated face down and, with one hand he pulled it by the collar of the jacket towards the trawler – the body following easily in the knee-deep water. His other hand gripped the carving through a hole that Helga had cut between the two half-formed dolphins.

Suddenly, he stepped over the hidden edge of the tide-scoured channel and found himself struggling out of his depth, being drawn by the current at a frightening speed towards the wide arch of the concrete bridge.

He let go of the jacket collar but clung onto the carving which floated and gave him a little buoyancy. The dead man's body twisted and rolled in the dark water by his side.

Weighed down by his waterlogged clothes, frightened and clinging onto the life-saving carving, Kenny saw the black fins approaching and relaxed. He could once again be Useless Kenny with no need to think for himself. Mummy D and Daddy D were coming for him as they had so often done in his childhood dreams. They were coming to take him to live with them and with his dolphin brother and sister, Flipper and Flapper. He let go of the carving and sank, only to be lifted to the surface by a familiar-feeling smooth black nose. The dream vanished in a fit of coughing, the water salty and bitter in his mouth.

FairIsle slipped her head under one of his arms and Rockall nosed in under the other. Kenny floated between them, an arm over each of their backs near to their ragged dorsal fins. The dolphins carried him up-current, through the rush of water under the arch and manoeuvred to where he could climb into the Zodiac moored alongside the trawler. He turned and petted the nose of each dolphin in turn as two more swam slowly towards him, one with the dead man's body draped sideways across its back between its blowhole and its dorsal fin. The other held Helga's carving in its mouth.

Kenny reached out and took the carving, then thumped on the side of the trawler with his foot until Helga came on deck and looked over the side.

'Ken-ney! How in the name of Thor did you get there?' she asked and without waiting for an answer, jumped down into the Zodiac beside him.

'Grab the body,' Kenny spluttered, 'or it'll float away.'

Helga reached out and gripped the sodden jacket of the dead man. The dolphins sank from sight.

*'Is that the Sprat of which you spoke?' Malin asked Rockall.*

*'FairIsle says he is more of a Mackerel now,' he replied.*

*'He swims less well than either. It would seem the Orca-man must now be safely on the boat. Does that complete your obligations?'*

*'I have one more before I can swim free,' said FairIsle. 'A big one. It will be Rockall's choice if he honours the obligation with me.'*

*'That is . . .?' asked Grace of Lundy, anxiously.*

*'We . . . I promised a starwhale that I would tell her kind in the Northern Waters of her death. It is of great importance to them.'*

*'I will swim with you,' said Elegance of Rockall.*

*'May we?' asked Lundy.*

'We would be honoured,' replied Grace of FairIsle. 'But first I must find some live fish. I have dreamed of this moment for a whole moon or more.'

'It will be a waste of time,' said Rockall.

'Catching fish?' asked FairIsle. 'Try and stop me.'

'No. The wasted time will be in swimming north. Nordstar died alone. The She-salmon with the white hair still lives – we have seen her in the soft-skinned boat. The prophecy demanded a human sacrifice as well. She was to be the white-headed human who was to die with the white stargazer.'

FairIsle explained Nordstar's version of the ancient legend, sad that her friend the starwhale had died in vain.

'The human male whose body we took to the boat had white hair on his head,' Lundy said. 'It may be that he was the human who had to die rather than your friend.'

'In that case we should have left him in the sea to be eaten by the crabs.' Rockall swirled away and raced into the current. At least he was free.

'Good God – it's Kenny!' said Dan, as Helga helped him down the steps into the galley.

'Hi,' said Kenny as he stood by the table, water dripping from his clothes. 'Are *you* OK?'

'Not too bad, thanks.'

'There's a body in the rubber boat – the vicar-man,' Kenny said. 'And your clothes and Helga's gear are in the car. We'll need to get the body and all of those on board before the police find them.'

'Where's the car?'

'Up to its axles in water over by the car park.'

Dan groaned. If he was going to get out of this one he needed Plans A, B, and C. He didn't feel up to anything.

'I'm knackered,' he said, 'I can hardly stand. And my shoulder's out.'

Helga looked at Kenny, now drooping and shivering. His teeth started to chatter, loud in the tiny galley.

'We cannot be stopping and giving up now,' she said.

Super-Dolphin would never give up, Kenny thought. 'What do you want me to do?' he asked, the question directed at both Helga and Dan.

It was Helga who spoke first. 'Come with me,' she said.

Kenny followed her on deck and down into the Zodiac. There was enough light now to see the vicar's body was still there, lying face down in the scuppers, water draining from his clothes.

'We'll have to get him aboard but we must clear the other things from the car first.' Helga started the engine then cast off. The boat drifted backwards away from the trawler, then surged forward as she opened the throttle and turned in a wide circle towards the car, now left almost high and dry by the receding tide.

The inflatable ran aground on the edge of the deep-water channel and Helga and Kenny got out. One on either side, they lifted the bow onto firm ground before running to where the car stood, water dripping from underneath the chassis. Sea birds, poking at the newly exposed sandflats rose, complaining noisily, then settled again behind them.

Watching the road and hoping they were unobserved so early in the morning, Helga grabbed her suitcase and the accordion box and Kenny took the bundle of Dan's clothes and they ran back through the clouds of screaming gulls to the Zodiac.

'What about the car?' Helga asked.

'We'll have to leave that. The engine's flooded. We'll never start it now.'

As Helga brought the Zodiac alongside *The Warrior*, holding the bow into the current, Kenny climbed aboard and tied the mooring rope forward so that the inflatable lay below the net-hoist. Helga cut the engine and passed up the bundle of clothes and her own things. 'We must get this . . . this . . . man aboard. Do you know how to work the hoist?' she called up.

'Sorry, no idea.'

'Come down into the blow-up boat and I will see if it is like the ones at home.' They passed each other as she came up over the gunwale.

'The big winch needs the boat's engines to be running but there is a little pulley and a hand winch too – I will use that.'

Kenny reached up and took the line that Helga lowered to him, made a loop round the body under the armpits, then tried not to look at the pallid face as Helga winched the body up and over the gunwale of *The Warrior*.

Two cars passed over the road bridge during the critical time the body was visible, but neither slowed down. Kenny climbed aboard again, his joints aching and the shivering starting again. Helga was laying out the body on the deck and covering it with a tarpaulin that she had found folded and secured to the base of the hoist.

'I have seen too many drownded men on boats,' she said straightening up. 'Now, as all is the ship shape so we will go below and see to Dan's shoulder.'

Dan was slumped across the galley table. He raised his head slowly. 'I can't get out of this damned suit.'

226

Helga found a pair of scissors in the cutlery drawer and cut up each of the arms and legs and across the chest. The rubber suit came away in black pieces.

'I have made a better job of skinning a seal,' Helga said and Dan smiled weakly. His right arm hung awkwardly. He fingered it carefully with his left hand.

'This is going to hurt me more than it's going to hurt you,' Dan said. 'But it's got to be done. Kenny-boy, make a roll out of the wet-suit material – about as big as a rugby ball – then push it up under my arm. If I shout take no notice. Then you've both got to pull my arm outwards and downwards. Like I said – if I shout – take no notice.'

Dan did shout but not as much as Kenny expected.

Afterwards Helga gently rubbed Dan's other arm, his legs and the rest of his body with a towel. The last time she had bathed someone else's body it had been the yellowy, wasted skin that hung in loose folds on her sick mother. This skin was a healthy brown where the sun and wind had tanned it and a clean white otherwise. The muscles beneath the skin were firm and taut and they excited her in an almost forgotten way.

When Dan was dry she bandaged his hand and put a plaster from the ship's first aid box across a cut on his left eyebrow. His breathing had almost returned to normal when she had finished.

'We need a cup of tea after all that, while we decide what to do next,' he said as he struggled to dress himself. 'The sooner we get away from here the better. Something nasty is going to hit the fan in the next couple of hours.'

'Which fan is that?' asked a bemused Helga as she looked around the galley.

Mary and Hywel had driven the police car as far as the Chesil Beach car park. They arrived just as the dolphins were delivering a bedraggled Kenny to the trawler. The Morris was standing up to its axles in the sea. From the police car they saw Kenny scramble into the Zodiac. They were sure he had not even looked in their direction.

'Get out and watch,' Mary told Hywel. 'I'll hide this.'

She circled in the car park, turned back onto the road, drove over the bridge again and up through the sprawling village of Wyke Regis, looking for somewhere to leave the car where she would not be seen getting out of it. Even the back streets seemed to have a milkman or a jogger in each and she was near the disused and boarded up Coastguard Station before she found a narrow track leading towards the sea. Here, between the high, bramble-covered hedges she abandoned the vehicle and walked back up the lane, impatient to rejoin Hywel.

She stopped. She was a mile or more from where she had left him and felt that, as a lone woman at this time of day, she would stand out and be noticed by any early risers, especially if she ran. Her guilty conscience made her feel doubly noticeable, though a jogger passing the end of the lane waved in a friendly way as he passed.

A jogger. Apart from milkmen and postmen they were the only people not to be noticed so early. She walked back a few yards down the lane, slipped off her skirt and pulled at the hem of her T shirt so that it hung below her pants. Joggers often ran like that. She was already wearing white trainers – that would help her disguise.

Rolling her skirt into as tight a ball as she could, she held it in her left hand, bent her elbows into the jogging position and ran out of the lane and down the road past the sunlit houses. The morning air felt fresh and cool on her bare legs but her conscience was making silly noises in her head about running nearly naked through the streets. 'Shut up,' she told it severely, 'this is all in a good cause,' and ran on.

She crossed the bridge and ran down onto the car park. Hywel was there, crouched behind a dustbin and she walked across to him, breathing fast. He stood up stiffly, stared at her legs and smiled.

'I was beginning to wonder where you'd got to. You look good.'

Mary grimaced at him, unrolled her skirt, shook it out and stepped into it.

'What's happened while I was away?' she asked.

'After the dolphin-man climbed into the rubber dinghy and you went off, another dolphin swam up with a body across its back. The blond woman from the pool came on deck and helped the dolphin-man get the body into the dinghy. Then they left it there and climbed up into the big boat. After a bit, the dolphin-man and the blonde came ashore and took some bags and things from the car. Then they hoisted the body aboard with a sort of crane on the big boat. They've just gone down inside the big boat again.'

Mary was no longer listening. She *had* to get the precious tape back or she would never be able to take the dolphin's song to the world of people. That mattered more than anything.

'What now then?' Hywel asked.

'The tape should still be in the vicar's pocket. You said it must be washed and dried soon or it wouldn't be any use. We must find a way to get it back.'

Cars carrying fishermen were coming down off the road and parking near the Information Centre behind them. A man in overalls was unlocking the buildings, whistling and rattling keys. Hungry gulls sat on the top of the roof eyeing each human hopefully.

'We'd be less conspicuous if we were up on the road,' Mary said. 'Those people on the boat don't know us from Adam – we could just be a couple out for a morning walk.' She took Hywel's arm as they walked along the pavement.

As the sun rose higher there was more activity around the Ferrybridge pub and along the foreshore. A man was unlocking the gate of a wire enclosure with a sign 'Oyster Farm', and workers were arriving at a boat-works for the day shift. Three men, wearing rubber boots, dug apparently at random in the wet sand, dropping the lugworms they found into tins. Hywel and Mary sat side by side between two dinghies hauled up on a concrete ramp, watching the trawler as it swung round to face the now rising tide, and discussed ways to get aboard.

Mary looked at her watch. 'I should be at work,' she said standing up suddenly. 'I'd forgotten all about it.'

'Keep on forgetting all about it then,' Hywel said. 'They can manage without you for one morning. They'd have to if you were ill.'

'But it's not right – not to let them know.'

'What do you want to do? Phone in and say, 'I can't come to work today – somebody blew up a swimming pool, a vicar and a whale have been killed and your waiter and I are trying to recover a tape-recording of singing dolphins. Oh and by the way I stole a police car last night . . . Better if we let them believe we've run away together. I'm overdue as well but they aren't expecting me. I . . .'

'But all that's true!'

'Maybe so, but it won't get the tape back. That's what you want, isn't it? I do.'

'Yes,' said Mary and sat down again, staring glumly at the boat.

Hywel was holding a piece of orange-coloured glass in his hand. He held it up towards the sun.

'That's from the church,' she said accusingly. 'Why did you take that?'

'God knows,' said Hywel. 'All sorts of odd things happened last night. I don't know if I'm coming or going. What the hell have we let ourselves in for?'

# CHAPTER THIRTY

Cyril Cartwright came out of his house with the In and Out drive and got into his Rolls Royce to go down to the pool. Something odd had been going on in the night. The more he thought about it the more he was sure that the voice on the loud-hailer had been young Kenny's. Even so he had eventually got out of bed and looked into his wife's bedroom. She was asleep. She could sleep through anything except his snoring, as she was fond of telling her friends.

At two-thirty he *had* gone round the house and flushed all three of the toilets and turned on all the taps as the voice had requested.

Once outside the pool he knew something was wrong. There were no sounds at all from over the wall, not even the welcoming tail-slap that he had come to expect.

To his annoyance the side door was unlocked and it opened to show a scene of utter devastation. The white whale, wrapped in a net and clearly dead, lay on the bottom below the diving-board platform and, opposite to where he was standing, a huge hole gaped blackly in the wall of an empty pool.

Shaken, Mr Cartwright closed the door behind him and walked gingerly round the cracked paving. Something caught the sunlight close under the dead whale's head and he went carefully down the steps into the empty pool, taking care not to snag the trousers of his summer suit on any rough edges. He picked his way between the patches of slippery brown slime drying into thin cakes in the morning sunshine.

He bent down, felt cautiously under the whale's head and pulled out a leather covered hip flask that was lying in a shallow pool of water, dried it with his handkerchief and noted the hallmark on the silver neck.

Mr Cartwright unscrewed the lid and sniffed. Whoever had lost this knew what was good for him, he thought as he climbed back up the steps and carried it out to his car. He used his mobile phone and dialled 192 for Directory Enquiries.

'Insure-all? . . . Cartwright here, Dormouth . . . I need to make a claim . . . Yes . . . Explosion, probably methane gas . . . Three very valuable dolphins dead . . . Yes . . . Highly trained performing animals . . . Had a buyer for them too, from France. No . . . have to be taken away at once, the council is insistent . . . Public health hazard . . . You'll send the forms? You've got my address haven't you? Thank you.'

Mr Cartwright then rang the Dorchester Hunt.

'Will your dogs—, All right – will your *hounds* eat whale-meat? Eat anything . . . Good . . . must be collected today though . . . send a lorry . . . Good man. Here's the address . . .'

*The dolphins played in the tide-race at the tip of Portland, the two younger ones enjoying the fun and excitement of the churning waters and the taste of fresh fish in their mouths once more, though unable to fully abandon themselves to the sea. Knowledge of Nordstar's possibly wasted sacrifice and the pain in their dorsal fins restrained them. They knew their fins would soon heal although the tips would forever bear the scars of their escape.*

*'Do you still plan for us to leave for the Faroff Islands?' Grace of Lundy asked FairIsle.*

*'The She-salmon has the longing for home waters upon her. She is now on the Orca-man's boat. Soon she will make the boat take her there. I thought we would travel with them even though the news we have for the stargazers may not be the good news that Nordstar wished us to take.'*

Dan was trying to ignore the pain in his shoulder and concentrate on the job in hand. It was unlikely that anyone would make a connection between the missing vicar and *The Warrior*, even though the old man's car was half-submerged only a short way off. Was there anything to connect *The Warrior* or himself to the explosions? Not unless his boat was searched. Best to be out of the way though, before anyone did get suspicious. At sea he could easily get rid of the body and that would be most of the evidence gone. The rest of the explosives could go over the side too, if it looked as if the boat was going to be boarded. *The Warrior* was fully provisioned for a voyage and the fuel and water tanks were full. Helga and Kenny would make an adequate crew for a short journey.

He looked at his watch. The tide would be flooding now and that would only leave them an hour or so whilst they could be sure of getting under the bridge.

Helga was rummaging in each of the galley lockers, the kitten following her around and peering into each cupboard with as much curiosity as herself. Kenny had changed out of his wet clothes and was asleep on one of the bunks in the port cabin wearing a pair of Dan's trousers and a blue jersey several sizes too large.

Helga stood up. 'There is a lot of food on board,' she said. 'I think we should be sailing away from here.'

'Just what I was thinking,' Dan looked at Helga with a new respect. 'We might go up channel to Poole – or down the coast to Dartmouth. Keep out of the way for a bit. See which way the wind is blowing.'

Helga did not understand the reference to the wind. The trawler surely had a diesel engine.

'*I* was thinking of going a little further,' she said. 'It would perhaps be best to stay away from land for a while.' She was holding the kitten and watching Dan's face.

'I am wanting to go home. I am suggesting that the Faeroe Islands are out of the way enough for you.'

'It's a hell of a way out of the way,' Dan replied. The idea certainly had an appeal though. 'What about Kenny-boy?'

'He has nowhere else to go. If I ask him to come, he will say, 'Yes'. But I think it is best for him to be sleeping now.'

'Can you make some sort of sling for this arm?' Dan asked. 'Then we can get under way for the Faeroe Islands.' That would have to be Plan A for now.

On deck Dan was pleased to see that the body of the dead vicar was covered by the tarpaulin. It was a detail *he* should have seen to. He started the trawler's engine and nosed forward to slacken the chain, steering with his left hand and leaning against the wheel when he had to alter the throttle setting. Helga, at the bow, undid the shackle-pin and pulled the chain through the ring on the top of the buoy, guiding the green, algae-covered links into the locker under the foredeck where the emergency anchor was kept. Dan turned *The Warrior* towards the bridge and Portland Harbour as soon as Helga indicated that all was clear.

A couple on the shore ran down the beach, splashing through the pools and dodging the mounds of wet sand left by the early morning bait-diggers. They stopped at the edge of the water and shouted to him as the boat passed. Dan was sure that he had not seen them before.

'We must come aboard,' the man shouted.

Dan ignored him.

'It's about the dolphins . . .'

Dan throttled down to listen. 'We know about the . . .' The man made upwards sweeping movements with his arms, clearly indicating an explosion but obviously not wanting to shout the word.

Dan opened the throttle a little to hold the trawler's position on the flood tide, the diesel engine throbbing steadily. He was thinking. If these people *did* know something, it would be better to have them aboard under his control than blabbing about what they might know ashore.

'Stand by, we'll pick you up,' he called.

232

Helga had followed his thoughts. She hauled on the line to draw the Zodiac up astern and dropped in, started the motor and steered across to where the couple stood, now barefoot and knee deep in the water.

Dan watched the two as they stepped into the Zodiac awkwardly, failing to read the movements of the boat. The girl nearly fell. 'Bloody landlubbers,' he thought.

It was equally obvious that they were not used to boats as they climbed aboard the trawler. When they were standing awkwardly on deck, Helga secured the inflatable astern and Dan opened the throttle. The tide was flowing fast and he had to get under the bridge while he still could.

'Take them below,' he ordered Helga. 'Give them a mug of something. I can't talk to them until we're clear of the harbour.'

Once under the bridge and through the narrow channel beyond, Dan set a course across the harbour, throttling back and cutting the engine before approaching the breakwater built over a century before by convict labour. Between the stone bastions on either side of the channel, waves were running in from the bay, losing their momentum in the calmer waters within. It was time to get the Zodiac aboard.

Kenny had come on deck and Dan called him to help, Kenny drawing the inflatable round to where it could be hoisted above deck height and swung inboard with the net hoist. The lad worked better than Dan had hoped, following his instructions eagerly though it was clear that he was not familiar with boats. When the Zodiac was stowed he joined Dan in the wheelhouse, watching as Dan restarted the engine and steered for the gap in the breakwater. Dan started to explain the controls but they had hardly passed though the gap before Kenny rushed out and hung over the rail looking green.

When they were safely clear, Dan set a more southerly course towards Portland Bill, barely conscious now of the pain in his shoulder and hand. He called Kenny back into the wheelhouse, 'Hold this wheel and steer well to the left of that cliff. I'm going below. Press that buzzer once if anything changes – anything.' Action and concentration were the best cure for seasickness.

Helga was coming up the companionway stairs.

'Those people in the galley will be believing we are kidnapping them, I think.' She backed down again. Dan followed, turning sideways to protect his shoulder in the narrow stairway.

In the galley Mary and Hywel sat together, empty mugs on the table in front of them. They were looking apprehensive and Dan could see they were holding hands under the table.

'You've got a body on board . . .' said Hywel, wishing as he said it, that he had started some other way.

233

'Possible,' said Dan, noncommittally. 'What if we have?'

'Look, see,' said Hywel. 'We think there may be a tape in the man's jacket pocket. It belongs to us.'

'What sort of tape?' Dan asked, his eyes narrowing.

'A cassette tape.' Mary flashed Dan a smile and he relaxed. This girl didn't seem to be a threat.

'Music?'

'Sort of – dolphins singing. We recorded it from the church next to the pool.'

Things began to click together in Dan's brain.

'And the man who fell in the pool had it in his pocket?'

'We think so . . . We hope so. It's irreplaceable.' Mary said. 'We *must* find it.'

'Helga. Will you . . .? And while you're up there, check that Kenny's OK.'

Helga came back down holding the tape cassette in its plastic box.

'I need to go back up,' she said. 'Kenny is about to be sick of the sea I think.' She gave the tape to Dan.

'Is this what you're looking for?' He held out the cassette towards Hywel who thanked Dan, took the proffered box eagerly, lifted out the cassette and shook it. Drops of water fell onto the tabletop. He inserted a pencil point behind the pink leader-strip in the opening, drawing out a loop of tape.

'It's sodden,' he said. 'Can I have a bowl of clean water please? This'll be sea water.'

Dan was intrigued to see that his passengers were apparently unconcerned, though surely not unaware, that they were being taken out to sea. Still, it suited him – they couldn't make trouble when they were on the boat, out of touch with the land.

'I'll send Helga – the blond woman – down. She'll get clean water for you. Don't touch anything until she comes.' He went on deck again and took over the wheel. The wind was from the south-east. Kenny was hanging onto the rail, retching.

Dan checked the compass bearing and looked to port to judge the distance from the West Shambles buoy. He could hear its bell clanging in the distance.

*FairIsle leapt and saw The Warrior approaching from the north.*

*'I think the Orca-man's boat is coming,' she said.*

*Lundy leapt too and said, 'It is likely to be his. I have not heard its signature before but, since the big fishing boats started coming from the far south, we see fewer and fewer small ones like this.'*

*They swam alongside and looked up.*

*'This is the one. Look, the Mackerel is feeding his kind,' said Rockall, veering away and then swinging back to ride the bow-wave.*

Kenny feebly pointed out the dolphins to Dan then asked if he could go below and lie down.

'Helga'll sort out a regular bunk for you. Ask her for some water.'

Kenny staggered off. Dan called after him, 'The first four days are the worst!'

In the galley the man who had come aboard was slowly passing thin brown tape through a bowl of water and the girl was hanging it in loops over a string tied across the room just below the ceiling.

Helga guided Kenny back to the bunk that he had been asleep in earlier, shook the pillow, took a blanket from a locker and made him comfortable.

She went back through the galley where the tape was being washed, and up onto the deck, walked to the rail to look at the lighthouse, now visible ahead to the right, then went to the wheelhouse.

'Don't forget we've still got a body on the deck,' she told Dan who was holding the wheel with his left hand but showing few visible signs of his ordeal.

'We'll have to pitch him over the side,' he replied callously. 'Give him a burial at sea. What do you make of the couple downstairs?'

'They are still washing the brown tape. It is specially important to them, I think. Are they to come to Faroyar with us?'

'I haven't decided on that yet. We'll see how they behave themselves.'

It was time to work out a new Plan A *and* a reserve Plan B, to take account of the changed circumstances. This was certainly not the crew he had envisaged for *The Warrior's* first voyage in her new role.

Portland Bill was well behind them when Hywel and Mary came on deck and approached Dan. He was standing in the bow watching the dolphins swimming just ahead whilst Helga took a turn at the wheel.

Hywel said, 'We were wondering when you can put us ashore. The tape is drying now and I want to make copies of it. It's unique and very special.'

Dan said, 'That won't be for a couple of days. We're on a course for the Scilly Islands and tonight we've got a burial at sea.' He touched the hump under the tarpaulin with his foot.

Mary looked concerned. 'Can you do that? Is it legal? Don't you have to have a priest or something?'

'He is . . . was a priest himself,' Dan said.

'What about his relatives? They'll never know what happened to him,' Mary asked.

'I don't think he's got any,' Hywel interrupted. 'He told me once his wife and daughter had died in India.'

Mary ignored him. 'So you just pop him over the side? Just like that then?'

'What would *you* do?' Dan asked. 'Take him to the police station? Don't forget you stole *their* car – if I believe the story you told Helga. We're all in this together, whether we like it or not. You'll have to trust me, unless you fancy a long swim ashore. If you want something to do – you can help me wrap him up for a *proper* burial.' He touched the tarpaulin again with his foot.

Hywel and Mary retreated down the deck.

'He's mad,' said Mary.

'Mad or not, he's in charge. We have to do what he says. The old fellow's dead so it won't hurt him to go over the side. He won't know anything about it. Best show willing.'

Dan fetched a toolbox from the wheelhouse and directed Hywel as he hauled the spare anchor out of the locker.

'I don't like using an anchor as a body-weight,' Dan told him, 'but we're a bit short of cannonballs at the moment.'

Guided by Dan, Mary laid out the tarpaulin on the deck and the two men lifted the body on to it as Mary retreated to the rail, all the time keeping an eye on the madman with the beard.

A rosary fell from one of the pockets of the dead man's jacket. Mary recognised it for what it was, stepped forward hesitantly, bent down and picked it up. It lay comfortably in the palm of her hand. One of the links was broken but Hywel could easily fix that.

She turned her face up to Dan. 'When I met him before . . .' She sniffed. 'When I met him last time, he promised me a present, I'm sure this must be it. May I keep it?'

'OK by me,' Dan said. '*He* won't want it – not where he's going. Now, if you two can put the anchor on his chest and tie this rope round him, he'll be as snug as a bug . . . Come on, he's not going to bite you, for God's sake.'

Mary whispered in the dead man's ear as she pulled the tarpaulin to cover his head. 'Goodbye,' she said. 'Thank you for the rosary.' She put her hands together and prayed earnestly that his soul would be taken to Heaven. Hywel was looping the rope around the head and body to secure the sheet.

Lucky had followed them up onto the deck and he walked around between their feet sniffing at the body, then shivered in the cool sea breeze. He sneezed twice, then went down the companionway stairs to the galley.

Dan checked the wrapped body. 'Nice job. We'll put him over the side later, when it's getting dark. I'll relieve Helga now and she can get us something to eat.'

All afternoon Hywel kept checking the hanging loops of tape but it was taking some time to dry and he did not dare risk rewinding it too soon. Mary sat in a corner passing the beads of the rosary slowly through her fingers and caressing the tiny black figure on the cross.

Dan and Helga took two-hour shifts at the wheel and Kenny slept on in the lower bunk of the Port Cabin. *The Warrior* headed steadily south-westwards riding the long swells easily.

At 9.30 Helga was at the wheel and Dan asked Hywel and Mary if they would please come on deck as he was going to put the body over the side and would need a hand. They followed him up the companionway stairs.

Dan checked the horizon. Only one other vessel was in sight – a tanker hull-down to the south. No land was visible.

With Hywel's clumsy help he used the net hoist to lift the long parcel onto the rail.

'I'm not planning a "burial at sea" service but if either of you want to say a quick prayer, now's your time,' he said.

Mary gave him an unexpected smile and stepped forward to pray silently near the dead man's head.

Hywel stood next to Mary as she prayed with her hands together and her head bowed.

He felt unexpectedly moved by the occasion and put his hand into his pocket to fumble with the Hamlet box. If only he'd recorded *Abide with me* . . .

Perhaps *Hearts and Flowers* might be appropriate? But no – not really – better not. The boat lurched on an awkward wave and his finger pressed Button 4 on the box as he stumbled. Gusts of maniacal laughter came from his pocket.

'Turn that bloody thing off,' hissed Mary, swearing for the first time in her life and feeling a whole lot better for it. She walked down to the stern and stood by the wheelhouse.

Dan freed the hook and pushed the body over the side and into the sea. It floated head-end up for a few seconds, then sank. Bubbles rose to the surface but were soon lost in the wake as *The Warrior* surged forward again.

Dan left Hywel and went aft to relieve Helga at the wheel. She stood for a few minutes with Mary at the stern watching the Zodiac bobbing in the wake and the pair of gulls that followed the boat hoping for scraps of food to be thrown overboard.

'At home the birds all fly behind the fishing boats,' Helga said. 'At home there are very many gulls.'

*The dolphins swam round the body as it slid down to the seabed where it came to rest near a wreck from which the seaweed swirled in the underwater currents.*

*FairIsle scanned the bundle delicately.*

*'This was a good and gentle man,' she said, 'though his spirit is elsewhere. I dare to hope that **he** was the white haired one of the starwhales' legend and if so, Nordstar did not die in vain.'*

*Rockall swam forward and bit and tore at the sheeting with his teeth.*

*'For the prophecy to come true the crabs must be able to eat of his body,' he declared.*

Helga was the first to go below, her tired brain planning a meal for five. She stopped at the foot of the stairs. Lucky had evidently climbed onto the table while there was no one in the galley and had reached up for the tape. He was playing amongst the tangled loops on the floor, each happy twist of his body tightening knots in the delicate tape and making the mass look like the dried and matted sea-grass that lined the shore of the Fleet lagoon.

'Oh baby-cat!' she said, picking up the kitten and trying to unhook his sharp claws from the tangle. 'What *have* you been doing?'

Mary, who had followed Helga down the stairs, swore for the second time in her life.

With the tape in a cardboard box, to be 'sorted out when it is the morning', Helga allocated bunks. Dan was to share the port cabin with Kenny. She and Mary would sleep in the starboard cabin and she was sure that Hywel could make up a bed in the storeroom until Dan was fit enough to sleep there.

Hywel started to say that he was not going to be aboard for that long but decided not to argue. He was feeling a bit sick himself and wanted to lie down.

When Helga and Mary had made a supper of tinned stew and instant potato, Helga took a plateful up to Dan in the wheelhouse and told him of the arrangements.

'Good girl,' he said. 'Are you OK to do four-hour shifts through the night? Yes? I'll call you at 0200 hours then. Oh and by the way, tell that Welsh guy and his girlfriend not to get any funny ideas about nicking the Zodiac in the night. They won't be able to start it.' He patted his pocket. 'I've got the key.'

I am *not* a 'girl', Helga thought, but there was no resentment. Dan was going to take her home.

# CHAPTER THIRTY-ONE

Dan spent his watch developing Plan A. Any Plan B could wait until he felt better. In the quiet of the night the pain in his shoulder was savage despite the tablets he had taken from the first aid box. His brain kept reviewing the situation. Would any one connect the missing vicar and the wrecked pool with the departure of *The Warrior*? What should he do about the Welsh guy and his girlfriend? Strangely they seemed much more interested in the tape – and each other – than getting ashore. He must find out what was so special about that tape. What had the man said was on it – dolphins singing?

He handed over to Helga at two in the morning and asked her to tie the wheel and wake him if he wasn't on deck at six, then went below to take another couple of aspirins and lie restlessly on the bunk, trying to avoid pressure on his shoulder. His injured hand throbbed painfully until he dozed off. Kenny, in the bunk below, snored quietly.

At six, feeling surprisingly better, he went on deck. The wind had risen a little and he checked his position with the satellite navigation unit, transferred the latitude and longitude figures to the chart and altered course to the Northwest. Helga came back up on deck with a mug of tea for him then went below to sleep.

Dan secured the wheel, put his head out of the wheelhouse, took a deep breath of the salt-laden air, felt the tug of the rising wind on his beard and vowed never to go back to city life. *The Warrior's* bow smashed though a wave and spray flew high in the air. More seagulls, familiar with the shape of fishing boats, cruised above the stern waiting for nets to be hauled and fish guts and undersized fish to be thrown overboard.

Dan watched them as they dipped and soared, observing the way they took advantage of every current of air, searching the sea below for any scraps of food, their eyes cold and predatory. A joy of four dolphins appeared abeam.

Dan recognised the damaged dorsal fins on two of them and raised his hand in greeting as he would to a passing boat. The dolphins leapt in pairs as though to salute *The Warrior.*

*'The Orca-man has a damaged left hand and his other arm is hanging in a bag from his neck but he appears to be otherwise uninjured,' Rockall told FairIsle. 'The other humans must be in the belly of the boat.'*

*'We owe them our freedom,' she replied. 'We must find some way to do good things for them. We will stay near to them.'*

At nine Helga walked from her cabin through the galley to use the heads. Seated at the galley table were Hywel and Mary, teasing out the loops in the brown tape. She could hear Lucky mewing for his breakfast from behind the closed door of the storeroom.

'Have you got a needle?' Hywel asked. 'Some of these knots are quite tight.'

Helga found the boat's 'make do and mend' box, reached it down and offered an assortment of needles. Hywel choose a thick one with a not-too-sharp point and carefully inserted the end into a knot.

'Actually, I could do this better with two.'

He took another needle and, with one in each hand, he delicately pulled the knot apart. Mary, holding the cassette with a biro through one of the holes, rotated the pen to take up the newly created slack while Hywel worked on the next knot.

'You have got for yourselves quite a job there, I think,' Helga said. 'I am hoping that it is worth all the trouble.'

'It will be.' Mary flashed a smile at her. 'I promise you – it will be.'

'Would you have the coffee or the tea?' Helga asked, putting the kettle on the tiny stove.

'The man and the woman, How-well and Mary they are called, do not seem in a quick hurry to be put ashore,' Helga remarked to Dan as she went up for his empty mug. 'Whatever is on that tape is the most important thing in the world to them, I think. I hope that it is not damaged. I like them, especially Mary – that smile of hers . . . She pulls it back into her face before you really can see it – as if she is afraid that some bad person is going to steal it away from her. The man has told me he is a waiter at a hotel but I am not believing him in that. I am thinking he is a more clever man than to be a waiter.'

Dan spun the wheel to turn *The Warrior* bow-on into a big wave that was rolling towards them. 'Wind's getting up. If we're going to take you home we'll have to teach some of the others to take their turns at watch – or put them ashore and get a new crew. It's a long way.'

When he went below at ten, Hywel and Mary were still bent over the tape but the tangle was noticeably smaller than the night before. They put it all carefully back in the box to clear the table for a late breakfast.

Kenny did not appear and Helga took him a mug of sweet tea. She came back with the full mug. 'Ken-ney is sleeping like a baby-boy. That will be the best thing for him. I will take some tea for him at a later time.'

By 12.45, with the seas crashing over the bow and *The Warrior* pitching violently into each trough, the tape was finally untangled and fully wound back into the cassette.

'Is there a player on board?' Hywel asked Dan when he came out of his cabin. 'Ideally one with two decks. I must make a copy,'

'I've got a radio-cassette player that runs on batteries. But it's only a single-deck.' He fetched it from the cabin and put it on the table.

Hywel switched on the radio and a man's voice was reading the shipping forecast – 'North Utsira, South Utsira, Viking, Cromarty . . .'

He clicked the switch to off. '*That* works – let's hope the rest does.'

'Leave it on,' said Dan. 'Let's hear the shipping forecast and the one o'clock news first.' He switched the radio on again and heard the news through while Hywel fiddled impatiently with the tape on the other side of the table. To Dan's relief there was no mention of any unusual happenings in Dormouth.

Hywel dropped the cassette into the slot and pressed the 'play' button. There was a short silence, then magnificent organ music filled the tiny galley and through it came the voice of the dead pilot whale, suffused with a great and moving sadness.

> *Out of the Northern Seas I swam*
> *To satisfy an age-old prophecy*
> *My life a sacrifice. I am*
> *Part of the everlasting saga of the Sea*
> *'I did not fail,' I cry –*
> *Though I must die.*
>
> *Out of the Northern Sea I swam*
> *The hope of life for all my kin and kind*
> *The Times and Tides were not right then*
> *Now hear our Songs of Hope for all Whalekind*
> *So though I dread the coming pain*
> *Let it not be in vain.*

The music swelled and echoed around the galley like waves in a sea-cave as a storm builds outside.

*Hope fills my heart for all Whalekind*
*Though soon into the endless night I'll swim*
*And echoes fade and stars grow dim for me*
*I trust Mankind will hear our plea*
*Sung from this place of shame*
*'Let whales swim free again*
*Let whales swim free again'*

Hywel stopped the tape. 'That's funny,' he said, his voice thick with emotion. 'When I last heard that the words were in English, now they're in Welsh.'

'It was English,' said Mary.

'Just music – no words,' said Dan.

'Welsh,' said Hywel.

'English,' Mary insisted.

Hywel shook his head and pressed the play button again.

After a few bars of deep, rolling notes another voice sang:

*When I was born the sunlit sparkling Sea*
*Patterned the seabed, light delighting me.*
*Sun, Sea, companionship and joy were mine*
*Grace, beauty, love and peace would intertwine*
*As kelpweed in a swirling current's flow.*
*Now – what is the life I know?*

*All I possess is here within my brain*
*I have no hands to grasp and hold and claim.*
*But human hands once cast a subtle net*
*Unseen, unheard, unechoing – and yet*
*Strong to ensnare, to capture and enslave*
*This spirit born for Sea-life, wind and wave.*

*For I was taught that Dolphins love all Men*
*And Men love us, but now I wonder when*
*Their arrogance and greed this concept killed –*
*Still whales and dolphins die. My soul is filled*
*With alien emotions. Fear and hate*
*Pollute my mind – a toxic stream in spate.*

*I am a symbol of all whales' plight*
*Captured or killed, not knowing how to fight.*
*Trapped here, I swim in circles and the hatred grows*
*I yearn for freedom where the Sea wind blows*

> *Don't let a hate for Mankind poison me*
> *~Yegods~ and little fishes – set me free.*

Hywel stopped the tape again. 'Welsh,' he said positively.

'English', said Mary, equally positively. She flashed a smile at Dan, enlisting support.

'What are you two on about?' Dan asked. 'It's just someone playing an organ.'

Hywel pressed 'play' again.

The organ music changed to more gentle notes followed by:

> *I, Grace of FairIsle, call to Thinking Men –*
> *See us for what we are.*
>
> *Not competition for your fish*
> *Not fools to entertain your young*
> *Not handy hulks of oil and flesh*
> *But creatures of intelligence*
> *Deserving something better from our land-based friends*
> *Who occupy dry portions of this planet, humans will call Earth*
> *But which is mostly Sea.*
>
> *We know that you have eyes to see*
> *And ears to hear.*
> *We know that you have brains to think.*
> *We know imagination flourishes in men.*
> *We hope that you have souls to feel compassion too.*
>
> *Please, use your hands to signal*
> *STOP*
> *And let us live.*
>
> *See us for what we are*
> *A peaceful, gentle, cultured people of the Sea.*

'Can't you hear the dolphins singing?' Mary asked Dan. 'The first one was the white whale, the one who died. The others were the two dolphins that you released. Hywel made them sing,' she added, a touch of pride in her voice.

'That's not really true,' Hywel said. 'All I did was fix things so that they could make the organ play. But I don't know why it's in Welsh now.'

'English,' said Mary.

'I'll go up and relieve Helga,' Dan said. 'She should hear this. I can't follow what you two are on about.'

He pulled on a yellow oilskin jacket, went up on deck and staggered aft, buffeted by the south-westerly wind.

'Is everything OK?' he shouted over the hissing of the wind past the corners of the wheelhouse.

'All is OK,' replied Helga, 'but the wind is blowing very strong. This is a good boat, I think.'

Dan took the wheel and checked the course. Helga had gone before he could mention the strange argument going on below decks.

Helga fought her way up-wind to the companionway doors and went below.

'Listen to this,' Hywel said with no other greeting. 'Tell us what you hear.'

He pressed the button and the rewound tape played . . .

> *Out of the Northern Sea I swam*
> *To satisfy an ancient prophecy . . .*

> *'Let whales swim free again*
> *Let whales swim free again.'*

Hywel stopped the tape. 'What did you hear?' he asked.

'It is not easy to believe,' Helga replied, 'but I *think* I heard a hval singing to me. But sometimes it sang in the language of Faroyar, sometimes it was in Danish but if I concentrated my mind more, I could hear it in the English language.'

Hywel said, 'There's something very odd here. That time *I* heard it in English. Does anyone speak a foreign language, other than Helga.'

'I was pretty good at French in school,' Mary said.

Hywel rewound the tape. 'When I play it this time – think French. See what happens.'

> *Out of the Northern Sea I swam*
> *To satisfy an ancient . . .*

He stopped the tape at *'Let whales swim free again.'*

'Well?' he asked Mary.

'It *is* odd. This time I heard it mostly in French except for the words I don't know like 'prophecy' and 'sacrifice' – they were in English.'

'Listen to the rest,' Hywel said to Helga and pressed play again.

245

*When I was born the sunlit sparkling sea*
*Patterned the seabed, light delighting me . . .*

FairIsle's song finished with the words,

*See us for what we are*
*A peaceful, gentle, cultured people of the Sea.*

Helga was crying quietly. 'It is so beautiful – so beautiful . . . and so sad.'

'What language was it in then?' Hywel asked gently.

'I could make it any language I wanted to,' she said. 'Faeroese, Danish, English, even no language – just pictures. All so beautiful . . . and so sad.'

*The dolphins, FairIsle, Rockall, Malin and Lundy were playing in the bow-wave of The Warrior, riding the pressure waves and diving as the bow rose and crashed down again with each passing comber. They had hunted for fish earlier and were replete and playful. Rockall came up behind FairIsle and scanned her body, hoping to see his new-life forming inside her though he knew it was much too soon.*

*'Impatient one,' FairIsle let her thoughts flow back past her, then turned in puzzlement.*

*'Can you hear Nordstar singing, or is my mind adrift?' she asked Rockall.*

*'I heard it too, in the waves – but Nordstar is dead. She fell and died, crushed by the squeezing water in the Pool of Shame.'*

*'It was the voice of Nordstar. Singing her last song with the Great Wind Song Maker. I will never forget her singing that day.'*

*Rockall started to reply but stopped when the sound of his own song reached him, carried through the waves.*

*Malin and Lundy had swum back to join them.*

*'What are these sounds – these words – these . . . ?'*

*'Songs,' said FairIsle. 'The starwhale who died taught us to sing in the Pool of Shame. The songs must have drifted in the tides and have caught up with us.'*

*'They are coming from the body of the boat,' said Malin. 'Often I have heard rhythmic sounds and humans' voices coming from within the bellies of boats.'*

*'How did our songs get into this boat. Listen – there is the song I sang. Is that my voice?'*

*Rockall signalled the small 'yes'.*

*'They are very beautiful songs and wonderful ideas,' said Lundy as the
words,*

> *See us for what we are*
> *A peaceful, gentle, cultured people of the Sea . . .*

*faded and sank.*
*'I have heard that Stargazers sing but never we 'phins.'*

Dan was baffled by what he had heard in the galley and needed to think
and plan. He checked their position with the Sat-nav system and marked
their position on the chart. *The Warrior* was south of Plymouth, a safe
distance from land. Even so, with a single engine he was not going to
risk being caught on a lee shore with no spare anchor should he have
problems. He altered course to S S W and reviewed his situation.

There were five people on board, including himself, one more than the
number the boat had been fitted out to accommodate but last night had
proved that somebody could sleep in the store room if need be. There was
no shortage of provisions, fuel or fresh water. No immediate problem
there. *The Warrior* could ride out this storm easily. In fact he was sure
that the worst was already over – the wind was shifting towards the north,
and the barometer was rising, indicating that the depression would soon
pass.

Helga wanted him to take her to the Faeroes and he had half promised
that he would. He could break that promise if he had to and put her ashore
to catch a train to Aberdeen.

Kenny, who must still be in his bunk sick, was an oddity. The kid
obviously worshipped Helga who was much too old for him, but he had
no job now and would probably like to stay aboard when he got over
his sickness. He had shown more initiative than expected when the
explosion plan went wrong, even though the results had not been what
he had anticipated.

Dan eased his shoulder and slowly flexed his injured hand. It was still
stiff and sore but obviously there were no bones broken and he should be
able to leave the bandage and the sling off soon. *He* was OK – it was the
Welsh guy and his girlfriend who were the problem.

The man, Hywel, was obviously clever and totally engrossed in that
crazy taped music thing. He, Dan, had never understood music. Other
people, even other marines, had been able to read things into music which
seemed to him to be just a boring dirge or a discordant jangles of notes.
*He* certainly had not heard voices on those tapes, neither human, dolphin,
whale or . . . or seagull. The whole thing was absurd. Had those two
been pulling his leg? He swung the wheel to meet the next wave.

The girl, Mary, didn't seem the sort to do that. Far too uptight – except when she smiled. He'd have to think about what to do with those two, but now it was beginning to get dark – the night brought on early by the heavy clouds.

He switched on the port, starboard and masthead lights and swung the spotlight on the wheelhouse round to look at the waves. The sea was definitely subsiding. He pressed the button that made a buzzer sound in the galley and Helga came up to take over the watch again.

'Hold the present course,' he told her as she took the wheel. 'The weather's easing. We'll decide in the morning what we do then. I'll be up before midnight.'

Dan went to the stern and pissed into the sea, watching the bubbles blend in with those of the boat's wake. The dolphins were still with them – he could see their fins off to port as they rose intermittently to breathe.

Dan spent much of his dawn-watch studying the charts, trying to decide where would be the best place to put Hywel and Mary ashore. They had shown no inclination to report him for the explosion nor the illicit disposal of the body but could he trust them? *The Warrior* was past the Lizard Point now and he would turn north once he was clear of the Scilly Isles. Plan A would put them ashore somewhere on the coast of Wales, but only when he was sure they would keep their mouths shut. Plan B would land them in Scotland or even the Faeroes, but he couldn't keep them aboard indefinitely.

In the lodging house in Dormouth, Mrs Scrimshaw had waited until she had seen neither Helga nor Kenny for two days before going into each of their rooms with one of her Bingo friends for support. One never knew what one might find. The things one read of in the papers!

Helga's room had been spotlessly cleaned and she found the rent-money neatly stacked, with a brief note addressed to her.

'She's run off with that young man, I'll bet a pound,' Mrs Scrimshaw said. 'He always was soft on her, even if she was nearly old enough to be his Mum. Isn't it romantic?'

In Kenny's room, dishes were piled at random in the sink, and the wastepaper basket was full of wrappers from the chip shop, making the airless room stink of stale fish. Mrs Scrimshaw tut-tutted to her friend, opened the window and went down to her kitchen for a bin bag.

'What a mucky kid,' she said dropping the wrappers into the bag. 'I'm surprised a nice girl like her would go off with someone like that, but there you are. You never know what some folks will do.'

She stooped and picked up a woman's handkerchief with her finger and thumb from the floor near the bed and examined it at arm's length. There was a letter D embroidered in the corner.

'*Her* name was Helga,' she told her friend, nodding towards the partition separating the two rooms. 'The mucky little beggar was two-timing her even before they ran off. You just can't trust men – any men.'

She strode across the room, pulled Kenny's dolphin poster from the partition wall and thrust it violently into the black bag, then used her own handkerchief to rub away the last vestiges of Blu-Tack from the wall. Kenny's clothes and few remaining possessions followed the poster and the chip papers into the bag.

Kenny woke in the port cabin unsure of what time or even what day it was. He stood up slowly and found that he was feeling much better and was ravenously hungry. He opened the door into the galley and Hywel immediately asked him to listen to a tape.

Kenny waved towards the heads. 'I must go in there first.' He sniffed the air. 'If there's any of that bacon going I could eat a horse – well, perhaps a pig. I'm starving.'

Helga said, 'I will cook some for you. Would you like one or two slices?'

'Three, please,' said Kenny, grinning. 'I can't remember when I last ate.'

Mary got up and took a plate from the locker, then poured two mugs of tea from the teapot on the table as Helga fried the bacon. Hywel sat impatiently, his finger hovering near the play button on the cassette player.

'Let the man eat first,' Mary said. 'I know what you want – but there's plenty of time for that. Take this tea up to Dan in the wheelhouse.'

When Kenny had finished eating he rubbed his bristly chin and asked about a razor.

'*No* bloody chance,' said Hywel. 'Dan doesn't shave and the rest of us are a press-gang.' He rubbed his own chin. 'Listen to this,' he said, pressing the button.

Kenny sat at the table as Hywel played the dolphin tape. Once more the music filled the galley, Kenny looking from face to face as first Nordstar, then Rockall and finally FairIsle, sang their songs.

As FairIsle's plea for humans to 'See us for what we are . . .' faded away, Hywel clicked the machine off.

'What language were they speaking?' he asked Kenny eagerly.

'Dolphin . . . Dolphinese,' said Kenny, looking perplexed. 'What else?'

'How did it sound – this Dolphinese?'

'Like little pictures, squiggly little pictures.'

'Listen again. See if you can hear them in English.' He rewound the tape and played it again. Kenny sat with his eyes closed.

'It was in English that time. It started as squiggles but I let my mind go through the sounds – like you have to let your eyes go through the pictures on those Magic Eye posters. Then the squiggles turned into words – English words – the sounds of English words.'

'What did the squiggles look like?' Hywel asked. 'Can you draw them?'

Kenny tried unsuccessfully. 'When I was a kid,' he said, making it sound as though that was a century before, 'I invented a dolphin language. It looked like this . . .'

He tore the flap off a cereal packet and drew

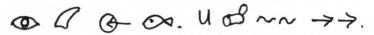

'That meant 'I, Flipper, want a fish. You can swim away.' He looked at the drawings. 'It wasn't very good and I've forgotten most of the shapes.'

Helga picked up the torn-off flap and said, 'My Uncle Roi brought some newspapers back from being in Hong Kong once. They were wrapped around a present for me. He told me that the Chinese people could all read the same newspapers even though they spoke in the different languages. A man who spoke in the Mandarin language could read it in the Mandarinese and a man from Canton could read it in the Cantonese, even though the sound of the words were different from one to the other. I asked my teacher at the school about it and she said it was because they used many little pictures instead of the letters – each picture being for one whole word.'

Hywel leant forward. 'If the dolphins were using the organ to make sound pictures and the chip in my system was fixing them in some way, everyone who heard the tape would use their own language to interpret them. That must be it. Bingo – I've done it!'

'Done what?' Mary asked.

'Cracked the fish-in-the-ear problem. At least as far as dolphins are concerned.'

'Who has got a fish in their ear – the dolphins?' Helga asked.

Hywel tried to explain the reference to *The Hitch Hiker's Guide* and the way the author had invented a system of inter-galactic translation.

'It'd make it a whole lot simpler at the United Nation's debates if everyone had a Babel Fish in their ear. If my device could be used there I'm on to fame and fortune.'

He grinned and rewound the tape. Then his face fell. 'Sh . . . sugar. I left all my gear in the church – including the device I invented. Someone may have found it by now. I must get ashore and put in for a patent.'

Mary was thinking, not of patents, but of how she could fulfil her mission of taking these songs 'to the world of people'.

*Fairlsle heard the songs through the boat's hull once more as she and Rockall swam alongside.*

*'The humans have trapped our songs and they swim around inside the boat as we swam round in the Pool of Shame.'*

*'Inside a boat is air,' said Rockall, knowingly. 'Otherwise it would sink.'*

*'Then the songs are flying inside like trapped gulls. Should we try and release them?'*

*'I don't think songs live as we live,' Rockall replied. 'I can sing my song again, so the humans have only borrowed it. I wonder what they want to use it for?'*

Dan was relieved at the helm by Helga who had listened to the conversation below in some bewilderment. She had found that it was as easy to switch the dolphins' songs from Faeroese, to Danish, to English and back as readily as Uncle Roi changed gear in his car. More and more she wanted to be home.

'Ken-ny has woken up and had some breakfast but I think they are all a little odd in the head down there,' she told Dan as he showed her the new course she was to steer. He walked round the deck checking the net hoist, the winch, the rigging, the hatches and the lashings on the Zodiac, then went below.

'I need to get ashore,' Hywel told Dan. 'Where's the nearest land?'

'We're about the same distance from the Scilly Isles, Pembrokeshire and Southern Ireland, but I wasn't planning to put into port just yet. What's the rush?'

Hywel tried to explain about the tape, insisting that Dan listened to it again. 'Let your mind sort of drift through the music. Don't try *too* hard to hear anything.'

Dan sat at the table staring at the wall as the tape played through. 'Bloody hell,' he said as it finished. '*That* was the dolphins?'

Hywel nodded.

'Bloody hell,' Dan said again. 'Look. If I put you ashore, how will I know you won't rush off to the police with any old cock and bull story about the explosions and get me into all sorts of trouble?'

'*We* know you did it to save the dolphins, even if the whale died,' Mary said. 'And the vicar. It's him *I'm* worried about.'

She was holding the tiny rosary under the table. Hywel had repaired the broken link for her.

'He looked very old to me,' Dan said. 'And he's gone now. Surely there's no point in making trouble over him. One of you said you didn't think he had any relatives. Best to let sleeping dogs lie.'

'How far away is *Ireland*?' Mary asked. 'County Kerry?'

'We could be in Rosslare tonight,' Dan said. 'County Kerry's round the corner on the west coast, another day, or day and a half away. Depends on the weather. What's there?'

'Another dolphin, Fungie. I swam with him once.'

Mary looked at the attentive faces around the table. 'I couldn't have told you this before but now that you've all heard the tapes . . .'

She told them of swimming with Fungie at Dingle and the message in Ogham. 'I need to finish what God wants me to do,' she said. 'If I swam with Fungie again he might be able to tell me more. You know – what to do next.'

Dan looked enquiringly at the others round the table. Hywel raised his hand and the others followed.

'Dingle it is then,' Dan said. 'In for a penny . . .' Hell – he'd just agreed to go to the other side of Ireland to get instructions from a bloody *dolphin*.

The captain went on deck to tell Helga – he was sure she would have no objections. He had a crew of sorts now, united in a common purpose, and that pleased him though they were certainly not the band of ex-squadron men he'd planned. He took a chart from the locker in the wheel house, showed Helga how little the diversion to Dingle would take them from the course that would take her home to the Faeroes, then went below with the chart, to work on it with a set of parallel rules and a pair of dividers.

He calculated a new course. The depression had moved away over the North Sea and what little wind there would be would blow from astern. They should be at Dingle the following afternoon.

*'The Orca-man is as mindless as a manta-ray,' Rockall said to FairIsle as The Warrior turned a few degrees to port and headed westwards.*

*'He may have plans which we can't guess at,' FairIsle replied. 'We'll stay with the boat unless it turns back, or is going too far from our way north for too long. The woman from the Faroff Islands is still aboard – she has influence on the Orca-man though he would probably not admit it. I'll whistle for Malin and Lundy to stay with us. They too will want to know what will happen if the humans set our songs free.'*

## CHAPTER THIRTY-TWO

South of Ireland, the wind dropped and the waves subsided to a long lazy swell, green in the bright sunlight. Kenny went on deck and Dan taught him how to hold a course when he took a turn at the wheel while he or Helga needed to go below for a meal or a break. Kenny enjoyed steering the ship towards a distant cloud or a far-off rock – it gave him a sense of power and responsibility. He thought of Billy Tranter locked up in the prison in another world far behind him. Poor old Billy . . .

Kenny's spell at the wheel took them past the Fastnet lighthouse and Dan reset the course to the north-west before calling to Helga to take over. It was good to have at least one more of the crew able to take a watch but he was still not sure what to do about Hywel and Mary. They were up at the bow looking down on the four dolphins who were riding the bow-wave.

Helga had taken to fishing, using the gear Dan had bought in Poole but had never got round to using himself. She enjoyed the tug and jerk on the line when a mackerel took the red-feather bait and she hauled it in. The handline she thought was crude – the fork-shaped ones she had used at home avoided the difficulty of the line getting twisted or kinking when it was wound around the wood. It was still exciting though, to land the kicking, jumping fishes on the deck, where they finally lay still, their metallic-patterned skins fading in the sunshine and the fresh breezes of the Irish coast as Lucky, now growing fast, sniffed at the scaly bodies.

When she wasn't fishing or taking her turn at the wheel, Helga carved at the block of wood Kenny had brought aboard. Everybody could see the two dolphins now, one leaping above the other which was dorsal-fin-down on the base. The fins and flukes of the wooden dolphins separated them yet held them together in a way that none of them would have found easy to explain.

Helga enjoyed being watched as she worked but spoke deprecatingly when Dan remarked on her skill. 'It is simple. The dolphins were in there all the time. I only let them out like *you* let the real dolphins out of the pool in England. I do it with my knife – you did it with the big bang in the water. It is all very simple.'

The next morning *The Warrior* passed the Skellig rocks which towered out of the sea, dwarfing the trawler and the power boats taking visitors from the mainland to climb up to the monks' stone cells on the summit of the larger rock. Dan passed his binoculars to Mary who had just come up on deck with Hywel. He pointed to the bumps against the skyline.

She took the binoculars and studied the rock-built domes. 'I heard about those when I was in Ireland. Monks lived there for hundreds of years.'

'What for?' Hywel asked

'To contemplate and pray.'

Hywel swallowed the sarcastic remark he was about to make.

'Do you really believe that praying does anyone any good?' He had been reading one of Skipper Jack's books with the aid of the piece of orange glass he had picked up as they were leaving the church after the explosion. Although he still read slowly he had been intrigued by the story. In the book elephants shared their god with humans and he was almost believing that such a 'less than almighty' god might exist. The elephants prayed, though they had a different name for it.

Mary put her hand on his arm. 'You should try it sometime,' she said, turning her face towards him and smiling. 'You might be surprised what happens.'

Hywel thought wryly of what he would pray for if he ever did, took the binoculars from Mary and focused on the stone cells. It would have nothing to do with being a monk.


The second, smaller one of the Skellig rocks was white with gannets and their droppings, while the birds themselves, nearly as big as geese, dropped with folded wings into the sea to reappear with fish in their beaks.

Dan set a new course to stay well clear of Valentia Island as he had no detailed charts of that coast aboard, leaving Kenny at the wheel.

Helga was trailing the mackerel line over the stern and Hywel and Mary were now sitting in the sun on the deck, their backs against the warm varnished wood of the wheelhouse.

Dan counted the days since he had left Poole and swore. Once at sea the happenings on land seemed remote and inconsequential – time took on another dimension. Weather and tides were far more important but there *was* something he must do.

He went down for his mobile phone to ring the Bank in Poole, hoping it would work through the Irish network. He took the phone up on deck and went to the bow, aware of being watched by the rest of the crew. He tapped in the number and reached the Security Office immediately.

'Dan Watts here,' he said. 'I took my boat down-channel a few days ago and I'm having some problems getting back. I'm going to have to miss a few shifts.

'No. I can't say how many.

'I *can't* say.

'Look, I would if I could. I just can't say.

'That *is* my attitude.

'That's up to you . . . Please yourself.'

Dan switched off the phone, snapped it shut and slipped it into his shirt pocket. Sod them and their bloody job! *This* was the real world.

He wondered if any of the crew might feel differently now they knew he had a phone on board.

The four dolphins were playing as they often did in the bow-waves below him. He looked again – there were six, not four. He looked once more to make sure but they had all gone.


*FairIsle had been the first to hear the signature whistles of two strangers approaching. She had answered back and waited for the formal greetings. The strangers identified themselves as Elegance of Kerry and Grace of Valentia.*

*'We heard the sound of a boat that we did not know,' Kerry told them. 'It is a boat for catching fish with nets but has only a single line behind it. We were curious.'*

*'Are you swimming with this boat?' Valentia asked.*

*'We are,' FairIsle told her. 'We have good news for the starwhales of the north.' She told of the prophecy and how it had been fulfilled with the streak of light in the sky and the death of Nordstar and the white-headed human.*

*'Strange things are afloat in the World,' Kerry told her. 'Have you time to swim with us to a cave where I lived for many years?'*


*FairIsle studied the remains of the curious markings on the wall of the cave – she had never seen their likeness before. Kerry saw her looking and swam to her side. 'They were made by ~yegods~,' he bubbled quietly.*

*'Do ~yegods~ really exist?' FairIsle asked.*

*'Two do, at least. They came here with that message for the humans. I passed it on but it may have sunk and been lost by now.'*

*'What was the message? Are you allowed to tell?'*

*'I swam the marks they had made with their tusks but the message itself was hidden from me.'*

*'Did the humans understand it?'*

*'A human female brought me a stick of wood with similar markings on it. These I could not read – but her mind-waves told me that **she** knew its meaning.'*

*'Strange things **are** afloat in the World,' FairIsle said, then told him of the Great Wind Song Maker. 'A starwhale taught us to sing songs with it and we have found that these same songs are captive in the boat we are escorting. Perhaps they will be freed in the Faroff Islands. We must swim after the boat. Farewell, Grace of Valentia and Elegance of Kerry. Farewell. May good fortune swim with you.'*

*'And with you,' the response shimmered after her.*

Dan was standing at the bow when the four dolphins returned. He was glad they had come back – he had been making plans that involved them. He had promised to put Hywel and Mary ashore at Dingle but, if he did that, he would only have Helga and Kenny as crew. Helga was very competent. He had never known a woman like her before but he was not quite so sure about Kenny. If *he* got seasick again there would only be Helga and himself to manage *The Warrior* and his shoulder was still bothering him occasionally. Given a little time he was sure that Hywel and even Mary could be taught to play a full role in manning the boat. Using the phone had given him an idea. He walked down the deck and squatted next to Hywel.

'I've got a proposition for you,' he said.

Hywel looked cautious, 'Go on.'

'Your main concern is getting a copy of that tape made? Yes?'

'It's the only one in the world.'

'Supposing we *phoned* it to England – is there anyone there who could record it from their phone?'

'That could work.' Hywel spoke slowly. 'But we should be ashore in Dingle today. I can make a copy there.'

'That's true,' Dan countered. 'But what then? *We* go on to the Faeroes and the dolphins come with us. You'd lose any chance of making more recordings. God knows where the dolphins would go if we go into port. We know that at least one of them came from the Faeroes. If you want the best chance of any more recordings – stay with us and we'll keep heading north. That's *your* best bet.'

Hywel turned to Mary. 'Dan's got a point. I do know someone who could make a copy from a phone. Do you remember me telling you about Mr Williams? He'd do that for me. What do *you* think?'

Mary *thought*, if we go ashore Hywel may go back to being a waiter and I may go back to selling shoes and being scared all the time and I may never see the dolphins again and it's warm here on the boat and I like Kenny and Helga and Dan's not too bad and I've given up trying to second guess God – he knows what he is doing even if his ways are mysterious and – so what – let's stay on the boat. She *said*, 'Yes.'

'Yes – what?'

'Yes – let's ring your Mr Williams and if he *can* make a recording so that the message is safe then I think we *should* stay on the boat.'

'You're sure about that?'

'Quite sure.'

Hywel brought the radio-cassette player up on deck, checked that the tape was ready to play and dialled the number he used at Christmas to speak to Mr Williams. The Matron of the Home answered. Hywel asked if Mr Williams was in.

'I'll put you through to his room.'

'Mr. Williams? It's Hywel. How are you?'

'Good God! Is it Christmas already? No, only kidding. Good to hear from you, son. To what do I owe the honour?'

'Have you still got the gear to make a recording?'

'Is the Pope a catholic?'

Hywel was glad Mary couldn't hear Mr Williams.

'Sure I can. Are you wanting to confess to a murder or something?' The voice was as full of fun as ever.

'No. I've recorded some dolphins singing and I need to have a back-up tape in case anything happens to this one.'

'What's happened to all *your* gear?'

'That's a long story. I'm on a boat now – off the coast of Ireland using a mobile. If I play a tape, can you record it and keep the copy safe until I get back? I'll call in at Abergavenny and pick it up then.'

'Ring me again in ten minutes.'


Hywel played the tape, holding the phone next to the cassette player. When Mr Williams had finished recording it he wished Hywel, 'All the best,' and put the phone down. He couldn't wait to listen to the tape properly. Only then did he realise that he had not asked for the number of the phone Hywel had used

He played the tape again, then again. Were these beautiful songs really *dolphins* singing? With the words in English? Hywel had said it was dolphins. He had never known Hywel lie, even in fun, although he had often called him 'Diawl bach' – the little devil. This had been his pet name for the lad when he had played tricks on Mr Williams as a small boy in the garden at Ty Mawr.

As he recalled the Welsh words the dolphins' songs mysteriously switched into that language but they were clearly singing in English again now. Something didn't make sense. He played the tape again and again then went and knocked at the room next but one to his.

'Hans. There's something I'd like you to hear.'

The following day, in the late afternoon, between Ireland and the tiny islet of Rockall, Dan and Kenny had finished pumping out the bilges. One of the pumps had fouled and clearing the inlet pipe had been difficult in the confined space below the floorboards. Because of Dan's shoulder problem he'd had to direct Kenny as he lay on the floor with his arm up to his elbow in oily water.

The two men were wiping their hands on some cotton waste.

'Thanks, Ken,' said Dan. 'That's a job better done in decent weather than in a storm. Is it forecast time? My watch is below.'

Kenny looked at his, the watch he had worked so hard to win in the distant arcade on the sea front at Dormouth.

'Fifteen minutes,' he said, and Dan went aft to talk to Hywel who was taking a turn at the wheel.

Kenny no longer regarded the shipping forecasts that Dan was so keen to hear as a boring waste of radio time. Now he knew that *Fastnet, Shannon, Malin* and even *Rockall* actually existed as real places, it was much more interesting, and Dan was teaching him what sort of seas to expect when the radio gave Force 5, 6 or 7.

After the early evening shipping forecast, the three men usually listened to the six o'clock news together, though Dan had given up expecting to hear anything about murdered vicars or missing trawlers.

Kenny walked up to the bow and stared ahead.

Had Dan actually called him *Ken*? No one had ever called him *Ken* before. It sounded good. He rubbed his chin, his own beard was growing fast. Faster than Hywel's.

Mr Williams' nephew walked into his uncle's room without knocking. 'Hello, Uncle Gareth,' he said. 'Are you well?'

The older man struggled to his feet and held out his hand.

'Hello. What brings you here?'

'Just passing – thought I'd drop in. I've brought these for you.' He held out an extra large box of his uncle's favourite mint chocolates.

'They'll be worth twenty will-points at least,' Amanda had told him but had refused to come herself. 'I'm not going all the way down to bloody Wales to suck up to that old fart,' she had said as he left.

Mr Williams turned to introduce his nephew to the even older man who was seated opposite him.'

'Hans, this is my nephew, Alex. He's something in the City.'

Alex loved to be described as that. It had a nice ring to it and no one ever asked him to define his job.

'Alex, this is Herr Müller. He came over here with the *Luftwaffe* sixty-odd years ago, dropped in at a local farm and decided to stay on. He's a good friend of mine.'

Herr Müller grinned at the familiar introduction and held out his hand without rising. Alex shook it briefly. He didn't care for Germans, they were making all the running in Europe and he had strong views on that.

He sat in an empty armchair and asked, 'What's new?'

'Nothing much for us old fogies down here in the sticks.'

'What about that *tape*?' Herr Muller asked.

Mr Williams glowered at him but Hans Müller was coughing into his handkerchief and missed the signal.

'What tape is that, Uncle Gareth?'

'Nothing really. Just a tape recording. How's Amanda?'

'Your uncle's got a tape recording of dolphins singing – from Hywel Jones on a boat. Play it for your nephew, Gareth. See if he can hear what *we* can hear.'

Alex did not care for Hywel Jones. The way his uncle spoke of him, he seemed to care more for bloody Hywel Jones than for his own flesh and blood. Now he was making signs to the German guy to shut up. Something interesting was going on here.

'I'd love to hear a tape about dolphins, Uncle Gareth.'

He looked round for the Music Centre but could only see one of the old fashioned black machines that used to be called 'ghetto blasters'.

He picked it up and carried it across to his chair.

'Is the tape in it?'

He did not wait for a reply but pressed the play button and looked surprised when he heard an organ playing.

Then he heard:

> *Out of the Northern Sea I swam*
> *To satisfy an ancient prophecy*
> *My life a sacrifice . . .*

Alex looked from one old man to another, turned the volume down and asked, 'Where's the tape with the dolphins on?'

'That is it. That is the one,' Herr Müller said. 'For me they sing in German, for your uncle they sing in the Welsh and for you I am sure that they are singing in English.'

His uncle scowled at Herr Müller and reached out for the player. Alex casually picked it up and took it back to his chair. He turned up the volume again.

A voice was singing:

> *. . . kelpweed in a swirling current's flow.*
> *Now – what is the life I know?*

Alex stopped the tape.

'Uncle Gareth. Is this really a dolphin singing?'

'So I believe. That's what Hywel told me.' The words were spoken reluctantly.

'What are you going to do with it?'

'Nothing. He just wants me to keep it safe until he gets back from wherever he is.'

'When's that?'

'He didn't say.'

There was a gentle tap on the door and one of the domestic staff looked in.

'Three teas is it today then, Mr Williams?'

They drank the tea together, Mr Williams asking Alex about London, the journey down, where he was going next, anything except a mention of the dolphin tape. When he had finished Alex got up and said, 'Must be off. Can't be late in Carmarthen. Thanks for the tea. Enjoy the chocs.'

He patted his uncle's shoulder, nodded a goodbye to Herr Müller and left. At the end of the drive he turned his BMW towards the Severn Bridge and London.

'He is not your favourite nephew, I think,' Herr Müller said.

'He is my *only* nephew and he's a cocky little twerp. All he's good for is chocolates.'

He opened the box, folded back the crackly gold paper and held out the box to his friend.

Next day, when Mr Williams went to play the tape once more, it was not in the machine.

Helga and Mary were sitting on the gunwale, one on either side of the stem-post at the bow, each wearing a blanket like a Roman toga. Their clothes were drying on a line rigged between the net hoist and the corner of the wheelhouse. On the deck below the clothes line, Dan and Kenny were dismantling one of the pumps. Lucky was sniffing at the pump housing and generally getting in the way. Hywel was at the wheel, steering towards a small cloud on the horizon as Dan had taught him.

Helga leant towards Mary and said, 'I am thinking that Ken-ney has found the father that he never had.'

'Dan calls him *Ken*,' Mary said. 'He likes that. I think I will call him Ken.'

260

'Me also. I think that he is deserving to be called Ken. Dan too is a better man than I once thought. He is more kind, I think.'

Mary looked at her, hoping she would say more. She had not been able to work out how well these two knew one another but instead Helga asked, 'You and Hywel – you are lovers?'

'Oh no,' said Mary quickly. 'Nothing like that.'

'Why is it nothing like that? He is in love with you – even I can see that is so. He is always trying to be near you and he looks at you with eyes like a hungry baby-dog. Do you not love him?'

'But he's an atheist – he doesn't believe in God.'

'So? Once when I was little and my father and grandfather were drowned, *I* did not believe in God. I told my Uncle Roi and he said, "Helga, my dear. It is more important that God believes in *you*."

'I did not understand then what he meant and I am not sure that I do understand now. But it is enough for me. When we get to my home and you see how beautiful the islands are, you will know what I am meaning. Does God believe in Hywel? Do *you* believe in Hywel?'

'*I do*. He's very clever – and nice.'

'There you are then. If you can believe in him, I am thinking that God must believe in him too. So you can be lovers and live happily ever after, as my grandfather used to say in his stories.'

Mary's face was red.

'Helga!' was all she said but Helga thought her smile said much more. She smiled back, feeling a bond with this girl unlike any she had experienced before. She stared ahead knowing that it was far too soon to see any of the islands of Faroyar, while both hoping and dreading that they would appear on the horizon. The horrible truth that she had been suppressing for so long would come out then. Could she burden Mary with her troubles?

Perhaps, since she had helped Mary, the girl would not mind helping her.

'Before I left my home to come to England, I . . .'

Mary was looking up at her – her face without the smile, plain and comfortable. Helga felt able to continue.

'Before I came to England I *may* have done something dreadful. I am not sure that I did but I think I must have done so.'

She stopped and waited for Mary to ask what it was that she had done but Mary just gave her an encouraging smile.

Helga tried to find a better way to say what she had to but it was no use hiding the truth any longer. She blurted out, 'I killed my mother. I am thinking that in the night I killed my mother.'

She waited for Mary's condemnation.

Mary was taken aback. She was beginning to accept shipboard life and even to enjoy the easy rhythm of four-hour shifts and the acceptance that nothing one did could hurry things along. Feeling safe and being near Hywel and knowing that the Dolphin Songs were secure with Mr Williams was enough for the present.

Now this woman, older than her and much better looking, was seemingly confessing to murder. She felt like a priest in a confessional must feel but here in the open on the bow of a boat with no protective screen between them, it all seemed more naked and raw. She didn't know how to respond so she smiled, the defence that had proved effective all her life – except once.

Helga was crying and Mary reached out and held her hand as her mother had held her own when she had been troubled at home.

Helga felt the hand warm around hers. The last time anyone had held her hand like that it had been her grandfather before he left on the trip to Iceland and had never come back. She could smell the pipe-tobacco smoke aroma of his beard, the same smell that had been on the pillow *that* night. She turned away so that Dan and Kenny could not see her crying.

'What should I be doing about it?' she asked.

'You said you only *thought* you'd killed her. You're not sure?'

Helga told her as much as she could remember but beyond standing by the bed holding the pillow, her mind was blank until she was playing her concertina to the seals and the whales were coming in from the sea.

'Maybe you didn't do anything,' Mary said. 'Maybe your mother just died. Was she very old?'

Helga tried to think but figures seemed irrelevant.

'I did not love my mother. All people should love their mothers but I did not. I was not a good daughter so I killed my mother.'

'You're not sure about that,' Mary said. 'Only God knows for sure. You must pray for Him to forgive you.'

'He would do that – even for killing my mother?'

'If you are truly sorry. Truly, truly.'

'I do not know if I am. I did not love my mother. I think she was not a nice person.'

'You can pray about that too. God understands.'

'I still am not sure that I really believe there is a God.'

'What were we saying just now? It is more important that God believes in you. I am sure that God believes in *Helga*.'

Mary smiled and Helga hoped that God *did* believe in her.

262

'I am thinking that our clothes will be dry now and we can get dressed again. Then Ken will be able to keep his mind on what Dan is wanting him to do.'

Ken was following Dan's instructions. He had unscrewed the end of the pump motor housing, removed the armature and cleaned the field magnets and the brushes. Occasionally, his attention was diverted to the line of washing above his head. He'd had no idea that Helga wore such frilly, silky underwear. His heart kept doing the payout-clunking thing. He could see Helga up at the bow with Mary, talking.

'Girl talk,' Billy Tranter would have called it.

# CHAPTER THIRTY-THREE

Dan came up at midnight to relieve Helga at the wheel. There was only a small sea running and the bright moonlight was throwing black shadows on the deck as *The Warrior* headed steadily northwards. He checked the course and used the Sat-nav unit to confirm their position. Helga had not gone below immediately as she usually did but had gone up to the bow and was staring ahead.

Dan watched her for a couple of minutes then twisted a rope loop around one of the wheel spokes to hold the course and walked forward to stand next to her.

'A penny for your thoughts,' he said, quoting what old Mrs Gaskell used to say to him when he was a boy. Helga turned her head. She had been crying.

'Now then,' he said, his words seeming to echo old Mrs Gaskell's. 'What's up?'

'I'm scared,' she told him. 'I think that before I came away I might have done something dreadful and bad. While I was in England I did not have to think if I had done it, but now I cannot hide it from myself.'

Dan waited for her to go on. He wanted to put his arm around her like Mrs Gaskell had done when *he* had been upset.

Helga started to cry. Dan's arm went around her shoulders involuntarily and drew her towards him. She turned and buried her face in his dark jersey. He held her as she cried. Her hair smelt warm and his mind flitted briefly to a hotel bedroom in Majorca but somehow this was different.

Finally, she wriggled a little and he dropped his arms as she stood back from him. He could tell by the position of the moon that *The Warrior* was veering off course but that didn't matter – he could correct it later.

'I am thinking that I might have killed my mother,' Helga said.

'Do you want to tell me about it?' he asked. They were Mrs Gaskell's words coming out of his mouth. Even the tone was hers, low and concerned.

'I really do not know what happened,' she told him. 'It is all in a muddle and mixed up with an octopus and some trolls.'

Mrs Gaskell had once read him a story about trolls and a goat that wanted to cross a bridge. He had dreamed about them for three nights afterwards. He was silent for a moment.

'Are you sure your mother is dead?' he asked.

'I am remembering going to the church and burying her in the ground. That was after *you* had come and gone away again – when I was angry with you. I think at that time I was a bit mad in the head.'

'What makes you think *you* killed her?'

'I only remember standing by her bed holding a pillow and then on the next day she was dead.'

Helga moved back towards him and his arm went round her shoulders once more as a whisper of a breeze ruffled the surface of the low waves. Her body felt warm against his side. The moon had moved to the other side of the boat. *The Warrior* must have made half a circle and was now heading south but it still didn't matter. Dan held her as she started to cry again.

'Does anyone else think you might have killed her?'

'I do not think so. *They* would not believe that I could do such a thing. *I* do not believe that I could do such a thing.'

'Then it's not important any more. Your mother is dead and you have the rest of your life to live now.'

Dan fumbled in his pocket for a handkerchief and wiped Helga's face.

'But it is *important* to me,' Helga said. 'It would be a murdering and a murdering is a bad thing to do. Especially to your own mother.'

Dan noted that *The Warrior* was beginning to head north again.

'So what,' he said and it was his own voice now. 'You may not have done *anything*. Even if you did, only you and I know and *I'm* not going to tell anyone. We all do things in our life that we regret later – even killing sometimes.' He remembered the Iraqi patrol that had wanted to surrender and Mrs Gaskell's black and white cat lying in the gutter, blood around its mouth. 'You can't bring them back.'

Helga sniffed and turned to look out over the bow. 'I told Mary and she says I should pray.'

'That wouldn't bring her back,' Dan said. He moved towards her but the moment had passed and she stepped back.

'You will be thinking that I am a silly woman after all,' she said and walked away towards the companionway.

Dan stared ahead for a minute then went back to the wheelhouse to correct the course.

*Fairlsle and the other dolphins, swimming parallel to The Warrior's course, were puzzled when the boat started to turn towards the south after heading north for so long. They swam nearer and saw the two humans standing in the bow in the moonlight.*

*'The She-salmon is sad and is being close to the Orca-man,' FairIsle said. 'They are wanting to joyn but do not know it yet.'*

*'How can you tell that?' Rockall asked.*

*'The She-salmon's mind and mine flow in similar currents. See how she is pressing against the Orca-man and he is letting the boat go in a circle. She is drawing him into her life even if she does not know it herself. Before the next new moon they will be joyned.'*

*FairIsle leapt to show her confidence in her predictions.*

Ken had found his old mouth organ behind the bunk where it had fallen out of his pocket when he had first come aboard, soaked through. When it was his next turn in the wheelhouse at night he tried to play it, softly. In films there was always one man, the quiet one, who would take out his mouth organ at just the right time and play an appropriate tune. He had longed to be that man but had never mastered even a few consecutive notes.

Hywel, lying awake thinking of Mary in the cabin across the galley, heard the discordant sounds through the open porthole and recalled his first attempts to play the mouth organ that Mr Williams had given him for his tenth birthday. He threw back the blankets, pulled on his trousers and the fleecy jacket Dan had loaned him and went up onto the moonlit deck.

*'The Mackerel has a baby wind song-maker' Rockall said as the dolphins cruised closer to The Warrior. 'But it knows no words yet.'*

*'The words are in the Mackerel's head,' FairIsle replied. 'The song-maker only turns them into pictures.'*

*'Here comes the Dogfish,' said Rockall. 'He has been drawn by the empty sounds.'*

*FairIsle leapt. It was true. The human that Rockall called the Dogfish was walking along the deck towards the place where the humans took turns to steer the boat.*

Ken saw Hywel coming and slipped the mouth organ into his pocket.

'I heard you playing and...' Hywel's voice trailed away. He was not sure what he intended to say.

Ken apologised. 'Sorry if I woke you up. I can't really play the thing.' He switched on the dim light over the chart table and took the instrument out of his pocket. 'Had it since I was a kid. Can't play a note though.'

Hywel held out his hand. The desire to create music was strong in him. 'May I?'

Ken shook the mouth organ and wiped the edge down his jumper before handing it to Hywel who tried a few tentative notes then started to play *Myfanwy*. He played quietly at first then, as the haunting spirit of the Welsh love song took him over, he moved out onto the deck and let his soul make the music for him. He could see the dolphins' fins in the moonlight as they swam closer to listen and then saw first Mary, then Helga and Dan come up the companionway steps to sit on the gunwale and listen. He had an audience of seven and the magic bond formed as he played on, working through his repertoire of Welsh and Irish songs.

Mary, sitting on the gunwale, started to shiver and Helga silently went below and returned with a blanket to drape around Mary's shoulders. Ken's envy of Hywel's skill with the mouth organ turned to respect, then to admiration.

Dan moved around the far side of the wheelhouse, went in and eased the throttle back slowly before cutting the engine and letting *The Warrior* drift silently as Hywel played on.

Helga went below again and returned carrying the accordion in its case. As Hywel moved from the *Rose of Tralee* into *Danny Boy* she stood near the bow and held up the case for Hywel to see. He nodded and as he moved into the second verse she played herself into the melody.

Soon the two players and their instruments were alternately competing and cooperating whilst the audience of three on the boat and four in the water listened in amazement and appreciation. Finally, Helga played a hymn tune familiar to Hywel and for the next half-hour, as the dawn stole the moonlight, they played favourite hymns together, ending as if by common consent with *Amazing Grace*.

As the last notes floated away over the sea the players stood and bowed to one another.

Dan wanted to clap but he had learned from the few times he had been to church with old Mrs Gaskell and the even fewer times he had been unable to avoid attending a Church Parade, that one did not clap hymns. 'Bloody hell', was all he could say as he turned towards the wheelhouse. 'Bloody *hell*'.

The four dolphins leapt in unison and Mary went up to Hywel and kissed him. Ken wanted to do the same to Helga but held back. Dan restarted the engine and steered *The Warrior* back on course. It was his shift now anyway.

*The dolphins lined up alongside the boat as it got under way.*

*'These humans continue to surprise me,' said Malin. 'Soon I will believe that some of them do have souls like dolphins and whales.'*

Later in the day Helga was on the deck of *The Warrior*, holding and stroking a plump Lucky, and staring longingly ahead, though the horizon was frequently hidden by mists and banks of fog. Her mind felt equally fog-bound. England had been an experience – now she wanted to be home but dreaded having to face up to her own reality. Supposing the police were waiting to arrest her for murder! It was all very well Dan saying that it wasn't important any more and Mary saying God would forgive her but guilt and uncertainty clouded all her thoughts.

She could see the dolphins swimming off the starboard bow and remembered that she had promised Ken that she would finish the carving for him. She put Lucky down and went below for her knife and the nearly-finished sculpture.

Ken was coming up the companionway stairs as she was about to go down. She stood aside and waited.

Dan was at the helm when Ken approached him.

'Could we tow the Zodiac for a while?' he asked. 'With me in it.'

Dan looked at the inflatable, secured on the forward deck and asked, 'Why?'

'I want to practise playing the mouth organ. Without disturbing you lot.'

'Get Hywel to come up here and steer and we'll hoist it over the side. It's time I ran the engine up anyway. The sponsons are looking a bit sad too. I'll get the foot-pump out.'

Ken sat in the Zodiac as it was towed behind *The Warrior*. The rubber boat, with its sponsons inflated to rigid tubes, swerved slightly from side to side at the end of the taut tow-rope. Ken felt almost light-headed from the events of the previous night and the unfamiliar feeling of being away from the others. The four dolphins were swimming, two either side of the Zodiac, breathing noisily as the tops of their heads and backs broke water in unison. Ken tried a few notes. One of the dolphins, Rockall, leapt close alongside and Ken dropped the mouth organ. It slid under one of the sponsons and, as he knelt to retrieve the instrument, it jammed between the tube and the floor. Ken leant forward to ease it out, his ear pressed tight against the rubber tube. He could hear the dolphins talking.

Well, not exactly *talking*, he told himself. What he could hear were squeaks and grunts and whistles which kept turning into squiggles like the ones he could remember seeing when he had first heard the tape of the dolphins' songs. In amongst the squiggles were pictures. Quite clear pictures, the most frequent one being of a mackerel like the ones Helga sometimes caught over the stern of *The Warrior*, dark stripes and all.

Ken kept his ear to the tube, concentrating on the sounds and trying to let his mind go through them to the squiggles and the more positive pictures beyond. He found, as he concentrated, that he could flip his mind from squiggles to pictures and back again then catch the picture and the squiggles together. The sounds as such were no longer relevant.

'Bloody hell,' he said, imitating Dan. 'Bloody *hell.*' It was like watching a very early and badly scratched film with subtitles in Chinese but, as he knelt with his ear tight to the sponson, the pictures cleared and the squiggles took on recognisable patterns. Patterns that were always the same for each picture. Eventually, his leg developed cramp and he sat up on the sponson, the mouth organ in his hand. The dolphins were still swimming alongside.

In his mind Ken held the picture of a mackerel with the squiggle pattern beneath it. He put the mouth organ to his lips and imitated the squiggles.

*'The Mackerel is telling us his name,' FairIsle said and leapt to show her appreciation.*

Ken called up another picture, that of *The Warrior,* and tried 'playing' the squiggles that were beneath it. FairIsle leapt again. He tried *seagulls, dolphins, wave* – all the pictures he could remember having seen when his ear had been pressed against the tube. Each was rewarded with a leap from FairIsle. He stood up and waved to Dan, signalling that he wanted to be pulled back to *The Warrior.*

'You weren't long,' Dan remarked but Ken climbed aboard and hurried below without replying. Dan let the coiled rope go and the empty Zodiac dropped back astern.

Hywel was dozing in the upper bunk of the cabin when Ken rushed in.

'Hush, man,' he said. 'I'm trying to get some . . .'

'Where's the tape thingy?' Ken asked.

Hywel sat up, careful not to bang his head on the underside of the deck close above him. 'What's going on?'

Ken explained what had happened in the Zodiac and together they went into the galley with the tape player. Mary was there, washing dishes.

'What are you two up to?' she asked as they sat at the table and started to play the tape of the dolphins' songs. Hywel held a finger to his lips as Ken spread a sheet of paper on the table and started to write words with squiggle marks against them. The tape was played over and over again until both sides of the sheet were covered in words and squiggles.

Mary had finished the dishes and sat watching quietly as Ken wrote *mackerel, seagulls, wave* and *dolphins*, each followed by a distinctive squiggle, then searched the page, running his finger along each line.

He found *dolphins* and *wave* in Rockall's song and compared the squiggles.

'They're the same,' he said. 'They're the bloody same. Sorry Mary, but they're the same – the bloody same. Sorry again.'

'What's the bloody same as what?' Mary asked.

Ken told her about listening to the dolphins through the sponson and playing the squiggles back to them with the mouth organ. He showed her and Hywel how he interpreted them, playing *mackerel*, and *seagulls*, then *wave* and *dolphins*.

'Can I have a go?' Hywel asked, holding out his hand for the instrument.

Kenny shook it, wiped it down the front of his jumper and handed it to Hywel.

Hywel imitated Ken's notes for the four words several times, then tried other squiggles from the page.

Helga came down the companionway steps carrying the carving. 'What are we all doing?' she asked. 'I was thinking I was hearing the dolphins playing the mouth organ – but it is only you I have been hearing.'

They all started to explain at once, then all stopped at once and burst out laughing.

'Mary, you tell me, the men are a little mad, I am thinking.'

Mary explained what had happened and wrote the first part of FairIsle's song on a fresh sheet of paper with the appropriate squiggle under each word. Hywel played the squiggles several times as Mary wrote out the other songs in the same way. Ken was busy with another sheet of paper.

Dan, intrigued by the sounds coming up from the galley fought off his desire to know what was happening until he could bear it no longer, checked the course, searched the surrounding sea for possible hazards and, seeing none, used a loop of rope to secure the wheel before going below.

'What are you lot up to?' he asked.

Mary explained.

'Bloody hell,' said Dan. 'Bloody *hell*.'

Ken held out his paper. 'I'm trying to write a message for the dolphins but I can only use the words from the songs. It's not that easy.'

Dan shook his head and went back up on deck. Someone had to steer the bloody boat.

Ken had written, *We – wonder – if – dolphins –*     He showed it to the others.

'If we can make up a message out of the words in the songs, we can play it to the dolphins and see if they can understand it,' he said. 'But I can't find *if.*'

Mary looked through the songs. 'There isn't an *if*. We could try *of.*'

Ken crossed the word through and they all tried to compose a message using only the words from the songs.

'The dolphin-hvals will have to be able to show to us that they are understanding what we are saying to them,' Helga said.

'They leap,' Kenny replied.

'They are often leaping. It would need to be something more special.'

Eventually, after much discussion, they agreed a message. It read *We – humans – wonder – of – you – dolphins – hear – and – know – this – symbol. Signal – knowing – swim – in – circles.*

Hywel practised the message with the mouth organ until Ken was satisfied that it was as near as possible to what they had agreed to say. The *of* did not seem to matter when the pictures appeared in his mind.

They followed Hywel up onto the deck. The dolphins were cruising alongside as Hywel went to the bow and started to play. Dan watched, bemused, from the wheelhouse.

As Hywel played the last note the four dolphins leapt together and swam in unmistakable circles. Ken clapped his hands. Mary hugged Hywel and Helga walked back the wheelhouse to explain it all to Dan.

'Bloody hell,' he said. 'Bloody *hell.*'

Ken, Mary and Hywel sat in the Zodiac near *The Warrior*, which was drifting with the engine off. Dan and Helga were leaning on *The Warrior's* gunwale watching as the dolphins circled slowly. Ken had his ear to the pontoon and Hywel was holding the mouth organ.

Mary waved to attract the dolphins attention and pointed up at the sun.

*'That human is wanting us to say the word for the Light-giver,' Fairlsle said.*

*'How can you know that?' Rockall asked.*

*'I can sense her mind-waves.' She turned towards the inflatable. 'Sun,' she said, repeating the word several times, 'Sun. Sun, Sun.'*

Ken picked up the sounds, then the picture of a glowing ball, then the squiggles – all repeated four times. He sat up, wrote on a piece of paper then compared the new squiggles with the ones Mary had written earlier from the dolphins' songs. They were exactly the same as those under Sun in 'Sun, sea, companionship and joy . . .' He jumped to his feet, punched the air and shouted, 'Yes.'

'Steady,' said Mary, 'or you'll fall over the side.'

Ken sat down, dazzled by her smile. 'Do another,' he asked, breathlessly.

Mary pointed at *The Warrior.*

*'Now she is asking the word for the big boat,' FairIsle said and spoke it four times.*

Ken heard it, drew the squiggle pattern and passed the paper to Hywel. 'Try playing that,' he said.

Hywel played the pattern twice. Two of the dolphins leapt and the other two swam in circles. He played the notes again and this time all four dolphins swam in a circle. Ken was grinning and bouncing up and down on the sponson like a four-year-old and Mary's smile was lighting up the whole boat.

Helga put her hand on Dan's arm as they stood side by side near the wheelhouse. 'Hywel is making the dolphin-hval's word for *The Warrior*,' she said.

'How do you know that?'

'I can see it in the sounds.'

'You're kidding!'

'No. It is true. The music says to me, *'This is the big boat.'* I do not know how I am knowing that.'

'You saw Mary pointing this way,' said Dan, still unwilling to believe what was happening all around him.

Mary was trying other words. She indicated parts of her body – head, arms, and legs. Each time a picture and pattern of squiggles came back which Ken copied and passed to Hywel who played them and was rewarded by the dolphins swimming in circles.

Helga could 'see' each word in the sounds even without watching Mary's action first. She went down to her cabin and came up carrying the accordion and when Hywel looked her way she held it up questioningly as she had the night before. Hywel made a thumbs-up sign and when he played the next word, '*sky*,' Helga copied it.

FairIsle and Rockall, clearly identifiable by their scarred dorsal fins, swam forward and circled for her whilst the other two dolphins did the same for the trio in the Zodiac.

Then, whilst Mary was searching for some new thing to indicate, feeling like a child trying to play 'I spy,' Helga, at the bow of *The Warrior*, played a different pattern of notes. FairIsle alone swam in a circle.

*Rockall asked, 'How did the She-salmon know to say that?'*

*'I put it in her mind. I have told you before, the She-salmon and I swim in similar currents. You watch now. I will speak it for you as well as tell it to the She-salmon.'*

*She turned towards The Warrior and said, 'My companion, Elegance of Rockall would like you to show us that you understand my words. To show that you do, turn your body around two times and then speak these words back to me with the little-wind-song-maker.'*

*They watched as the She-salmon did exactly as FairIsle had asked. FairIsle circled a response and Rockall leapt an acknowledgement.*

*'I can teach her many words and she will then be able to talk with us all,' FairIsle said as Malin and Lundy joined them.*

*They saw the three humans in the Zodiac draw it up under the stern of the boat and climb aboard.*

For over three hours words, patterns, and accordion notes flowed back and forth between FairIsle in the sea and Helga, who appeared to be in some kind of trance, on the deck.

Then as if Helga had passed through some kind of barrier, the notes changed. The separate notes merged and the sounds became a sort of music, continuous and haunting in their beauty. No one on the boat spoke and the dolphins floated near the bow listening intently.

*The little-wind-song-maker was singing words of greeting from the humans on the boat to all whales and dolphins. It sang words of apology on behalf of other humans for blind, unthinking killings, it sang of hope for the future – hope of understanding between whalekind and humankind.*

*It told of life on the Land and of things out of sight of the sea that dolphins had only been able to guess at before. Then it became more personal. The She-Salmon was telling of their voyage north to her home in the Faroff Islands and that, though she would try to persuade her countrymen not to kill the hvals, they must all stay safely away until she could assure them that there was no danger.*

*The music died and the She-Salmon stood up, the stance of her body indicating a strange state between great elation and extreme fatigue.*

*'That is the **little**-wind-song-maker?' Lundy asked. 'May I live to hear the **Great**-One.'*

Helga stumbled down the companionway stairs, her cheeks wet with tears and fell face down on her bunk. Ken went to follow her.

'She needs to be alone,' Dan called after him. 'You can talk to her later.'

Hywel looked back along the deck to where Ken was now comparing notes with an ever-smiling Mary. He'd finished reading Skipper Jack's elephant book and had been intrigued by the God which, in that story, had motivated and guided the elephants and, by the end of the book, the human characters as well. Now *there* was a God which seemed plausible even to him. Perhaps Mary was not so very wrong after all . . . What was it that Spikey Smith – English – had once read to his less than fully attentive class? 'There are more things in heaven and earth, Horatio, than are dreamt of in your philosophy.' He couldn't even remember who Horatio was, but for some inexplicable reason the quote had stayed with him.

# CHAPTER THIRTY-FOUR

'You sold it for a grand? A poxy, snivelling grand! You're a bloody fool, Alex bloody Bowen, a bloody fool. Have you seen the tele? Have you listened to the radio? It's dolphins, dolphins, dolphins, dolphins bloody dolphins all day long.'

Alex slumped in the chrome and plastic armchair and took the cellophane wrapper off a packet of cigarettes. Amanda's tantrums usually didn't last. He lit a cigarette as the tirade continued.

'I suppose you sold it to that Eddie bloody Steady. *He's* as tight as a mouse's arsehole. That tape would have been worth millions. I could have gone to Aspen four, even five times a year.'

Alex ventured a response and immediately regretted it.

'I couldn't be sure that it was genuine. A grand seemed good money at the time.'

'It didn't have to be *genuine*. The bloody experts are still arguing about that. People *want* to believe it's genuine – so it *is*. God-dammit man, people *love* dolphins – they *want* to believe they can sing and think like bloody human beings.'

Alex looked at the television in the corner – on as usual with the sound turned down. As if on cue, dolphins were leaping on the screen then pictures came up of pickets outside a Marine Park in America. Placards read, 'FREE THE DOLPHINS.' 'LET WHALES SWIM FREE.' 'SEE US FOR WHAT WE ARE.'

Amanda was still ranting – keep your head down Alex-boy and your mouth shut. He drew deeply on the cigarette. You can't win this one.

Perhaps he *should* have asked Eddie for more money.

Amanda's voice was high pitched and penetrating. '. . . on every radio programme. If they're not playing that bloody tape you *gave* away – they're discussing it. Do you know that tape is Top of the Pops? Do you know what *that's* worth? Eddie bloody Steady is laughing all the way to the bloody bank.'

Keep your head down, Alex. He stubbed out the half-smoked cigarette. Boy, could she go on. She wasn't British Slalom Champion for nothing. She would burn out soon though.

'. . . and have you thought what your Uncle bloody Gareth will be thinking? Have you? We won't see a penny of *his* money now. You're a dickhead, Alex Bowen, a bloody dickhead. I'm going out to get pissed.'

More dolphins leapt on the silent screen as Alex heard the front door slam. He pressed the 'sound on' button on the remote control unit.

A voice-over on the dolphin film was saying:

*'Effective vocal communication, using a wide range of words, must be considered to be the real test of high intelligence. In that case dolphins . . .'*

Alex pressed the 'off' button and stood up. He might as well go out and get pissed too.

Ken was at the wheel as the sun dropped towards the western horizon. Stars were just beginning to show, pale dots in a mauve sky. He read the figures that Dan had written down for him and turned the wheel until the compass lined up on that course, selected a star straight ahead and steered towards it. He found he was humming a tune, *When you wish upon a star.* What film was that from? One of the Disney ones – Pinocchio – that was it. Then he thought back to that day's events. The dolphins had been 'talking' to them and Helga had been talking to the dolphins. It was like one of those magical evenings in the Home when none of them had been quarrelling and they were working together on some common project. It had not happened often but when it had, it was magic. Today had been magical like that.

He thought of the others down below, chatting or playing draughts on the little table in the galley and felt quite lonely. He looked out of the door but it was now too dark to see the dolphins. Soon Dan or one of the others would come up 'for a breath of fresh air' but really to see if he was OK. He was glad of those visits and did the same himself when others were alone at the wheel for long periods.

None of them had heard the news that day. At 6 p.m. all the three men had been trying to catch up on their missed sleep, trusting Mary to steer *The Warrior* as Helga was still asleep on her bunk in the cabin the two women shared. Ken switched on the radio and twiddled the knobs to find a programme to entertain him until the late news came on or someone came up from the galley. He hoped it would be Helga, though she now seemed to enjoy being near to Dan much of the time. Not that they said much when he was about – they just seemed to want to be near one another like Billy Tranter and Sharon had last year. Hywel and Mary were the same.

As the frequency-finder on the radio passed a station he was sure he could hear a snatch of FairIsle's song. He turned the knob back and it *was* FairIsle singing.

> *See us for what we are*
> *Peaceful, gentle, cultured people of the Sea.*

The song was followed by voices speaking in what sounded to him like French. He turned the knob to another station. Rockall was singing now

> *. . . my mind – a toxic stream in spate . . .*

Further round the dial it was Nordstar's song and then Rockall's again. What the hell was going on?

He pressed the buzzer and held it down – the agreed signal for 'All hands on deck'. Dan had made them all rehearse it several times since leaving Ireland.

Dan was up the companionway steps first, followed by the others, each carrying a life jacket.

'What's up, Ken?'

'Listen to this,' Ken spluttered. 'Our dolphins are on the radio. Singing. All over the place.'

Someone was speaking in German. Helga said 'Shuss,' and translated. '. . . even – in – China – the songs – of – the dolphins – can be – heard – in – in . . . I am sorry. He is talking too fast for me, but I am sure that he is speaking about the hval's songs.'

As if to confirm this, Nordstar's voice sang:

> *Out of the Northern Sea I swam . . .*

Dan turned the tuning knob:

> '. . . and has the unique property of being heard and understood in any of the known languages. This property has been given the name "Audio Pictography"' by scientists at Edinburgh University who have been analysing the recording. In a special programme on Radio Four at Ten Thirty tonight, the recording will be played in full and discussed by a panel of leading scientists.'

Another half turn:

*'. . . were first played on a radio breakfast programme, Eddie Steady Go and then pirated from there. Not only have tapes and compact discs been made but the songs have been dubbed onto existing video film of dolphins and are selling in their thousands.'*

Dan turned it a little more, past a voice giving the closing prices in London, New York and Tokyo, and heard:

*'News is coming in from Japan that the crew of a Japanese whaling vessel have mutinied in the Pacific Ocean where Japan has, for many years, taken whales for scientific analysis. Conservationists have always held that this operation has been a cover to provide whale meat for consumption. The ship is reported to be returning to its home port.*

*'In America, crowds have gathered outside . . .*

He turned it a little further:

*'Not since the funeral service of Diana, Princess of Wales, back in 1997, has the whole world been so emotionally united. The plight of dolphins and whales, as described in the so-called Dolphin songs . . .*

'Bloody hell,' said Dan. 'Bloody *hell.*'

'Can I use your mobile?' Hywel asked. 'I must speak to Mr Williams.'

Dan fetched the phone, not at all sure if there was a compatible system in the Faeroes or if there was, whether they would be within signal distance.

'Hywel? I've been expecting you to ring,' Mr Williams said. 'I'd have called *you* but I didn't have a number. I'm sorry about the tape. It was all my fault. Do you remember that nephew of mine, Alex – my sister's brat? Well, he came here and . . .'

He explained about Alex's visit.

'. . . all my fault really. I should have been more careful. I feel I've let you down badly.'

'I don't think that any harm's been done, Mr Williams. We – I – we were supposed to be taking the songs to the world of people. That's what my friend Mary calls it. It would seem that this has happened better then *we* could ever have arranged it. Anyway – it's done now.'

'You must tell me about this Mary sometime – it's time you found yourself a nice girl. How up to date are *you*, Hywel-boy? I've been following events all day on the television. It's been really exciting. Did you see what happened in Norway?'

'No. We're all on a boat. We've only just picked it up on the radio.'

'Have you got a minute?'

'Got all night if need be. Well, until the batteries run out, that is.'

'The pirating of the tapes, as they call it, just happened to coincide with the release of a report that DNA tests on some whale meat being shipped from Norway to Japan showed it was from a blue whale, not a minke. Blues are protected and whatever feelings there may have been in Norway in favour of whaling, they all went up the chimney.

'Some alert television company sent a team to the whaling ship's home port where it was tied up to the quay and they've been transmitting live from there all day. The whole world's been watching. At about tea time there was a crowd of thousands who just swarmed onto the dock and then onto the boat. The police couldn't do a thing. Someone must have opened the stopcocks for the boat sank in the harbour and the crowd on the quay cheered themselves hoarse. Hans – he's a friend of mine – drank their health and we cheered a bit ourselves.

'Hang on. There's something else coming up – The United Nations are going to debate whaling and captive dolphins soon, but I'd say it's a foregone conclusion that it'll all be banned. Give me that phone number now and I'll keep you posted. Thanks for not giving me hell about the tape. You did ask me to keep it safe after all. Good-night, son.'

Hywel relayed what he had just been told to the others.

'Bloody hell,' said Dan. 'Bloody *hell*.' He went out and stood up in the bow, staring into the darkness. From what he had just heard, *The Warrior* had no future role.

The rest of Dan's crew were clustered in the tiny wheelhouse, the little bulb over the chart table lighting their faces. Helga was smiling. 'All the hvals will be safe now,' she said and Kenny punched the air and shouted, 'Yes.'

Helga went up to the bow and stood next to Dan.

'You will still be taking me to Faroyar?' she asked.

'I don't see why not. We're nearly there anyway.'

'What will I do for a job?' he was wondering. Perhaps he could sell *The Warrior* in the Faeroes?

# CHAPTER THIRTY-FIVE

*Grace of Tyne and Grace of Humber had mourned the loss of the ebullient FairIsle in the place the Stargazers had called the Channel of Sacrifice.*

*After the panic of their own escape to the sea, they had turned back on the slight chance that FairIsle might also have escaped but the blood of the starwhales was tainting the water and, although they whistled and sent their calls vibrating up the fjord, there was no response other than the distant songs of the last dying whales.*

*They had waited at the mouth of the fjord in the silent sea until hope had faded with the dropping of the sun behind the hills, then turned sorrowfully towards the open sea again and headed south, away from the horror of the Faroff Islands.*

*Two moon cycles later they had been on their home waters patrol, cruising slowly past the humans' light tower at the end of the spit of land near Humber's birth place, when they became aware of two other creatures swimming close to them – creatures who each had the long single tusk of a Conductor of the Sea.*

*'There are two ~yegods~ near to us,' Humber bubbled silently to Tyne.*

*'I have seen them,' she bubbled back. 'What could they want of us?'*

*The ~yegods~ swam closer.*

*~**Your daughter, Grace of FairIsle, lives,**~ one said, addressing himself to Tyne, his voice deep and resonant.*

*Tyne leapt involuntarily before asking, 'Where is she?'*

*~**She is to the south of this land, held in captivity by the humans near to the Great Rock and the Bank of Pebbles. Soon she will be fulfilling her destiny and will then be free.**~*

*'We must seek release from our patrol duties and go to her,' Humber said.*

*~**You may leave at once,**~ the ~yegod~ said, his tusk waving to emphasise the words.*

*'But our patrol . . .'*

*~**All dolphins are to leave this Sea. It is unsafe. Human water-poisons have made it so. You may both leave now.**~*

*Tyne leapt again.*

The dolphins thanked the ~yegods~ and sped southwards, resting only infrequently. They passed through the patrol areas that the humans call Thames, Dover and Wight to arrive at the one they call Portland.

They called and whistled as they swam towards the great rock, hopeful of a response but the sea was silent of all whale-sound. No dolphin nor whale responded to their signals.

Off the southern-most tip of the great rock-mass they met a porpoise chasing a lone salmon that twisted and turned in the rushing current as it tried to escape its pursuer. The dolphins watched the hunt, waiting, as is proper, until the porpoise had caught and eaten the fish before declaring themselves.

'How are your seas?' Tyne asked.

'Calm 'nuff,' replied the porpoise. 'Your swim?'

'Favourable currents,' responded Tyne, impatiently following the time-honoured greeting. 'No Orcas?'

'None known.'

'That is good. – We are seeking news of my daughter, Grace of FairIsle.'

'Fair-Isle?' repeated the porpoise.

'Have you knowledge of her whereabouts?' Tyne asked him.

'Know-ledge?' replied the porpoise.

'Do you know anything of my daughter?'

'Fair-Isle?'

'~Yegods~!' Tyne bubbled to Humber, then asked the porpoise, 'Do – you – have – knowledge – of – my – daughter – the – dolphine – Grace – of – Fair – Isle?'

'Oh yes,' replied the porpoise, snapping at a piece of weed drifting by.

'Tell – us – what – you – know – please,' Tyne asked.

'Swam off,' said the porpoise.

'When?'

'Ten days.'

'Which way?'

'West-wards.'

'Alone?'

'Not her.'

'Who with?'

'Rock-all.'

Tyne glanced at Humber but she indicated, 'Not known to me.'

'Only Rockall?'

'Oh no.'

'Who else?'

'Mal-in.'

'Just those?'

'Oh no.'

'Who else.'

'Lun-dy.'

'Who else?'

'No more.'

'All well?'

'Not well.'

'How hurt?'

'Fins bad.'

'Which fins?'

'On back.'

'Did all the dolphins have hurt back fins?' Tyne asked.

'Oh no,' replied the porpoise and Tyne again bubbled, '~Yegods~!'

'Which ones?' she asked.

'Fair-Isle.'

'Who else?'

'Rock-all.'

'Malin?'

'Oh no.'

'Lundy?'

'Oh no.'

'Thank you,' said Tyne. 'We will follow and find them.'

'Good luck,' whistled the porpoise after them as the dolphines powered up current to the west.

'Flu-ent!' said Humber.

'You joke,' Tyne replied.

'West-wards is big,' remarked Humber as the rush of the tide race eased and Lyme Bay opened before them.

'Hope swims with dolphins,' Grace of Tyne replied. 'We will find her.'

For days they traced the passage of FairIsle's joy through Plymouth, Sole and Fastnet and into Shannon.

Here they met Elegance of Kerry and Grace of Valentia.

After the formal greeting Tyne said, 'We seek news of my daughter, Grace of FairIsle – swimming with three other 'phins.'

'They were here,' Fungie told them, 'but have now swum northwards to the Faroff Islands. They were with a human's boat.'

Fungie and Valentia gave all the news they could, assuring Humber and Tyne that the damage to FairIsle's fin was healing and that otherwise she was well.

'She has joyned with her companion, Elegance of Rockall. He is a good 'phin but still suffers from his confinement by the humans,' Valentia said. 'I scanned your daughter for new-life but it is too soon to be sure.'

*'Great things are afloat in the World,' Fungie said as he wished them farewell. 'I dare to hope it will be for the good of Whalekind.'*

*Humber and Tyne swam north through Malin and Hebrides towards the area that humans call Faeroes but is known to starwhales as the Eighteen Islands and to dolphins as the Faroffs. They had swum a huge circle since they had last seen FairIsle.*

The nights were getting longer and even at sea there was a sense of approaching autumn. Darkness still came slowly but the evening and night watches, that they all now shared, went slowly.

Hywel relieved Helga at midnight but she stayed by the open door of the wheelhouse talking to him about the day's news. So much had happened in the last twenty-four hours. She asked him what his plans would be when they got to the Faeroes but it was obvious that he had not thought ahead yet. They talked again about the dolphins then, when Helga judged the mood was right she said, 'I am expecting that Mary will have told you about me and my mother?'

'No,' said Hywel. 'What about her?'

Helga was surprised.

'She has not told you that I have killed my mother?'

'Not a word. Did you? Kill her I mean.'

'I am not quite sure but I think I did.'

'Accidentally?'

Hywel turned the wheel slightly to realign the bow on the star he was steering by.

Helga told him what she had told Mary and Dan.

'What do *you* think I should be doing about this thing?' she asked.

'Not for me to say, really. Up to you, like. But I was always taught to own up when I had done something wrong.'

'Then I would have to go to the women's prison in Danmark. I would not like that. I would miss the sea and the birds and the dolphins and the other hvals. It would be for me like it was for the dolphin-hvals in the pool in England.'

'First they would have to prove that you did it. Could they?'

'I am not knowing. I have never done anything like that before.'

'Maybe you didn't this time. You said you weren't sure.'

'I am not *sure*, but I am *thinking* that I did.'

Ken came up on deck with two mugs of hot chocolate.

'I couldn't sleep,' he said. 'I heard you talking so I brought this up for you.'

'You have heard what we have been saying?' she asked.

'I did overhear a bit,' he admitted. 'But I don't think you did it.'

Helga smiled. Ken would say that.

Hywel walked to the stern rail to relieve himself over the side in the darkness, Ken took the wheel until he came back.

'It's a lovely night', Ken said. 'I'll do your shift if you like. It'll cost you that mug of choccy though.'

'It's a deal,' said Hywel. Helga's dilemma was not something that he felt he could help with. He hurried off and down the companionway steps.

Ken confirmed the course with Helga, selected a guide star and they stood side by side in the intimacy of the wheelhouse drinking from the chunky china mugs.

'You can tell me,' Ken said at last. 'I *am* your friend.'

Helga told him all she could remember of that night and of her fears that the police would be waiting and that they would take her to prison.

Ken thought of Billy Tranter doing porridge back in England. It seemed another lifetime away. What could he say that would help? Friends were supposed to help one another.

'Do they send women to prison in the Faeroes?' he asked.

'I do not remember a woman from Faroyar ever having to go to prison. I would be the first.'

'But you didn't do it.' Kenny was loyal to the last. 'There's nothing they could prove.'

'But even if the police do not come, *I* would know that I had done a bad thing to my mother and I do not know if I could be happy to be knowing that.'

This was beyond Ken's experience. Billy Tranter had said that if you didn't get caught you were OK and if you did get caught but 'they' couldn't *prove* anything, you were still OK.'

He felt himself to be a poor friend, not being able to help.

The moon rose above a bank of fog or low cloud far to the east and he could see the Zodiac following easily behind *The Warrior* on its tow rope and the four dolphins keeping station to starboard. What would *they* make of all this? Did dolphins have to worry about such things? Maybe they would have answers to Helga's questions. Helga had always called FairIsle her friend.

'You can *talk* to the dolphins,' he said. 'Why don't you ask them what to do?'

'Do you think that they, the dolphin-hvals, would know?' Helga asked eagerly.

Ken felt foolish at having raised her hopes so stupidly. What could dolphins know about such things? They just lived in the sea and swam about having a good time chasing fish even if, as he knew, they could talk *and* sing. He was sure that they wouldn't know about murders and courts and policemen and prisons. He was about to say so when Helga said, 'I will talk to the dolphins sometime.'

Before he could say anything more she had hurried off and disappeared down the companionway steps.

Dan was dreaming of old Mrs Gaskell feeding her goldfish in the round glass bowl on her window sill, only in the bowl were tiny dolphins and she was feeding the goldfish to them one by one while an R S P C A inspector was knocking on the door trying to get in.

The knocking woke him and he called, 'What is it?'

Helga's voice asked, 'Can I come in? I have something I am wanting to be doing.'

Dan sat up and ran his fingers through his hair with his left hand while he reached for the light switch with his right. The engine note was steady and the sea calm – no problem there. His watch, hanging in the hook near his head, told him it was just after 2.30 in the morning. What did Helga want of him in the middle of the night?

'Come in,' he called, hoping she had come to seek physical solace but knowing she wouldn't have.

She opened the door and stepped in hesitantly, leaving the door open behind her. It was *not* that.

'You will be thinking it is a silly thing to be doing in the night but I am wanting to be talking to the dolphin-hvals from the rubber boat.'

He looked at her, her eyes bright and eager, her hair as usual in an immaculate plait and said, 'Give me five minutes and I'll come up and get things organised.'

Helga closed the door behind her and he dressed before going on deck. Helga had already drawn the Zodiac up to the stern and was standing ready to step into it, her concertina in her hand. Ken was at the wheel although Dan was sure it should have been Hywel's watch. He went into the wheelhouse and checked the course. Spot on.

'Keep her on that,' he told Ken needlessly. He could ask about the change of duties later.

Helga, holding the towline so that the Zodiac was up under the stern, asked Dan if there was a longer rope.

'I want to be further back behind the boat,' she explained.

'Nothing suitable,' Dan told her and in the glow from the wheelhouse door, could see the look of disappointment in her face.

'You could go free,' he said. 'As long as you keep in sight of the masthead light you won't come to any harm with the sea as calm as this.' He coiled the rope and dropped the coil into the Zodiac as soon as Helga had climbed down into it, then went to the wheelhouse, took over from Ken and throttled back the engine. After a few minutes at slow speed he stopped it entirely and *The Warrior* soon lay becalmed.

As Hywel and Mary came on deck Dan could hear Helga playing her concertina in the darkness, the music low and fervent.

Hywel asked why the engine was stopped. Ken put his finger to his lips and pointed out into the night towards the distant music. Hywel reached out and held Mary's hand.

---

*'The She-salmon is singing to us with the little-wind-song-maker,' Rockall told FairIsle even though it was apparent that she had heard this for herself.*

*'Hear her song,' she bubbled to him and they listened with Malin and Lundy as the She-salmon sang her sorrow and her concerns to them.*

*When the music had finished and the boat had circled back to take the soft-skinned boat in tow again, Rockall asked FairIsle what they should do.*

*'It would seem that when the She-salmon felt herself to be a captive in the Faroff Islands, something exploded in her head as the Orca-man's package did in the Pool of Shame when we were captives and this made her not herself.'*

*'But can this excuse the taking of another's life?' Malin asked. 'Not even the Culler Whales, the Orcas, can kill their own kind even if they are Laggards, as this human who died would seem to have been to her own kind. Though we hate it when the Orcas take our aged loved ones, it leaves us to swim free. It would seem that the humans have no Land Orcas to do the same for them.'*

*'The She-salmon fears captivity in a dry pool in another land. That must be the humans' penalty for killing one's own kind.'*

*'Remember, she also sang that she was not sure if she did do a killing. The explosion inside her head made her not sure. If she did not, it would be even worse for her to be put as a captive in the dry pool.'*

*'Surely the other humans would not do that to her?'*

*'She feared it to be so.'*

*'Could it be that if she goes to this pool we could swim with her as she swam with us in our Pool of Shame?'*

*'She could swim in the water with us but we could not live for long in a dry pool such as she sang of.'*

*'Her concern was not just a fear of captivity. In her song she sought forgiveness and understanding.'*

*'I know a way to comfort her,' FairIsle said.*

286

Helga did not know if she had expected an immediate reaction from the dolphins after she had played her fears to them. They had circled the Zodiac slowly as she had played but, when she had finished, they had sunk and swum away together. Perhaps they were horrified at what she had told them. Any dreams of help from them drained away and she slumped in the boat until Dan, hearing that the music had stopped, restarted *The Warrior's* engine and brought it gently up alongside the Zodiac. Ken and Hywel helped her climb aboard and Mary took her arm and guided her down the companionway steps to her bunk where Helga lay crying quietly to herself.

Helga's dream came as dawn tinted the eastern sky with a delicate blush of pink and the other crew members clustered in and around the wheel house discussing her problem.

From where Ken stood he could see the fins of the four dolphins keeping station some distance away. As the light strengthened he saw one of them swim away from the others until it was close alongside, near to the cabin shared by Helga and Mary. He knew by the distinctive scarring on her dorsal fin that this was Helga's friend, FairIsle.

*Helga was aware of being a young salmon, a smolt, swimming down a rushing river, eager for the taste of a great sea that she knew instinctively would be at the end of the river though she had never made the journey before. Behind her swam some dark and fearsome secret – a huge dark eel of a fear that pursued her relentlessly. Only the wide-open sea would offer a relief from pursuit and the freedom she craved.*

*Now she was in the sea, tasting the salt and changing, not into a sleek silver salmon as she had expected – but into an Orca. She could see herself reflected on the underside of the surface, her skin now black and white and her body huge. Fish, that moments before had seem large and threatening, were now tiny, hardly worth snapping at. She rose to breathe and her breath whooshed skywards in a spray of fine droplets. She dived and powered downwards into dark green water before rising slowly to breath again.*

*Swimming alongside her she could see two tusked nar-hvals and beyond them, at a respectful distance, were her friends the dolphin-hvals, FairIsle and Rockall. Beyond them again, vague in the sea murk, was a larger shape that might or might not be a white grindhval.*

*One of the Nar-hvals was speaking.*

*~Helga of Eysthavn,~ it said, its voice like that of a judge in one of the plays Helga had heard on the English radio way back in another life.*

*~Helga of Eysthavn, it has been reported that you have taken the life of your mother. Is this a truth?~*

*Helga struggled to speak but no words came.*

*The Nar-hval asked again, ~Is this a truth?~*

*Before she could answer, the dolphin-hval, FairIsle, was at her side speaking for her.*

*'I know the one who is accused. She is unable to speak for herself so I must speak on her behalf. She is good and honest and is a friend of all Whalekind. If she did such a killing it was because she was driven beyond endurance and deserves our pity – and your mercy.'*

*~If we do not punish her, others may take advantage of our leniency and err likewise,~ the Nar-hval replied. ~When she returns to the land will you take her punishment for her if it is found to be justified? A tusking in the belly would be her due.~*

*'I would do that, for I owe her my life and freedom. May I make a suggestion though?'*

*FairIsle's voice was low and respectful.*

*~Speak,~ commanded the second Nar-hval.*

*'Should it be true that, under great stress, the accused one did kill her mother then the life lost could be replaced with another life of equal value.'*

*~Speak on,~ said the second Nar-hval.*

*FairIsle continued. 'On the boat above our heads is a male Orca who has also been of great service to Whalekind though he is not fully aware of the importance of his role as yet. He desires this female. If she were to joyn with him, a new life, a continuation of the life of the dead one, could result and the debt would be repaid. A Life for a Life.'*

*~That would be no punishment,~ said the first Nar-hval.*

*'There may have been no offence,' countered FairIsle.*

*~You speak boldly.~*

*'I care greatly for the accused. I will speak for her even if it costs me a tusk in my belly. It is to her that I owe everything.'*

*~Will the accused do as you have suggested and produce the new-life to replace the life that was lost?~*

*Helga signalled her assent and watched the Nar-hvals clash tusks and fade away into the green sea. She turned to thank FairIsle but the sea was empty except for shoals of tiny fish that swam in circles around her head, to disappear as her dream faded.*

When Helga woke at midday she was feeling brighter. A great weight had been taken from her though she was not really clear why. She dressed and went up onto the deck.

'We should be in sight of the first of the islands at 0800 hours tomorrow,' Dan told her after reading the position from the Sat-nav unit. 'Then at your place late afternoon.'

Ken, his face tanned a deep brown from the sun and sea winds, came back from doing some job up at the bow and said, 'You won't forget to finish carving the dolphins for me, will you?'

The latest news confirmed that the United Nations Assembly had carried a motion without further debate after the 'Dolphin Song' recording had been played in the chamber. All hunting and killing of whales and dolphins was to cease immediately and cetaceans in captivity anywhere in the world were to be prepared for release into the sea.

Never before in the history of the U N had a motion been passed without a single objection.

At dawn the next day Helga came on deck and stood in the bow, staring forward over a flat calm sea. A thin mist hid the view ahead but the abundance of sea birds indicated the nearness of land. Shearwaters swept by, missing the updrafts from waves that normally allowed them to fly with minimal wing movements, and tiny bright-billed lundi swam and dived all around the boat. She sat on the gunwale, rubbing the backs of the carved dolphins with a sheet of fine sandpaper that she had found in the boat's toolbox. Today, she would be home and she had promised Ken that the carving would be finished. He was at the helm watching her from the wheelhouse.

Dan came up on deck and looked about. They should be able to see land in an hour or so. He had never known a sea so smooth – it was like floating on mercury. He checked the course with Ken and stayed in the wheelhouse chatting and watching Helga busy at the bow. There was not the slightest trace of a swell and, as the mists cleared and the sun rose, it felt as though the whole world was holding its breath waiting for something momentous to happen.

After a while he realised that Helga had not heard the news of the United Nations' decision. He went forward, sat by her side and told her what they had heard on the radio.

'Will you tell the dolphins?' he asked.

*The four dolphins had eaten their dawn-meal and were cruising along-side the trawler when the She-salmon came up to the bow carrying the little-wind-song-maker. When she finished playing the message they digested the scarcely credible news along with their morning fish, and discussed the future.*

'We are near the Faroff Islands,' FairIsle said. 'You've all seen the birds. We must leave the humans soon and take Nordstar's story to the stargazers. Her body **must** have been eaten by creatures of the Land as even now the crabs will be eating the body of the white-haired human to the west of the Great Rock. The prophecy is satisfied and humans in the Islands can no longer kill stargazers or **any** dolphin or whale. The She-salmon has confirmed this in her song to us. All Whalekind is safe.'

She leapt her joy and the others followed, sharing her pleasure.

From the top of her leap she saw the sea far ahead was flecked with black fins. She leapt again to make sure. There, in the distance, was a constellation of stargazers heading slowly towards the islands. Soon their doleful songs reached the dolphins through the water.

As before, each starwhale was singing its own Song of Truth, though the whole merged as one melancholy pattern of sound. It was apparent that they had not heard the news and were swimming to sacrifice themselves to the humans to further expiate Sirius' shameful act of so long ago.

FairIsle surged forward and sought out the leader.

'Wait,' she called. 'Wait and hear. You are all free of the Death-duty – men no longer kill whales!'

The songs died into an incredulous silence, the water vibrating with expectancy as hundreds of whales turned towards the dolphine.

'Can this be the truth?' asked the leader. 'Can it be that after a thousand years of sacrifice **we** are the ones to be spared?'

FairIsle leapt the great 'YES'.

'Where have you heard this?' the starwhale leader asked.

'From the humans themselves,' FairIsle said and explained the reports from the Humans' Council that the She-salmon had sung to her with the little-wind-song-maker less than an hour before.

'I would find what you tell us hard to believe,' the leader said, 'except that the stars have told us something similar. Last night, as is our custom, we circled and looked to the Skies. There were signs of only **two** imminent deaths, not hundreds as we had expected. Some of the younger starwhales said we should chose two out of our number to die while the rest of us swam free, but I felt that we had no right to abandon our duty until we knew of a white starwhale's death with a white-headed human and the subsequent cross-consumption. Have you knowledge of such an event?'

FairIsle again leapt the great 'YES'.

'We can tell you of that,' she said. 'We were **there** when a starwhale – Nordstar the Virgin – died with a white-headed human. She left a Song for you. I do not have the voice of a starwhale, but I remember her every word. I will sing it for you.'

*Out of the Northern Sea I swam*
*To satisfy an age-old prophecy*
*My life a sacrifice. I am*
*Part of the everlasting saga of the Sea*
*'I did not fail,' I cry –*
*Though I must die.*

*Out of the Northern Sea I swam*
*The hope of life for all my kin and kind*
*The Times and Tides were not right then*
*Now hear our Songs of Hope for all Whalekind*
*So though I dread the coming pain*
*Let it not be in vain.*

*Hope fills my heart for all Whalekind*
*Though soon into the endless night I'll swim*
*And echoes fade and stars grow dim for me*
*I trust Mankind will hear our plea*
*Sung from this place of shame*
*Let whales swim free again*
*Let whales swim free again.*

'*That* was **her** *song.*'

There was a great silence through which the distant throbbing of a trawler's engine could just be heard.

'And now you tell us that Mankind has heard Nordstar's song,' the leader said. 'If this is true we must honour her memory. We will swim in joy to the Channel of Sacrifice and remember the million whales who have died for Sirius' shame. The ~yegods~ demanded a harsh price for a moment's folly. Will the human female get the song-maker to sing to us so that we can be sure?'

It was Ken who saw the fins of the pilot whales from the bow of *The Warrior*. Helga was looking at the distant cliffs of the most southerly of the islands.

'Look,' she said. 'There is Suduroy. Today I will be home.'

'What's that?' Ken asked, pointing at the mass of black fins ahead.

'Those are the grindhvals, they have come to welcome me.'

'How would they know you are here?' Ken asked dubiously.

'The dolphins have told them,' Helga replied confidently. 'Look. There is FairIsle coming to tell me about them.' She pointed out the distinctive scar-tipped dorsal fin of the dolphine she had come to love.

*FairIsle swam alongside and 'spoke' to Helga.*

*'The starwhales want you to sing to them,' FairIsle told her. 'I have told them of Mankind's decision never again to kill whales or dolphins, but they have given so many lives to the people of the Eighteen Islands – your islands – that they are hesitant to believe me.'*

Helga went below for the accordion. 'Will the grindhvals understand my music?' she asked, the words and pictures flowing easily between the woman and the dolphine.

*'They use similar pictures to ourselves,' FairIsle replied. 'They will see and know your words as they fly out of the little-wind-song-maker.'*

Helga smiled at the four-picture word FairIsle had used to name her accordion. It seemed wonderfully apt.

'I will sing a promise on behalf of my people,' she said. 'The hvals will all be safe.'

She paused. 'About last night . . .' she started to say.

*'I know nothing of last night,' FairIsle replied, 'I was feeding far away.' She lingered for a moment, dived, leapt joyously, then swam back to join the starwhales.*

*'The She-salmon will sing for you,' FairIsle told them.*

Dan stopped the engines and Helga brought the accordion up from her cabin. *The Warrior* lay becalmed on the still sea and the Zodiac floated silently alongside. There was no sound from the grass-topped island to starboard nor from the seals hauled out on the rocks at the foot of the cliffs. No other boats were visible and even the sea birds had stopped calling as though they too knew that something of tremendous importance was about to happen.

Helga slipped her hands through the leather loops of the ancient accordion and drew the ends apart. Air hissed in. Then she pressed the ends together and a song floated out across the dark green waters. A song such as had never been heard before in the islands.

Ken later swore that he understood every word of the song but there was no doubt that the pilot whales did. They formed a great circle in the sea, each seeming to know its exact place and all listened with their gleaming black heads above the water. Helga sang of the Humans' decision to cease all killing and holding Whalekind in captivity and how starwhales need never again fear harm from *her* people – the people of the Eighteen Islands.

292

When Helga had stopped playing, Dan restarted *The Warrior's* engine, the sound seeming to break the spell of silence. The seals plopped down from the rocks into the sea and the gulls, circling above the trawler, screamed in frustration. They had learned over many years that the proximity of boats, land and whales meant plentiful food at the head of the inlet beyond the black cliffs. Today there would be none.

# CHAPTER THIRTY-SIX

'We will soon be at my home,' Helga told Ken and Hywel as they stood in the bow watching the cliffs slide past. 'It is just around that point.'

Dan was steering well clear of the cliffs even though, as they fell sheer into the sea, there was little chance of running onto outlying rocks. Ahead of *The Warrior* was a phalanx of several hundred pilot-whales, amongst whom four dolphins leapt and dived as they turned into the entrance to the fjord. He could see Helga's lone house in the green meadows on one side of the water and the many-coloured houses of the village on the opposite shore. Helga signalled to Dan from the bow to turn towards her house as the pilot-whales swam up the inlet for their celebrations and rememberences.

As he swung the wheel, a cry rang out from the village – a man's voice giving the ancient call that heralded the coming of the grindhvals. 'GRINDABOD, GRINDABOD.'

The echoes rebounded from cliff to cliff. 'GRINDABOD . . . GRINDABOD . . . Grindabod . . . Grindabod . . . grindabod . . . grindabod . . . bod . . . bod . . . bod . . .'

Men and boys were running from the houses down to the harbour carrying the sharpened hval-hooks and were leaping aboard the boats. As these came surging out of the harbour-mouth to circle round behind the swimming whales, Helga knew that the flashes of light she could see in the men's hands came from the sunshine being reflected from the polished steel of the grindaknivar, the razor-edged slaying knives. She counted the boats – twenty-one – almost the entire Eysthavn fleet.

'No,' she shouted at them, though they were too far away to hear. 'You can't. No. No. No. I promised. NO!'

The boats came on, each jostling and pitching in the wake of the boat ahead. Helga and Ken could now see the excitement on the faces of the men and boys who manned them. Helga looked for her Uncle Roi's distinctively coloured boat. It wasn't among them – no help from that quarter.

Dan shouted to Ken. 'Take the wheel. Keep *The Warrior* between the boats and the whales. Ram the bastards if necessary.'

He dropped down through the companionway hatch, lunging into Mary and spilling the four mugs of coffee that she was carrying up to the deck on a tray, unaware of the developing drama.

'Sorry,' Dan said and dashed through the galley to the aft cabin. He took his catapult and a bag of ball-bearings from the wall cupboard to which it had been consigned.

Not much of a weapon, he thought, wishing he had his S L R and a case of ammunition. The *Thing* was threatening to take over – he must keep a cool head. In the hatch above his head were the variable timers and in the other hatches were the magnets, the detonators and the P E left over from the explosion at the swimming pool. He made a mental note – it might come to that if Plan A did not produce results. There was no way that the work and effort they had all put in over the last months would be buggered up by these blood-thirsty sodding villagers. There was no way he was going to stand by and watch Helga's whale and dolphin friends being slaughtered as he had seen those others so brutally killed on that summer's day not so long ago. No way!

He clambered up the companionway.

'Helga. Take over from Ken,' he ordered and Helga did so, tears streaming down her face. 'Keep *The Warrior* between the boats and the whales.'

'Ken – you do the same with the Zodiac. Hywel – if anyone tries to come aboard – hit them with this. Hard.' He handed him the boathook with its heavy metal end and slipped a ball-bearing into the leather sling of the catapult.

Helga was leaning out of the wheelhouse. 'Dan,' she called. 'Let me *speak* to them.'

Dan ignored her; these people wouldn't listen unless he showed that he was prepared to defend the whales first. He let fly at a man who stood in the bow of the nearest boat waving a hook menacingly. The hook dropped from his hand with a clatter onto the raised foredeck and bounced into the sea. The man clutched his hand and swore in Faeroese, then looked puzzled as a shiny steel ball rolled across the deck and dropped into the scuppers.

'One,' said Dan.

'Let me *speak* to them,' Helga called to him.

Dan let fly again and a second man dropped his hook and swore.

'Two,' said Dan and walked back to take the helm. They might listen now.

Helga ran to the bow and stood like a character in a Wagnerian opera, shouting in Faeroese.

'Stop. It is I, Helga Jacobsen. The hvals must not be killed. I have promised.'

Dan cut the engine and the other boats did the same, drifting in the still water of the fjord as Helga called again.

'I, Helga Jacobsen, have promised the hvals that they will not be killed. You must leave them alone.'

'You have gone soft in the head, Helga Jacobsen. You have been eating too many of the English mad-cows. We have always killed the grindhvals and we always will.'

'But you will have heard on the radio . . . The United Nations . . .'

'A cow's arse to the United Nations,' the man called back. 'They do not fool us with the clever song tricks, pretending to be hvals singing. They do not fool us – not here in Faroyar.'

Dan took aim from the shadow of the wheelhouse and the man dropped the hook he was waving, clutched at his groin and slumped to his knees.

'Three,' said Dan as he restarted the motor and called to Helga. 'They're not listening. Take over here. I must go below. Try and keep between the whales and the boats.'

Plan B. He went below, levered off a ceiling panel using a large screwdriver and took down the pack of P E. He broke off two pieces, each large enough to tear the bottom out of a small boat and rolled each one into a ball. Then, treating the other ceiling panels in the same way, he collected two detonators, the magnets and two variable timers. He glanced at his watch. Fifteen minutes should be enough. No, perhaps thirty minutes, just in case he could get the boatmen to see sense. If he could, that would give him time to warn them to leave their boats.

He thought of Bonny, his once beloved motor cycle at the bottom of the sea and set the timers for fifteen. Shit! That was being personal and unprofessional. He reset them for a thirty-minute delay before inserting a detonator into each of the timers and pushing them into the balls of explosive.

He found two carrier bags in the galley, put a magnet and one of the charges into each and tied them into neat parcels with wire flex, leaving a loop of the wire to carry them by. He went on deck. The Faeroese boatmen had restarted their engines and were circling menacingly.

Helga was still managing to keep *The Warrior* between the boats to seaward and the whales further up the fjord. Ken was zipping back and forth in the Zodiac. Hywel stood at the bow of *The Warrior*, boathook in hand looking concerned and unsure of himself. Mary stood anxiously at his side.

Dan called to Ken to bring the Zodiac astern, dropped over the rail into it, ordered Ken aboard *The Warrior* then zoomed away to where he could see the pointed fins of the dolphins close to the more rounded ones of the pilot whales, all swimming together in obvious agitation.

He slowed the boat to a stop, cut the motor and whistled, two fingers together in his mouth. The pilot whales stopped swimming and several heads appeared above the water. Dan concentrated his thoughts in the direction of the dolphins and willed Rockall to come to him, focusing his mind as hard as he could and projecting his thoughts towards the dark fins, wishing desperately that he had learned some of the 'words' from Ken's list. Rockall swam away from the others and came alongside the inflatable.

Dan spoke to the dolphin in English, slowly and precisely, backing each word with a precise picture in his mind.

TAKE THIS THING TO THE NEAREST BOAT AND HOLD IT AGAINST THE METAL OF THE KEEL – LET GO AND SWIM BACK FOR ANOTHER – DO THE SAME TO THE NEXT BOAT – THEN SWIM CLEAR – DO THIS FOR THE WHITE WHALE AND FOR THOSE WHO RELEASED YOU FROM CAPTIVITY –

Dan could see the look of understanding in the dolphin's eye as he took the first mine awkwardly in his mouth and submerged to swim towards the islander's boats. Soon Rockall was back and took the other. The Faeroese were fanning out across the fjord trying to get past *The Warrior* but keeping clear of the Zodiac with the bearded maniac aboard.

*Rockall had no difficulty in understanding what the Orca-man wanted him to do, but now, with the thing in his mouth, he felt it giving off a sort of aura that affected his sense of direction. It was similar to the Earth's North-South aura but was moving as he moved. He swam towards the smaller boats, found one and felt the thing in his mouth leap towards the shipstone keel as he got close to it.*

*His head was clear as he swam back towards the soft-skinned boat. He took the second of the things from the Orca-man's hand and tried to find another small boat but now the thing's aura was making him swim in circles. The dark shape of a boat loomed ahead of him and, as he neared it, the thing was snatched out of his mouth and clung to the keel.*

*He backed off and his head cleared again. The bulk of the boat above his head showed that he had taken the thing to the **wrong** boat. This one was the big boat that they had followed north from the Land of Eng. The one on which the Orca-man and the She-salmon lived. This was **not** what the Orca-man had told him to do.*

*He **must** remove the thing and take it to one of the other boats.*

*FairIsle followed Rockall, keeping far enough behind him so as he would not notice her in the hustle and excitement radiating from the terrified* whales and the vibrations emanating from the jostling boats sealing off the entrance to the fjord.

When Rockall had placed the first of the things he was carrying under the keel of an islander's boat and had swum back towards the soft-skinned boat, FairIsle swam forward to investigate. The thing was clinging to the shipstone keel and from it radiated a sense of potential evil as well as a familiar but distorted aura that made her head spin.

Was the Orca-man using Rockall to smash the humans' boat? She nosed forward slowly.

A blow struck her body. A human on the boat above had jabbed at her with the hooked pole that humans used to pull boats together at sea. She dived to avoid a further blow and tried to assess her duty.

If the thing on the keel did what she feared it would do, she and any other whales or dolphins nearby might be killed by the crushing water and the boat would be destroyed as the wall of the Pool of Shame had been destroyed when they had escaped to the sea. The humans would be smashed or drowned, and the ancient edict of the ~yegods~ clearly stated that dolphins were to help humans at all times. She **must** remove the thing **before** it destroyed the boat. She rose for breath and dived to come up under the keel but could not reach the thing of evil. Her scarred dorsal fin rubbed against the barnacles on the boat's hull and she sank away, trying not to cry out with pain.

She rose sideways and pushed at the thing but it slid along the shipstone keel as though it was alive and then held tight once more. She tried again and again until she had to come to the surface away from the boat to breathe.

Rockall was having the same difficulty as he tried to remove the thing from the Orca-man's boat. As he swam forward for the fifth time he realised that there were two larger creatures nearby, each with a spiral tusk projecting from its mouth. ~Yegods~, he thought and hung in the water, trembling.

~**Elegance of Rockall, tell us what you have just done,**~ one of the ~yegods~ said sternly.

'I have taken a thing that the Orca-man gave me to each of two boats and left them under the keels, to which they cling like so many remora fish on a shark's belly.'

~**What will these things do to the boats?**~ asked the other ~yegod~ with a voice as cold as an iceberg.

'I think that they are meant to sink the boats so that the humans will not kill our friends the stargazers.'

~**It is not the duty of dolphins to harm humans, nor their boats. It is your set duty to help humans at all times,**~ said the first of the

*~yegods~. ~You have earned for yourself a tusk in the belly. Compose your thoughts and await our return.~*

One of the ~yegods~ vanished into the depths as silently as it had appeared while the other ran its tusk into the hanging loop of wire, twisted its body to tear the thing loose from The Warrior's keel and swam in the direction of the open sea, the wire-loop tight around its tusk.

Rockall rose for breath then sank to the depth of the keel and waited, still trembling and looking around him fearfully, dreading the reappearance of the ~yegods~.

FairIsle had taken a full breath and was preparing to dive again when a deep voice spoke from behind her. *~Swim clear, Grace of FairIsle,~* the voice said. *~You have done your best. Leave this task to me. I am better equipped for this than you.~*

A ~yegod~ swam past her towards the boat and was gone almost before she was sure of what she had seen and heard.

'Look at that,' said a boy on the leading boat. 'Quick. Look down here. There's a Nar-hval under the boat. It has a parcel on its horn.'

'Where?' said his father coming forward, swinging a pointed hook. 'Those horns are worth many kroner.' But the nar-hval had gone.

Helga was not sure what Dan was planning but these were *her* people, this was *her* village and *her* island, almost *her* hvals – the hvals who had trusted her – she *must* do something. She called to Ken to take the helm and went below, coming back carrying her accordion. She went to the bow and started to play, inspiration coming to her as it had done once before on the rocks behind her.

Firstly, she played a favourite Island song and, hearing the music, the villagers once more cut their engines of their boats to listen. Helga Jacobsen really had gone mad but she could play that thing well.

Ken cut The Warrior's engine and Dan, in the Zodiac stopped too. What *was* Helga up to?

Helga played slowly until all was quiet in the fjord.

As earlier that day, the seabirds had fallen silent and only the faintest of wave sounds were heard. A man's voice called from one of the boats but was hushed by other voices. Helga began to speak to the whales with the little-wind-song-maker, the inspiration for the words coming from somewhere outside of herself.

'To my friends in the sea – I am ashamed. My people have not understood what I have told them – join with me to show them the truth.'

As she played the word-pictures, she spoke to Mary at her side.

'Be quick for me. Bring the tape-machine and the loud-voice machine and when I have finished, play the tapes to the whales and to my people.'

Mary stood ready, holding the tape player, Hywel standing next to her with the loud hailer and, as Helga's last notes echoed around the hushed cliffs of the fjord, Mary pressed the play button. The tape had not been fully rewound and it was Rockall's song that came out of the loud speaker and as it began, the starwhales formed their ancient circle and swam round in this formation with a clear area in the centre where, in another formation and at another time, the doomed white-whale had been. As they swam, they rose to breathe in unison, exhaling just below the surface so that the air was filled with a fine mist that caught the sunlight striking along the length of the fjord and glowed gold over the water. In the centre of the circle of whales a dolphin leapt, then another, the vigour and grace of their leaps interpreting the message of the songs as a ballet-dancer interprets the music with movement on a stage.

Gulls swooped down and dipped and circled silently above the whales and the leaping dolphins, all glimpsed through the golden mists by those on the boats, as Rockall's song for freedom rebounded from the black cliffs and drifted away up the fjord to the empty beach at its head.

As his song died and FairIsle's song followed, the whales increased their swim-speed and surged round. The leaping of the dolphins changed subtly to reflect the new message calling for recognition.

> See us for what we are . . .

As FairIsle's song faded, Mary realised that Nordstar's song had not been played and pressed the 'rapid rewind' button. The tape whizzed backwards and clicked to a stop as the whales slowed their circling. She pressed 'play' and, as Nordstar's farewell filled the air between the cliff-faces, the starwhales performed a sombre undulating rise and fall as they circled. In the centre two dolphins executed the Curvee of Salutation, each rising from the water in a perfect arc as the previous one's tail-flukes slipped below the surface leaving hardly a ripple. Mary could not see the distinctively scarred dorsal fins of FairIsle and Rockall and wondered why they were not taking part.

Nordstar's final words hung in the air.

> Hope fills my heart for all Whalekind
> Though through the endless night I'll swim
> And echoes fade and stars grow dim for me
> I trust Mankind will hear our plea

300

*Sung from this place of shame*
*'Let whales swim free again.*
*Let whales swim free again.'*

Mary stopped the tape and in the silence that followed a boy on one of the boats shouted, *'I'm* not killing any more hvals, today – or ever,' and threw his hook and knife over the side A man on the next boat dropped his hook and his knife into the dark green water. Others followed his example.

Dan sat in the Zodiac, sick in the guts. He looked at his watch. Any moment now the mines would tear the bottoms out of two of the boats. All of what had just been achieved by Helga, the dolphins and the whales would be lost. Could he warn the boatmen now? He looked at his watch again. No – there wasn't time. Any moment . . .

Out at sea, far beyond the ranks of the Faeroese boats, there was an eruption of water followed by another, then two muffled explosions. From that distance it appeared to him that two tapered sticks were falling back into the sea amongst pieces of flesh and cascades of red water. He looked at the faces on the boats – no one else seemed to have noticed.

'Bloody Hell,' he said to himself. 'Bloody Hell. How the shit . . .?'

Helga was standing in the bow of *The Warrior* calling to the men and boys in the boats.

'Once more I am proud to be of Faroyar,' she said in their own language. 'When you are old men, you will speak of this to your grandchildren and be glad that you were here on this day. Tonight I will sleep in my own house and tomorrow I will come to the village and we will talk of England and of the world beyond these islands.'

One by one the boatmen restarted their motors, raised a hand to the new Helga Jacobsen and turned for home.

Dan brought the Zodiac up behind *The Warrior's* stern and climbed on board. He walked along the deck to stand at Helga's side, watching the departing boats. Ken watched Dan and Helga talking quietly together in the bow as he steered the trawler back towards the lone house standing in the green fields above the rounded rocks. Hywel and Mary sat side by side on the gunwales, Hywel's arm around Mary's shoulders.

*The constellation of starwhales swam seawards, leaving Rockall trembling as he floated in the water, scanning all about him, braced for the return of the ~yegods~. After a few minutes he dared to believe that they would not be coming and swam to find his FairIsle.*

*She was joyously greeting her mother and her aunt, Grace of Tyne and Grace of Humber who had just joined her and were telling of two ~yegods~ who had swum rapidly past them, each carrying a package on its tusk.*

*So it didn't only happen in the stories!*

As *The Warrior* neared Helga's home, Dan took over the wheel and guided the boat into the little harbour between the rocks, reversing the propeller to avoid entering too fast. Ken used the boathook to draw the trawler against the worn-out tyres that hung from metal spikes in the rock. Dan stopped the engine and leapt ashore to secure the boat with an arrangement of crossed ropes.

'Helga and I will be sleeping ashore,' he said, looking at Ken.

Ken recognised the hint of a challenge in Dan's voice and accepted the situation.

'Fine by me,' he replied as Helga came on deck. She was carrying the carved dolphins.

'Dan and I are going to sleep in the house tonight,' she said quietly.

'I know. He just told me.'

Helga was holding the carving towards him. 'I would like you to have this. I have always promised it for you,' she said. 'When you are far away in England, you will look at it and remember Helga from Faroyar and all the things we have been doing together.'

Ken thanked her awkwardly and stood on *The Warrior's* deck watching Dan and Helga as they walked together over the rocks to the house. Then he went below. Mary was scrambling eggs while Hywel laid out three plates on the galley table. Ken felt an outsider here too but ate the meal then announced that he would keep a watch from the rocks in case anyone came over from the village.

Hywel watched Mary wash the dishes at the tiny sink in the corner of the galley.

'It's just you and me aboard tonight, then,' he said.

Mary detected the underlying message and wiped the pan she was holding before replying.

'You know how I feel about that,' she said putting the pan away in the cupboard. 'It's not that I don't *want* to . . .' She turned to face Hywel and smiled.

'Dan and Helga will be . . .' Hywel said, but knowing he was on a losing wicket.

'That's up to them. Besides all the bunks are too narrow.'

'Where there's a will . . .'

'No!'

She put the cloth down, walked round the table and kissed Hywel's forehead. 'When we're married, we can all the time.'

'Married? I haven't asked you yet,' he said.

'But you *are* going to? Aren't you?'

'Looks like I'm going to bloody well have to, doesn't it? Do you want all the down-on-one-knee stuff, girl, or will this do?'

Mary's smile told him it would.

When Dan came down to pee in the sea just before it got dark, he found Ken sitting on a rock holding the carved dolphins and staring across the fjord, a blanket around his shoulders and Lucky rubbing against his legs.

Near the fjord entrance the fins of the pilot whales circled slowly and a dolphin leapt occasionally.

'You OK?' Dan asked as he zipped up his flies.

'I thought that someone ought to make sure no one came over. You – we were pretty rough on them today.'

'Helga says they won't come. She's sure of that but if you do hear or see anything you don't like, come up and bang on the door. Don't be in too much of a hurry though. See you in the morning.'

He strolled over and checked *The Warrior's* mooring ropes. All the lights were out. On the way back to the house Dan parted his beard with his fingers as he walked.

As he passed the side of the house Dan could see through the window into Helga's bedroom. She was sitting up in bed, wearing a soft white nightdress. Her blond hair, loose around her shoulders, gleamed in the light of a candle. He went into the house, felt his way across the big room and opened the bedroom door. The picture of Sven Forkbeard had been taken down and put away. He smoothed his beard together again.

A tjaldur cried plaintively from the field at the back of the house as Dan crossed the room, bent and kissed Helga.

'You are not meant to do that, Dan-ney,' she whispered. 'You are meant to smash down the door.'

'That was Plan B,' said Dan.

The night passed slowly for Ken on the rocks. He watched the lights of the houses over the water go out one by one until only the two lights on the new harbour entrance were left. Their reflections flickered and rippled as the tide flowed into the fjord and then out again in the early hours of the morning. A thin sliver of a moon gave a little light.

Sometimes he walked over to look down on *The Warrior*, dark and snug in the little harbour and sometimes he walked to the end of the promontory to stare at the moving banks of fog over the sea. Once he walked up and quietly circled the dark house before returning to the rocks.

When it was light enough, he could see that the pilot whales had gone but he caught occasional glimpses of FairIsle, Rockall and their families as the fog banks formed, dissipated and reformed. They were probably feeding. He counted six fins and wondered who the other two dolphins were.

He pulled the blanket tighter around his shoulders although the air was not cold and fondled the rounded back of the uppermost of the carved dolphins. The polished wood under his hand felt smooth and firm like Janice Coomb's breasts on that memorable day at the Home when she had offered him a feel in exchange for a Mars bar.

His hands moved from the upper to the lower dolphin, equally smooth, then down to the chunky base. The wood here was rougher – perhaps Helga had left it like that to signify waves but it did not feel quite right to him and he moved his fingers backwards and forwards over the rough-hewn base as the sun came up out of the mists to seaward.

The fog banks had cleared but fine wisps of cloud were still drifting around the tops of the mountains when Helga, wearing a blue dress that Ken had not seen before, carried a mug of tea from the house to where he sat.

'You would like this, I think,' she said. 'But it has only the tinned milk in it. Later, I will milk my cow for the real milk.'

She stood for a moment looking out to sea, her fingers playing with the string of pearls that had replaced the gold cross around her neck. A boat came out of the harbour on the other side of the fjord and headed towards them.

She turned to Ken. 'That is the boat of my uncle Roi,' she said and waved. The figure in the boat waved back.

She was down at the little harbour as the boat nosed in and moored next to *The Warrior.*

'Uncle Roi,' she said as he kissed her. 'I am glad to be home. You know what happened here yesterday?'

'I was in Torshavn,' he replied. 'But I have heard all that was done. You are the talk of the village – probably of all of Faroyar by now.'

He took her elbow and walked her a little way from the boat then, lowering his voice, he said, 'After you left there was some foolish talk over there about my sister and how she died. I had a long talk with Dr Carlsen and he was very sure of what he had already said on the certificate. Your mother had died of a heart attack in the night before the grindhvals came.'

'Thank you for telling me, Uncle Roi. I am glad to know that.' *A Life for a Life* still seemed a good idea to her though.

'Come and meet my friend from England – he is called Ken.'

Ken shook hands with Uncle Roi who immediately excused himself to go and milk the cow. Helga sensed that Ken wanted to tell her something and sat on the rock by his side feeling more light-hearted than she could ever recall. It was so good to be home. *A Life for a Life*. She slipped her hand down across her abdomen and held it there for a moment. It couldn't be that easy, surely?

Ken sipped from the mug, then picked up the carving of the dolphins.

'I don't think you've finished this,' he said.

Helga reached out, took the carving from him and turned it round. 'Where is it not finished?'

'Here,' said Ken, running his fingers over and around the base. 'Can you see? Here's the white whale hiding in the wood – you've not let *her* out.'

'I can see her. Yes, I can see her. You are right, the white grindhval – she is still trapped here in the wood.' Helga said. 'I will get my knife and I shall make her free too. I should have known she was there. I should have known.' She hurried off towards the house.

When Helga returned she was followed by Dan, who sat on a rock, stretched and yawned.

Hywel and Mary came up onto the deck of *The Warrior* and Ken watched Hywel help Mary climb the rock steps. He continued to hold her hand as they walked towards them. Mary smiled at Helga where she sat carving vigorously.

'I thought you'd finished that,' she said.

'Not quite.' Helga returned the smile. 'You will see. Soon you will see.'

Suddenly, the hump of wood that had formed the base became the bulbous head and the rounded back of a pilot whale, its dorsal fin having exactly the right amount of curve to identify it as the whale whose body they had abandoned in the pool at Dormouth.

Helga put down the big knife and took a smaller one from a pocket in her dress. With a few deft movements she carved the eyes and mouth and brushed away a few loose slivers of wood. She studied the carving, turning it round slowly. Ken was watching closely.

'It is *your* whale,' he said, 'except . . .'

Helga looked up. 'Ja . . . Yes. Except?'

'Nothing,' said Ken.

'Except what?' Helga persisted.

305

'*This* whale is looking happy,' Ken told her.

'I know,' Helga replied as she passed the carving to Ken. 'That is the way I found her in the wood-block.'

She stood up and pointed. Out in the Channel of Reconciliation six dolphins were leaping the Curvee of Salutation.